"Could . . . . s a madcap South American adventure story in the tradition of *Robinson Crusoe*. . . . Unputdownable." —*The Sunday Telegraph* (London)

"*The Dolphin People* is a great big tidal wave of a book that will pick you up and whisk you along for the two or three days that it takes to read [it]. You'll read it in bed, at breakfast, and on the bus. . . . Torsten Krol has an almost limitless supply of surprises to spring, each of which puts everything that went before in a new light. . . . Impressive. . . . The series of climaxes with which the book ends will have you holding your breath. . . . There is a minor but fascinating genre including such books as Paul Theroux's *The Mosquito Coast* and Barbara Kingsolver's *The Poisonwood Bible*, and *The Dolphin People* is a distinguished addition to it."
—Brandon Robshaw, *The Independent* (London)

"A splendid yarn to be read when the nights are drawing in; H. Rider Haggard with a bitter modern twist."
—*The Times* (London)

"Philip Roth once complained that modern reality in all its manifestations had outstripped the capacity of the novelist's ability to imagine. Torsten Krol's bizarre, thought-provoking, and funny book *The Dolphin People*, a highly unlikely tale featuring Nazi doctors, headhunters, hermaphrodites, piranhas, and the penis-dwelling candiru fish, shows how wrong he can be. . . . A postmodern novel par excellence. . . . [Krol has an] admirably breezy writing style. . . . An exuberant novel, fast-paced and clever." —*Sydney Morning Herald*

"A fantastic adventure story set against the backdrop of a jungle village deep in the heart of Amazonas."

—*Bookseller* (Booksellers' Choice)

"A coming-of-age adventure story.... Interesting and compelling, as the characters discover themselves, and one another, in the space between two historical worlds—the Stone Age and the age of industrial warfare.... Extremely realistic ... and, at the same time, highly suggestive."

—*The Daily Telegraph* (London)

"Readers won't be disappointed.... *The Dolphin People* is what would happen if the TV series *Lost* met *Life of Pi*; a postmodern, grown-up Boy's Own tale.... The clash of tribal culture and supposed civilization adds to the novel's depth, while the author's delight in the grotesque and the bizarre enhances further still this most superior adventure novel."

—*Metro* (London)

"Krol wastes no time in propelling the action.... The reader is compelled to page-turn."   —*The Age* (Melbourne)

"Revealing the powers ... of storytelling, this absurd fantasy is related in such extraordinarily vivid detail that the reader remains hooked to the brutal end.... [The] powerful motif of castaways, employed by stories from *Robinson Crusoe* to *Lord of the Flies*, is used to devastating effect in Krol's unflinching story of madness and murder, which lays bare both body and mind."   —Anita Sethi, *The Independent* (London)

The Dolphin People

ALSO BY TORSTEN KROL

Callisto

The Dolphin People

A Novel

TORSTEN KROL

HARPER ● PERENNIAL

NEW YORK ● LONDON ● TORONTO ● SYDNEY ● NEW DELHI ● AUCKLAND

HARPER ● PERENNIAL

First published in Australia in 2006 by Picador, an imprint of Pan Macmillan Australia Pty Limited, Sydney.

First published in trade paperback in Great Britain in 2008 by Atlantic Books, an imprint of Grove Atlantic Ltd.

FIRST U.S. EDITION

Library of Congress Cataloging-in-Publication Data is available upon request.

ISBN 978-0-06-167296-5

09 10 11 12 13 RRD 10 9 8 7 6 5 4 3 2 1

ONE

THE TOPS OF THE WAVES as they curled were pale green with a ridge of white foam, but just below the green they were deep blue. Giovanni, the sailor who liked Zeppi and me, told us it was Atlantic blue, different to Mediterranean blue, which we had already seen, and he was right. Atlantic blue was darker further north, almost black sometimes, but the further south we went, the greener the blue.

I told Mother about the difference, but she said it was all the same, and we only thought the waves were different because we were both excited. Zeppi was excited, yes, but not me. He was only twelve, and being four years older made me different to him, less of a child. To Mother, though, we were the same, just like the waves. Giovanni said all mothers are alike that way.

It was an Italian ship, *Stromboli,* and under its name on the stern it said *GENOA,* which is where we got aboard, Mother and Zeppi and me, for the trip to Venezuela. Uncle Klaus was waiting for us there. Mother was going to marry him because my father was dead, killed on the Russian Front in '43, and she was too young to be alone in the world with two boys. That was how she explained it to us when the letter came with Uncle Klaus's proposal of marriage.

She read it to us, leaving some parts out. Uncle Klaus told her his brother's two fine sons deserved a father, and Helga deserved a man who would look after us all now that the war was lost and the Führer dead. He was very matter-of-fact about everything – the war, the Führer, the reasons why Mother should think seriously about marrying him and raising us boys far away from the ruins of Germany and everything that had gone wrong there. She should do it for Zeppi and Erich, he said in the letter, and for Heinrich, his dead brother buried under Russian mud, a hero who deserved to know his family would survive without him.

That was how he put it, and after Mother read it again to herself, she said that in the Bible a widow often married her dead husband's brother. Mother was sometimes religious and sometimes not, so I could tell that she was trying to make up her mind. She took four days, then wrote back to Uncle Klaus in Caracas, and six weeks after that we got steamship tickets in the mail. Mother sold some items that were too big to take with us, the furniture and things that were still left after all the bombing, and we set off.

Getting out of Germany was not so easy, with the Americans and British running everything. You couldn't just get on the train and go to Switzerland the way you could before the war. Mother said Klaus had made all arrangements to smuggle us across the border, and he must have known a lot of people on the Swiss side because we were taken close to it in a car, and then led across on foot by a guide, with just our suitcases, in the middle of the night. From there on it was as if we were in a different world, with nobody telling us what to do or demanding to see our identity papers, except when we crossed into Italy a day later. By then we were just a woman and her two boys on holiday. It was Klaus who made it all possible, Mother kept reminding us.

All the way from Italy to the Strait of Gibraltar, Mother was seasick, even though the waves weren't very high. The cabin smelled bad, so Zeppi and I spent a lot of time on deck, where we met Giovanni. He told us where everything was that we needed to know about, where to assemble for lifeboat drill in case the ship sank, where the galley was, and the mess-room where passengers had their meals.

There were only eleven of us because *Stromboli* was a cargo vessel with just enough room for a few paying passengers. There was only one other lady aboard, and she spent some time with Mother, then told me I had to look after her like a good boy because of the seasickness. She said Zeppi had to help too, but as usual he wasn't listening, so it was me who went down to the cabin two or three times a day to ask Mother if there was anything she wanted, which there never was, she was too sick.

When we passed through the strait, Zeppi and I were on deck to watch, even though it was after dark. We expected something more interesting, tall cliffs with foam smashing against the rocks on both sides, with barely enough room for the ship to pass through, but it wasn't like that. The Pillars of Hercules, that was what we wanted to see, like something from a storybook, but it was foggy and all we saw were the lights of Gibraltar on the right as we went slowly by. Zeppi said he didn't think we'd really gone between the Pillars of Hercules, but I told him we had, and he should stop whining about how disappointed he was and go below to sleep. I was disappointed too, but Mother always said I had to set an example for Zeppi.

I stayed on deck for a long time, feeling the water beneath us get deeper as we passed into the Atlantic. The waves were bigger and longer there, invisible in the fog, but I could feel them and hear them crashing into the bow and sliding along the hull in the darkness. These were the waves we would ride all the way to Venezuela, blue-green Atlantic waves. I went to the stern to see the last of Europe, but it was already gone.

Mother said we would never return, never see the Fatherland rebuilt, if it ever would be. She said the Russians and Americans would divide it between them like a cake, cut it in half right down the middle, and it would never truly be Germany again, so it was better to leave and start our lives over. Uncle Klaus was a doctor and a fine man. He would be a father to us in a land where the sun always shone and the air was filled with coloured parrots and the smell of bananas. I'd had a banana once, when I was much younger than Zeppi, but I couldn't remember the taste of it. In Venezuela everything would be different, and I would grow up to be a man like my father, who died in the snow.

There was a storm halfway across the Atlantic, and Mother, who'd been feeling better for a while, became sick again, and Zeppi too. I had to empty their buckets into the lavatory and flush their vomit away. I got sick once myself, but it was the smell, not the ship going back and forth. When Mother and Zeppi had no more inside them to come up, I went away and watched the storm through the mess-room windows.

Giovanni told me not to go out on deck or I might be swept away, so I stayed there all afternoon watching the waves and listening to the wind howl.

All the passengers but me were sick, and the sailors were busy, so I had the mess-room to myself. I had to brace my legs wide apart and hold onto the railing under the windows. It was a wonderful feeling to be thrown this way and that, and I felt strong. My father told me before he went away for the last time that I must always be strong, and this was the first time I had felt that way. I wondered if he could see me standing on my feet in the middle of an Atlantic storm. Mother said the dead were in heaven, watching over us, and we mustn't disappoint them by behaving in a way they wouldn't approve of. I wondered if my father approved of us going to Venezuela to be with his brother, and whether I would still have to be strong after that, when I had a new father to be strong for us all.

I'd met Uncle Klaus once or twice before the war, and he came to visit us after Father was killed, to express his condolences. He looked exactly like a doctor ought to, very tall and straight and intelligent, and very handsome too, more so than his brother, who favoured their mother, not their father, who had been in the army in 1916. My uncle the doctor looked like a soldier, but my father, who was a soldier, looked like a railway porter, which he wasn't – he sold insurance policies. He was very brave, anyway. He gave me the Iron Cross that was pinned on him by the Führer himself for killing a lot of Russians. He killed them with his tank, and the Führer gave him the Iron Cross and smiled at him. My father told me it was the greatest honour that could be given to a German.

Now I had the decoration in its leather box in my trunk, hidden away down at the bottom where a thief might not notice it. Father gave it to me when he told me I had to be strong, for the sake of the family. Once I tried it on and looked at myself in the mirror. It didn't weigh very much. I felt guilty wearing it when I had no right to, and put it back in its box. Mother never wanted to see it again after he was killed. I knew Uncle Klaus would want to see it. I would hand it to him and watch him open the box. 'My father won this,' I'd say, 'and he'd want you to see it.'

A long wave came across the decks below me and ran away over the side in sheets of foam. It was washing away the past, I thought, sending it all over the side to sink to the bottom of the ocean so everything could be new and better for us. Mother had already told me it wouldn't be polite to compare Uncle Klaus with my father, since it was pointless. My old father was dead, and my new father would be the closest thing on earth to my old father because they had been brothers. It was the best way out of Zeppi and me having no father, and Mother having no husband.

I asked her, 'Do you love Uncle Klaus?' She said she had always respected him and admired the way he joined the Party in 1933 to be a part of the Führer's march toward a golden tomorrow for all Germans. Father had never done that, and I knew from overhearing arguments between them that Mother thought he'd let himself and the family down by not being a Party member like his brother, but he still wouldn't join. She was very proud when he signed up for the Wehrmacht, though, and kept a picture of him standing on the turret of his tank on the mantelpiece, until that side of the house was blown apart by American bombers.

I told myself, watching the storm, that I would do what Mother advised. Uncle Klaus had been kind enough to offer us a new life away from all the bombed-out cities and starvation and a Germany that was divided in two like a cake. Everything we had ever known was gone forever, and Uncle Klaus was the last piece of whatever remained from the past, a hand reaching out to us, pulling us up from a dark hole. He was a good man, Mother said, who didn't have to do what he was doing, and we should all appreciate it. Our family name would remain the same, which was also good. I would still be Erich Linden, not someone else with a name that might be ugly or stupid. Uncle Klaus was the perfect answer to everything, really. I tried hard to remember the taste of bananas, but couldn't. That was gone too, but there would be the chance, less than a week away now, to taste them again.

We could smell Venezuela before we saw it. Zeppi was the one who asked Giovanni what the heavy, dank smell was, and Giovanni said it was land, but we wouldn't be able to see it until the next day.

Zeppi said to me, 'It doesn't smell very nice. It smells rotten.'

I told him it only smelled that way because the ocean smelled so different, and it wouldn't smell so bad once we were back on land. 'I don't like it,' he said, whining the way he sometimes did when things weren't the way he wanted, so I told him, 'Listen, little idiot, you can't change it, so you'd better get used to it, and don't go crying to Mother about how anything smells or I'll twist your ear.'

He knew I meant it, so he stuck out his bottom lip to show me how upset he was, just as if he was still seven, not twelve. 'Grow up,' I told him, and he stuck out his tongue, then ducked away, laughing, before I could grab his ear.

Mother came up on deck a few minutes later and said, 'What's that strange smell?' I told her it was Venezuela, and she didn't say anything.

Next morning I was on deck at first light, and there was land ahead, with low clouds covering it. The air was hotter than it had been, and the smell was much stronger. There were birds flying around us, but they weren't parrots, not yet, just seagulls. I could feel my heart jumping in my chest. My new country was before me, waiting, and somewhere behind that long green line was Klaus.

I'd decided the night before to stop thinking of him as my uncle, and since he wasn't married to Mother yet he couldn't be called Father, so he'd have to be just plain Klaus until everything was settled. It made me feel closer to him, using only his name, as if he was a friend, someone I'd known for more than just a few days at a time over the years. Maybe he'd want to be called Father once the marriage ceremony was over. That would be strange, and not right somehow. I wanted him to tell me from the very beginning to call him Klaus. It would start things off the right way between us. If he insisted that I call him Uncle, then Father, I'd be – disappointed.

Zeppi was beside me. 'It smells worse,' he said, wrinkling his nose, 'like a rubbish bin with old turnip skins inside.'

'You'll get used to it.'

'I won't. I don't want to.'

'Then you'll be very unhappy, with no one to blame but yourself.'

'I don't care.'

'Shut up, little boy.'

He punched me on the arm as hard as he could. 'Don't say that!'

'Little girl, then. You look like a girl, did you know that?'

He knew it, all right. Zeppi was the prettiest boy I think I've ever seen. Sometimes I was jealous because he looked so pretty. He got that from Mother, while I took after our father. At school, Zeppi would get teased about his cupid's-bow mouth and the length of his eyelashes and little seashell ears, until his face would turn red and he'd almost cry. That was why he got teased, to make the tears come, and if they did he looked even more like a girl, and somehow prettier than ever. He was never good at games, and I'd always avoided him at school, embarrassed by his prettiness and delicate ways. But he was my brother, just as Klaus was my father's brother, so I had to love him and look after him, especially now that a new life for us was about to begin.

'*You* shut up!' he said, and I turned away, wanting the fight to be over before it really got started.

'Look,' I said, pointing, 'a pelican!'

'It isn't. It's a crane.'

It was definitely a pelican, but I said nothing, and Zeppi cheered up a bit.

'When do we get there?' he asked. 'I'm sick of this stupid ship.'

'Giovanni said we have to sail up a river to get to where we're going. It'll be days yet.'

'But Caracas is by the sea. We saw it in the atlas. It's the capital.'

'We aren't going to Caracas, we're going to some other place called ... Bolivar, I think. The river takes ships as big as this all the way inland, two hundred kilometres. There'll be jungle on both sides of us.'

'With monkeys?'

'And parrots, and anacondas that squash you to death then swallow you whole.'

'I won't let them!'

'You can't stop them. They drop out of the trees and grab you in their coils and squeeze and squeeze until your guts burst and your eyes pop out of your head. You can't get away from an anaconda unless there's someone else there with a gun to kill it before it starts breaking your ribs.'

'I'm going to have a gun then, and you have to get one too, so we can save each other. We have to be together if we're under trees.'

He was serious, so I didn't laugh.

'What river?' he said. 'The Amazon?'

'Idiot. Remember the atlas? What was the big river in Venezuela?'

'The Amazon,' he insisted.

'That's in Brazil, genius. The one we're going up is the Orinoco.'

'Orinoco,' he said. 'Orinoco . . .' Zeppi's face had the faraway look it sometimes got, as if he wasn't there any more, he was half asleep. I used to tease him about it until Mother told me not to. 'He's a little dreamy, that's all,' she said, 'so leave him alone. He might be a great thinker when he grows up.' I didn't believe that part, of course, not Zeppi. Maybe he'd be a film star like Rudolph Valentino if he stayed pretty enough, but Zeppi couldn't work his way through a simple crossword puzzle without help.

I sometimes wondered what Mother imagined I'd be when I grew up. Once I told her I'd command a tank like Father, and she said, 'No! Never again!' That shows how hard she took his dying, and explained why she never wanted to see his Iron

Cross. It also explained why she said, when she told us she intended accepting Klaus's proposal of marriage, 'A man of healing, that's something to be proud of. A healer, not a destroyer.' I'm sure she didn't mean to insult Father by saying that, it's just that with the war over and Germany in ruins, being a tank man didn't seem to have any point, in her eyes, anyway.

A man of healing, that was an expression I liked. Klaus was a healer of men, and of women too, if he made Mother happy again the way she used to be before the war changed everything. Maybe he wouldn't want to see Father's Iron Cross after all. It was hard to say in advance just what Klaus might want. I imagined him greeting us wearing a white coat, the kind doctors wear, with a stethoscope around his neck instead of the Iron Cross a destroyer of men might wear.

'Do snakes swim?' Zeppi asked.

'Some of them do.'

'The big ones? The anacondas?'

'I don't know.'

'We have to stay out of the water too,' he said, frowning.

Stromboli passed through a maze of channels where the Orinoco met the Atlantic. I couldn't tell if the jungle I saw was part of the mainland or an island in the estuary, and Giovanni didn't know either. He said the river pilot knew the way. The pilot was a man with dark skin like Giovanni's, and a sailor's cap like his, only there was a bigger badge on the front of it because a river pilot's job is more important than a sailor's.

After a whole morning the channels were behind us and the river was a lot wider, so wide it didn't seem like a river at all, and the jungle was just like it looked from the ocean, a thin green line, only on both sides of the ship. After a while it was boring, but Zeppi and I stayed on deck anyway because below decks it was too hot now, not like when we were at sea. Mother stayed on deck with us, and the rest of the passengers too, all gathered together in canvas chairs under an awning Giovanni and some others set up for shade. We still hadn't seen any parrots, so maybe they don't like to fly above water.

Even when we came through the channels we weren't close enough to the jungle to see anything interesting. I didn't feel that we'd really arrived in Venezuela yet because of the parrots. When we finally saw one, we'd be there. I wanted it to be one of the red and blue ones, or yellow and blue, with a black beak, like the pictures I'd seen in books. I already wanted one for a pet. We used to have two cats, then a dog, but they all died in the war. They weren't killed by bombs, though. Mother said someone ate them, which made Zeppi cry. I didn't want a dog or cat again. A parrot would be a wonderful thing to have. I'd train it to sit on my shoulder like a pirate's bird, and teach it to say clever things.

When night came we were still on the river, and there were lights along the shore, but not many, and very far away. Some passengers slept on deck the way the sailors did. Giovanni told us we were lucky the river was so wide, because if we were close to shore we'd be eaten alive by mosquitoes. I watched the stars above us all night, not sleeping because the deck was so hard, but I didn't care. The ship's engines seemed louder than they had at sea, maybe just because I couldn't sleep and nothing around me – the stars and the jungle smell in the air and the sound of the engines – could be got away from by sleeping. It was all more real than before, and behind the sound and the smell of the night there was another thing inside my head to keep me awake – tomorrow we would see Klaus again for the first time in three years.

Would he still look the same? Would he still smoke his cigarettes through a long yellow cigarette holder made from genuine ivory? Father had called it an affectation but Mother had said the long cigarette holder was sophisticated, not like the pipe Father smoked. The cigarette holder made Klaus look young and debonair, she'd said, and the pipe just made Father look like an old man. They hadn't spoken to each other for two days after that.

The river port where we docked was called Ciudad Bolivar and was filled with dark-skinned people, Spanish types and Indians, and we couldn't understand any of the words they yelled as the wharf labourers began swarming aboard to unload the ship's hold. I watched Giovanni helping to roll back the sea hatches and saw a blast of hot air come out each time as the cargo holds were opened. The air above them rippled as the heat came rushing out. That was the last time I saw Giovanni, even though I'd promised myself to tell him goodbye. Mother had everything packed and ready hours before we docked, and a sailor came to take everything down the gangway and onto the wharf, with the three of us hurrying along behind.

That was when I saw my first parrot. It was sitting on a wharf post with its head cocked to one side, looking straight at me. Its feathers were red and blue, and its wings had been clipped short so it couldn't fly away, which meant it was someone's pet. I made up my mind never to clip my parrot's wings when I got one. They looked short and stumpy and ugly. My parrot would love me so much he wouldn't even

want to fly away. When I got closer I saw that the parrot had
pulled out a lot of his own feathers across the chest, and his
skin showed through, all puckered and pale like an uncooked
chicken. I'd wanted to touch the parrot, but now I didn't want
to.

'Erich, don't go wandering away!'

Mother was looking anxious, holding onto Zeppi's hand
and turning her head to see if Klaus was coming, but he
wasn't. Sweat was rolling down my ribs under my shirt, and
my feet were hot inside their socks. My face and neck were
wet. I wanted to throw myself off the wharf and into the water
to get away from the terrible heat, but when I looked down
the water was dirty and brown, with all kinds of rubbish
floating in it.

'Erich, stand over here so we're all together.'

I went to her and we waited. Zeppi sat on the largest trunk,
looking miserable, hair plastered across his forehead with
sweat. Some of the other passengers spoke to Mother, saying
goodbye and good luck and so forth. They said the same to
Zeppi and myself, and we said goodbye to them, then they
disappeared along the wharf with their luggage being pushed
on trolleys by the wharf men. Then there were only the three
of us left, and the wharf was a lot quieter. A sailor shouted
down to us that we should go along to the customs shed
where there was shade. He yelled at a man to come and put
our trunks on a trolley and follow the rest of the passengers,
which is what happened, and soon we were inside a very big
tin shed with a long counter where some of the passengers
had their bags opened for inspection.

We were the last ones through. Nobody really looked
inside our trunks at all, and a man wearing a dirty uniform

stamped Mother's papers very slowly and carefully, breathing on the stamp every time before he brought it down onto the paper. Still no sign of Klaus, and Mother was looking worried.

An hour went by. Zeppi started complaining about the heat and how hungry he was until I told him to shut up. I was getting angry myself – Klaus should have been there waiting for us. It was a bad beginning. I think Mother was holding back tears just like Zeppi.

A lemonade seller came inside the customs shed and we bought three small bottles from him. He looked at our money and made it clear it wasn't acceptable, and pointed out the moneychanger over in the corner. The customs men hadn't even bothered to come over and tell us we needed to change our marks into whatever the Venezuelans used.

Mother didn't have very much left of the new money after she'd paid the lemonade man, so I think he took more than he should have. I didn't like him after that. He was a Spanish-looking man wearing clothes that hadn't been washed in a long time and a straw hat with a hole in the top. He tried to sell us some more lemonade and got loud and angry when Mother said no. He started to argue with her in Spanish and I wanted to hit him, kick him in the shins under his cut-too-short pants. He had sandals on, not real shoes. Someone like that had no business being rude to my mother.

It wouldn't have happened if Klaus had been there. My opinion of him was slipping, and my opinion of Venezuelans too. Nobody told the lemonade man to go away and stop pestering Mother. They just stood there, those men in uniform, and watched what was happening, probably enjoying it because there was nothing else to do.

It was midday by then and very hot. There was a large

window in the side of the shed, and I saw big black birds shuffling back and forth along the roof of another building across the street. Another one came down from the sky with its wings flapping like a broken umbrella. It landed clumsily and sat on the roof with the others, shifting around on its legs, moving its ugly head from side to side. If I'd had a gun I would have shot it, and the others too. The lemonade man had been silent for a half minute or so, then he started telling Mother to buy more lemonade, this time being nice about it, trying to take the rest of her money with a smile, and still nobody came and told him to go away, so I went over and pushed him.

He wasn't expecting it and fell against his little broken-down pushcart filled with bottles, making them clink against each other. Then he started shouting at me, and shouting at the customs men to do something, but they just kept on watching the show, smoking or picking their teeth, their caps pushed to the backs of their heads. The lemonade man got even angrier then, and turned back to me, shaking his fist, so I put up my fists like a hero in the films, even though I've never learned how to fight properly.

'Erich, no . . . Stop that. I don't want any trouble here.'

'He won't go away, Mother. He's awful, and those other men won't do anything.'

'Just ignore him and he'll go away.'

'He won't!'

'Yes he will. Don't even look at him and he'll leave us alone.'

I put down my fists then because I felt foolish, and it hadn't made the lemonade man stop talking his angry babble. I didn't know what to do next. Then I saw Klaus. He was halfway across the room, striding along quickly on his long legs. It was the cigarette holder that made me recognise him.

Everything else about him was new and different. He had on a creamy white suit made of baggy material that looked cool and comfortable, and he had on a wide-brimmed hat of yellow straw the same colour as his cigarette holder. He was walking so fast the smoke went straight back into his eyes, but he didn't blink.

The cigarette holder jerked up and down, dislodging ash, as he barked something in Spanish at the lemonade man, who jumped at the sound of his voice and turned around. Klaus barked at him again and he began slinking away like a dog with his tail between his legs, pushing his pathetic little bottle cart.

'Klaus . . .' said Mother, just staring at him. She was even closer to tears by then, but it was because she was relieved to be seeing him at last.

'I'm so sorry, Helga,' he said, 'there was a snag at the works office. I had to sign some papers and the fools were wanting to take their siesta. Are you all well? How was the trip? A fair crossing, I hope? Boys, you've grown several feet since I last saw you.'

'Oh, Klaus . . .' said Mother, beginning to sound weepy, 'we were starting to worry . . .'

'My fault entirely. I should have known they wouldn't have the paperwork done on time, today of all days. They insist that everything be done in triplicate, even if they lose it all later. But never mind all that. You must be hungry. I've had a snack prepared at the hotel to keep us going till dinner. Everything's waiting. Leave all this here for the time being.'

'Leave it?' Mother looked at our trunks with doubt in her eyes.

'It'll be perfectly safe. Just a moment.'

He went over to the customs men and said something to them, then came back.

'It's all arranged. They'll keep an eye on everything. Come along.'

He offered Mother his arm and she took it after hesitating for a second or two.

'We'll have to get everyone hats,' said Klaus. 'You can't walk around under the sun here without one or you'll get sick.'

We marched out of the customs shed into the afternoon's bright light and heat. Zeppi and I hadn't said a word so far. I pointed to the broken-umbrella birds on the roof across the street. 'What are those?'

Klaus looked. 'Vultures. Ugly devils, aren't they? You'll get used to them. Was anyone seasick on the way over?'

'Not me,' I said. 'The others were.'

'Let's walk on the shady side,' he said, escorting us across the street. There was no one else out walking and the shops had their shutters down. 'Siesta,' said Klaus. 'You've heard of it, I'm sure. Everything shuts down until late afternoon because of the heat, a necessary part of life here, I'm afraid.'

'Where are we going?' Zeppi asked.

'To the hotel, for a bite to eat. I've reserved rooms there for all of us. My god, Zeppi, you've grown. Do they still call you Zeppi, or are you Freidrich now?'

'I don't care,' said Zeppi. He was embarrassed at being asked about his baby name, but I knew he hated being called Freidrich.

'Did you know it was me who named you Zeppi? Just after you were born I dropped by to see the new baby and they said, "Klaus, this is little Freidrich," and I said, "What's little about him, he's more like a balloon. No, a zeppelin," and that's when everyone started calling you Zeppi. Did you know that?'

'Yes,' he said, but I knew he'd forgotten.

'Erich, you used to carry your baby brother around in your arms like an oversized watermelon, pretending he was a zeppelin travelling through the clouds. You made a very interesting buzzing sound as you swooped among the furniture. You made everyone laugh. You were still very young yourself. Your mother was always warning you not to drop him.'

'I don't remember.'

'There's a lot to catch up with on both sides,' he said. 'All the old family history.'

He was looking down at Mother, who noticed and looked up, then looked away again – blushing, I think, or it may have been the heat.

'See that gentleman on the horse?' said Klaus, pointing. We were entering a court, which was called a plaza here, and there was a statue at the centre of it, a noble-looking man holding up a sword. The horse under him was bulging with muscles and its thick mane seemed to fly sideways on a non-existent wind. 'Simon Bolivar,' Klaus told us, 'who liberated Venezuela from the Spanish yoke more than a hundred years ago. You'll see statues and pictures of him everywhere.'

'Like the Führer?' asked Zeppi.

'Sort of,' said Klaus, 'although there's no comparison, really. The Führer's plan was much grander in scale, of course. Still, everyone here admires Bolivar, so it's considered polite for foreigners to act the same way. There are lots of things you'll find out as we go along.'

'I'm thirsty again.'

'The hotel's just around the next corner.'

It stood behind a row of palm trees with very fat trunks covered in what looked like upside-down fish scales. There were clusters of orange berries or fruit up high, just under the fronds. I think they were date palms, because coconut palms are taller and skinnier. The sign along the front said: *HOTEL CONCORDIA*. We went up the steps and inside to a big lobby with a long desk made from very dark wood. Large fans hung down from the ceiling with their paddle blades turning slowly. I couldn't feel any breeze coming from them, but it was cooler inside. There was nobody behind the desk. Klaus led us up a winding staircase, letting us know this was the best hotel in Ciudad Bolivar, and we'd be staying there for two days until the river boat left.

'Where are we going?' I asked.

'Further inland. I have a job with Zamex, the second biggest oil company in Venezuela. Their head office is in Caracas. It wasn't until I got the job that I sent for you. A married man must have steady work.'

I looked at Mother to see how she reacted to this first mention of marriage to Klaus, but her face told me nothing. Klaus went on, 'There's a good position just opened up at a new field they're establishing inland. The pay is better there because the conditions are a little harder. That's how it is down here. The further away from the coast you travel, the more difficult things become.'

'Will there be snakes?' Zeppi asked.

'Certainly, and alligators. They call them caymans here.'

'The big snakes that squeeze you to death?'

'Perhaps. With a little care you can avoid being a snake's supper, Zeppi. I don't want you to start worrying about things like that before you need to. There aren't any snakes around here for you to be concerned about. Now, I think you'll find these accommodations nicer than your cabin aboard ship.'

The room we entered was quite large, with an overhead fan. Klaus turned a switch on the wall and it began turning. The ceiling was very high. There were shutters outside the tall windows, closed against the heat so it was almost gloomy inside, but that made it feel cooler. There were two large beds with bright orange and yellow covers.

'We have adjoining rooms,' Klaus explained. 'I hope the three of you won't mind sharing this room for one night. My room is through that door. Tomorrow you boys can have this room to yourselves. Helga, I've made all the arrangements. The ceremony will take place in the morning, before the heat builds up. A little church, just a short walk from here. It'll be a modest affair. I hope you didn't have anything too grand in mind. It's a question of money, you see. You won't be marrying a wealthy man, I'm afraid.'

'Everything will be satisfactory, Klaus. Please don't worry. The boys and I are grateful just to be here, aren't we, boys?'

I said yes. Zeppi nodded his head. Mother's smile was very nervous. I tried to imagine how she must feel, to be standing next to her brother-in-law, knowing that tomorrow he'd be her husband. Klaus seemed a little nervous too, with a smile that didn't quite fit properly on his face. For a moment no one said a word, and things were getting awkward, so I said, 'What about that snack?'

'Erich,' scolded Mother, 'don't be rude.'

'No, no,' said Klaus, 'Erich has things in order. You must all be hungry, I know I am. It's all set up next door. Go through, it isn't locked.'

Klaus's room was almost the same, with the ceiling fan

already turning and the windows shuttered against the heat. There was a small table set up in the middle of the room that looked as if it didn't belong there, and on the table was a plate of sandwiches covered by a hooped wire and cloth contraption to keep flies and insects away from the food. There was a bowl filled with ice, with bottles of lemonade poking out of it. Zeppi went directly to the table and lifted the sandwich cover.

'Zeppi! Wait until you're invited', said Mother. Her voice almost cracked when she said it, so her nervousness wasn't going away.

'No need for that', Klaus said. 'Everything's informal here. Eat, everyone, please. Erich, bring over another chair, would you?'

We sat and ate. The sandwiches were very good, with meat and salad and small pieces of fruit along the edge of the plates as well. The lemonade was the same kind as the man at the customs shed sold us, but the bottles were a larger size. Mother ate slowly, trying hard not to tell Zeppi and me to eat like gentlemen, rather than swine. Klaus ate very little. I think he knew he hadn't ordered enough food when he saw how Zeppi and I tore into the sandwiches, so he let us have the lion's share. I thought that was very considerate of him. I'd already forgiven him for being late at the wharf.

I asked, 'Why are you going to work in an oil field if you're a doctor?'

'Erich', Mother warned.

'It's a good question', said Klaus. 'The fact is, I'll be working as a doctor, not a driller. Accidents happen on any site where men and machinery come together.'

'But you're a surgeon', I said. Mother had always told the

neighbours about her brother-in-law the surgeon. It sounded like a higher calling than someone who bandaged cuts and delivered babies.

'And my surgical skills will come in handy on occasion, I'm sure.'

'But don't surgeons work in big hospitals?'

'Generally speaking, yes, but in my case I feel I must try my hand at something new, something less glamorous, if you like. There were plenty of Berlin surgeons who cared less for their patients than for their bank accounts. That's human nature, unfortunately. I'd like to contribute something toward the betterment of man. In a new country one feels a certain yearning for a new life entirely. You may experience this feeling yourself in time. Does that answer your question, Erich?'

'Yes,' I said.

He went on, 'You boys are very lucky, being so young and being here. Germany is exhausted.'

Mother said, 'Some things are best forgotten . . .'

'No, Helga. Erich has a shrewd mind, not unlike my own at his age, and I'm sure Zeppi will be the same some day. All questions posed in genuine need of an answer should be confronted.' He became very serious then. 'Nothing back there will ever be the same. The Communists will take over, that much is certain. The Americans and English are too soft-hearted to beat them back, and they'll be accommodated out of political weakness. I want no part of a Europe overrun from the east. Some of those Russians, those Slavs, you know, are no different to the Mongol hordes of history. Far better to be away from all that. Whatever culture flowered over there will now be crushed. Here, there's freedom to begin again. You boys will find in due course that I'm right.'

He smiled. 'And now the lecture is over. Has everyone had enough to eat?'

'I have,' said Zeppi.

'Excellent. Now I recommend that you follow the practice of the locals and stretch out for a nap. You boys may have a bed each if Helga would care to use my room. I have business to attend to elsewhere,' he added, 'siesta or no siesta.'

'When will you be back?' asked Mother.

'Early this evening. Rest yourselves, please.' He stood up.

Mother stood up too. She looked a little panic-stricken. 'Of course, Klaus,' she said, 'we're in your hands.'

'A safe place to be, I assure you,' he said, smiling. He looked even more handsome when he smiled. Some people have faces you trust automatically, and Klaus was one of those people. His hair was a little longer than it had been back home, and this gave him the appearance of a hero from some old tale, someone from beyond the bounds of civilisation. He was three years younger than Father, so he was thirty-six, but he looked younger because of his untidy blond hair and tropical suntan and white teeth, and his eyes were very blue also, the kind of blue girls go for in a fellow. Klaus had never married, or even thought about it before, so far as I knew, and I suppose he thought the moment had come to do what most men do, and at the same time rescue the surviving members of his family from a Communist Mongol Europe.

He reached for his hat, then he was gone. The room felt very empty without him.

In the evening, Klaus took us out to eat in a restaurant that served German food. He seemed to know several people there, including the owner, a fat man from Bavaria who came to our table to welcome us to Venezuela. He gave Mother and Klaus a liqueur glass each of some special schnapps, then Klaus asked if we boys could have something also, because of the circumstances, and the restaurant owner sent for two tiny glasses and a bottle of kirschwasser. It tasted of cherries and was sweet and bitter at the same time. I liked it but Zeppi didn't, and everyone laughed at the face he pulled.

He didn't get upset, though, the way he might have done ordinarily, being as sensitive as he is, and the meal went on with lots more laughing after that. There was a dance floor and a band too, and Klaus persuaded Mother to get up and dance with him. They looked very nice together, twirling slowly around and around. Mother seemed very much more relaxed, what with Klaus doing all the talking and making Zeppi and me laugh at his jokes, which weren't very funny really, but somehow he made it easy to laugh when you were with him.

We went back to the hotel through streets that were very crowded and noisy, not like in the afternoon, and we petted a monkey on a man's shoulder. It had a little waistcoat and hat on and was very friendly. It even jumped onto Zeppi's head and started screeching in a funny little monkey voice, hanging onto Zeppi's ears. Zeppi didn't like that, so the man lifted it off and the monkey calmed down again. Klaus said the man said the monkey liked Zeppi very much.

Our luggage had been brought from the wharf and put in our room. We had to wait in Klaus's room while Mother got undressed, then Klaus left us to go down to the bar while we got into our pyjamas. We went through to the other room, where Mother was already in bed but not asleep.

She asked us, 'Do you like your Uncle Klaus very much?' We both said we did, and she asked, 'Enough to live with him from now on, until you're old enough to leave home and start families of your own?' We said yes again, and I could tell she was relieved.

'What about you, Mother,' I asked, 'do you feel the same?'

She thought about it, really thought about it, then said, 'Your father was a fine man, and Klaus is in no way trying to replace him, you do understand that. Life is sometimes hard and things don't work out the way we plan, and when that happens you have to do things differently than you ever intended. But that isn't necessarily a bad thing. I think, yes, I think we can all be happy together.'

'I think so too,' Zeppi announced, and Mother hugged us both, then we got into bed. Mother fell asleep almost immediately. I had to wait until Zeppi was asleep before I could push him over to his own side of the bed. He likes to wrap himself around you if you let him. Then I lay back and listened to the music that came through our window from the street, very nice music that sounded happy and carefree. I couldn't sleep because of everything that had happened that day. I wondered what would happen to me in my life. Maybe I'd be a doctor like Klaus, even though I don't like looking at blood. He could teach me a lot. That would be a good thing to be, a doctor. Everyone respects a doctor.

Much later on I heard Klaus come into his room. He banged into something in the dark, then I saw a line of light under the connecting door. He started humming a tune but I couldn't recognise it. When the light under the door went out, I fell asleep.

T W O

THE CHURCH WAS ONLY a little way off, just as Klaus said. Mother made us dress in our best clothes, which were too heavy for the heat, but she insisted, no matter how Zeppi whined about it. Klaus said we'd go shopping for more suitable clothes after the ceremony, so we had to walk down the street to the church with sweat pouring off us and our socks going *squish, squish* inside our shoes and our necks sawed in half by collars and ties.

It was awful, and I stood there inside the church thinking about cool mountain streams and ice cream while the priest droned on and on, his voice echoing in the empty church, making it even harder to hear, plus he was talking in Spanish. I didn't understand a word of it, but Mother made all the right responses, with encouragement from Klaus.

There was no one in there to witness them getting married except Zeppi and me, and, of course, God, who saw it all from above, or so they want you to think. I've never believed anything about God myself, even when Mother used to take us to church once in a while. I don't think she really believed any of it either, but sometimes she pretended to because you're supposed to believe, the way everyone else does. Wouldn't it be funny if nobody at all believed in God, but pretended they did because they thought everyone else believed?

After the rings were on their fingers and the priest had droned on some more, we went back outside. At least in the church it had been cool.

'Now then,' said Klaus, 'what shall we do for the rest of the morning?'

'I'm hot,' said Zeppi, his voice starting to whine all over again.

'Ah, yes, the new clothes I promised. You fellows look like a pair of baked piglets. Helga, surely they can remove their ties and jackets?'

An hour or so later, Zeppi and I were comfortable in short pants and short-sleeved shirts, all in white and made from lightweight material. We had broad-brimmed straw hats on our heads and sandals on our feet. Our arms and legs looked very white, almost as white as our clothing. Klaus said we looked like a pair of peeled bananas now, and Mother laughed.

We went to another store then, and Klaus bought some things for Mother too. We had to carry our old heavy clothes back to the hotel in a paper bag, and by then it was almost time for siesta. We ate in a small cafe next to the hotel and drank lots of lemonade, then went back up to our rooms, only this time Mother went into Klaus's room. When Zeppi realised she wasn't with us any more he went to the door between the rooms and turned the knob, but the door was locked. He started banging on it and calling, 'Mother! Mother!'

Klaus opened the door and Zeppi ran past him into the room. I wanted to see if Mother was in Klaus's bed, which she had every right to be, of course, so I followed Zeppi through, pretending I was chasing him. Klaus didn't try to stop me. Mother was sitting by the shuttered window, still with all her clothes on, which was strange, I thought, because Mother was very beautiful, and now that she was married to Klaus it seemed like a waste for them not to be in bed together. Maybe they wanted to wait until they thought Zeppi and I were napping.

Zeppi ran to her and flung his arms around her. 'Where did you go?' he said, which was the stupidest question.

'Only in here,' she said. 'This is my room now, as well as Klaus's. We're married, you understand that, don't you, Zeppi? That means you and Erich will have the other room all to yourselves until we leave. You can have a bed each, won't that be more comfortable?'

'No!' said Zeppi, being a brat. 'I want you to come back . . .'

'Now then, Zeppi,' said Klaus, 'don't you want Helga to be happy? Grown-ups are happiest when they're together as man and wife, you see, and that's what happened this morning. You were there, you saw and heard it all. A man and his wife have a life together, as well as a life with their children. You'll understand it all better when you're a little older. Erich, you understand, don't you?'

'Of course.'

'Perhaps you could explain certain facts to Zeppi.'

'No,' said Mother. 'I will. Klaus, Erich, please leave us for a little while.'

Klaus and I went back into the other room. Klaus jammed a cigarette into his yellow holder and lit it. We could hear Mother's voice through the door. Klaus blew smoke and said, 'Zeppi is very young for his age.'

'He's always been like that. He needs time to get used to things, that's all.'

'I hope so. We have one more night here, then tomorrow we leave for the new Zamex drilling site. Helga will have other duties now. Zeppi must grow up. It isn't right that a boy his age should need his mother so, don't you agree?'

'I'll talk to him.'

'You know, Erich, you and I are going to get along, I can tell that already. We're pragmatists, and pragmatists cope best with life. Circumstances change every day, and we must change with them.'

Zeppi came through the door, not looking at us, and Klaus went back into his room without another word. Later on, when bars of sunlight burned through the slats of the window shutters like molten ingots and Zeppi was asleep, I was still listening for signs of physical activity in Klaus's room, but I heard nothing. In the end I fell asleep too.

In the evening we went to the same German restaurant and the owner sent over more schnapps and kirschwasser. I said to Klaus it was time I had a real drink, and he let me have some schnapps. Zeppi said he wanted some too, but Mother said he was still too young, which made Zeppi start pouting to punish her. She ignored him, though, and that made him grumpy. He said he wanted to go back to the hotel, just because nobody else wanted to. Klaus and Mother got up to dance so they could get away from him, and I told Zeppi to stop being such a baby.

He wouldn't look at me while I lectured him, and didn't say anything more, even when Klaus and Mother came back to the table. All three of us had to pretend Zeppi wasn't there, trying to make his little angel face into a mask of disapproval. I sneaked another shot of schnapps behind everyone's back, and the whole situation began to seem a lot funnier than it was. Zeppi was being a spoilsport, that was all, and failing miserably at it. I almost felt sorry for him. It made me feel quite grown up to take the side of Klaus and Mother against him, even if nobody was saying a word about it. The band was playing very loudly, and I was getting a headache.

We left after a while and began walking back to the Hotel Concordia. Zeppi found his tongue again and wanted to know where the man with the monkey was. He knew it was a stupid question, and when nobody bothered answering, he shut up and didn't say another word all the way back to the hotel and up the stairs to our rooms.

Klaus told us, 'Boys, your mother and I have something important to say to you. Please sit and pay close attention. Zeppi, are you ready to listen to what I have to say?'

'Yes,' he said.

'First, I have a surprise for you. There's been a change of plan. Tomorrow morning, when we leave for the Zamex site, we won't be going by river. Can you guess how we're going to get there? It's a long way from here, so don't tell me you think we'll be walking.'

'We're going by truck,' I said.

Klaus shook his head. 'No roads.'

'By boat?' said Zeppi, and I felt like smacking the back of his head.

'He already said we're not going by river.'

'I meant a boat that goes on the ocean!' Zeppi shot back.

'It won't be any kind of boat', said Klaus, settling it.

I thought for a moment. 'Mules? Horses?'

'Try again.'

'A plane!' Zeppi shouted. 'We're going by plane!'

'Correct', Klaus said. 'Helga tells me you haven't flown before, so this will be a special treat for all of you. We'll be flying down to Amazonas State, that's the southernmost part of the country, and it'll take most of the day.'

Zeppi instantly became tremendously excited, jumping up out of his chair, his bad mood forgotten.

'Good', said Klaus, 'you like the idea. Now then, about the other thing I have to tell you . . .'

'Zeppi', ordered Mother, 'sit! Be still and listen.'

He went back to his chair. Klaus cleared his throat. 'This may strike you as unusual, boys, but from now on you won't be called Linden any more. As of today, the family name will be Brandt. You'll be Erich and Friedrich Brandt.'

'I hate Freidrich!' said Zeppi.

'Zeppi Brandt then', said Klaus. 'The fact is, I've been going under the name of Klaus Brandt, ever since coming to Venezuela. It's important to remember this change. Whenever anyone asks you your name, or my name, or your mother's name, it's Brandt, is that clear?'

'But why?' I said. 'Your name's Linden, the same as our father's. You're his brother, so how can your name be Brandt?'

'Because I choose to make it so.'

'You'll have to tell them why', Mother said.

'Very well.' Klaus started pacing about the room. 'As you know, we have lost the war. When a nation loses in battle against other nations, it loses everything. Not just its armies and their equipment, not just its planes and submarines. A defeated nation loses its freedom. Our enemies control every aspect of life in Germany, and one of their first acts has been to assign blame for the war to individual Germans.'

'But the war ended more than a year ago,' I said.

'They insist on prosecuting innocent Germans,' Klaus continued, as if I hadn't spoken. 'They will have blood – our blood – to atone for their own misdeeds. There's nothing so weak, so defenceless, as a nation recently defeated. They can do what they want with us, you see, and we have no way to retaliate.'

'The names,' Mother reminded him.

He stopped his pacing and took a breath. 'The plain truth is, I've been informed by certain loyal Germans living here in Venezuela that my name is on the list of the accused. I was shocked when I learned of this, as you can imagine. Boys, I have no intention of surrendering to our enemies. In my position, wouldn't you do the same?'

Zeppi nodded, his mouth hanging open, and from my own throat came a dry little 'Yes . . .' My head was swimming. How dare they accuse my uncle, my *new father*, of doing anything wrong!

'Of course,' Klaus continued, 'there can be no doubt as to who is behind all this. Only one body in the world has the power and the determination, the complete mastery of everything that shapes public opinion, the sheer ability and *will* to spread lies and misinformation to this extent. Erich, who am I referring to?'

'The Jews . . .' I breathed.

'Correct. They'll be looking for a single man named Linden, not a married man named Brandt. You see how important you all are to me? My family will be my disguise. Will you help me, boys?'

'Yes!' I said, and Zeppi said it too. Suddenly Klaus was cast in a more heroic light than before. He not only looked like a hero, he *was* a hero, an innocent man falsely accused, like the Count of Monte Cristo. The Jews were trying to kill him, make him appear evil, but he was outwitting them, using his brains and courage just like a hero is supposed to do. And Mother and Zeppi and I were helping him do it! I was so proud, and then I was a little bit ashamed, because Klaus was so much more of a hero than my father had been. A dead hero is less interesting than a hero who still has trouble and injustice to overcome, especially if that hero is standing right before your eyes, looking handsome and determined and asking for your help.

'Thank you,' Klaus said, smiling with his white teeth. 'Together, we Lindens . . . excuse me, we Brandts, will run rings around our enemies. They're no match for us, no matter how many newspapers and governments they control. The war may be over, but the battle is not yet lost, nor will it ever be for as long as fellows like me stay free, hidden behind other names, in distant places where Jews don't have the nerve to follow. Make no mistake, boys, Amazonas is no place for weaklings. Helga has done me the honour of becoming my wife, knowing full well what lies ahead, and now I have a similar pledge from you both. At this moment I'm the proudest man in Venezuela. Boys, Helga, I truly feel invincible!'

Zeppi ran to Klaus and flung his arms around his waist,

sobbing. I'd never seen him so worked up. It was a peculiar and moving thing to see, and Klaus appreciated it, I could tell, because he gently stroked Zeppi's blond hair. There were tears in Mother's eyes, and one or two trying to squeeze out of my own. We were united against the Jews, the four of us, and we would win. This was a wonderful moment. I hadn't expected anything like this all the way from Germany to Venezuela, thinking all the while that maybe Klaus could be an acceptable new father, but possibly wouldn't be, and now I could see that all my sceptical thoughts had been wrong. Now we could all be heroes in the service of Klaus, helping him win the fight against all odds. And to top everything off, we were going to fly in a plane!

That night when I went to bed I did a strange thing – I put on Father's Iron Cross. I didn't want anyone to see it pinned to my shirt, I don't know why, so I got some ribbon that came tied around a clothing box Klaus had bought Mother. There was a very nice white dress in the box, and the ribbon was green, so I looped a length of it through the cross's pin and tied it behind my neck. Father's decoration hung over my belly, and the green ribbon wasn't visible inside my collar if I kept the second-to-top button on my shirt done up.

I think I wanted to wear the cross out of respect for Father, now that Mother was married to another man. I'm sure Father wouldn't have minded that she had married Klaus, who was his own brother after all, and preferable to any other man. But still, I wanted to keep a part of Father, the only remaining part, next to my skin, to make his ghost feel better about everything. It was strictly between Father and myself.

*

The airport was not very big, just a few small buildings and a
wind sock. There was only one plane there – ours. Big orange
letters ran down the fuselage – *ZAMEX*. It was a wonderful
name for something as ordinary as an oil company. How
many words have a Z and an X in them? It was like the name
of an Indian god. Zamex, lord of the jungle and mountains. A
god like that would demand human sacrifice, hearts ripped
out of living chests and held up to the sun. Zamex, the savage
god.

'We're the only passengers,' Klaus said as we climbed
inside. There were boxes and crates with Spanish words sten-
cilled on them lashed against the walls. 'Drilling equipment,'
Klaus explained as we squeezed past everything along a narrow central aisle.

Our baggage was passed through the door behind us and
an airport man started lashing it all down with canvas straps
and netting. It was a twin-engined plane, with retractable
undercarriage, and the inside smelled of spilled oil and dirty
metal and sweat. Mother had a handkerchief with some per-
fume on it held under her nose, and Zeppi was saying, 'What
a stink!'

'The seats are up the front,' Klaus said. He was carrying a
solid-looking black bag, the kind that opens out like a clam at
the top, a doctor's bag. 'Nothing too plush, I'm afraid,' he said,
and he was right. They were just metal buckets bolted to the
walls with a safety belt across the front and no cushions to
make them more comfortable. I sat in one, and it was like sitting on the iron seat of a farm tractor.

'Oh, dear,' Mother said. 'This doesn't look very nice at all.
How long will the flight take, Klaus?'

'Six or seven hours, depending on the winds. It'll pass

quickly enough. I've seen passengers fall asleep on shorter flights than this out of sheer boredom.'

'I'm not going to fall asleep,' Zeppi said, 'and anyway, it won't be boring.'

'That's the right attitude,' Klaus encouraged. 'Pick out a seat for yourself and make sure you buckle the belt tightly. We'll be bouncing around quite a bit, I can assure you. Helga, why don't you sit here next to me, and the boys can sit together on the other side. Everything has to be balanced as much as possible in a cargo flight.'

'Then there should be one adult and one child on each side,' I said, 'or it won't be balanced.'

'It's close enough,' Klaus said, settling himself beside Mother. 'I just meant we couldn't all sit along one side.' He put his black bag under the seat where his legs could wedge it against the wall behind him.

Zeppi poked his head through the curtains separating us from the cockpit. There was a doorway but no door, just curtains, dirty ones with a pattern of laughing clown faces on them, not what you'd expect to see in a plane. Maybe the pilot's wife made them.

'Zeppi,' Klaus cautioned, 'stay out of there. No interference with the pilots. Buckle your safety belts, everyone.'

I could hear voices in the cockpit. The pilot or co-pilot put his head through the curtains and asked something in Spanish. Klaus replied and the man went past us back along the plane and slammed the door with a loud bang, then came pushing through the aisle again and disappeared behind the curtains. There was some more talking up there, then the engine on the right wing started coughing and clattering and broke into a roaring that hurt my ears, followed by the engine on the left wing, which sounded even louder because Zeppi and I were sitting on the left side. Zeppi put his hands over his ears, which is what I wanted to do but couldn't because he did it first. Mother had her hands over her ears too, and was laughing, but I couldn't hear it. Klaus was grinning at her. The sound of the engines got louder and louder, and the seats shook so hard it was more like shivering.

Then we started to move. It was just a dirt airfield, so the ride was very bumpy as we taxied toward the end of the strip. With the cargo loading door shut it was hotter inside the plane than before, and I felt a little sick. Klaus was saying something to me, maybe even shouting it, but I couldn't hear a word, so I just nodded. He was probably saying it would get smoother and quieter and cooler when we were airborne; at least, that's what I hoped he was saying. The plane suddenly spun in a tight half-circle and I knew we must have reached the end of the strip. We stopped for a moment, then the engines got even louder and we started to roll along the ground faster than before. The whole plane levelled out as the tail wheel lifted, and a second or two later the wheels under the wings lifted too, and a lot of the vibration running through me was gone.

I looked through the little round window next to me but couldn't see much except for the ground falling away beneath us. My guts settled deeper into my belly for a moment, a very strange feeling, then the plane banked to the left and started climbing slowly.

I saw the wheels and struts folding up into the engine pod to make us more streamlined; then the flaps extending along the wing's trailing edge were cranked inside the wing somehow, pneumatic pressure lines, I think. After a minute or so the engines were throttled back a bit and we levelled off. Outside the window I could see three things – blue sky and white clouds and green jungle.

Zeppi was squirming in his seat, trying to see outside, but he was further from the window than I was, so he started unbuckling his safety belt. Klaus shouted at him to leave it alone, and I could hear his words this time, so it was definitely a little quieter in the plane. Zeppi either couldn't hear Klaus or else was pretending not to, because he kept pulling at his belt, so I leaned over and smacked his hands away from the buckle.

'Leave it alone!' I yelled at him, and he smacked my hands away, so I smacked him harder than before and he tried to punch me in the chest, so I punched him in the chest instead. His flesh felt surprisingly soft before my knuckles came up against bone. Zeppi howled, and Mother began shaking her finger at us both, telling us to behave ourselves. Zeppi was crying by then, and got in one good punch to my shoulder before hugging himself for comfort. It didn't hurt. His punches never did, he was so soft and girlish. What he really needed was a good hiding to make him grow up and stop acting like a silly little boy. He was irritating that way, and Mother let him get away with far too much, in my opinion. It was a good thing we had Klaus to set the rules from now on. Klaus would make Zeppi start acting his age.

The same man came through the curtains again, smiling at us, this time with pillows in his hands. He gave one to each of us, then went away. My pillow was very greasy and smelled of hair oil, and the others looked just as bad. Mother pulled a face and set hers on the floor. Klaus told her, 'You'll appreciate it before too long, mark my words.' Mother just shook her head.

I knew she'd never let anything so filthy touch her skin or clothing for more than a few seconds. Father always said she was neat as a pin and an excellent housekeeper. Everything was always spic and span at home, even after the bombings knocked out a wall.

Zeppi held out his hand. 'I want it!' She picked it up and tossed it over to him and he put it under his arse, and his own pillow behind his back. I put my pillow behind my head and leaned back against it, feeling the vibration of the fuselage through it at the back of my head. It was relaxing in a way, and I imagined a hand, a strange quivering hand, reaching through my skull to take hold of my brain. Just thinking about that made me sleepy. The air in the cabin had cooled a little, and the monotonous roaring of the engines was almost soothing.

I pointed to the black bag under Klaus's seat. 'Do you keep your equipment in there!' I had to shout to make myself heard.

'Yes!'

'Scalpels and needles and things?'

He just nodded, unwilling to hold a conversation at the top of his voice.

For hours we droned along in the air. After we left Ciudad Bolivar there were hills to break up the landscape, then everything became more or less flat. Every time I looked out the window I saw the same thing: a land of green with here and there a silver thread running through it, with the shadows of clouds passing across the jungle like the shadows of whales passing across the sea floor. No matter how long I waited in between peeks through the window, nothing ever changed. My eyes closed often and I dozed, like everyone else. There was nothing to say, and the engines were too noisy anyway. We were trapped inside a long tin can flying above a sea of green that seemed to stretch out on all sides of us forever.

After a longer than usual nap, I opened my eyes and saw Mother and Klaus sleeping upright in their seats, like the king and queen in a fairy story I read a long time ago, sleeping side by side on their twin thrones, under a dark spell that made them sleep away the centuries in their silent castle. I tried to remember if the king and queen had two sons, or just one. The prince or princes had something to do with the spell. I was little when I read it, or maybe Mother read it to me. Zeppi might not have been born yet.

I turned to look at him. He resembled a little prince with his pretty face. He noticed me watching him and turned to look at me. I winked at him and he tried to wink back at me, but winking and whistling are two things Zeppi has never been able to do. When he tries to whistle he just blows tuneless air, and when he winks, he winks both eyes at once, which looks like a facial tic. He saw by my smile that he'd done it again, made himself look idiotic, so he stuck out his tongue to show me he didn't care. I yawned to let him know his behaviour was very boring, then looked away. It was hard to think of Zeppi ever growing up. When he was twenty he'd still act like a spoiled brat and still be making a fool of himself, but probably everyone would forgive him because he'd be so handsome. Certainly, women would. He'd be more successful than me with women, the little shit. It wasn't fair that he got all the looks while I got all the brains. Still, good looks fade after a while, but you can stay smart all your life.

Zeppi was saying something to me. I leaned closer and he put his lips to my ear.

'I don't like this flying.'

'It's fun,' I told him, but he shook his head.

'It's too noisy and there's nothing to do.'

'Go to sleep then,' I said.

'I can't. I hate this plane. I want to get off.'

'You know where the door is. Bye-bye.'

'Shut up.'

'Shut up yourself and stop whining. You told me once you wanted to be a pilot.'

'I don't want to any more. It's awful.'

'There's nothing I can do about it, and anyway, I like it, so keep your complaints to yourself.'

'I hate you,' he said.

'See if I care.'

Zeppi looked to see if Mother was listening, which she wasn't, being asleep, then he called me, 'Shitface, shitface, rotten shitface . . .'

I wanted to give him a smack, but that might have made him howl, which would have woken up Mother. There was really nothing I could do but say to him, 'Someday when you're all grown up you'll wish you hadn't said that to me. It should happen in about fifty years, little boy.'

'Shitface.'

'And the same to you, pipsqueak. Now stop bothering me or I'll twist your ears.'

'You wouldn't dare. Mother would punish you.'

He was right, so I ignored him. Just to be sure he knew how I felt, I closed my eyes again. Behind my eyelids, with nothing to look at, the sound of the engines was louder somehow. I imagined us being chased across the sky by flying Jews, huge and dark in their black coats and hats, like thunderclouds, their long beards and sidelocks streaming behind them. They puffed their hairy cheeks and tried to blow us out of the air with great gusts of poisoned breath, making our little plane buck and lunge, but we kept on flying, determined to outrace the flying Jews with our roaring engines, chopping off their desperately reaching fingers with our spinning propellers, sending their silly black hats flying with our backwash, always staying just a little ahead of them, making them angry with our little silver plane so they gnashed their teeth that were red with the blood of Christian babies, their lips blackened with lies about Klaus.

Then the biggest Jew of all came hurtling along from behind and opened his mouth till it looked like a dark green tunnel in the sky, hoping to swallow us whole, and I jumped up in alarm, reaching out to slap at him and make him go away.

My safety belt cut into my lap as I lurched forward, then I was snapped back into my seat and the back of my head hit metal. Where was my pillow? Where was the sunlight that had been streaming through the little window beside me? The engines were straining, the fuselage shaking. Mother was looking at me, her face white. Klaus was holding her hand. I turned to look at Zeppi just in time to see a jet of vomit come straight from his open mouth and splash across his knees. He started crying, or maybe he'd been crying all along.

The plane was lunging down, then up, then from one side to the other. It was far worse than the storm on the ship. I saw rain pelting against the windowpane. It was dark inside the cabin, then brilliantly lit by a lightning flash. The smell of Zeppi's puke filled my nose, and for a moment I wanted to vomit too, but managed to hold it back. My pillow was on the floor, but it jumped out of reach as the plane was kicked sideways by a thunderclap louder than anything I'd heard before in my life. The pillow was in the air, hanging like a fat magic carpet, then it lifted to the ceiling and flattened itself against the curved metal there, then it fell away toward the rear of the plane, followed by one of Zeppi's.

Something was filling my chest, a feeling I recognised from the bombing raids – I was afraid. It was like a fist clenched around my heart, this fear I knew from the past. The flying Jews had caught up with us and were pounding on our plane with their giant hands, trying to swat us out of the sky, pressing their tangled beards against the windows, covering us in darkness. Zeppi threw up again, over me this time, but I didn't hit him. I was too scared to blame him. Mother was scared too, I could tell by her face, but Klaus wasn't. He sat there holding Mother as best he could, both of them separated from each other by their safety belts, and his face was worried without looking panicky. He saw me watching him and smiled for my benefit, a tight little man-to-man smile that made me feel better.

There was a terrifically loud bang that shook the plane, as if it had run into a brick wall in the sky, and the inside was lit up for a second by the most brilliant light, like a camera's flashbulb, and I knew it could only have been because we'd been struck by lightning. Mother's long hair was streaming from her head in all directions. Even Klaus's hair was standing out from his scalp like iron filings on a magnet, and Zeppi's too, and mine. I felt a kind of shivering pass across my skin, from my head to my toes, but it wasn't unpleasant. Zeppi gave a little yip of terror as he felt the same thing, like a frightened puppy.

Then a ball of light appeared by the curtain with the clown pattern on it, as if the nearest clown had performed a trick and popped a glowing blue soap bubble from his grinning mouth. The ball hung in the air without moving for a few seconds, then began moving slowly toward the rear of the plane. It passed between us in silence, lighting our faces with a lovely blue light. Zeppi's jaw had dropped so far he looked almost comical, but he wasn't afraid of the ball because it looked so wonderful. Then it simply vanished. I waited for another one to appear, but that was the only one. It must have been something to do with the lightning strike, a little piece of electricity that found its way inside the fuselage, hanging in midair like a bubble until it popped.

The pilot and co-pilot were yelling at each other. Up till then they'd been fighting the storm in silence like real professionals, but now they could be heard above the sound of thunder and engines. It was then I realised that one of the engines had stopped, the one on the right wing. I looked at Klaus to see if he'd noticed. His head was cocked to one side as if he was listening, and he looked across at me to see if I knew. Mother and Zeppi hadn't noticed yet, and Klaus's look told me it wouldn't serve any purpose to tell them. Zeppi looked terrified enough already, and I could tell by Mother's clenched eyelids she was praying to the God she only half believed in to save us.

This situation lasted for perhaps ten minutes, then the other engine stopped, and this time the sound of the storm wasn't enough to hide the fact that we were without power. Of course, now we could hear each other.

'Klaus . . .' said Mother, 'what happened . . . ?'

'It's temporary,' he assured her. He was an excellent liar, and for a moment her face relaxed, then became anxious all over again when she saw how bad Zeppi looked.

'Zeppi? Zeppi! It isn't anything to worry about. It'll be all right in a minute . . .'

Zeppi just stared at her, then he turned to me. He wanted me to say the same thing, so I told him, 'If they don't start up again we'll just glide.'

That made Zeppi feel better. He knew what gliding was because we used to watch the local glider club take their long-winged sail planes into the sky and swoop and soar for hours. He didn't know enough about planes to be aware that a metal plane can only glide for a short while, depending on its altitude. I wanted very much to hear the engines start up again, and every second that passed in silence, with just the thundering outside to listen to, seemed to stretch for an impossibly long time. It was so quiet, compared to when the engines were running, that we could hear the pilot and co-pilot, who weren't even yelling any more, just talking back and forth in quick sentences. I could hear the strain in their voices as they tried various ways to make the engines start up again, but none of them worked. We must have been gliding for two or three minutes by then without power. How close was the ground, I wondered?

The same man who had brought us the pillows came through the clown curtains, this time without smiling. He said something to Klaus, then went back into the cockpit.

Klaus said, 'We're going to land,' as if this was an everyday thing.

'But where?' said Mother. 'Have we arrived?'

'There's a river beneath us wide enough to risk a belly landing.'

'A river . . . ? But Klaus . . .'

'We can't put down among the trees. A water landing will be the safest thing. There's very little risk. Boys, as soon as we're down and have stopped moving, unbuckle your belts and go to the door in the rear. Don't hesitate for a second. We may not have very much time before the plane sinks, do you understand?' Zeppi and I nodded dumbly. He continued, 'I assume you can both swim?' We nodded again. 'Good,' he said, 'then there shouldn't be any problem. Helga and I will be right behind you. Swim to shore without looking back.'

The plane tipped over onto one wing, then straightened out. I heard a grinding noise as the wing flaps were extended. We were very close to the ground now. Through the window I could see the jungle lit by lightning flashes, but not the river, which must have been directly below us. The tallest of the treetops looked alive as they thrashed in the wind.

The pilot shouted something and Klaus said, 'This is it! Put your head in your lap and fold your arms over the top! Do it now!' I heard Zeppi whimpering beside me as I bent over, arms across the top of my head. It didn't make me feel any safer. Nothing happened for several seconds, and I wanted to look up and out through the window again, but didn't want Klaus to catch me doing it.

Then there was a terrible thump from below my feet and I was jerked sideways, toward the cockpit. Zeppi's body was flung against mine and I heard him yelp, then we both went back the other way and my body hit his, but with less force. If we hadn't been wearing the safety belts we would have been flung around like dolls. Another thump, not so loud this time, and we lurched forward again. The plane had hit the water a second time and didn't lift off again.

We slowed very quickly then, and I took my arms from around my head. Klaus was telling us to unbuckle our belts, and I didn't need to be told a second time. When I stood up, I saw that Zeppi was just sitting there, doing nothing, while Klaus and Mother were attending to their belts. 'Help him!' Klaus said, and I got Zeppi free of his belt. The pilots were still in the cockpit, not saying anything, so I thought they must be doing whatever pilots do after a belly landing in the water.

'Go to the door!' Klaus yelled, so I grabbed Zeppi by the arm and started dragging him to the rear. Some of the cargo had burst free from the netting and straps, and the aisle between the crates had disappeared, but we were able to scramble over the loose stuff without too much trouble. I got to the door and pulled the handle down, then pushed. It opened easily enough. I saw water, lots of water all whiskered with raindrops, and beyond the water I saw trees. They weren't very far away, so we wouldn't have to do a lot of swimming. Water was already running over the bottom of the doorway.

'Get out!' Klaus shouted. He was making his way over the tumbled crates with Mother, the medical bag in his hand. 'Don't stop!' I took hold of Zeppi, who was shaking with fright, and flung myself through the door.

The water was warm, like bath water. I went in over my head and lost my grip on Zeppi, then came to the surface and found him still beside me, hair hanging in his eyes, mouth open gasping for breath. 'That way!' I told him, and we started swimming. Both of us had always been good swimmers, although Zeppi liked to stop when he got even a little bit tired. I made sure I didn't get ahead of him in case he got into trouble, but he didn't panic or start thrashing about the way I thought he might. He was like a little dog that knew only one thing – he had to reach the shore, so that's where his eyes were set and what his legs were kicking for.

I looked behind us just once. The top of the plane was still above water like a silver whale swimming just below the surface, and I saw two heads in the water between the plane and us, so Mother and Klaus had escaped all right. Klaus was holding his black bag above his head, swimming with one hand. I couldn't see anyone else, but the pilots had a little door of their own in the cockpit, so maybe they'd got out on the other side. Even as I was looking, the roof of the plane slid under the water and out of sight, followed by the tail. I started swimming again.

Zeppi was a little ahead of me by then, and I caught up with him to let him know he wasn't alone, but he didn't even look at me. He'd stopped swimming properly and was just dog-paddling. I could hear his breath blowing in and out much too fast, so I could tell he was close to panicking. 'Slow down!' I shouted. 'We're almost there!' But he wouldn't stop. His hands slapped the water like the wooden blades on a paddleboat you ride at the seaside, and his breathing had turned to panting. Another few seconds and he'd start to sink. I stopped swimming and prepared myself to support him, and when I did that my feet touched the river bottom. Zeppi kept on paddling and reached the shore before me. I saw him go up the bank on hands and knees without looking back. I waded from the shallows, watching him collapse sideways, chest pumping in and out.

I made sure the Iron Cross was still around my neck, then turned to the river. Klaus and Mother were struggling ashore together, but there was still no sign of the other men. Soon all four of us were standing on the muddy bank, watching the water. The sky continued pelting us with rain, the clouds so dark it was as gloomy as evening except when lightning flickered and flashed. Zeppi was hugging himself tightly and shivering.

'Where are they?' Mother asked. 'Did they get out?'

'They might have swum to the other side,' Klaus said. 'Their door was on that side of the plane, I think.'

'But it's so much further that way. They must have wanted to put us down close to this side. Why would they have swum to the other side?'

Klaus shook his head. 'Who knows what happened. Being in the front, they may have taken much more of the impact than we did.'

Mother swept sopping hair back from her face. 'What does that mean?'

'Possibly a pair of broken necks, I have no way of knowing. Perhaps their door jammed and they drowned inside the plane, or they might have got out and been swept downstream, I just don't know.'

I said, 'They wouldn't have been swept away, the current's too slow.'

Klaus said nothing. He opened his doctor's bag and began inspecting the contents.

I asked him, 'Is everything all right?'

'Certainly. Not a drop of water came through, and everything is in place. Your grandfather gave me this bag when I graduated from medical school. It was expensive, the very best. You get what you pay for.'

Mother went to Zeppi and knelt beside him. She put her

arms around his shoulders and leaned her head against him, then both of them began to sob. It wasn't so much for the two pilots, I think, as a delayed reaction to everything that had happened. I was shivering all over, not because I was cold but because I'd come close to dying.

Klaus put his arm across my shoulder. 'We're lucky,' he said, and he was right.

THREE

THE CRASH HAD HAPPENED midafternoon. When the storm passed we saw light return to the sky, but the sun was lowering by then. The river was brown, the jungle green. The air was filled with a fine warm mist that seemed to rise from the rain-soaked ground into the still air and be swallowed by it. Mosquitoes found us and started biting.

'Make them stop it,' Zeppi moaned, slapping at his bare arms. Mother shooed them away but others moved in to take their place. Klaus suggested rubbing mud onto our exposed arms and legs, but Zeppi wouldn't, saying the mud was smelly. 'Then be bitten,' Klaus said, 'but stop making such a fuss about it. Insects are the least of our problems at the moment.'

I smeared mud over my skin, including my face. Klaus gave me an approving look but didn't take his own advice, either because he wasn't being bitten as much as the rest of us, or else because he didn't care. Mother was dabbing mud onto her arms and legs while Zeppi stood pouting, watching her do it. I knew she'd start putting mud on him before long, and he'd let her. I said to Klaus, 'Should we stay here, or start walking? Do you think they sent a radio message before we went down?'

'They might have. Then again, lightning may have knocked out the transmitter. I don't think we can count on an SOS having reached anyone. It's always safer to assume the worst, you know. I think the war has taught us that.'

'But what should we do?'

'Let me think.' He turned to the jungle behind us, a ragged green wall that didn't invite entry into its shadows. 'That's the enemy,' he said. 'Once you set foot inside there you haven't a chance, not without supplies and a compass and gun. We have nothing, so for the moment we should stay right where we are. If I'm wrong about the SOS they'll send search planes along our flight path. There's a reasonable chance we'll be seen on the river bank, none at all if we take to the jungle.'

'So we stay here?'

'Erich, your guess is as good as mine. If you can think of a better plan in the next few days, I'll listen. Meanwhile, yes, I'm fairly sure our best bet is to remain here.' He lowered his voice. Mother was five or six metres away, daubing mud onto Zeppi's arms as I'd predicted. 'And listen, Erich, don't let on any of my doubts about the radio to your mother or Zeppi. You and I can discuss all the possibilities, including those we don't want to think about, but the others need . . . protecting from the hard facts, at least for the time being, all right?'

'Yes.'

'Good man. The situation is bad, but it could be worse. We have no injuries, we have no losses, at least among the family.'

'We have no food,' I said. He looked at me, wondering if I was trying to be funny.

'Food is something a healthy human can do without for three weeks or more, provided he has access to water.'

Just thinking about the possibility the pilots didn't send out a radio message made me feel afraid. No food, and worst of all, our location known to no one except ourselves. How could we possibly survive? We had no gun to shoot animals, no hook and line for fish, nothing but some medicine in Klaus's black bag if we got sick. I wanted to cry, but didn't, because of what Klaus had said to me. I had to act like a man, the way he did. Mother and Zeppi were under our protection and would have to be jollied along with brave smiles and hearty words of hope.

Zeppi was our weakest point. He simply didn't have any kind of guts, nothing that would make him act brave even if he didn't feel it. All through the war the Führer told us to be strong, but his words never seemed to apply to Zeppi, who acted all along like someone who lives in another world, who isn't connected to what's actually happening around him. Even when he gave the salute in school assembly he looked silly doing it, as if he was imitating what the other students did without knowing why. Zeppi had always been an embarrassment that way. If he'd ever been invited to visit Hitler for a face-to-face talk, he probably would have looked at the walls and ceiling and not even bothered noticing the leader of the Fatherland right in front of his eyes.

Sometimes I thought Zeppi was simple-minded. Otto Fruenmeyer who lived down the street from us was simpleminded, a complete idiot who couldn't tell you what day it was, and he was taken away to the asylum. His mother told us later he died there, of pneumonia and deliberate self-starvation, and it only took a week. It must have been the pneumonia that killed him, not the self-starvation, because Klaus had told me a healthy man could last three weeks without food.

Anyway, Zeppi wasn't as bad as Otto. Otto was ugly, with big, loose lips and eyes that never stayed still and crooked teeth that his mother never bothered to have straightened because even with good teeth he still would have looked like an idiot. As Zeppi was as pretty as a girl, his silliness would always be forgiven. There were other retarded people in our town who went away to the asylum before the war, and they all died there, the ones Mother told us about.

As I thought about all this, Mother was looking after Zeppi like the big baby he was. Without Mother he wouldn't last for more than a week, I calculated, because Klaus and I wouldn't fuss over him the way Mother did. I felt uneasy thinking this way, Klaus's way, the straightforward honest way, because Zeppi was my brother. Sentiment was invented for people like Zeppi. In an unsentimental world he had about as much use as a flowery hat when what you really need is a tank or machine gun. In a way, it was a miracle that Zeppi had even come out of the war alive, like a single pink rose left standing in a garden blown apart by bombs, swaying prettily in the breeze and not knowing a thing.

Mother would try to survive, if only for Zeppi. Maybe also for me, since I was her other son, even though I wouldn't need looking after, and for Klaus, now that she was his wife, even if he was the most likely of us all to survive.

Soon the sun began to go down. We'd all managed to dry off quite a bit by then, but not completely because of the heat that made us sweat all the time. Watching the big yellow ball sinking behind the treetops was depressing, but Klaus didn't allow us to watch it for long. 'We need shelter,' he said, 'something to keep us dry if it rains again during the night. Come on, everyone, lend a hand. You too, Zeppi. Let's organise ourselves and do something useful.'

We went a little way into the jungle, just far enough so we couldn't hear the river and the air seemed less damp, and found a small clearing. There we started to build a shelter out of fallen branches and fronds and so forth. New green fronds would have been better, springier and less brittle, but we didn't have a knife or an axe to cut them down. In the end, what we had by sundown was a rough lean-to set against a fallen tree trunk. It was filled with holes and wouldn't have stopped any rain from coming through, but it was better than lying down under nothing. It was small, so we had to huddle together to cram in beneath it, but being so close was probably a good thing once it got dark, because we had no way of lighting a fire and night in the jungle isn't as warm as you might think, especially if you have to lie on the ground, which is usually damp. That's why I ended up squatting on my haunches with my back against the tree trunk, forehead on my knees and my arms wrapped around my legs to keep me from falling over. I was so hungry my stomach hurt, and Zeppi wouldn't shut up about food until he finally fell asleep. Klaus and Mother spoke very little, not wanting to waken Zeppi again, but before I nodded off I heard him say to her, 'Happy honeymoon.' She actually managed to laugh, just a chuckle or two. I admired them both tremendously for that.

Several times during the night I woke up, once to piss and

once because Klaus opened his bag. The clasp made a loud click, or maybe it was the movement itself that woke me.

'What is it?' I said.

'There's something moving around among the trees,' he whispered. 'Be very still. I have a scalpel in my hand and I don't want to cut you accidentally.'

'Something big?' I whispered back.

'I can't be sure. Hush.'

We listened together. I heard the sound a moment later, a snuffling, swishing sound, definitely a creature of some kind moving through the undergrowth. I could smell it too, a sort of rank animal smell, a combination of earth and fur. At the same time it became silent, probably smelling us, and then it moved away, very likely as scared as we were. 'Be still, my heart,' Klaus said, and I laughed, but not so loud as to wake up Mother or Zeppi.

'If only we had a fire,' said Klaus. 'It would make all the difference in the world. I imagine our ancestors thought so too, in their caves and hideaways, knowing there were sabre-toothed tigers about.'

'And bears,' I said. 'There used to be giant bears that are extinct now.'

'Indeed, and here we are, trembling at the approach of an anteater.'

'Was that what it was?'

'Possibly. A carnivore would have shown a lot more interest in us, I think.'

'Tomorrow we need to make one of those things they make fire with, you know, the stick that you rub between the palms of your hands with some dried grass under the point of the stick?'

'Friction fire,' said Klaus. 'But one of those little bow things would be better, where the bowstring is looped around the stick. That's a lot faster and easier.'

'We don't have any string.'

'I have surgical thread, old-fashioned stuff made from horsehair.'

'Really?'

'We'll make a fire bow tomorrow. That'll be the first order of the day.'

Zeppi groaned then and we stopped talking. I thought about how the fire bow would be made. Just imagining it working, producing smoke and flame from dried grass, made me shiver with happiness. After that we'd make some spears, and some real bows, and arrows to go with them, of course, and build a real hut with a rainproof roof of thatched fronds. We'd be the Swiss Family Robinson, only in the jungle instead of on an island.

Before I fell asleep again I wondered how it was that I'd made myself accept so quickly the fact that there would be no rescue, no search planes anywhere near where we came down. It went against human nature to be so pessimistic, so why had I accepted it? Then I realised it was Klaus's words and Klaus's attitudes that had made me think that way. Klaus had called himself a pragmatist, and certain notions go along with such descriptions. Klaus was talking to Mother and Zeppi in terms of rescue, I'd heard him, but to me he made no bones about our chances. To me he said, in so many words, we would have to rescue ourselves. He trusted me with the truth. Truth was for men to share, and the women and children could only be led to it slowly, by degrees, because they couldn't face it directly.

In Zeppi's case this made sense, but I thought Mother could face the facts without losing heart because she'd already been through so much that was bad. Still, if that was how Klaus wanted to handle the situation, it was fine with me. His trust made me feel good enough that I could forget my growling belly and lay my head down again on my knees. Just before my eyes closed I asked myself whether, for all of Klaus's pragmatism, we would die anyway, because nature doesn't care what kind of label you put on yourself. I didn't like that thought, so I shoved it away, out into the darkness under the trees where invisible creatures roamed and hunted and killed.

In the morning, Zeppi cried because he was thirsty, but he wouldn't go to the river and drink because he was afraid an anaconda would leap out of the water and drag him under. Finally, Mother had to take him by the hand and lead him down to the river's edge and scoop out some water for him, which he drank from her hand like an injured dog. I told him to stop worrying about snakes in the water, and was about to tell him the problem with the water was the alligator things, the caymans, but then I thought better of it. If I said a word about them he'd never go near the water again, and Mother would have to hand-spoon him water all the time just to keep him alive. It was ridiculous.

Klaus gave us a little talk later on. We had words instead of food for breakfast, but it gave us something to be going on with. He called it The Plan.

'While we wait for the search planes to find us, we have to keep ourselves busy. What should we do with our time?

Obviously, we must find food. There are probably edible plants in the jungle, but I have no idea what they look like, and the chances are we'd eat something poisonous instead, so plants are not the answer. We need to hunt game. Meat we understand. How do we hunt when we have no weapons to hunt with? We make those weapons. Bow and arrows, spears, that kind of thing, and with them we'll hunt until we make a kill. We have no choice.'

'But how do we make such things, Klaus?' asked Mother.

'Leave it to Erich and me. While we're doing that, it might be a good idea for you and Zeppi to weave a fish trap out of twigs and vines, you know the kind of thing, a funnel shape with a cage at the end.'

'Perhaps if you draw a picture . . .' said Mother, who'd clearly never heard of such a device. Klaus said he'd draw a picture in the dirt in a minute, when he'd finished talking about The Plan.

'Finding food is only the first step. The next thing is to find a way out of here. Traipsing through the jungle is pointless. It's impassable in many places, and we don't have a compass, so we'd end up going in circles.'

'The planes . . .' said Zeppi. 'They'll find us . . .'

'We must certainly hope they do, Zeppi, but a prudent man always has an alternate plan prepared and that's what we're discussing at the moment. How do we get out of here, you ask? By way of the river. All rivers in Amazonas, even the smallest stream, flow into larger rivers, and those flow into rivers larger still, and eventually it all finds its way to the Orinoco. Once we get that far, we'll be seen by the river traffic and picked up.'

'But we have no boat, Klaus.'

'Then we'll make one, or rather, given that we're without

the proper tools, a raft. Something simple, made from fallen trees lashed together with vines.'

Mother and Zeppi didn't look reassured.

Klaus said, 'We have a choice – either we do as I've suggested, or we simply stand about and wait to die of starvation. Zeppi, do you want to stand about and slowly die?'

'No . . .'

'Helga?'

'Of course not . . .'

'Then the choice is made. Erich, you're in agreement with this plan?'

'Yes, it makes sense.'

'Naturally. Man has a brain, and the brain tells him what he must do to survive. So, we must begin immediately, before we lose strength. Erich, search for suitable branches or saplings to make a bow and arrows. Make sure the wood is supple. When you find it, come to me and I'll give you a bone saw from my bag.' He squatted on the ground, cleared a section of twigs and leaves and began sketching with a stick. 'Helga, this is what a fish trap looks like.'

I walked away into the trees, feeling important. Klaus had chosen me to find the right tree to make a weapon from. Without the weapon there would be no hunting, no food, and without food we couldn't survive to build a raft and float downriver to safety. Everything depended on me, really.

After I'd gone far enough into the jungle to lose the sound of voices, everything felt different, more dangerous somehow. The air was already thick with heat and the buzzing of insects, and very still, as if the closeness of the trees stopped it moving around. It was like wading through invisible water, exploring a submarine jungle.

I looked at the ground often, worrying about snakes, not anacondas but little ones that hid in the leaves and couldn't be seen until you were right on top of them. My feet, sockless inside their sandals, felt very exposed and white. I pictured a snake fastened onto my instep, sinking its fangs deep into my flesh, injecting me with poison that paralysed me instantly, and the picture was so real, so vivid, I stopped walking, couldn't take another step. I was breathing hard by then, every bit as terrified as Zeppi, and I was ashamed.

I stood like a statue, afraid to move even my eyelids. A tiny bird, green and red, flew past my head, its wings moving so fast they were a blur, then it turned around and came back to hover right in front of my face. A hummingbird, I thought. How beautiful it was . . . then it was gone. I couldn't even turn my head to watch it fly away. The situation was ridiculous. Klaus was expecting me to find the right piece of wood for a bow, and I hadn't gone more than fifty metres from the river yet. I couldn't even raise my hand to brush the sweat from my brow, from where it was running down my nose and into my eyes, stinging them, making the greenery around me swim with flickering shapes that moved in ways no bushes ought to. There were animals prowling around me, carnivores anxious to leap from cover, pull me down and tear chunks of flesh from my body. I could feel my bowels loosening with fear. I wanted to cry out for Klaus to come, but no sound came. My throat was plugged with terror; I could feel those beasts moving closer on silent paws, drool hanging from parted lips.

Then I saw the man. A naked man, with fat earrings that had little yellow feathers stuck in them. He didn't have a stitch on his body and he was watching me steadily. A pale brown man, not tall, with black hair combed down from the top of his head and cut straight across just above his eyebrows and the tops of his ears. Dark eyes watched me without blinking.

The man was uncircumcised, not like me. Klaus had recommended circumcision for Zeppi and myself for reasons of hygiene, despite it being what the Jews did with their baby boys. A circumcised penis is a penis that can be kept cleaner, he had told us. Father had said no one would mistake us for Jews, because we were blond. The brown man had a penis that was smooth all the way down, like a sausage. In his hand was a long straight stick twice as tall as himself. I knew its purpose from pictures in natural history books in the school library – a blowpipe. Now I saw the little quiver of darts slung around his neck, decorated with more tiny feathers like the ones stuck in his earrings, which I now saw weren't rings at all, but tubular plugs crammed into big holes that stretched his earlobes.

We watched each other without moving. He'd been there all along, from the moment I had stopped walking and started worrying about snakes, but I hadn't seen him there in the green shadows any more than I'd taken notice of individual tree trunks. He was part of the jungle, and I'd only come to be aware of him after I stopped moving. I had the feeling that he was the one who made me stop, so he could study me, and after he was done with that, he let me see him. I don't know why I felt that way. And as we stared, I became aware that I wasn't frightened any more. This was a man, not a jaguar. He wouldn't harm me. There was no hatred in his eyes, and no fear, not even curiosity. He just stared, with no expression at all on his face.

Then he turned and vanished into the greenery as if he hadn't been there at all. And I could move again, as though his disappearance had released me somehow. I went directly back to the others, my heart hammering with excitement.

At the edge of the clearing I started to run. The lean-to was there, but no one was around, and I began to panic. Had there been other naked brown men who had come and taken everyone away while I was paralysed with fright among the trees? Was I alone now?

'Klaus! Mother . . . ! Where are you!'

I heard voices not far away, to the left of where I'd come bursting from the trees, and I ran toward the sound, still calling for Klaus and Mother. I saw Zeppi first, then the others, and stopped dead, panting, sweating, suddenly feeling like a fool. They were looking at me in astonishment.

'Erich, is something wrong?'

'Klaus . . .'

'Speak up. What happened?'

I pointed into the jungle. Klaus turned to follow my finger.

'Did you find a suitable tree? Erich, what's the matter with you?'

'Did you see a snake?' Mother asked. 'Oh, Erich, you didn't get bitten, did you?'

'There's a man . . .' I said at last, pushing the words out past my teeth.

'What man? You've only been gone for five minutes.'

'A man,' I insisted, 'out there, with a blowpipe!'

'Blowpipe?'

'And no clothes. A brown man. He saw me. He went away.'

Mother said, 'Are you sure you weren't imagining things?'

'No! He was there, a brown man with no clothes and a blowpipe. He went away.'

Mother turned to Klaus. 'Is this a good thing?'

'Perhaps, perhaps not. If he was naked he's obviously not a mission Indian. That means he's wild, unfortunately. Did he seem hostile?'

'No, he just stared at me.'

'There are probably others,' said Klaus. 'He'll fetch them and come back.'

'What should we do?' Mother asked, going to Zeppi and placing a hand on his shoulder. Zeppi seemed not to understand what was happening, just stood looking at us in turn as we spoke.

'The best thing would be to wait. We can't run away. If they come back, show them no fear. Treat them as you would a growling dog. Look them in the eye and don't move. I suggest we wait by the lean-to. This might be the best thing that could have happened, if they're friendly.'

'And if they're not? Klaus, will they kill us?'

'Calm yourself, Helga. The Indians aren't savage every hour of the day. They'll be curious, I expect, especially if they haven't seen whites before. There are said to be tribes that haven't. That might be the best thing, in fact. They'd probably be scared of us.'

I said, 'But then they might kill us, if they're scared.'

'Possibly,' he admitted, 'but let's not assume the worst just yet. In all likelihood they'll be friendly. They'll feed us! Who isn't hungry?'

He was trying to be jolly for Mother and Zeppi. We stood together by the lean-to, then waited, facing the trees. Zeppi was frightened to the point of shivering. I was nervous myself.

Mother concentrated on keeping Zeppi calm. Klaus did a strange thing – he put his cigarette holder in his mouth. His cigarettes were gone, of course, ruined in the river, but he placed the long yellow holder between his teeth anyway, as if presenting himself to the Indians that way would impress them. He didn't have a gun, but he had his cigarette holder. I understood what he was doing without talking about it to him, and Klaus, in any case, was in no mood for conversation. He stared into the shadows beneath the trees like a man intent on seeing what he knows to be there, even though it isn't visible.

And I began to feel myself that we were being watched. They were right in front of us, but hidden by the greenish gloom of the jungle. I felt their eyes, many eyes, taking us in as we stood there exposed to their poisoned darts, showing no fear, or trying not to.

'I think I see one . . .' said Mother. '. . . No, it's just a tree . . . Klaus, is anything there, do you think?'

'I can feel them watching us. Be still now and wait. Zeppi, you will immediately cease that ridiculous noise.'

Zeppi was moaning in the back of his throat. He stopped.

They came from the trees, five of them, small and naked and brown. Two carried blowpipes, the other three carried bows. None had arrows nocked to their bowstrings. They came toward us slowly, never taking their eyes from ours. I tried to detect anger in them, in the way they walked and carried their weapons, but felt none. They were wary of us, that was what I felt, not afraid exactly, but apprehensive, and I began to think Klaus was right – they hadn't seen white people before. We were something new and strange, and they weren't sure how to approach us. This was good news, probably. I felt a little less afraid as they came closer, five metres, then four, then three, two, one . . . and then they were beside us, peering into our faces, sniffing loudly, as if trying to find out by way of their noses what kind of humans we were.

One of them reached out slowly and touched my hair. His fingers were gentle, rubbing the long hair over my forehead between the fingertips. His fingers then touched my cheek. I could smell his hand, a warm and sweaty smell, slightly sour, but not horrible. His face was close to mine, examining me intently, a broad face with slightly slanting eyes that made me remember my history lessons about Asiatics crossing the frozen Bering Strait from Siberia tens of thousands of years ago to populate the Americas, north to south over more thousands of years. His face was completely hairless, but I was sure he was an adult, even though the top of his head only came level with Klaus's shoulders.

He fingered the material of my shirt, then leaned close to me and licked my cheek. The touch of his wet tongue almost made me cry out and jump away from him, but I stopped myself and even let him do it again. He lifted my upper lip and looked at my teeth, tapping a fingernail against them when I gave him a smile. The smile made no difference. None of them was smiling. Klaus and Mother and Zeppi were all getting the same treatment, a slow and careful touching and feeling and prodding that was insulting in a way, but never rough or hurtful. I saw one of them touch Mother's breasts under her dress and squeeze them gently in a thoughtful kind of way. She flinched and closed her eyes, but didn't make a sound.

Another, I think it was the one I'd seen in the jungle, bent down to look at Zeppi's face more closely. Zeppi was trying hard not to be afraid, but I could hear his breath panting in and out. He still had hold of Mother's hand. The man licked his cheek with a long wet tongue, passing it from Zeppi's jawbone clear up to his ear. Zeppi gasped. I waited for him to scream, which might have upset everything.

The tongue licked him again in the same place . . . and Zeppi started giggling. He laughed! It was a silly little laugh, an embarrassed laugh, the kind that wants to hide itself away before it gets any louder, but can't. I held my breath. Would Zeppi's laugh offend the men? They were all five looking at him, and Zeppi felt their eyes boring into him, I could tell, because his own skittered from one to another while the laugh kept trickling from his lips, a girlish tittering that made me want to give him a smack to shut him up. He stopped. They continued looking at him.

Then Zeppi did the most stupid thing he could possibly have done. He poked out his tongue and blurted at them. It was the kind of sound, along with lots of spittle, that little boys make when they want to insult each other. Zeppi made it as disgusting as he could, then stopped, drew breath, and started again. I heard the air catch in Klaus's throat at Zeppi's foolishness, but he didn't move or speak. Zeppi blurted loud and long, then stopped. We waited for a reaction from the Indians. I was afraid all over again. Everything had been going along smoothly while they sniffed and licked and touched us, then Zeppi had to go and behave like a stupid little schoolboy and put us all at risk.

One of them blurted back at Zeppi, then the others did too, making their blurts as loud and long and wet and disgusting as they could. And Zeppi blurted right back at them. They started to laugh then, at each other and at Zeppi, who stopped blurting and laughed also, a high-pitched whinnying laugh that ordinarily would have irritated me, but under the circumstances was the most welcome sound I could have imagined. He almost screamed with hysteria, and the Indians laughed harder than before, pointing at him as if he was the most hilarious object they'd ever seen, and every time one of them pointed at Zeppi the rest of them started laughing all over again.

Klaus must have decided that laughter was the one thing that would unite us all as human beings, so he started too, a very fake laugh that sounded as if it was being cranked out of him with a handle. Mother took the hint and made the strangest noise, halfway between a laugh and a scream. It was my turn then, so I took a deep breath and pumped out the silliest laugh I could produce, a hyena sound that was so exaggerated it got me laughing real laughter. One of the Indians began rolling on the ground, trying to laugh and blurt at the same time. His friends found that very funny

Then, as quickly as it had started, all the laughing stopped. The Indians spoke among themselves, a soft babbling sound like running water, then one of them turned to us and pointed at the trees. Some of them started walking, the others waited for us to move. Klaus picked up his medical bag and told us to get going. The rest of the Indians followed along behind.

'Should we do this?' Mother asked Klaus.

'What alternative is there? They seem friendly enough.'

'Where are we going?' Zeppi wanted to know.

'We'll find out when we get there,' Klaus told him. 'It might be a long way, and it might take a long time, so you have to be strong, Zeppi. That means no complaints along the way. Will you do that for me?'

'Yes', said Zeppi, but he didn't sound happy about it.

The jungle seemed less threatening with the Indians along. They moved quickly, not bothering to push through the thickest scrub. They never stopped once to consider which way they should go. It was as if they knew every little gap and space between the trees, although I couldn't see anything that looked like a pathway. They kept up a steady pace, and Zeppi started to puff and pant, but to give him credit, he didn't complain, and even refused Mother's hand over some of the rougher sections. Sweat was pouring from me, and my hunger pangs were so bad I had a headache as well as a stomach ache, but I concentrated on putting one foot in front of the other.

The further we got from the river, the less dense the undergrowth became, and we travelled faster between the trees, some of which must have been at least fifty metres tall. I could hear loud shrieking above us – monkeys, I thought – but I saw nothing. We walked and walked, sometimes speeding up to a fast trot in the more open areas, and I had a sense of urgency, of hurrying toward whatever place it was they were taking us. We were being swept along, herded like sheep by silent but watchful dogs.

The land began to rise a little. I was exhausted by then, and so was everyone else, especially Zeppi, whose face was twisted with misery. But he'd kept his word about complaining. I felt sorry for him and said, 'It isn't much further now', even though I hadn't any idea how much longer it would take. The strange thing is, I was right. Just a few minutes later we stopped on a low rise with some open land before it, and saw something two hundred or so metres away the like of which I'd never seen before.

It looked like a giant wasp's nest built on the ground instead of in a tree, greenish-brown in colour, a kind of dome shape with a hole in the top from which smoke trickled out, which made me realise this was a place where people lived. It was something like an Eskimo's igloo, only a hundred times bigger, and made out of what looked like giant leaves. Further away down the slope I could see a river glinting behind the trees. The Indians were watching us as we stared at the place.

'What is it?' Mother asked.

'Their village, I presume,' said Klaus.

Zeppi asked, 'Can we stop walking when we're there?'

'Of course we can. You've done very well, Zeppi.'

We started moving again, but slowly now, going down the slope toward the village. On our left was a garden of some kind, not with flowers but with what looked like banana trees. There were some naked women there collecting big bunches of little green banana things. I looked at their breasts for as long as I could as we went past, and the women stared back at us. One little girl pointed and screamed. Zeppi looked behind us to see what the girl was pointing at. He didn't understand that she was screaming about us.

As we got closer to the dome I saw how it gave the impression of a wasp's nest because of the lumpiness in the walls and roof. It was a higgledy-piggledy place, but very interesting to look at because of the size. When we were close enough I saw a hole appear in the wall, not a big hole, just wide enough for us to bend down and enter. Someone inside had taken away a few dead thornbushes that blocked the hole, and that's what allowed us through. When we were inside it was blocked again behind us.

The men who had brought us there started making

whooping sounds as loudly as they could, probably to let everyone know they had something very important with them. They were showing off, just like a winning soccer team, jumping up and down and making as much noise as possible.

It was like being inside a giant ball, just the top half, with a big hole cut away at the highest point. The whole structure was made on a circular branch-and-pole frame that must have taken forever to build, and then thatched with big flat leaves on the outside of the frame to keep the rain out. Most of it was open space, but further back under the roof I could see hammocks slung from what I suppose would have to be called rafters. There were small fires burning here and there, and most of the supporting poles were hung with arrow quivers and bunches of the banana things, only yellower or browner than the ones I saw outside, so they must have been riper.

There were lots of naked people everywhere, dozens of them, men and women and children, all staring at us. Some of the men picked up bows and blowpipes and ran at us, yelling and shaking their weapons. The men who had brought us inside were acting like our protectors now, holding the other men back and screaming at them. A few even got into a shoving match.

It was clear that nobody was supposed to touch us until permission was given. The men who had brought us into the village were acting superior to the rest and weren't about to let just anyone come near the strange white people they'd found. It was almost funny to watch them acting that way. The women and children had come closer, staying clear of all the shoving, and I looked from one set of titties to the next. Most of them were very disappointing to look at because they sagged and were more like upside-down beer bottles, but the younger women and girls had nice plump ones that stuck straight out.

Then a man came forward, naked as the rest of them, with the same bowl-cut hairstyle, but there was something different about him. For one thing, he wasn't yelling or shoving. He wore the same feathered ear plugs as the other men, but was a little taller, and very well built, solid like a wrestler, while most of them were more on the skinny and wiry side, like cyclists. Everyone stepped aside a little as he came closer, even the men, and by the time he was standing beside us most of the noise had calmed down. There was some excited talking and lots of arm movements as the men who brought us in described to him what they'd done – at least, that's what I thought they were doing.

While they spoke he looked us up and down, one at a time, then came closer and touched us and smelled us and tasted us, just as the others had done. This time nobody started blurting and there was no laughter. Zeppi was staying as close to Mother as he could, his eyes wide. Mother looked worried, but Klaus didn't. He looked bored, but I think he was putting on an act to let the chief – that's who the solid-looking man had to be – know he wasn't afraid of him. I decided to model my behaviour on Klaus's. I didn't have a cigarette holder to put between my teeth, but I could stand with my hands on my hips and my chest out like him.

The chief looked up into Klaus's face, then he slowly reached up and carefully plucked the cigarette holder from between his teeth. He looked at it closely, feeling the smooth ivory, then he sniffed at the wider end where the cigarettes were plugged in, and nodded his head as if he understood what it was for. He pushed the wide end up his left nostril and huffed a few times to see if he could breathe through it. This should have made him look as silly as a schoolboy who shoves pencils up his nose to look like a walrus, but nothing this man did seemed foolish in any way. He left the holder there, I suppose because he didn't have any pockets to put it in.

I looked at Klaus to see if he was annoyed at having his holder taken away, but he seemed calm, and was even smiling a little, as if to say to the chief, 'You're very welcome, I'm sure.'

All of us had our blond hair fingered by the chief, and Mother had her breasts squeezed again, but there was nothing offensive about it. The chief just wanted to be sure she was a woman under all that cloth. I think if she'd been naked like all the Indian women he wouldn't have touched her. Zeppi, whose hair was blondest of all, almost white, was given another very close inspection, and I could tell his fear was giving way to grumpiness again.

As the chief's face came closer to Zeppi's a second time and his mouth began to open for another lick of my brother's smooth-as-marble cheek, Zeppi pulled away. 'No!' he said directly into the chief's face. Zeppi then turned to Mother. 'Make him go away!'

'Zeppi, please . . .'

'He smells!'

Klaus said, 'Zeppi, control yourself.'

'I don't like him!'

'Would you like him to pop you in a big pot and eat you?'

'Klaus, don't say such things!'

'He must learn to behave.'

Zeppi gasped at Klaus's words, then shut up. The chief didn't seem to be affected in the least. He straightened up and went to the largest fire, then sat down. The men who had brought us followed, and we went along as part of the group. Everyone sat, then some women started bringing us food, those little banana things first, then some meat that still had fur on it. It had been cooked, but they hadn't bothered skinning the animal first, whatever it was. The fur was short and dark grey, so I thought it might be monkey. I couldn't eat it even though it smelled good. My stomach was in knots just looking at it. Mother and Zeppi were the same. We'd eaten the bananas, but all they did was let our guts know it wasn't enough.

Finally, Klaus picked up a chunk. 'Like this,' he said. He turned it over and began eating, holding onto the furry side as the Indians did, burying his face into the meat the way you might eat the middle out of a halved orange. His example was all we needed. Along with Mother and Zeppi, I started eating. The meat was good, whatever it was, very tasty and with lots of juice. I had a second piece, then a third. We all did. The Indians stood around or squatted and watched every move we made. Zeppi was so hungry and so happy to be eating he did so with his mouth open, a habit Mother had worked hard for a long time to break him of, but she didn't notice.

From where I sat on the ground I could see up between the legs of all the women who were standing. They had hardly any hair, and their private parts weren't very interesting, just a sort of fold in the flesh that went all the way around to the bigger fold behind. I preferred looking at their top parts, but the funny thing is, after seeing more tits in five minutes than I'd ever seen in dirty books at school, I didn't really bother looking any more. They were just tits. It was the same with all the cocks hanging this way and that. Back home, in the shower room after a game of football, everyone sneaked a look at everyone else's to see if it was bigger than his own, but here the cocks were so openly on display they weren't really interesting at all. I started paying more attention to the faces. They were the thing to study if you wanted some clue to who was in front of you.

I noticed that some of the Indians wore paint on their faces, mostly in straight lines with a few twirls here and there, in only two colours, black and red. Some had armbands made of what looked like woven grass with feathers stuck in them, and others had red-coloured mud or something on their hair to keep it in place like a sticky helmet. They all smelled of sweat, but apart from some little babies who crawled around in the dirt they seemed clean enough.

I was getting full, but kept eating. The meat was gone, but I had three more little bananas. Zeppi had already stopped and was looking at the Indians. 'Look at all the willies,' he said with a straight face, and Klaus and Mother actually laughed, although Mother's laughter was almost hysterical.

The chief spoke often with the men who had found us. I paid no attention after a while. My legs were cramped after all that sitting, so I stood up and started walking around, never moving too far from the others. Some little children followed me, staring and pointing and giggling among themselves.

I strolled deeper under the slanting roof. There were dozens of hammocks slung there from various struts and supporting poles, and lots of weapons leaning nearby. There was no privacy at all, nothing like a room or even a curtain to separate one section from the next; in fact, there wasn't anything you could call a section. It was a huge circular room with a sloping roof, with no furniture apart from the hammocks. I wondered where we were going to be put, and if we could stay together.

One of the hammocks was occupied by a sleeping man. I went closer, not sure why it was that I wanted to get a better look at him. It wasn't until I stood right beside him that I realised what it was that made him different to the other Indians. This one had a beard, and his hair was long, not cut into a bowl shape. He was as naked and brown as the rest, and his hair and beard were black, but I knew he wasn't an Indian.

His face was shiny with sweat and his arms and legs shook sometimes, little tremors that came and went, the way a horse will make its skin shiver to shoo away a fly. I watched him sweat and shake, and listened to him murmuring in a language I couldn't understand. His eyes opened and he saw me. He stopped breathing, then started again, and sat up in the hammock. He stared and stared at me, delighting the children who were watching. They seemed to understand that he was even more amazed to see me than I was to see him.

He said something to me and I shrugged to let him know I didn't understand. He said something more – in Spanish, I think – and I told him, 'Excuse me, I don't speak that language.' He gave out a gasp, then smiled at me.

'Whose child are you? Where did you come from?'

His German was good, but he spoke slowly and a little clumsily, as if he hadn't used it for a long time. I looked around for the others. They were still by the fire with the chief and most of the adults. Zeppi had wandered away and was looking for me. When he saw me he ran over.

Noticing him, the bearded man said, 'My god, there are two of you ... and more? Are there more? Please answer me.'

'Yes,' I said, 'Mother and Klaus.'

'Klaus? Klaus who? Give me names, boy.'

I didn't think it was any of his business, but he looked so anxious I told him anyway. 'Klaus . . .' I almost said Linden, '. . . Brandt. He's our new father.'

'So, this one is your brother.' He leered at Zeppi, who backed away several steps.

'No need to be afraid of me, sonny. I'm like you, a German. Wentzler, Gerhard Wentzler. Tell your father to come over here. I can explain everything you people will need to know. Run and get him, Goldilocks.' He said that to Zeppi, who asked me, 'Why does he look like that?'

'Go and fetch Klaus,' I told him. 'This is important.'

'Fetch him yourself,' said Zeppi, sticking his chin out.

I said, 'If you don't, I'll tell the Indians to eat you.'

His mouth fell open. 'You would not.'

'Yes I would. Do as I say.'

Zeppi went slowly away.

'Big lad for his age,' said Herr Wentzler.

'He's twelve, he just acts as if he's nine.'

'Aha, and may I ask how it is that you and your family are here?'

'We were in a plane. It crashed into the river.'

'The river, yes . . . Perfect!'

I didn't know what he could possibly mean by that, and wondered if he was a little bit crazy. His eyes were dancing around with excitement as he got himself up and out of the hammock and stood there, his skinny legs shaking. I saw the grey in his beard and hair now, and knew he must be a lot older than I thought at first, maybe in his forties.

'Here they come, here they come . . .' he said.

Klaus and Mother and Zeppi were approaching, along with

at least a dozen of the Indians. They all gathered around Herr Wentzler, who held out his arms as if greeting long-lost relations. Nobody stepped forward to be embraced by those arms, which were as skinny as his legs. 'My good people ... my fellow Germans ... welcome! Gerhard Wentzler, Professor Wentzler, Heidelberg University. May I say how utterly remarkable it is to see you!'

He was shaking from top to toe. I thought he might fall down.

Klaus said, 'Thank you, Herr Professor, and may I say how remarkable it is to see you here also. Klaus Brandt, University of Frankfurt. My wife, Helga, and our boys, Erich and Freidrich.'

'No!' said Zeppi.

'Who likes to be called Zeppi, I must add. Herr Professor, I'm curious to know if there are other white men here, or nearby perhaps? We've had a terrible accident.'

'So your boy said. Yes, terrible, but you know, it was meant to be, this crash, at least in the eyes of the Yayomi.'

'Pardon me?'

'They knew it, spoke of it beforehand, at least two days ago. You crashed when?'

'Yesterday. What is ... Yayomi?'

'These,' he said, sweeping his arms around the inside of the circular village, 'these are the Yayomi. This is only the second time they've encountered white people, the first time being their introduction to myself, of course.'

'But you said they knew of the crash. They saw it happen, do you mean?'

'Nothing of the sort. They talked of it at least a whole day prior to that, not about the plane crash, no, I don't believe they've ever seen a plane, or could possibly understand what a plane is, but you, *you* they know of, do you see?'

Klaus smiled at him. 'Certainly,' he said. He'd reached the same conclusion as me – Herr Wentzler was not in his right mind. Klaus went on, 'Are you well? You seem to have a fever, Herr Professor.'

'Wentzler, just Wentzler. What could a title possibly mean here? The Yayomi have no titles. Even the chief, the fellow beside you, is known to one and all by his chosen name, Manokwo. But I'm wandering, aren't I. Yes, they knew you were coming. Noroni saw it in a dream, the arrival on the river bank around the bend of the four dolphins.'

Mother looked at Klaus. 'What does he mean?' She was taking great pains not to look at Wentzler's private parts, which were uncircumcised, like those of the Indians.

'What I mean, charming lady,' said Wentzler, 'is that you four are the dolphins, you see?'

'I'm afraid not,' said Klaus, still smiling.

'Freshwater dolphins, usually found further south than here, in Brazil, but not unknown hereabouts from time to time. They're very pale, you see. Four white dolphins, yes . . . You comprehend?'

'We are the four white dolphins someone saw in a dream?'

'Found exactly where you ought to have been, not far from here, just around the bend in the river to the east, am I correct?'

'I have no idea what bend of what river we were found beside, but we're certainly not dolphins, can't they see that?' Klaus smiled at the Yayomi, nodding pleasantly as he spoke, as if they might understand his words and be offended by his doubt.

'Creatures may on occasion take human form, Herr Brandt. You are dolphins, and as such you're honoured guests. The one who saw you coming, Noroni, will enjoy great status among his people because of this. You'll find he wants to be your friend. Some of the others may be a little fearful at first. That's Noroni, there.' He pointed to one of the men who had come to find us by the river, the same one I'd first seen among the trees. I was beginning to be able to tell the difference between some of them already.

Klaus said, 'Herr Wentzler, you haven't answered my question. Are there other whites nearby, a mission, perhaps?'

'Nothing for three or four hundred kilometres in every direction. This is so very strange ... They tell all kinds of stories about the supernatural, but one doesn't expect to see any of it made into flesh, not even myself, who has been here so long. Remarkable circumstance ... truly remarkable. You'll forgive me if I sit?'

Herr Wentzler collapsed back into the hammock, his breathing ragged, sweat pouring from him. He smelled very bad, like old laundry allowed to get damp and left for a week or two. One of his scrawny legs dangled from the hammock, toes touching the ground, and he used this to create a gentle swinging motion that seemed to calm him. His eyes closed. A shivering, hissing sound came from his lips, and he appeared to pass out.

Klaus moved closer and checked his pulse. It was the first doctorly thing I'd ever seen him do. He opened his bag, which had never left his side from the time we departed the river bank, and out came the stethoscope. He planted the circular plate onto the sick man's bony chest, then listened. He thumbed back the eyelids and lowered them again. 'A low-grade fever, that's all I can say for certain.' He opened his bag a second time and took out a little bottle of white pills. 'Erich, find me some drinking water, please. I want our friend here to get well. Think about it, Helga, a white man who knows these people and speaks German too! I can't believe our luck. Erich, some water, quickly.'

I went looking and found a big clay water bowl back near the fire where we'd eaten, with some little bowls around it. I brought back as much as one of these would hold to Klaus, and he forced a pill down Herr Wentzler's throat after a lot of spilling and spluttering. The Yayomi watched all this with great interest, but things took a bad turn when one of the men reached into the open medical bag behind Klaus's back. I saw it happen. The man was looking at Klaus, not where his hand was going, and he suddenly let out a loud yelp and snatched it out, bleeding from a cut between his second and third fingers. He howled and yammered and made a tremendous fuss, although the wound didn't look so bad, and pointed at the bag a lot.

'Serves you right, my friend,' said Klaus, smiling as always. 'Never reach idly into a bag containing scalpels and bone saws.'

The Yayomi backed away to a respectful distance, and at first I thought they'd grown afraid of us, but the direction of their eyes told me it was the black bag they were scared of, which was perhaps a good thing in that they probably wouldn't go meddling with it again. Klaus was very protective of his bag.

Soon their interest in us began to wear off, and the Yayomi moved away in ones and twos to do whatever they would ordinarily be doing, I suppose, although this didn't seem to be very much. Most of the men, including the chief, went to their hammocks and fell asleep, this being the hottest part of the day. It was interesting to see that the Indians did the same thing as the Spanish Venezuelans. Left alone, we gathered around Klaus to see how he summed up the situation.

'The only thing better than what we find here would be a mission station, and I believe Herr Wentzler when he says there's no such thing anywhere near. Wentzler himself is our missionary. With his understanding of these Indians, we'll coexist with them a lot more easily for as long as we remain here. It's my hope that this will not be for long. With luck and Herr Wentzler's gift for the Indian lingo, I'm sure some of them could be persuaded to take us by river as far at least as the Orinoco. We're fortunate, believe it or not. Providence has taken us out of a sinking plane, allowed us no more than one uncomfortable night alone in the jungle, sent Indians to bring us here, where at least there's food to be had, and on top of all that we've been given a guide who'll lead us through what might otherwise have been a minefield of misunderstanding.'

'Thank God,' said Mother.

'God,' said Klaus, 'doesn't live here, and never has.'

Noroni came over and beckoned to us. We followed him across to where several empty hammocks waited. It was clear he wanted us to use them. Mother said, 'I'd love to go to sleep. Last night was so awful.' Klaus spread the width of the nearest hammock for her to get in. 'Here, make yourself comfortable, my dear. A word of advice, don't try to turn over in bed, or you'll find yourself on the ground.' She got into the hammock, with Klaus's help, and said it was quite comfortable. Noroni looked pleased, although he can't have followed what she'd said, and led us to the next hammock.

Klaus said, 'It looks as though there are only three available for our use, so you boys will have to share this one. You first, Erich. Zeppi, don't go squirming around or you'll tip both of you out. Our friend Noroni has probably told his own family to vacate their hammocks for us. This is an honour, boys, so appreciate it.'

Zeppi got in at the other end and our legs lay alongside each other in the middle. I would have preferred a hammock of my own, but it wasn't too bad. Klaus got into the third hammock and stretched out his long body until his legs dangled over the end, almost touching the ground. Noroni and a boy and girl about my age who must have been his children squatted close by and stared at us. Maybe they were proud to have dolphins in their hammocks, or maybe they wanted them back so they could have a siesta. I didn't care. I had a full belly and every confidence in what Klaus had told us about getting away from here. Zeppi's eyes were already closed.

I closed my own.

FOUR

I WOKE UP WITH A terrible bump. Zeppi had woken before me and started wriggling around, so both of us were tipped out onto the ground. It was less than a metre, but long enough for me to dream that I'd been thrown over the edge of a pit that bored down through the earth to hell. I woke up fighting for breath, terrified.

Zeppi was sitting up next to me, rubbing a bump on his head and looking puzzled. 'Idiot,' I said to him, but he was still so dazed from sleep he didn't hear me.

I looked over at Mother, who still slept, then at Klaus's hammock, which was empty. The Yayomi were up and about, and the sun's rays were coming through the giant hole above at a lower angle, so it must have been midafternoon by then.

'My head hurts,' Zeppi grumbled.

'I wonder why,' I said, and went to look for Klaus. In a circular dwelling it doesn't take long to see where everyone is, and Klaus, predictably enough, was by the side of his patient. I joined them.

Herr Wentzler was sitting with his skinny legs dangling over one side of his hammock, talking with Klaus, who squatted Indian style beside the nearest supporting pole. He turned as I walked up to them. 'Erich, imagine this – a fully accredited professor of anthropology decides to abandon his sinecure and go to the Indians, actually live among them, as they do, without clothing, without the least little thing from the outside world, not even a notebook!' He turned to Herr Wentzler. 'But doesn't that interfere with your study? How on earth do you expect to remember everything you've learned without notes to refer to?'

'I was given a mind that recalls with absolute clarity,' Herr Wentzler said with some pride. 'Everything that has come to pass these last eleven years is inside here,' he tapped his temple with a long forefinger, 'complete in every detail. When I return home it will all be regurgitated, so to speak, as I work at my typewriter. Nothing will be lost, I assure you.'

'Eleven years?' I said.

'I've kept count of the dry seasons by cutting a notch for each one in a tree trunk,' he explained. 'I came here in '35. It's now 1946, correct?'

'Correct,' said Klaus. 'Herr Wentzler, have you had no contact with the world at all in that time?'

'Call me Gerhard, please. Formality among these surroundings is so foolish, don't you think? No, no contact at all, by design. I wanted to be absorbed completely into the Yayomi culture, you see, and forays outside what I refer to as Yayomiland would have distracted me, diluted my total immersion in things Yayomi. As an anthropologist of the modern type, I was prepared to make all necessary sacrifices, the better to understand them. I did tell some of my colleagues what I intended doing, and they called me a fanatic – imagine that. These were desk dwellers, of course, whose knowledge came from books written by greater men. To study the Indian, one goes among them, naturally.'

'So you have no idea what's been going on back home, or anywhere else?'

'None. Have there been any developments I should be made aware of?'

I started to laugh. Klaus stopped me with a look, then said to Herr Wentzler, 'As a matter of fact, there have.' He then told the professor about the war – how the Jews, with a little help from the Communists, had started it, and how the Führer had tried to wipe Europe clean of their poisonous stain once and for all, only to be stopped by the intervention of the Americans. 'If the Japanese had confined their own war to Asia and left Hawaii alone, the Americans would have stayed at home on both fronts, wringing their hands a little, perhaps, but they never would have come to the aid of yellow races on the one hand and Jews on the other. Unfortunately, that was not the case, and now the Führer's master plan to rid us once and for all of the Jewish problem has been torn to pieces by those irresponsible Japanese. I was glad, personally, when their stupidity was rewarded with annihilation by atomic weapons. There was rough justice in that.'

'Atomic weapons?'

'My dear Wentzler ... Gerhard, the world has been turned upside down in your absence. Nothing is the same, believe me. Millions are dead. Germany itself was bombed into rubble and the Führer is no more. The Fatherland is occupied by

American farm boys and Russian peasants, both looking at each other with hatred. It's the end of everything that seemed so achievable when you came here.'

'Hitler is dead?'

'He held out to the very end. If he could have kept his strength, not just his physical health but his strength of purpose, we might have prevailed. A new world order would have come into being.'

Herr Wentzler looked away from us for a moment, his forehead creased with thought, then he turned back and asked, 'Herr Brandt . . . may I call you Klaus? What of my home town, Dresden? Surely no bombs fell there? Such a pretty place.'

'Destroyed completely, and for no reason at all. It was like running a steamroller over a gingerbread house. Dresden is gone forever, I regret to inform you.'

'No! This is a shock . . .'

'While you studied these primitive people, civilisation itself came crashing down, almost to the point of extinction. The last decade, my dear sir, has been a turning point from which mankind will take a century or more to recover.'

Herr Wentzler had a strange look in his eye. 'Dresden,' he said, 'of all places . . . I had hoped to return there to write my book . . .'

There was silence for a while and I glanced over at Mother. Zeppi was standing by her hammock, poking her, trying to wake her up. He could never feel secure without her near him. I sometimes wondered what his chances were of ever being anything but a mama's boy, even when he grew up. I was glad I wasn't him, tied to another person that way, even to someone as worthy of admiration as Klaus. He wouldn't want it, anyway. Klaus, I had a feeling, was looking for an equal, a friend who was more than just a friend, closer, in a way, than a man could be to his wife. That was my role, I saw at that moment, watching Zeppi bothering our sleeping mother while the words of Klaus continued in my ear.

'Our problem now, Gerhard, and I refer to myself and my family, is how to get back to the civilised world. No doubt you'll want to be left alone with your natives for further observation, but for us, hot water and electricity beckon. Is there a chance some of your friends will take us by canoe to the Orinoco, or the nearest trading outpost?'

'It's doubtful,' said Herr Wentzler. 'They don't like to venture far from home, you know. These are not an exploratory people. They believe they inhabit the finest part of the world and that to go away would bring about calamity. They move their shabono every few years, of course, but usually less than ten kilometres away. Their plantain gardens become exhausted after a time, and sometimes the population grows to a point where the tribe is better off splitting into two distinct groups. Everything is so much more easily managed when the shabono numbers fewer than a hundred. This particular group split away from a larger group six years ago. I went with them, to study the effects of resettlement on them. By and large, the effects have been good.'

'Shabono?'

'Excuse me, I must remind myself you're a stranger here. This dwelling place is the shabono.'

I asked him, 'What's a plantain?'

'Plantains are the small bananas they cultivate. They're very nutritious.'

He went on to other topics that he intended putting into

his book about the Yayomi. I got bored and walked away. Mother was awake and talking to Zeppi, so I went in another direction. Some children followed me, making swimming motions with their arms. I suppose they were asking me to turn back into a dolphin. I made the same movements myself, and they laughed. One of them had a parrot, a bright green one, sitting on his head, and I asked him if I could touch it. He understood when I reached for the parrot, and took it from his hair to place in my hands, upside down. The parrot was not at all upset to be handled this way and simply pulled itself upright in my hands, then looked at my face. It let out two or three loud squawks and all the children laughed, probably thinking the parrot was saying, 'Look at this thing, it's a dolphin!'

I carried the parrot around perched on my hand. There were pets everywhere, I now saw, most of them parrots of all sizes and colours, and even some little monkeys with white faces that scampered here and there, screeching and stealing food from the women preparing it. I even saw a lady with a tiny baby monkey on her tit and it was sucking milk from her, just like the human baby on her other tit. I looked at that for a long time but the lady didn't get embarrassed. She just stared right back at the dolphin. There were skinny dogs all over the place too, but they weren't friendly, probably because I smelled strange. All in all, the shabono was a very active and noisy place, with all kinds of interesting smells and sights.

Later, Klaus and Herr Wentzler collected Mother and Zeppi and myself and we went out through the hole in the leaf wall where we'd come in, and followed a path down to the river, with Herr Wentzler giving us a lecture about how the Yayomi always built on high ground so they and their gardens didn't get flooded out during the rainy season. It was the dry season at the moment. When we got to the river I saw seven or eight canoes, made from hollowed-out logs, pulled up on the bank, and I asked Herr Wentzler, 'If they were expecting four dolphins on the river bank just around the bend, why didn't they paddle around and pick us up instead of walking through all that jungle?'

'The bend in the river,' he said, 'is long, far too long to paddle. The river goes north then turns in a vast loop before coming back this way, almost touching itself when it gets back here. The distance between the shabono and the place where Noroni knew he'd find you is quite short across country. It was much faster that way.'

'About how far is it by river to the Orinoco?' asked Klaus.

'So far as I know, there's no direct link between this river and the Orinoco. You'd have to portage between river systems. I don't know that anyone here has ever done such a thing. Crossing the land of a neighbouring tribe is considered very bad form unless you take along plenty of gifts to bribe them into allowing it without bloodshed, and the nearest tribe in the direction of the Orinoco is the Iriri, who don't take kindly to strangers, even strangers bearing gifts. It's easier for the Yayomi to stay home. They have everything they need right here, you see.'

'But Herr Wentzler,' said Mother, 'we must be taken away from here.'

'Do you have anything to bribe the Yayomi with? They might do it if you flatter them with gifts, plus gifts for the Iriri whose land you must cross. It would have to be something very special, or it wouldn't be worth the risk.'

'We have nothing,' she said, and that was when I saw Herr

Wentzler shrug his shoulders. He didn't care! That's what started me thinking he might be mad. It wasn't impossible. Maybe he'd been there so long he considered himself a part of the tribe, and the Yayomi probably wouldn't want to see their walking dolphins leave – not yet, anyway.

Klaus had said we were lucky to have Wentzler to translate for us, but who really knew what he might tell the Yayomi? He might tell them we liked it here so much we never wanted to leave. He might want to keep us here for company but never admit it to us. It suddenly seemed to me that we couldn't trust him.

I looked at Klaus, the only other person whose opinion I truly valued, but he seemed not to be taking part in the conversation, and was staring instead at some children and adults who were splashing around in the water together. I stared too: adults and children playing together is something you don't ordinarily see, unless it's a father teaching his son how to kick a ball or something like that. But this was different. They were playing together as if there was no real difference between them. I realised then that the Yayomi were nothing like us; in fact, it occurred to me they might be better than us if the grown-ups could frolic around, splashing and laughing with their children.

Klaus saw me looking at him and the Indians, and knew what I was thinking. That's the kind of mental communication that was developing between us. He said, 'You don't see that at the local pool, do you?'

Mother said to Klaus, 'If the Indians don't want to take us away from here, what will we do?'

'We'll have to borrow a canoe and take ourselves away,' said Klaus, as if the problem was of no real significance.

'That would be stealing, Klaus.'

'And failing to oblige us in our wish to leave is imprisonment by another name. Which crime is greater? They can always make themselves another canoe, but we can't stay here forever.'

Mother looked at Wentzler, trying to see by his expression what he thought about this. He must have heard what Klaus said, standing right beside us as he was, but he pretended he hadn't heard a thing. Absolutely nothing showed on his face, and I wondered if maybe he was embarrassed that his Yayomi friends wouldn't do the right thing, and embarrassed again because his fellow Germans intended doing the wrong thing. He was caught somewhere in between, so he acted as if none of it was happening.

I turned back to the bathers. The day was still very hot and my clothes were sticking to me. I wanted to take off all my clothes and jump into the river too, splash about like the rest of them. Of course, then everyone would have seen that I was wearing the Iron Cross, and that was still my secret. The water looked wonderful, though, despite being very brown. Maybe if Mother hadn't been there I would have gone swimming.

It seemed silly, given that all the Indians were completely naked and wouldn't think twice about it if I stripped off and jumped in, because I was a dolphin, after all. But I just couldn't do it with Mother there. Klaus I didn't care about, or Zeppi. I hadn't seen Zeppi naked for years, but I had a feeling that if he saw me naked he'd want to strip off and jump in too. His face was very sweaty and he was watching the Yayomi enviously, just as I was.

'Why don't you go on in?' said Klaus, reading my mind again.

I shook my head. He understood. Klaus understood everything.

The rest of the afternoon was more of the same, with Zeppi starting to relax enough to go around with the other children, playing with their parrots and monkeys, and enjoying being the centre of attention as usual. Klaus and the professor talked and talked, a couple of real university intellectuals, and I stayed within earshot most of the time. Mother kept an eye on Zeppi. It had been a long and strange day for us all, and by the time evening came we sat down to eat with the rest as if it was something we'd done many times before.

Everyone watched us eat, probably waiting to see if we'd do anything dolphinish. It seemed a shame to disappoint them, and I thought hard to recall what I knew about dolphins, which wasn't very much, except that they aren't fish, they're air-breathing mammals, and they talk to each other with squeaks and clicking sounds. And that made me remember a newsreel I saw before the war, about two trained dolphins who'd come when called, and begged for fish by standing on their tails.

I recalled the funny sounds they made, and wondered if freshwater dolphins made those same peculiar noises. At the time I'd irritated Mother by making those sounds for days afterward, and I decided to give it a try now, just to entertain the Yayomi, who'd been very nice to us and deserved some kind of reward.

I opened my mouth, clenched my throat the way I remembered having done years before, and pumped out a squeak or two, the second one louder than the first. It worked! I did it again, then did the clickings, much harder, and they came out pretty much the way I wanted. I did it all over again, concentrating so hard on producing the sounds that I wasn't aware of the effect I'd had until I stopped to catch my breath and relax my throat, which felt as if someone had grabbed it and squeezed hard from the inside.

They were all looking at me, each and every Yayomi, young or old, with wide-eyed surprise, or maybe it was fear – who could tell with them.

Mother said, 'Really, Erich, that's the sort of thing I'd expect from Zeppi.'

Zeppi took that as a challenge and imitated me, probably not even aware that he was supposed to sound like a dolphin. The Yayomi didn't move or make a sound, only stared at us. Zeppi, true to form, liked the attention and made the squeaks and whistles again. Frankly, I think his were better than mine, his voice being pitched higher, and he simply wouldn't stop once he'd started, until his face got red and he ran out of breath.

'Very clever,' said Wentzler, 'very clever indeed. I see what you intend to accomplish. A confirmation of their mistaken belief, yes? You want them to have no doubt you're dolphins, am I correct? I haven't heard a dolphin in my life, but the looks on their faces tell me you must have been very close. It was deliberate, was it not?'

'Of course,' I said.

'To what end?' he asked.

I shrugged. 'I don't know. To give them a laugh.'

He shook his head, as if that was the wrong answer to a trick question. 'Never confirm an incorrect belief without a pressing need to do so. Now, should you ever want them to consider you nothing but human, assuming that was possible, they simply won't swallow it, young man. You've just erased any last doubt that some of them may have had that you *are* dolphins.'

'Is that so bad?' asked Klaus.

'One never knows. The Yayomi are a serious people who take their own mythology with no grain of salt whatsoever. They have four dolphins by their fire, eating their food, sharing their shabono. They're wondering, as we speak, what purpose you have for coming to them, for telling Noroni in his dream that you would be found where you were. They're wondering what you require of them. Soon they'll ask me what it is that you want, and I must have a story prepared. If I say you're merely four humans like myself, they may become very angry and do you harm, I can't say for certain. In future, please consult with me before engaging in such antics. Playful acts committed in ignorance can have far-reaching, sometimes devastating, effects here. This is not your world, so I beg you to tread carefully.'

'They're just silly,' was Zeppi's comment, and that made Wentzler angry.

'Any silliness is your own. You simply have no idea what kind of people you're dealing with. They have a different set of beliefs to yours. If I was to tell them that the god of white people sent his son down to earth and allowed humans to kill him, and did nothing to punish those humans, they'd consider him a weak and foolish god. The Yayomi live for revenge against their enemies, anyone who has transgressed their territorial boundaries or their taboos. They're warriors of the first order, and for them to allow an act of murder to go unpunished would be to abandon everything they believe in.'

'But, Herr Wentzler,' said Mother, 'what does it matter what they think?'

'It matters a great deal. To them, the Christian world would be a world turned upside down, where the weak and forgiving dominate. It would be a blasphemous world. They'd be enraged by it. Certainly, they'll kill any missionary foolish enough to come here. The Yayomi might not have any idols, or particular places of worship, but they exist in a world of all-pervasive, never-ending spirit and the colour of that spirit is blood red. Theirs is a philosophy of endless atonement for crimes committed in the past. The blood feud is their cultural mainstay. They live to kill their enemies. It defines them. Without intertribal killing, their lives would have no purpose. Women have babies so the boys will grow up to be warriors and kill more enemies, and the girls will grow up to give birth to more boys who'll grow up to be warriors . . . and so on, the way it's always been.'

He stopped. His face was very red.

'But how awful,' said Mother.

'Not a bit of it,' snapped the professor. 'Haven't I been told today by your husband that the world has fought itself to a standstill after killing millions? What was that for but the pursuit of the Führer's ideal, a world without Jews?'

I stepped in. 'That means the Yayomi would approve of what the Führer did, doesn't it? He wanted to get rid of the enemies of his people, and that's what they do.'

Wentzler considered this for a second or two, then said, 'Yes, they would approve. Naturally the sheer numbers involved would be beyond their understanding, but the essence of what you say is correct.'

Zeppi, who'd started all this, hadn't followed most of it, and Mother obviously didn't approve of the Fatherland's brave storm-troopers being compared with painted savages. Klaus and I understood, though. I pictured God, Mother's Catholic God, swooping down from the sky, huge and naked and painted red and black, thirsting for the blood of those who'd nailed his son to the cross. He'd reach down with a mighty hand and crush them like ants, those murderers, teach them not to do that to his flesh and blood. But he hadn't done that, had he. That had always been the thing that had stopped me believing, even a little bit as Mother did, in God. The Yayomi were right – that kind of a god was useless. Better to make the killing itself your god, the way they did. But then, if the most important thing was killing, what value did anything else have?

The Yayomi continued staring at us, waiting for Zeppi and me to make dolphin noises again.

'I think,' said Wentzler, 'that you're all on dangerous ground.'

'Explain, please,' said Klaus.

'You see my skin, how dark it is? That isn't sunburn, I've always been dark. And my hair was black as you please when I came here, a trifle grey now, I admit. The point is, our hosts do not equate you with me. You four are dolphins made human, while I have to accept my lowlier status as merely human. I'm an outsider who wormed his way into their shabono by not offending them. Originally I was a curiosity but now I've become a member of the tribe, insofar as that is possible. They won't allow me to marry any of the women, because I'm useless, from their point of view. I can't hunt because my eyesight is poor and I lost my only pair of glasses shortly after coming here. More importantly, I don't join in their warmongering. That's the thing that makes me about as valuable as one of their pet monkeys. They view me with affection, but I don't have their respect.'

He seemed a little embarrassed to admit this but went on anyway, obviously wanting us to understand. 'All of this is acceptable to me because my aim is not to become a Yayomi but to observe them. This is a concept they could never understand, since they relate only to themselves and their neighbours. The situation is acceptable to both the Yayomi and myself because, as I said, I'm only another human of inferior type. But you four – what a difference! Pale skin, blond hair, these are things they've never seen before. You truly are dolphins in their eyes and, to be frank, I haven't the faintest idea what they intend doing with you. Noroni's vision has given you credibility as envoys of the supernatural. That will be to your advantage, until and unless you let them know you're no more unusual a specimen than myself. If that happens, if you disappoint them, they may become angry. I tell you this to warn you. You must all behave correctly.'

'But what kind of behaviour could be termed correct,' Klaus asked, 'if they think we're dolphins? How the hell does a dolphin with arms and legs behave?'

Wentzler shrugged.

Mother looked upset. 'This is impossible,' she said, with a tremor in her voice. 'You said they won't go beyond their own territory to return us to civilisation, and now you say they'll hurt us if they stop believing the stupid thing they believe about us. How can we go on like this?'

'My good lady, I'm nothing more than a visitor here myself. I can't wave a magic wand and transport you to where you wish to go. Please appreciate the true nature of the circumstances.'

Mother glared at him. I think she hated Wentzler because he was perfectly happy to be there and she wasn't, and also because he still hadn't bothered to hide his nakedness from her. That was the worst part, from Mother's point of view.

Klaus said, 'What do you propose to do, Gerhard? There'll come a time when you feel you've learned all there is for an outsider to know about the Yayomi, and you'll want to leave here in order to write your book. I'll be expecting an autographed copy, incidentally.'

Wentzler laughed. 'When the time comes, my friend, I'll be in need of divine intervention. My predicament is not so very different to your own. There are no guarantees of anything here.'

Klaus leaned forward. Several of the Yayomi leaned forward too. They were listening closely, even though they couldn't understand a word. 'I have a proposition to make,' he said, 'and it's this. You've been among these people for eleven years now, and I'm sure there remains very little you don't know about them. This tribal culture, it's not like studying Renaissance Italy, is it, Gerhard? In your heart you're aware that the time has already come to leave and write your book. I suggest to you that we dolphins can help you escape.'

'You presume too much, I think,' said Wentzler, smiling. 'My studies are not necessarily complete.'

'I suggest to you that they are,' Klaus insisted, smiling also. 'I further suggest that if you want medical help from me – recall your feverishness this morning and the pill I gave you – then you should perhaps be more amenable to my plan.'

'And what plan is that?'

'The one you and I will concoct together, my friend.'

Wentzler's smile disappeared. 'My dear Klaus, I do thank you for your little pill. Certainly it made me feel better. What was it, quinine? I believe my periodic bouts with fever are malarial in nature. The Yayomi haven't been able to stop it with their herbal medicines, so it must be something from the outside world. Fortunately for them, malaria is not communicable, that's correct, isn't it, Doctor? If I feel weak and shivery again, I need only go to your handsome bag there and take another pill, I think. As a doctor, your Hippocratic oath obliges you to heal me with whatever means you have at your disposal.'

'Perhaps it does, and perhaps it doesn't. I'll be the sole judge of what to do with my medical supplies. Tell me, Gerhard, do you speak or read Portuguese?'

'No.' He looked puzzled.

'Because all my medicines are Brazilian in origin, and so labelled. I have many pills, and they're all alike to look at. You'll need your doctor's help in distinguishing between what's good for you and what's deadly.'

Wentzler laughed again, very briefly, then he seemed to collapse a little, as if his skinny naked body slumped inside its own skin. Even his penis suddenly looked smaller.

'That bag,' he said after a little while, staring at it where it sat like a black dog beside Klaus. 'The Yayomi think it's alive.'

'Alive? How could that be?'

'They tell me that Waneeri – that's the gentleman on your left with the watchful look in his eye – reached into your bag and was bitten. The bag, he says, has teeth inside, therefore it's alive.'

'I suspect he was pricked by an unsecured scalpel.'

'I'm sure, but for him, and the rest, the bag is evil – a black demon, if you will – and one that's directly under your control by magic, since you weren't even touching it when Waneeri was bitten. That's powerful magic you have there,

Doctor. You appreciate, of course, that I was under no obliga-
tion to tell you of this great weapon you have in your
possession, but now I've done so. Why? To make you aware
that whatever differences you may or may not perceive
between us, I happen to be a white man, a fellow German, and
I resent any suggestion from you or your wife that I'm in collusion somehow with the Yayomi.'

'Nobody made any such suggestion.'

'It was implied,' insisted Wentzler.

'All I intended suggesting,' said Klaus, 'was that we have a
mutual need to get away from here. My family and I need
your expertise on native ways, and you need the help of four
dolphins who have the locals flummoxed and possibly a little
bit terrified. A symbiotic relationship is what we have here,
would you agree?'

'Perhaps.' Wentzler still wasn't happy.

It was getting dark inside the shabono, with the cooking
fires burning here and there like yellow flowers in the gloom.
The hole in the roof still showed light in the sky, and a few
clouds with their western edges touched with gold, but all of
that faded away very quickly and soon the hole turned from
grey to black, and the stars came out. The hole looked like a
velvet bag dusted with tiny particles of glass, and it made me
shiver.

When the food was done with, the Yayomi began drifting
away to their hammocks, talking among themselves, ignoring us at last, because how long can you look at a dolphin
without getting bored? They started going to bed. There was
hardly anyone moving around now, just dozens of vague
human forms lying in hammocks, some of them swinging a
little, but mostly they were still. Klaus and Mother got into

the same hammocks as before, and I could see the one Zeppi and I had used. We got into it carefully, Zeppi going first.

I saw Noroni and his son and daughter lying on the ground nearby and felt guilty for having taken their hammocks, but they seemed comfortable enough, with Noroni snoring lightly. He didn't seem to have a wife, only his two children. I could barely make out the boy, but the daughter was still awake. It was hard to tell how old she was in the dark, and I'd barely taken any notice of her earlier, apart from looking at her tits, the way I looked at every female's. I couldn't remember if she had nice ones or not, I'd seen so many all at once, and it was too late now to have another look. She had her back against one of the bigger supporting poles and I swear she was looking at me. I lay down with my legs alongside Zeppi's and waited for him to stop squirming. She was still looking at me as my eyelids grew heavy. A baby somewhere cried for a little while, then stopped. I imagined him being put onto a nice juicy tit to suck and keep him quiet.

I closed my eyes and shut everything out of my mind. I could hear mosquitoes, but they didn't seem to bother me, and I realised why it was that the Yayomi had their hammocks slung as close to the fires as possible. The smoke felt like tiny fingers passing over my face and entering my nostrils, looking for a way up into my brain. The tiny fingers would steal around in there and know what I was thinking, maybe even change my thoughts by fingering this little bit of grey matter or rubbing that piece against another until I wouldn't be able to tell if what I thought came from my everyday self or from some other, darker part of my mind where the thoughts had never seen the light of day. There was a secret pit at the very centre of my brain filled with dark thoughts waiting to be discovered and released.

I told myself I was being silly. It was the smoke that was making me think that way. I drifted away at last, but not before the Iron Cross around my neck shifted and settled alongside my ribs, square and sharp at the edges, but warm and somehow comforting.

FIVE

AT FIRST I THOUGHT Professor Wentzler was jealous of us because the Yayomi found us more interesting than him, but it was Klaus who pointed out what the real situation was.

'The man is studying us,' he told me in confidence. 'He's watching what happens between us and the Indians. Observing, if you will. Waiting to see if this encounter between primitives and civilised men will result in worship or bloodshed, or both.'

'They wouldn't harm us. They think we're dolphins.'

'Erich, for all I know, Indians *eat* dolphins if they can catch them.'

We had been at the shabono for four days now. I'd taken to wearing only my sandals and shorts, and Klaus wore the same. Both of us were getting very brown across the chest and shoulders. I saw his little SS blood-type tattoo on the inside of his upper arm. He saw me looking and said, 'This little reminder from the past could get me into trouble if the Jews ever saw it.'

'Why?'

'Because it identifies me as a member of the Waffen SS. No one gave the Jews a harder time than us. We were the ones responsible for rounding them up and relocating them. They'll never forgive us, not for generations to come.'

We were sitting by the river in the morning sun, watching the sluggish waters roll by. Sometimes I thought I saw a cayman, but when it came closer it was always a tree trunk. Wentzler had told us there were no caymans around here, which was one reason the Yayomi had picked this spot to live.

'Why didn't the Jews want to be relocated?'

'Because it wasn't to settlement areas of their choice. They all want to go back to Palestine and live together as they did in the Old Testament. A pipedream. They had to be forced, you know. God, I miss my cigarettes.'

'And your cigarette holder.'

'Herr Manokwo is welcome to it. What good is a cigarette holder without cigarettes? Have you seen what he's done with it? The simpleton went and bored a hole through the septum of his nose and pushed it through. Can you imagine the pain involved? The facial nerves are plentiful and extremely sensitive. These people are from the Stone Age.'

We watched the water sliding by. The opposite bank was at least a hundred metres away, a line of thick green jungle, just like this side. A flock of yellow and green parrots flew past. I'd promised myself one for a pet, but when Zeppi said he wanted one too I decided against it; he was such a little copy-cat.

'You're aware, Erich, that your mother is not happy.'

'I've noticed. The only thing she does is watch over Zeppi all day long. Not that he doesn't like the attention, the little egotist.'

'Now, now, he's your brother, even if he is a little immature.'

'A little? He's just a mama's boy, and she won't even let him take off his shirt. I know he wants to, but she won't let him.'

'Helga will allow Zeppi to grow up when she herself is happier, and that can only happen when we're away from here, back where we belong. She loses herself in her son in order to blot out everything else. It's not a healthy position to be in.'

This was an adult conversation. Klaus respected my intelligence enough to tell me something about my own mother that was a little bit disturbing. It made us very close. Klaus wanted me to understand things, from big historical questions about the Jews to the more personal things, like how Mother was unhappy in her heart. It was their honeymoon, but she and Klaus hadn't had a private moment, so far as I could tell. I couldn't help wondering if they'd gone to bed together yet, or, since there weren't any beds for hundreds of kilometres, whether they'd gone off into the jungle like the Yayomi did.

That very morning I'd seen couples going off together into the trees, and you could tell just by looking that they were going to do it when they got far enough away. I thought they must do it standing up or leaning against a tree trunk or something, because the ground is either too hard and covered in dead twigs and leaves if it's dry, or too muddy if it's wet. I had a plan to follow some of them the next day. Early morning seemed to be the time they preferred to do it. I thought it must be a Yayomi custom, not like the civilised races that do it at night under cover of darkness.

I'd been thinking a lot about Awomay, Noroni's daughter. She was really very pretty, with the whitest teeth I'd ever seen, and wide brown eyes, and exceptional breasts, exactly the right type for me, not too big or too little, and always on display. I hadn't noticed them at first, because the interesting thing about her, the thing that would get your attention first, was the three little carved sticks that were stuck into three little holes in her face, one on either side of her mouth, and another just below her bottom lip. I wondered, when I first saw them, whether they hurt her, sticking into her flesh like that, but then my eyes moved on to the rest of her body and I forgot about the little face sticks.

She'd seen me watching her, I could tell. Those white teeth had been flashing at me a lot over the past few days. Her family had made themselves new hammocks out of some kind of split plant fibre the women used to weave things out of. All three of the new hammocks were slung alongside the old ones where we slept, so Noroni and his family were always closest to us through the night, and for quite a bit of the daytime too. Sometimes the men went out hunting with their bows and blowpipes, but a lot of the time they seemed to laze around the shabono doing nothing but chat with each other about God knows what. Possibly us, the dolphin guests.

'Of course,' said Klaus, 'she's blamed me for this, ever since I was foolish enough to tell her we could have reached the new Zamex drilling site by river steamer. If we'd done that instead of taking the plane, we'd be there now, with me practising medicine on a lot of rowdy oil-driller types and your mother at home in the company bungalow preparing supper. She's right, I have to admit.'

'But you couldn't have known the plane would go down.'

'Nevertheless, it did, and here we are, and your mother is greatly displeased.'

'Then we have to leave,' I said.

Klaus picked up a pebble and threw it into the water. It plopped quietly under the surface and ripples began to spread before being overtaken by the current and swept away. Three seconds after the pebble hit, you wouldn't have known where it landed in the water.

'To leave, yes, but how? Wentzler's made it clear he has no actual influence over these people. He's in for a shock when he wants to leave himself and write that precious book.'

A sudden thought made me catch my breath. 'He isn't ever going to leave,' I said. 'That's why he doesn't care that they'd never take him across Iriri territory to the Orinoco.'

'And what makes you say this?'

'Just a feeling, but it's a strong one. He's a criminal, a murderer, I bet, and the reason he's here in the first place is because he's on the run from the police, not because he's studying the Yayomi. What's there to study? They eat and hunt and gather food and sleep and . . .'

'And procreate. I agree, it's a pointless existence, but there are men who genuinely take an interest in such simple-minded cultures. Wentzler would disagree, naturally. I was speaking with him yesterday, and I happened to state my opinion that the Indians were utterly different to ourselves. That got his back up and he said – picture him drawing himself up to his full height and looking along his nose at me – he said, "The Yayomi are the same as you and me, but they have no metal." Can you imagine a more ridiculous statement? The same as us! And not so long ago he was telling us how different they are. The fellow's a walking contradiction.'

'That's because he's not an anthropologist like he said, he's a murderer! He came here to hide away from the world and escape punishment.'

'You think so?'

'I bet I'm right.'

'You have nothing to place a bet with, unless it's your Iron Cross, and I doubt that you'd want to part from that.'

'It's not *my* Iron Cross, it's Father's. I'm just . . . keeping it for him.' I don't know why I said that. Father gave it to me, after all, and a few months later he was dead. If the cross was anybody's, it was mine. Since taking off my shirt I'd removed the long green ribbon, snipped off a short bit and wore the medal on that. I wore it proudly, and all the Yayomi looked at it, even stopped me and fingered it sometimes. I intended giving the spare ribbon to Awomay, the way Americans in the Fatherland were known to give women chocolate and nylon stockings to make them take their clothes off and lie down. I had the green ribbon folded carefully in the pocket of my shorts, waiting for the right moment to dazzle her and be led into the jungle for some standing-up lovemaking.

'I wouldn't share your theory with anyone else, Erich. We need to be in Wentzler's good graces for the time being.'

'All right, but I'm not going to change my mind about him.'

'No one's asking you to.' He flicked another pebble into the water. 'If only I had a cigarette I wouldn't care if he *was* a murderer.'

I didn't take him seriously, of course.

Later in the day I was walking beneath the shabono's sky hole when Mother called out to me, 'Erich! Erich, come here!' Zeppi was with her, and I knew in advance what the matter was.

I went over. Mother rarely set foot outside the shabono except for relieving herself, only she refused to make use of the community shitter. The Yayomi had a good idea there. Everyone shat in the river a short distance downstream, and the crap was carried away instantly. A large tree with a long straight trunk had fallen into the water, and it was a simple matter to go out along it a little way and squat above the water. There were knobby projections along the trunk where boughs had rotted away and fallen off, and these made good handholds so you wouldn't topple backwards into the river.

As for pissing, everybody pissed anywhere, so long as it wasn't along any of the well-worn paths crisscrossing the area between the shabono and the plantain garden and the river. It was all done in plain view of everyone else, and within a day or so I'd accepted the custom as being natural. Not so Mother, who wouldn't do anything in front of anyone else. She went into the jungle to relieve herself. I'd overheard Klaus telling her that when in Rome, one did what the Romans did. Mother had said the Romans were decadent killers of Christians and she wouldn't do anything their way, which was an argument about history, not about shitting, but you couldn't make Mother see what she didn't want to see.

'Erich, Zeppi has to go.'

Zeppi was beside her, looking sheepish, digging the toe of his sandal into the dirt.

'Then let him go,' I said.

'He wants you to take him.'

'He knows where the tree is, I've taken him there plenty of times.'

'He wants you to be with him when he goes. Don't argue

with me, please. Things are difficult enough without you disobeying me. You have a duty, Erich.'

'To take him to the potty like a baby?'

She smacked me sharply across the cheek. 'How dare you mock him!'

'I wasn't . . . I was . . . He should go by himself, that's all.'

I felt close to tears. It had been ages since Mother had hit me, and then it had been a whack across the seat of the pants for doing some stupid thing or other that all boys do. This was different, but I wasn't going to let her see how much she'd hurt me. The Yayomi nearby had seen it too, and I didn't want them to know I was embarrassed.

'Come on,' I said to Zeppi, and turned away.

He followed me outside the shabono, trotting so close behind me his sandals kept scraping the backs of mine. 'Don't do that! Walk alongside me, you idiot!'

'If you call me that, I'll tell Mother.'

'Tell her whatever you please. This is the last time I'll take you to the tree, do you understand? Why do you act like a baby all the time? You're twelve years old and you still can't go for a shit by yourself? It's ridiculous.'

'Mother said . . .'

'Mother said what? Come on, spit it out.'

'She said that I shouldn't do anything the dirty people do.'

'Dirty people? The Yayomi, is that who she means?'

'I don't know.' He sounded so miserable I lost my anger and felt sorry for him.

'Listen, Zeppi, you aren't tied to Mother with invisible strings. You don't need to stay in her shadow all day long. You should come out and walk around in the open air and go swimming like I do. And for Christ's sake, take off that shirt!

You can't possibly be comfortable in it, and in any case it stinks from being on your back all the time. You smell like an Armenian's armpit, if you want to know the truth ... and so does Mother.'

Zeppi gasped. Open criticism of Mother was never allowed while Father was alive, and we'd continued the rule after he'd died, out of respect.

I said, 'She ought to go swimming too. Everyone else does, and they don't smell bad.'

'You used to think they did.'

'Well, I don't any more.'

When we came to the tree, a woman was using it. When she was done and had walked back along the trunk to the shore, Zeppi went out, not walking upright with grace and confidence like the woman, but edging his way along on hands and knees. It was a sad sight. When he was halfway along the trunk he turned around and started to wriggle his shorts down around his ankles while holding onto one of the stumps for support. When he was ready he said, 'Don't look!' I turned away.

I stared at the trees and tried to decide if I was happy or sad. Bathing every day helped me feel happy because it cleaned me, but I didn't do it where any of the Yayomi could see me. Maybe Mother would feel better if she took her clothes off and did the same, but I knew she would never do that. She was afraid of water snakes, she said, but more than that, she was afraid of revealing herself to the Yayomi. The day before, I overheard her tell Klaus it was disgusting the way Wentzler refused to cover himself when there was a white woman inhabiting the same space he was. Klaus had said it was Wentzler's business if he chose to look like an Indian, but

Mother disagreed. I couldn't support her over this business of nakedness; in fact, what I really wanted to do the next time I came out of the river was not put my shorts back on.

I'd already abandoned my shirt and underpants, leaving them behind in my hammock one day. An hour later I saw the shirt tied by the sleeves around the waist of a woman, with the rest of it hanging over her arse, and the underpants were wrapped around the head of Kwaytcha, Awomay's brother. He looked like the kind of fool who puts underwear on his head to get a feeble laugh out of his friends at school, but the other Yayomi seemed to think he looked very nice. He was about my age, and he was Awomay's brother, after all, so it was in my own best interest to let him keep the underpants if he wanted to.

Wentzler had already warned us that anything not actually being worn on our bodies or in our hands (with the exception of Klaus's fearsome demon bag) would be communal property within minutes, and it was certainly true in my case, but, as I said, I didn't care. I intended leaving off my shorts so Kwaytcha or someone else would steal those too, then I could go around naked and be a lot more comfortable. Shorts that haven't been washed chafe across the thighs and between the legs. There was absolutely no reason for wearing them in a naked society. Mother wouldn't have agreed, of course.

I heard a splash and turned around. Zeppi had fallen off the tree trunk and was splashing about in the water. He knew how to swim so I wasn't worried, and he was only a few metres from shore. He found the river bottom with his feet and started wading ashore, his filthy shirt plastered to his body, and as I watched him struggle through the shallows, a word that had been on my mind a lot lately came into my thoughts again. The word was tits. My brother had tits. I could see them clearly under the wet shirt plastered to his chest like a second skin. Zeppi had tits. Little ones, yes, but they were definitely tits. And watching him come stepping up onto the bank at last, dripping and embarrassed, I knew why he hadn't taken off his shirt despite the heat and humidity and its filthy state. He didn't want anyone to see his tits!

I was close to panic. Was my brother really a girl? But that couldn't be, because I remembered seeing his cock now and then when we were little, and those things don't just drop off and turn into a crack. But there were the tits, right before my eyes, and now Zeppi was aware that I'd noticed them, because he wrapped his arms around his chest like someone who's cold and shivering. He stood there looking at me, and I stood there looking at him, not knowing what to say. Finally he started walking away, back toward the shabono. When he was a little way off, I called out, 'Take off your shirt! You'll dry out faster!' He ignored me.

When he was gone I took a walk along the bank to sort things out. How was it that I'd never noticed Zeppi's chest before? Had the tits only sprouted recently? That would make sense, given that he was twelve, almost thirteen, the age for pubic hair and tits on a girl. But he *wasn't* a girl! These weren't just lumps of fat stuck there, the rest of him wasn't pudgy. These weren't a fat man's tits. They were female tits. How was that possible?

Some of the younger Yayomi were bathing in the usual place and they called to me as I came closer. 'Eri! Eri!' Wentzler had told me they could begin a word with a hard sound but they couldn't end a word that way, in fact, they pre-ferred to avoid hardness in their names, so I was Eri, Klaus was Klow, Helga was Hella and Zeppi was … Zeppi, a very Yayomi-sounding name if you think about it. I looked at them splashing around, about a dozen of them, and saw that Kwaytcha was there. He stood out because my underpants were still on his head, that is, until one of his pals pulled them off, which started a game of catch-the-underpants. Awomay was there too, and that decided me – no more private bathing!

I took off my shorts. Now I was naked in front of the girl I wanted, except for my Iron Cross. My body isn't bad. I was good at gymnastics at school, and my cock was a reasonable size, so far as I'd been able to judge by sneaking looks at others in the showers. Joachim Kirst's put everyone else's to shame, but whenever he wagged it at us to make us feel small it was pointed out to him, 'You couldn't fuck anything with that but an elephant,' which upset him no end, the show-off. The showers were always an embarrassment for me, with my Jewish-looking cock. Every time someone asked me why I had a Jew cock, I had to explain to them that my uncle the doctor had recommended it for reasons of hygiene, which didn't help much when the usual reply, 'What would the Jews know about hygiene?' came back. But there were no Jews in Yayomiland, so it didn't matter.

I knew Awomay was looking at me as I stood there, but pretending not to. I waded out into the deeper water where everyone was gathered, still chucking Kwaytcha's underpants around, then dived under in my best dolphin style. I'd always been pretty good on the school swimming team, and knew some strokes the Yayomi didn't. Surprisingly enough, they weren't very good swimmers at all, for people who lived beside a river and had canoes that sometimes overturned. They say that sailors in the old days never learned how to swim either. The Yayomi could stay afloat if they wanted to, and do a strong dog paddle, but they had no real technique at all, no breaststroke, not even any kind of freestyle. It was easy enough to impress them by knifing through the water, literally swimming rings around them, with the Iron Cross trailing between my shoulderblades.

I dived, swam as far as I could underwater and surfaced right beside Awomay, blowing out stale air and taking in fresh air, just like a dolphin. She looked at me and laughed, then said something with my name in it. Eri had never sounded so good coming from anyone else's lips. Being that close to her, seeing her smile with those white teeth, her breasts bobbing in and out of the water in a teasing kind of way that was intentional, I think, and listening to my name on her lips, there was nothing I could do but fall in love with her. I'm serious. It was more than simply wanting her. From the shallows of lust I plunged headfirst into the depths of love.

She was right next to me, brown and lovely, absolutely irresistible, and I felt I was swimming in my own blood that lapped and hummed around me like liquid electricity, making me dizzy with longing. I felt a little sick, the feeling was so intense.

Then I saw what was happening on the bank. One of the older men was inspecting my shorts, and I knew what that meant. If he liked them, the way Kwaytcha had liked my underpants, they were his, and I couldn't let that happen, not because I wanted the shorts any more, but because the green ribbon was in the pocket. I turned away from Awomay and swam ashore.

Coming up the bank with long strides, I tried not to be angry. 'Hey!' I said.

He turned to face me. I came up to him and held out my hand for the shorts. His face told me he didn't want to give them back. Other people had my shirt and underpants, so why shouldn't he have my shorts?

'They're yours,' I said, 'but I have to empty the pockets first.' His expression was sullen, and the small blue birthmark on his temple seemed to darken. I smiled to try to make my point, but it made no difference. He clearly had no intention of handing the shorts over. Was this any way to treat a walking dolphin, I thought crossly, a guest of his people? The man was being rude, in my opinion, so I took hold of the shorts. He wouldn't let go. I smiled even wider and gave them a tug. He still wouldn't let go. Others were coming out of the water now to watch what happened next, all talking excitedly. It was something important, this dispute over the dolphin's shorts.

I tugged again and he hissed at me like a snake. His grip was strong and the muscles in his arms were bulging. We were surrounded by a crowd now. I couldn't just let him have the shorts, even though I was perfectly happy to let him have them after I'd got the ribbon. It was a contest, to see who would back down. There had to be a winner and a loser. No other outcome would be acceptable. It was up to me to make a move that would establish my right to my own property, but I couldn't think what to do. I knew the man was stronger than me, and I didn't want to lose any kind of fight that might start. If strength wasn't on my side, brains would have to be.

'Excuse me,' I said to him, looking over his shoulder and giving a little nod to the invisible person standing there, 'I think the conductor wants your ticket.'

He turned. I put my right leg around his and pushed hard against his chest. He went down hard, giving up his grip on the shorts to break his backward fall with both hands. There were 'ooohs' of amazement at my cleverness from the crowd. The man on the ground stayed there only a few seconds, then bounded up again like a tiger, hissing with anger. I took the ribbon out slowly, like a magician taking a rabbit from a hat, then handed him the shorts. 'This is all I wanted,' I told him. 'You can have these.' He wouldn't accept them, he was so angry. I pushed them against his chest and his hands came up automatically to take them. As soon as he touched them I let go the shorts. Now they were his. He didn't look at them, just kept glaring at me.

If I kept on looking at him it would turn into another contest, so I turned away and searched among the faces for Awomay's. Finding her, I went over and handed her the ribbon. She took it instantly, in fact, she snatched at it so fast I was a little offended, but I put it down to a difference in cultures. Wentzler had said that some things we did without thinking twice would offend the Yayomi, and the reverse certainly applied, so I told myself her snatching wasn't rudeness, it was happiness that I'd offered her something so wonderful.

The ribbon was a metre or so long, and she tied it without hesitation around her waist where I wanted my arms to be. I heard a sound behind me and turned, expecting to find the man attacking me, but all he'd done was throw down the shorts and start walking away. I turned back to Awomay to find she'd already begun walking off with some of her girlfriends. Again, I had to remind myself that Yayomi ways were not German ways, and what looked like ingratitude was simply a different way of behaving. She'd definitely liked the ribbon, I knew that much. In a way I was grateful to the man who'd tried to make off with my shorts, because if we hadn't had our silly confrontation I probably wouldn't have handed over the ribbon to Awomay. But at the same time I'd made an enemy as well. And the incident had shoved from my mind the thing that now came flooding back – my brother had tits.

It was several hours later when I entered the shabono. Zeppi had come back inside after his dip in the river and was near Mother as usual. Mother took one look at me and gasped. Strange as it may seem, I'd forgotten I was naked. We looked at each other. No doubt she saw a white savage. I saw a woman in an asylum, her hair all snaggled and dirty, her dress grey with dirt and sweat, her expression one of horror and outrage over nothing at all. It was hard to say who was more shocked. Another strange thing – I wasn't ashamed to stand naked before my own mother. Even yesterday I wouldn't have been able to do it. Something had changed inside me.

'Get dressed!' Mother snapped.

'I don't have any clothes.'

'Find them and put them on. Do it immediately.'

She was trying to control herself, keeping her voice down, not wanting to create a display in front of the neighbours, so to speak. It was as if we were back home and she'd found me staggering up the garden path drunk, with the whole street watching.

'My clothes belong to other people now, Mother.'

It wasn't a lie. My shorts had been left behind at the river, and by now would certainly be the property of someone else, I wouldn't know who until I saw them worn in some silly way by the new owner.

'Get them back. Get everything back and put it on.'

Her voice was harder than I'd ever heard it before. She was

deadly serious, and ordinarily I would have been a little
afraid, but considering what she was talking about, and the
fact that it didn't mean anything to me any more, I felt I had
to stand firm. I'd just done exactly that in front of a grown
man, and I wasn't about to back down to my mother. I was a
naked person now, like the Yayomi, who were sensible about
the climate and matter-of-fact about their flesh. Mother was
the one acting stupidly. To obey a stupid order is to be stupid
oneself. So I did nothing.

Mother had been taken over by a demon of righteousness
that had probably crept inside her when she was a little girl in
church with her father, a devout Christian who would probably have shot me for appearing naked and unashamed in
front of my mother. That demon, the little imp who
demanded buttoned collars and hymns on Sunday, simply
didn't belong here. Let her keep her little demon of good
manners and correct appearance, feeding him her rage and
frustration until he got so big he would burst. It had nothing
to do with me any more.

'Erich, do as I say.'

'No.'

'You will get your clothes, which Klaus has paid good
money for, and you will put them on and not remove them
again without permission.'

A feeling of sadness came over me. My mother, my lovely
mother who had cared for Zeppi and me and had suffered the
death of her husband and was a brave and good woman, that
person was gone, replaced by the crazy woman I saw in front
of me, humourless and inflexible as a school nurse with hair
on her upper lip, someone to be a little bit afraid of but who
had no authority beyond her little antiseptic-smelling sick

room. This was not my mother. This was another woman entirely, and it was my nakedness that allowed me to see her, because it was my nakedness that brought her out into the open. All of this must have shown on my face, and been interpreted by her as a weakening, a sense of shame, which it most certainly was not.

'Yes,' she said, with a tight little smile, 'yes, you should be ashamed, going about like that. Have some decency. Have you forgotten who you are? Get your clothes back on this instant.'

I wanted to explain to Mother that the things she cared about so passionately were worthless, things carried across the ocean in our trunks from a far country with different ways, things with no purpose here. Mother was living still inside the trunks that now rested on the river bottom along with the plane that carried them. Mother was drowning in meaningless customs, but to her I was the one sinking into the mud of savagery.

I looked around for Klaus, who was the only one who might have been able to talk some sense into her, but there was no sign of him. I hadn't seen him since our talk by the river this morning.

'Go on. Do as I say.'

Zeppi was standing in the shadows behind her, frightened by her behaviour.

I said, 'Mother, I learned something strange today.'

'Then unlearn it. Be true to yourself and where you came from and stop this . . . this terrible thing you've done.'

'No, it isn't that, it's Zeppi . . .'

'Zeppi?'

'Mother, Zeppi . . . Zeppi has . . . breasts. I saw them.'

She whirled to face Zeppi. 'Did you take your shirt off!'

He shook his head quickly, afraid. 'No . . . I kept it on all the time.'

'It was when he fell in the river,' I said. 'His shirt was wet. I saw them. What does it mean?'

She turned back to me, her face white under the coating of wood smoke and dirt. 'Nothing . . . It means nothing. Say nothing, do you hear me?'

'But Zeppi's a boy . . . He can't be like that, he —'

'Be quiet! Hold your tongue when I say so!'

She was upset, but it wasn't about me being naked now, it was because I'd seen Zeppi's tits, which meant Mother already knew and was not happy about it. What mother would be? I didn't know what to say. Mother was looking around the shabono, eyes darting this way and that, making her look even more crazy.

'Erich, say nothing of this to Klaus. And that man Wentzler, he mustn't know either. For Zeppi's sake, do as I say. Tell me you'll do as I say.'

'All right.'

'On your word of honour.'

'On my word of honour.'

She looked at my body, then quickly away. 'Why have you done this to me?'

'It's cooler and more comfortable. It makes sense, Mother.'

'I don't recognise you any more. You're someone else.'

What she said was true, but I knew that agreeing with her would have upset her even more, so I said nothing. She seemed to sag a little, and went to sit on her hammock, eyes staring at the hard earth beneath her sandals. I still wore my own sandals, and had done so even as I swam, for fear of something I'd been warned about by Mother as a child –

broken glass left by thoughtless people using the beach. There was no broken glass in the river. I'd swim without sandals next time, and leave them off for as long as I felt like it through the day from now on, to harden my soles until they were Yayomi feet, but I'd tie the sandals around my neck so they wouldn't be stolen until I was good and ready to give them up. I wasn't an Indian yet, not by a long way, just enough of one to upset Mother.

'Where is Klaus?' she said. 'Why isn't he here?'

I looked for the black bag. It wasn't by Klaus's hammock.

'Would you like me to go and look for him?'

'Yes . . . yes, do that for me. I'm too tired.'

She tipped herself back into the hammock and lay like a dead woman, staring at the leafy thatch above. Zeppi's eyes flickered back and forth between Mother and me. I wondered how long she'd been telling him not to reveal his chest. It couldn't have been too long because I'd seen him in nothing but pyjama bottoms last summer when it was so hot and we could hear the cicadas rasping all night long through the open window. This was something new. He must have gone to her in tears, saying, 'Mother, what are these? They weren't there before, Mother . . .' Poor little Zeppi. What would happen now?

Mother's eyes had closed. I beckoned to Zeppi and he followed me outside the shabono to search for Klaus. We went to the plantain garden but he wasn't there, or down at the river. I counted the canoes, thinking that maybe he'd stolen one and abandoned us, but when I saw that all eight were present I was ashamed of having thought that about him. Still, it was a puzzle, his disappearance.

We ran into Wentzler in our rambling and he seemed

taken aback at my nakedness. 'Well, well, young man. So you've accepted the inevitable, eh? Will the rest of your family be following in time?'

'I don't think so, Herr Wentzler. Have you seen Klaus? Mother wants him.'

'It so happens I've been having a long conversation with your father. You'll find him just a little way along this path. Keep straight on and you'll find him. And you,' he said to Zeppi, 'wouldn't you like to take off those sticky clothes and feel the breeze on your skin?'

'Yes,' said Zeppi. I hadn't expected that, and neither had the professor.

'Well, then,' he said, 'take them off, do. You'll be so much more comfortable, and I'm sure your brother can tell you that being without clothes in front of other people is something you get used to very quickly, isn't that so?'

'Yes it is,' I said, waiting to see if Zeppi would follow his own wishes.

'I can't,' he said. It was a forlorn little sentence. He was suffering for Mother's sake. It all seemed so ridiculous, and Wentzler obviously thought so too. He shook his head then pointed up the path again. 'That way,' he said, and walked on.

'I want to,' Zeppi said to me, 'but Mother says not to.'

'I know. It's silly. You'd be much better off without clothes. Is it because of the . . . you know. Is that what's stopping you from disobeying Mother?'

'I don't know. Why are they there, Erich? They're what ladies have.'

'We should ask Klaus. He's a doctor, after all, and this is a biological problem.'

'Mother said not to.'

'Listen to me, Zeppi. Something strange has happened to you. I don't know if it's a good thing or a bad thing, but I do know that Mother doesn't know either. All she has is an opinion, not any real knowledge. She hasn't a clue, so she wants to hide it away and make a secret of it, but that's bad for you, because you can't possibly be comfortable with clothing on. She's being selfish and ridiculous, so we have to ask Klaus what to do. He has knowledge because he's a doctor. Do you understand what I'm saying?'

'Of course I do! I'm not stupid! You always think you know everything!'

Obnoxious Zeppi was preferable to timid Zeppi, which was what Mother had made him. I put my arm across his shoulder, something I hadn't done in a long time, and gave him a quick hug.

'Come on,' I said.

Zeppi followed me willingly. He even took my hand, which he hadn't done in years. We stayed with the path as it wound among the trees, up toward the slightly higher ground from which we'd first seen the shabono. The trees thinned a little, and we saw Klaus sitting beneath one, wearing only his underpants and sandals. He had his medical bag with him, so he must not have completely trusted Wentzler's statement about the Yayomi being afraid of it. They would overcome their fear some day and take it for their own, even if it was filled with snapping teeth.

He saw us coming and waved. He seemed not to be shocked that I was naked.

'So, a move in the direction of the practical, I see.'

'I like it better this way.'

'I'm working up the nerve to do the same,' he said.

'Go ahead', I told him, 'it really does make all the difference in the world.'

'I believe you, but what will your mother say? I can't quite picture her in a nudist colony.'

'She's already seen me. She was angry. I'm not putting my clothes back on, though. It's too late for that. Everything's changed.'

He nodded as if he understood what I myself still didn't understand, not completely anyway. 'You must do as you see fit, Erich. It may be that Helga will adjust to this place in time. And you, Zeppi, how do you feel about this question of clothes or no clothes?'

'I want to go swimming', he said, 'but Mother says not to.'

'And why is that? What's wrong with a little swim?'

'It's not the swimming itself,' I said, and Klaus looked at me, waiting for more. I said to Zeppi, 'Show him.'

Slowly, reluctantly, Zeppi took off his soiled shirt. And there they were, quite a bit bigger than they'd appeared under his wet shirt. His nipples were very pretty, I thought, and blushed. Klaus's face drained of blood, not the reaction I'd expected. Nobody said anything for a long time. Zeppi was waiting to be told everything was all right, but Klaus simply stared at the lovely smooth breasts on Zeppi's chest.

Finally he said, 'This is most unusual...' His voice was tight, strained. He was trying to be nonchalant, but wasn't quite convincing. 'Very rare indeed...' Klaus continued, and then his whole manner changed, and he was like a doctor in his surgery, very calm and asking all the right questions. 'Come closer', Klaus told him, and Zeppi stepped forward. Klaus reached out and casually felt his tits. 'Absolutely normal outer appearance and inner development, so far as I can see and feel,' he said. 'Zeppi, where on earth did you find these pretty things?'

'I don't know,' said Zeppi. 'They just started growing, and when I showed Mother she said never to tell anyone . . . I don't want them if people are going to laugh at me!'

'No one will laugh at you, Zeppi. You're much too attractive a youngster to be laughed at. You may think it strange to hear me say so, but the fact is, you're better off here in the jungle with the Indians, with these . . . splendid appurtenances, than you would be in the city. The Yayomi may think nothing of them, nothing at all.'

'But when we go away, what will happen then?' Zeppi wanted to know.

'Getting away is a bit of a problem at the moment, I must say. Zeppi, if you want to take off your clothes and be comfortable like Erich, don't hesitate. You'll feel a little self-conscious at first, but I'm sure you'll get used to it.'

'What about Mother?' I said.

'Leave that to me. Zeppi, I have a question that will sound silly, but I need to know if . . . well, if everything is as it should be inside your pants. May I have a quick look? This might be the time to take off all your clothes, in any case, if that's the decision you've made.' Seeing Zeppi hesitate, Klaus stood and removed his own underpants. His cock was a healthy size and his balls hung low in the heat, like mine. The hair was blond and curly, a shade darker than the hair on his head.

'There,' he said, 'that certainly feels better. Zeppi, I invite you to step into the world of practical comfort. Don't be shy.'

Zeppi carefully unbuttoned his shorts and let them fall, then slid his underpants down. Even though I remembered having seen his cock in the past, I was surprised to see that he had one. It wasn't very big at all, and looked a bit defenceless, like a cock on a statue. He had balls too, but the bag was small, and he had no hair at all. His skin was very white all over, like marble, apart from his arms and legs which had tanned. There was something not quite real about the picture he presented, neither male nor female, glancing nervously at Klaus and myself, wanting to hear us say he wasn't a freak of nature.

'You look very nice, Zeppi,' I said. I couldn't think what else to say.

Klaus said, 'A textbook case.' Zeppi looked at him questioningly, and Klaus went on. 'You aren't the first to have this happen to him, not at all. There are recorded instances going back to ancient times. It's extremely unusual, certainly, but not unheard of, by any means. The word used to describe your condition, Zeppi, is hermaphroditism. It's a hard word to say if you've never heard it before. You have the sexual characteristics of both male and female. This happens sometimes in nature, nobody's quite sure why. Once in a great while, a young fellow reaches puberty and hey presto! the young man is surprised to find he's become a young woman also. That is your condition, Zeppi. It's described in all the medical literature.'

'I don't want it,' said Zeppi. 'Can you make it go away?'

Klaus paused, then said, 'I'm afraid not, Zeppi. Some experimentation has been done with a view to eradicating one set of characteristics present, but it's a very new process. I know that Muller in Berlin was working on a young person when the war began, but I failed to follow his progress, and I believe the Americans have also done some interesting work in that direction. The surgery is very complex, virtually a new science, you understand. I myself have read a little about it, but never . . . I'm sorry, Zeppi, but there's nothing I can do. I advise you to accept your condition and be happy.'

'Happy?'

Zeppi's eyes were brimming. I put my hand on his shoulder again and felt him trembling. Happiness was not part of what he was feeling.

'If not happy, then reconciled,' Klaus offered. 'When nothing can be done about a particular situation, misery is wasted, you see? You should perhaps take heart from the fact that you're a very special young person in this world, Zeppi. There are probably no more than a dozen or so like you anywhere at any given time. Does that cheer you up?'

'No. I don't want to be . . .'

The tears were flowing now, rolling down his cherubic cheeks, and his body was racked with sobs that couldn't be held back any longer. His little cock danced up and down as he wept, and I felt like crying myself at the way my brother had been put inside a prison nobody could break him out of, not even a surgeon like Klaus. It was a terrible thing to think of, and even Zeppi could see that Klaus's words about being happy were empty. How could he be happy if he wasn't entirely male or female? He was trapped by those nice little titties into being something that nobody else he would ever meet in his entire life would be.

I wanted to tell him it was better than being a hunchback or a legless person, or blind, but the words wouldn't come out, because deep inside I knew there could be no comfort for Zeppi, no words that could cheer him up and be true at the same time.

Klaus said, 'Now, about this problem with your mother. I can see why she's upset, but she shouldn't be, not really, so I'm going to have a word with her, all right? You two take your time coming in. That'll give me a chance to make her see it isn't anything to be . . . worried about.'

He'd been about to say 'ashamed of', I think, but stopped himself in time.

'So, as I said, take your time, and I'll see you both later on.'

He walked off down the path without looking back. He carried his black bag but he'd left his underpants behind. That's how I knew he was as hard hit by Zeppi's revelation as Mother had been, but at least he'd done the sensible thing and explained it as best he could, not just tried to sweep it under the rug.

Zeppi asked me, 'Can he really not do anything?'

'No, he can't. I'm sorry, Zeppi.'

He made a big effort and stopped crying. 'Do you still like me, Erich?'

That almost made me start bawling myself. 'Of course I do! You're my brother and I love you very much. Whatever else happens, that'll always be true . . . so there.'

'All right,' he said, looking down between his breasts at his little willie. 'If you say so.'

We walked along the path together, surrounded by a sudden gathering of brilliant blue butterflies. There were so many you could hear their wings. They touched our skin, dozens and dozens of them at once, the lightest touch you could imagine, so light it tickled. I think they might have been drinking our sweat. It was like being attacked by feathers.

Zeppi and I stood absolutely still. 'Aren't they beautiful, Zeppi?' I whispered.

The butterflies moved on, a shining blue cloud that

merged with the green around them and then vanished. I
knew it was something I'd always remember. Even when I was
old I wouldn't forget the butterflies.

When we got back to the shabono I was disappointed to
see that Klaus had put his shorts on. The first thing he said
was, 'You didn't happen to bring my underpants with you, I
suppose?'

'No.'

Mother sat on her hammock glaring at Zeppi and me. She
blamed me for the fact that Zeppi was now as naked as myself,
and for disobeying her and telling Klaus about Zeppi's problem.

The Yayomi had begun to notice that they had a white dolphin among them that was different to the other three. They
stared at Zeppi and talked excitedly among themselves,
touching their chests and their crotches to make the point.

'How can I call you my son?' said Mother. At first I thought
she must be asking Zeppi, for obvious reasons, but she was
talking to me. 'You have betrayed me.' She spoke it like a line
in a film, with lots of drama and passion, and the way it came
out made me embarrassed for her. Klaus was looking more
and more uncomfortable as the Yayomi crowded around us.
'See what you've done?' Mother accused. 'Now he'll have no
peace! Your own brother – how could you have done this?'

'Helga, please, what's done is done . . .' Klaus was kneeling
by her side, touching her, trying to make her less angry, but
she flung his hand off.

'No! You come here, *finally*, and tell me there's nothing to
worry about? How dare you! Where have you been for hours
on end? Why do you leave me here with these filthy things?
Don't touch me!'

'Helga . . .'

'No!'

I'd never seen her so angry before in my life. Even when she got the news that Father was dead she'd only sobbed for a long time, never screamed like this. She was blaming Klaus as much as me, which wasn't fair. He couldn't help it if I'd told him about Zeppi. I felt sorry for him, and the screaming brought more Yayomi across the shabono to stare at Mother.

Klaus didn't know what to do. Maybe Mother had been like this with him before, only a little quieter, and that was why he'd been going off by himself. He probably shouldn't have done that, because they had only been married a little while ago. I suppose he should have been holding her hand and telling her everything would be all right, or whatever it is that husbands are supposed to say. Now I felt sorry for Mother, but at the same time I wanted her to stop behaving like this.

Wentzler showed up beside us, and as soon as she saw his skinny naked body Mother shut her eyes so she wouldn't have to talk to him.

'Is something wrong?' asked Wentzler, but nobody answered him. Then he noticed Zeppi was naked. 'Aah, a sensible move . . .' Then he noticed the other thing about Zeppi. 'But what does this mean . . . ?' he said, pointing at his chest just like the Yayomi had done. 'I don't understand . . . Herr Brandt?'

'I'll explain later,' Klaus said, concentrating on Mother. 'Can you make them all go away, please?'

'Well, I can ask, but it won't do any good. They're curious, you see, fascinated in fact, by the young . . . fellow here. This is really quite remarkable. A case of hermaphroditism, isn't it?

I've never seen the like; some rare photographs, perhaps, in a medical text, I think, long ago. But to see it in the flesh!'

He was every inch a professor as he stared openly at Zeppi, who must have felt like a museum exhibit, because he began to sniffle and cry.

'Just shut up about it!' I said to Wentzler, which upset him.

'Yes, well . . . perhaps I should have expressed myself with more moderation.'

The chief, Manokwo, came through the crowd then, and listened as his people told him about Zeppi. Zeppi was staring at the ground, trying like Mother to shut everything out. Manokwo squatted in front of Zeppi and very gently squeezed his tits, then inspected his cock and balls the same way. Zeppi was shivering all over, but he didn't back away. Then the chief looked at my cock too, and it was clear he was interested in the way Zeppi and I had been circumcised. Nobody I'd been swimming with earlier had really noticed, given that I was in the water most of the time, and then there'd been the argument with the man who'd wanted to take my shorts, so again nobody had had a chance to see that I was different to them.

But now they did, all of them, and I was almost as big an attraction as Zeppi. Then Manokwo indicated that he wanted to see Klaus's cock as well, and when Wentzler translated, Klaus obliged him by slipping down his shorts. Mother opened her eyes briefly to see what was going on, and a shiver of disgust or dismay passed through her, then she shut her eyes again, as if everything around her was too horrible to look at.

Wentzler gave a little cough. 'Manokwo wants to know why the two boys have misshapen penises, and he particularly wants to know why the youngest appears to be both male and female.'

Klaus asked, 'What should we tell him?'

'I have no idea. A lecture on surgical procedures and human genetics wouldn't be understood. Manokwo would think you were trying to conceal something from him. They can be very suspicious of things they don't comprehend.'

Klaus thought hard but said nothing. I had the impression things were beginning to overwhelm him, which surprised me, but then he was concerned about Mother as well as everything else, so perhaps it was understandable.

The silence stretched on, until finally I said to Wentzler, 'Tell him these are special dolphin penises and Zeppi is the most special kind of dolphin of them all, a male and a female, and that we all ... worship him or something. I don't want them thinking he's not supposed to be the way he is. That's the important part. Go on, tell him.'

Wentzler drew himself up a little. 'Kindly address me as an elder. I had the respect of students older than you, young man.'

I was a bit taken aback, then I wanted to hit him, the scrawny scarecrow, but instead I said, 'I'm sorry, Herr Professor, I'm a little bit worked up.'

He sniffed, then spoke to Manokwo, who listened carefully and nodded. The others had all been listening too, and word of Zeppi's specialness spread among them like the buzzing of insects. More of them began touching his privates, and I told Zeppi not to mind them, that they thought he was a very remarkable boy. I said he was not just a human and a dolphin, he was a boy and girl besides, and that made the Yayomi think of him as better than the rest of us, who were only human dolphins after all. I don't think it helped a lot. He shivered every time he was touched, and the touching went on for a long time.

I was surprised that Klaus hadn't been the one to tell Wentzler how to explain things. It's a very strange feeling when you know you've taken action that an adult should have. It made me feel bigger, and at the same time it made Klaus appear smaller somehow.

The Yayomi began drifting away. It seemed that they accepted miracles very quickly, which is only natural, I suppose, if you don't have any science. When the last of them had gone about their business, apart from a few little children, I looked again at Mother. Her eyes were open now that we weren't surrounded by Indians. Wentzler had stayed and was waiting to see what happened next. I think we all were. We couldn't move, it seemed, until Mother spoke.

'You'll take me away from here now, this instant,' she said at last. It wasn't clear who she was talking to. No one said anything. A pet monkey was being chased by a pup, and it scampered across the ground and leapt into Mother's lap, thinking it would find shelter there. Instead, Mother screamed, and her whole body gave a great shudder. The monkey squawked and ran off with the pup still in pursuit.

Klaus said, 'As you know, Helga, we have no actual means of escape from here at the moment. We must be patient and see what develops.'

'Fix it,' said Mother, not looking at him, not looking at anything, really.

'Not so easily done,' said Wentzler. 'Here there are no police stations or courts of appeal for those who believe they've been wronged. Actually, nobody has been wronged, but I have the impression, Frau Brandt, you wish to blame someone . . .'

'I blame you,' said Mother, 'and you, and you.' She blamed all of us except Zeppi, who seemed relieved. I'm sure his tits made him think everything might be his fault. I felt that we were surrounded by ugliness, just as a half-hour ago Zeppi and I had been surrounded by loveliness in the form of big blue butterflies. I was suddenly very tired. Too much had happened, and none of it had answers.

Wentzler looked at Klaus, who gave no sign of taking charge, then continued, 'My dear Frau Brandt, you must adapt to your new circumstances. You didn't choose to be here, but here is where you are, and here you'll remain for some time, I'm afraid. This isn't such a bad place as you seem to think. You have food, you have shelter and companionship. These are enough, dear lady.' No reaction at all from Mother, but he went on, less like a lecturer now, with something like pleading in his voice. 'I understand your distress over the lack of modesty here, but really, what are these people but original Adams and Eves, living their lives in an earthly Eden? I ask you, can this be a sin? Won't you allow your family the simple comfort of nakedness, Frau Brandt, and yourself? It's been remarked upon that you refuse to take off your clothing even to bathe.'

He waited for a response, but Mother said nothing. He went on, 'This is something the Yayomi simply don't understand. They're a clean people, sometimes bathing two, even three times a day. Frankly, Frau Brandt, it's considered ill mannered to allow yourself to . . . stink. There have been complaints, and you're in danger of becoming the subject of jokes. They say – and I apologise for the intrusive nature of the subject matter – they say that you've made yourself smell so bad because you don't ... desire your husband and want to keep him away from you. I know this isn't the case, but the Yayomi have no conception of modesty such as we're used to. This is a society of skin, not clothing. You really must abandon your old ways, or suffer the consequences to your health and even the social standing of yourself and your family.'

Still not seeing any reaction, Wentzler addressed the rest of his remarks to Klaus. 'This is a serious matter. You're dolphins, not people, and for the Yayomi to see any one of you behave in an offensive manner may harm you. Supernatural beings must have an air of mystery about them to command respect. The young man here with his ... unusual characteristics has today risen greatly in the esteem of the Yayomi, but I must warn you that there has been a proportionate lowering of the status of your wife. She's in danger of being taken for a dolphin no longer, just a woman, and an offensive woman at that. She's become, if you'll recall the phrase, the guest who wouldn't leave. Hospitality here isn't extended for its own sake, but in expectation of reward. To stay with the Yayomi you must bring gifts, and the only gift your party has brought is your celebrity as dolphins. Kill that illusion and anything may happen.'

Klaus appeared to be thinking. Eventually he said, 'You're telling me my wife is a liability to us all, is that it?'

'With regret, that's exactly what I'm telling you.'

'What gifts did you bring, Gerhard?'

'Machetes, coloured beads, some ribbon, the usual bits and pieces.'

'And that was enough to guarantee their hospitality for eleven years?'

'That has proved to be the case, yes.'

'And simply by not bathing, Helga will undermine their goodwill?'

'I ask you to exercise your rights as a husband and command her to do what's right, for the sake of your family.'

They were talking about Mother as if she wasn't there, and the sad thing was, she *didn't* appear to be there. She stared at the ground with her lips pressed together, not listening, or not seeming to. If someone had told me a week ago that Mother would look and behave like this I wouldn't have believed it. She wasn't Mother any more, she was someone else, a very angry woman who seemed to think she lived in a cage.

Klaus was considering Wentzler's advice. I could see determination building in his eyes, then he said. 'Boys, you might have to assist me in this.' He turned to Mother. 'Helga, you'll come with me to the river and you'll bathe. It will make you feel much better. This isn't a suggestion, this is an order, for your own good and the good of us all. Do you hear me, Helga?'

She didn't blink an eye. Klaus sighed, then said to her, 'You give me no choice. I do this for you, Helga. If you struggle I'll have to use force. Do you want to make a spectacle of yourself in front of all these people you despise? Do this with dignity, I beg you. Now stand and come with me.'

She wouldn't, simply kept on staring at nothing. 'Very well,' said Klaus, and with one smooth movement he scooped her up out of the hammock and lifted her in his arms. She hung there like a life-sized rag doll, not resisting, but not cooperating either. Klaus started walking toward the hole in the shabono wall. I hurried ahead to clear the bushes, followed by Zeppi and Wentzler.

Klaus carried her down to the river, followed by a stream of Yayomi. I don't think they were as interested in seeing Mother naked as they were in seeing her get washed. For myself, I have to admit that somewhere inside I had a great curiosity to see Mother naked, and by this I don't mean some kind of mental sickness of the kind you read about sometimes. No, it was just that I'd seen everyone else without clothes on and now it was Mother's turn.

What I hoped for was that, once naked and washed, she'd become her old self again. It was a good sign that she wasn't struggling in Klaus's arms. Deep down, Mother must have been ready to give up her silliness and submit to nakedness, or she would have been kicking up a fuss about it. Klaus had done the right thing. He looked like a hero, taking her down to the water that way, like something on a film poster.

Klaus entered the river and carried Mother out to waist depth, then lowered her into the water. As it closed around her, Mother's arms came up and held onto his neck. Then she was standing upright in front of him, still holding on that way, and Klaus was unbuttoning the front of her dress. The Yayomi stood along the bank in droves, watching in silence as the dress was peeled off and allowed to float slowly away. Then he took off her brassiere, which I could see was a dirty grey colour instead of the usual white, and then he reached down out of sight below the surface and pulled off her panties.

These and the brassiere drifted after the dress, and then Klaus took off his own shorts, lifted them above his head like a trophy, and flung them far out into the water. I was pleased to see the clothes go drifting off. If the Yayomi had got hold of them they would have worn them in some stupid way, like

Kwaytcha with my underpants on his head, and made themselves look silly. It was much better that they looked like themselves, just naked with some feathers attached to their ears and their bodies painted black and red. That was the way they were supposed to be, and now, with Mother naked at last, maybe we could be like them, for as long as we were here, anyway.

Klaus ducked below the surface and came up with his hair streaming, then encouraged Mother to do the same. Her lovely blond hair had begun to look like a straw broom lately, and it must have made her scalp itch not to wash it through with running water. Her head went completely under, then came up, then went under again. She did it four times, then stayed up, gasping for breath, her hair lying over her face like an eyeless mask. She reached up to push it back, and I saw her breasts for the first time since I was a baby sucking on them, which of course I couldn't remember. They were very nice breasts with wide pink nipples, not brown like the Indian women's breasts, and I definitely heard Wentzler, who was standing next to me, take a breath.

Klaus began leading Mother ashore. When the water was only waist high she hesitated, then went on, and soon everyone could see every part of her. I must say, I hadn't expected her to be so bushy down below. The crinkly hair stood out a lot and was slightly darker than the hair on her head, just like Klaus. They looked like brother and sister as they came wading through the shallows and up the bank onto dry land. I heard the Yayomi making sounds of interest and appreciation, and felt good about it, because it meant that they were agreeing that my mother was a beautiful woman.

I asked, 'What are they saying, Herr Wentzler?'

He said, 'Perhaps you shouldn't know.'

'In the name of scientific curiosity, Herr Wentzler?'

'Very well. They're all tremendously impressed by your mother's pubic hair.'

'Really?' I should have expected it. The Yayomi women were practically hairless there, and Mother's bush was a fairly spectacular growth, I had to admit. Wentzler went on, 'Among the Yayomi, if you're interested, pubic hair on a woman is considered a sign of great sexual appetite. They have a number of ribald stories about encountering jungle creatures which transform themselves into humans, in much the same way that you and your family are assumed to be dolphins, and the women transformees are invariably equipped with masses of pubic hair. I'm afraid this might mean trouble.'

'Why? It makes us seem more like dolphins if Mother looks like something they tell stories about. You were worried about her looking too much like an ordinary human, and now she doesn't.'

'You don't quite follow. These stories, they're told by the men primarily to excite themselves. The creatures turned into women in these stories are voracious ... copulators. They'll expect her, in their fantasies at least, to engage them all in sexual activity, you see. That's what I mean by trouble. Fortunately, they understand that she has a husband. The bushy-haired women in the stories are alone, usually. Of course, there are stories in which the animal-turned-human's husband is ... killed, so the Yayomi may copulate en masse with his widow. Perhaps this is better not dwelled upon.'

'Why would they tell dirty stories like that?'

'Why do white men embrace pornography and visit

brothels? There's a common element that makes all men the same. A shame it isn't of a higher order.'

Klaus and Mother walked through the admiring crowd and began heading back to the shabono, their skin shining with water, like a pair of dolphins.

'This is a delicate matter, Erich, but I judge you to be mature beyond your years. Will you do something for me?'

'Of course.'

'I want you to encourage your father and mother to ... make love, and make love often. They must be sure the Yayomi are aware of them doing it. They should engage in amorous activity early in the morning, in the jungle a short distance from the shabono, the way the Yayomi do. This is important. If the men suspect that your mother is being sexually neglected, they won't hesitate to take over your father's marital duties. They may do so with some trepidation, since they don't know what reaction to expect from a dolphin, but they'll do it anyway, because Yayomi men are like men anywhere – they follow their pricks rather than their brains.'

'Maybe you should be the one to tell them, Herr Professor, you being the expert.'

'I think you may have noticed that Frau Brandt doesn't like me. Any suggestion that comes directly from me would likely be resented or ignored.'

'Then you should talk to Klaus, man to man. Really, it'd impress him more than if it comes from me. What would I know about things like this?'

'You could say that the information came from me.'

'I think you should tell him yourself, if it's that important.'

He didn't say anything. Everyone but Wentzler and Zeppi and myself had followed Klaus and Mother back up the path to the shabono. 'In any case,' said Wentzler, sounding far away, 'this has been a day of fabulous intensity for them, the Yayomi, I mean. First young Zeppi here astounds them with his uniqueness, then your mother, who was fast becoming a figure of fun, reveals herself instead to be a figure of great sensuality, according to their somewhat bizarre standards, I hasten to add. When your mother came out of the river naked, it would have appeared to the Yayomi men as it would to other men that their favourite movie star – Hedy Lamarr, for example – or even Venus Aphrodite herself, had suddenly appeared among them in the flesh, with the light of sexual favour shining in her eyes.'

Mother, by doing what everyone had been urging her to do, had put herself in danger, just because she had a really bushy bush. It was funny in a way that I hadn't anticipated, and yet not funny at all.

SIX

WHEN THE LAST OF THE clothing came off our bodies there was a change in all of us. I was the first to go fully naked, and Mother was the last, so it was only natural that I'd be the one to adapt sooner than the rest, and that Mother should lag behind. The problem was, between me taking off my clothes that day and Mother doing so was only a few hours, but her adaptation lagged for a lot longer than that. Even as much as a week later she still wasn't comfortable without her European covering. She finally used the tree that hung over the river like everyone else, and she bathed every day, but only when Klaus agreed to go with her.

Zeppi was better off without clothing because of his strange body, not despite it. The Yayomi found him fascinating, so much so that his only real problem was the way they'd follow him around, wanting to touch his tits, which he hated at first, then got used to, especially after someone gave him a little monkey for a pet. He called it Mitzi.

After getting Mother to behave normally, I concentrated on my own needs. I didn't waste time thinking about search planes (we hadn't seen any) or rescue parties, or wondering if and when we would leave this particular bend of the unknown river the Yayomi called theirs. It was pointless worrying about all of that, and acknowledging this was the second step of my adaptation. Without the anxiety that waiting to be taken away would have caused, I was free to think about other things. Like Awomay.

She knew very well that I wanted her because of the green ribbon, which was still around her pretty waist, sliding about above her gorgeous behind. Before she wore the ribbon all I looked at were her tits, but with the line of green separating her into halves, so to speak, I became more interested in the lower half. She slept in a hammock only a metre or two from my own, which was torture. The Yayomi had no privacy at all inside the shabono and so had to find it in the jungle where they went to make love, usually in the early morning, as Wentzler had pointed out, and as I'd seen for myself. I wondered if the thing to do was simply to follow Awomay when she left the shabono while the morning fires were getting built up and there were still little streamers of mist lying along the ground from the cooler night air.

I did it one morning but was too slow and ran into her coming back toward the shabono after she'd relieved herself down at the river. There was no one else in sight, and I waited by the pathway, hoping she'd stop and talk to me. I didn't know a word of the Yayomi tongue, but everyone knows that the language of love is universal. I practised some lines from the films I'd seen – 'Darling, you look so lovely. My heart is yours forever, my sweet,' that kind of nonsense – so as not to stand there like an idiot, saying nothing. She came toward me, tits swaying a little as she walked, and her thighs brushing together below her almost invisible crease, and the look of her made me want her right there and then, in the worst way.

All those lines flew out of my head as she came closer, crowded out by visions of Awomay and myself locked together on the ground like rutting cats. She stopped, all right, but her eyes didn't meet mine the way I wanted. Instead, she was looking at my cock, which had risen like a railway signal to stand straight out from my body. She said something and laughed, then walked on, and the opportunity was gone. I felt like an idiot, even if she was in no doubt now, if she ever had been, over how I felt about her.

How did the Yayomi go about winning someone, I wondered? The person to ask was our resident professor of all things Yayomi.

'Herr Wentzler, may I ask you a question?'

He was lying in his hammock during the midday heat, eyes half closed.

'What is it?'

'How do they . . . well, what's the correct way to go about . . . you know . . .'

'No, I don't know. Be specific, please.'

'How do I . . . get a girlfriend?'

'You get on a plane and fly to Caracas. I'm told the young ladies there are no better than they ought to be, among the lower classes anyway.'

'That's funny, Professor, but I meant right here. How does it happen if there's a problem with the language?'

His head rolled sideways so he could look directly at me. 'Language, young man, would be the least of your problems.

Like most Europeans, you have the erroneous impression that nakedness among these people indicates a lack of morals, or at the very least a willingness to copulate, willy-nilly, without fear of any consequences. In fact, the Yayomi are no more or less promiscuous than the rest of humankind. Their sex lives are quite rigorously predetermined by their social status, which is determined by whose daughter or sister they are, in the case of the females. I assume these are what you're interested in.'

'Of course.'

'Then my advice to you is to make love frequently to Lady Hand and her five daughters.'

'That's funny, Professor. I don't want to do that, though.' I was thinking that Wentzler, being told by the Yayomi that he couldn't have one of their women for his own in all these eleven years he'd lived here, was probably very intimately acquainted with Lady Hand. What had been good enough for him was definitely not going to be good enough for me, being at least twenty years younger.

'There's a particular girl. I know she likes me, Professor. She smiles at me, and she accepted a gift from me, but I think she's waiting for me to do something else, some special thing that you might call a formality. Could you tell me what that might be?'

'Pay close attention while I save you from yourself, Erich. All young women and girls are the wards of their fathers, brothers and uncles. They may have a yearning for some good-looking young fellow who takes their fancy, but they don't go dashing off into the trees with him for some sexual high jinks, not if they value their future.'

'Why not?'

'It's all arranged, set in place beforehand, sometimes years beforehand. Men bargain with men for the right to cohabit with – or marry, if you prefer – the young lady of their dreams. The young lady in question may express an opinion on the matter, but the men who are her protectors, for want of a better word, will ignore her wishes if the match is a good one.'

'How could it be good if she doesn't love the man?'

'Good for the family and the tribe, the shabono at large, not necessarily good for the young lady. Her preferences are taken into consideration sometimes, but only if they don't conflict with whatever her protectors have determined is best for the Yayomi as a whole. Will the intended fellow be a good provider for the young lady's family by bringing them lots of fish and monkey meat? Is he a good fighter who'll play his part in defending the shabono and the family if attacked? Is his company enjoyable? Does he tell funny stories and get along with all the future in-laws? Will he be acceptable to all?'

He must have seen my face fall, but that didn't stop him. 'You, for example, would be turned down as a suitor for any female bar some old thing whose husband has died and whose family have moved away over the years to establish another shabono. Some withered hag nobody else would be interested in, because she's basically a liability, you see. That'd be the kind of woman for you. I see you're shocked. Let me assure you, Erich, that love's young dream plays no part in the way such things are arranged here. Sometimes girls still in babyhood are promised as brides to a suitable man if the family happens to be in his debt for one reason or another. A girl often winds up with a fellow old enough to be her father. It's all as cold-blooded and unromantic as a sales transaction.'

'But you're talking about marriage, I think.'

'Aha, and all you want is a quick roll in the hay?'

'Well, no . . . more than that.'

'More than that means marriage, and you're eminently unsuited for matrimony in this society. No reflection on you, Erich, no need to take any of this personally.'

'Of course not.'

'You don't know how to use a bow and arrow or zabatana, and your prowess as a warrior is, shall we say, untested.'

'Don't know how to use a what?'

'Zabatana. The blowpipe. You'd be a liability to any family you married into, quite useless, in fact.'

'But I told you, I'm not interested in getting married.'

'Exactly.'

I decided he was telling me this because he was jealous of my youth and the fact that Awomay liked me. I hadn't seen any of the women give Wentzler the glad eye.

'Herr Professor?'

'Yes?'

'Could you ask her brother to teach me about bows and arrows and the zabatana?'

'And who is the "her" to whom you refer?'

'Awomay. Her brother is Kwaytcha. He took my under-pants.'

'So matrimony is your intention after all?'

'No, I just want to learn. It'd be fun to go hunting, and we should contribute something to the pot, I think.'

'I haven't done so in eleven years.'

I could have asked why not, but didn't, not wanting to suggest that he was lazy, but I couldn't resist saying, 'They must like you very much.'

'I tell them stories, Erich. They love my stories much more than they love me. I must have run through the tales of the Brothers Grimm and Hans Christian Andersen several dozen times by now. They never tire of hearing about Hansel and Gretel, or Little Red Riding Hood, or the Ugly Duckling.'

'See? You're paying your way with stories, but we aren't paying our way with anything. Sooner or later they're going to get sick of having dolphins around, eating their food and giving nothing back.'

He looked uncomfortable, and I saw I'd scored a point. He said, 'I'm not at all sure that it's a good idea for a dolphin to go hunting like any other Yayomi. As supernatural royalty, it's understood by all that you should be provided for.'

'But I'm bored. And what happens if they decide one day that we aren't dolphins any more? We'd just be . . . what was it you said about Mother? The guests who stayed too long? We should know how to make a contribution.'

He thought about it for a moment.

'Fetch him over,' said Wentzler.

I found Kwaytcha asleep in his hammock and wakened him. He wasn't put out by having his siesta disturbed, and he understood that I wanted him to come with me. We both went to Wentzler's hammock, and a rapid conversation took place, then Wentzler said, 'It's all arranged. Go with him, and be careful of the tips of his darts, they're dipped in curare. One scratch and you'll die horribly.'

'Thank you, Herr Wentzler.'

'I'm very fond of monkey. Get me a young one, nice and juicy.'

'I will.'

He laughed.

Being in the jungle with Kwaytcha was a quiet business. From the moment we entered the darkness beneath the trees he put his finger to his lips, like a European would have, and went, 'Ssssss.' We moved deeper into the gloom, Kwaytcha in the lead. Every now and then he'd turn to me and glare at my feet, which were still in sandals and probably making a lot of noise that I hadn't even noticed. I'd have to start toughening up my soles if I wanted to be a real hunter.

I couldn't hear Kwaytcha moving at all, only the sound of a million buzzing insects and screeching birds. He carried a bow and arrows and a blowpipe, but he never once got them tangled in the branches above. The trees themselves grew taller and straighter after a while, and the undergrowth thinned out.

We went deeper and deeper, away from the river, and the air beneath the canopy of trees became very sluggish and humid. Soon he stopped in a small clearing, set down his bow and arrows and took several blowpipe darts from the little quiver around his neck. There were two types, those tipped with a black substance and those not. He took one of the unpoisoned darts and put it into his blowpipe, which was about three metres long and perfectly straight. The blunt end of the dart had a puff of what looked like baby bird down stuck to it, so it fitted snugly into the pipe. Kwaytcha lifted it to his lips and aimed across the clearing, filled his lungs with air and blew. The dart flew out so fast I didn't even see it, and he had to walk across and show me where it had lodged in the side of a brownish-yellow fruit of some kind in a tree. He pulled out the dart and came back, then handed the zabatana and dart to me.

I put the dart inside the end of the pipe as he'd done, and

lifted it up to aim at the same piece of fruit. The zabatana, for all its slenderness, was heavier than I expected, and I had a hard time getting the far end to stop wobbling about. Finally I had it aimed, took a breath and blew. The dart was gone instantly, but not into the fruit. Kwaytcha put a hand across his mouth and bent his knees several times to let me know what a laugh I'd given him, then he went to fetch back the dart, which he'd been quick enough of eye to follow. It was in a tree trunk at least a metre to the left of the fruit, and another metre or so higher. I felt myself blush. This was not going to be anywhere as easy as I'd thought.

We repeated the practice at least a dozen times, and on the second to last and very last shot I hit the fruit both times, but only just, not dead centre the way Kwaytcha had. The basic trick to using the zabatana was judging the difference in the angle between the line of flight from the blowpipe to the target and the line of sight from your eye to the same target. Once you had a feel for that, it wasn't so hard. When Kwaytcha was satisfied that I'd improved a little, he replaced the dart in his quiver and we went on.

After twenty minutes or so he gestured me to absolute silence, then took out one of the black-tipped darts and loaded it into his zabatana. Slowly, carefully, he raised it until the pipe was aimed almost straight up into the trees above us. I couldn't even see what he was aiming at, and assumed it was a well-camouflaged bird or some kind of tree dweller. I heard the *pffffft* sound of the pipe, but couldn't make out where the dart went. Kwaytcha looked pleased with himself and kept peering up into the treetops, as if the dart was still rising toward its invisible target. It was obvious he must have missed whatever he aimed at, because another minute passed without him doing anything but look above us at a particular spot that appeared no different to me than any other patch of leaves and vines.

Then the monkey fell. I heard him come smashing down through the narrow lower branches and looked up just in time to step aside as a bundle of fur the length of my leg came dropping from above to land at my feet. The monkey's mouth was moving, but no other part of his body was. The eyes were still open, but even as I watched they slowly began to close. The dart was between his shoulderblades, angled up into the greyish fur, in a place where the monkey hadn't been able to pull it out despite his long skinny arms. Maybe it wouldn't have made any difference even if he had pulled it out, because already the curare poison would have entered the bloodstream. His eyes closed at last and the monkey was dead. Kwaytcha seemed especially pleased to be able to retrieve his dart. He put it back in the quiver and slung the monkey across his shoulder, then we began walking again.

I had no idea at all where we were. One stretch of jungle looked exactly like another to my eyes, but Kwaytcha led the way without hesitating once, and sooner than I would have thought possible, we were back at the river, although nowhere near the shabono. He set down the monkey and the zabatana that had killed it, took up his bow and nocked an arrow to it. This arrow wasn't like the other three, which had points. Instead it had a half-dozen sharp prongs that splayed out from the tip. He waded into the shallows, peering into the water, then pulled back the string, aimed and released.

The arrow disappeared into the water, then bobbed back up with a fish caught on the prongs. Its tail was still twitching as he removed it and threw it to me. I caught the fish and set it beside the monkey, then did the same for three more as Kwaytcha aimed and fired. The fourth fish was a lot bigger than the rest and was twitching with more energy when he came off the prongs, and he kept up his flopping around when I dumped him with the others.

Kwaytcha seemed satisfied with his catch after that, and beckoned me out into the knee-deep water. He nocked the same arrow to his bow and handed it to me. I held it as he had, and waited for a fish to swim close enough to take a shot at. I soon saw a silvery-grey one like the first three, so pulled back the string and let the arrow fly. To my surprise, it entered the water and then seemed to change direction, going nowhere near the fish. Then I remembered the lesson our Science master Herr Hoche taught us about the refraction of light in water. Learning from my mistake, I tried again. As with the zabatana, it was a question of adjusting for the difference in angles. I came close to a fish twice, but didn't hit any. Kwaytcha got bored watching me and took the bow and arrow away.

It was quite a bit later in the afternoon by then, but the sun was still high enough to throw shadows at our feet, and Kwaytcha wanted to cool off. He flung himself into the river with a splash, not caring now if the fish were scared away, and I jumped in after him. We started horsing around, splashing each other at first, then coming to grips in a friendly way to see who could wrestle the other down into the water. Kwaytcha was amazingly strong for someone so thin, and won every time until I did what I'd done to the man who wanted my shorts, and tripped him with a simple leg hook. Down he went, and to cover his annoyance he started jumping up and down by himself in deeper water, making a whooping sound.

I needed to piss and started hosing the river around my shins, saying, 'All right, if I can't shoot a fish with an arrow, I'll poison the water and watch them come belly up.'

Kwaytcha, seeing what I was doing, immediately came splashing toward me, shouting and waving his arms. I kept on pissing, a fine steady stream that hissed very satisfyingly into the water, wondering what it was he was so excited about. When he reached me he started batting at my piss with his hands! I've never been able to stop pissing once I've started, so I just kept going, asking myself whether this was some kind of game, or if pissing in the river was against Yayomi rules. I didn't see why it should be, if shitting in the river was allowed.

When I finally ran out of piss, Kwaytcha stopped yelling at me, but his face was still angry. He went to the bank and picked up his weapons, then pointed to the monkey and fish he'd caught, making it clear that I was to carry them. It seemed like a fair arrangement to me, so I picked them up and followed him back into the trees.

At the shabono, which we entered as the shadows began to lengthen, Kwaytcha began to strut and boast as soon as we were inside. I came through the hole like his manservant, carrying the catch. I got rid of the fish and monkey as quickly as I could, dumping them by the fire used by Noroni's family, then went across to Mother. I was pleased to see that Zeppi wasn't with her, which meant he was slowly becoming more independent.

'What have you been doing all day, Erich?'

'Hunting with Kwaytcha. One monkey, four fish.'

'You shot them?'

'No, he did. He's teaching me how to use the blowpipe and bow.'

'Have you seen Zeppi?'

'No.'

When we spoke we looked into each other's eyes and never let our gaze drop from there. It was a habit started by Mother, and one that I adopted immediately, knowing what it meant to her. It was her method of ignoring the fact that we were naked, mother and son, in a way that would have been unthinkable back home. It was silly, but I did it for her sake.

'He disappeared hours ago. And Klaus, have you seen Klaus? You all leave me for hours at a time with nothing to do and no one to talk to.'

'Well, I'm here now. I'll tell you all about what happened with Kwaytcha —'

She held up her hand, the one with the wedding ring on it. 'I'm not interested in hearing about hunting. Go and find Zeppi for me, and Klaus, find Klaus and tell him he's not to do this again. Hours on end with nothing to do and no one to talk to, do you know how wearying that is? Do you?'

'No, Mother.'

'It has to stop. At least one of you must be with me all the time from now on. I won't be left alone while you three go roaming around at will, doing your best to avoid me. I've done nothing to deserve this kind of behaviour.'

'Yes, Mother. I'll go and look for them both right now.'

'No, Erich . . . Erich! Come back!'

I pretended I didn't hear and kept walking. I went to the hole and stepped through, then wandered around until I saw Zeppi and his monkey. He was feeding it bits of plantain and talking to it, holding it against his tits like a baby. I half expected it to start sucking, but it didn't. 'Zeppi, have you seen Klaus?'

'He's over there.' He nodded his head in the general direction of the plantain garden.

I said, 'Mother's upset because nobody stays with her.'

'She just sits there,' said Zeppi. 'She talks about home all the time, about things that happened when we were little, and when I tell her I don't remember any of it, she tells me I do remember, I'm just pretending not to so she'll get angry. Why would she say that about me? Why doesn't she get up and *do* something?'

I had no answers for him.

'How's Mitzi doing? Have you taught her any tricks?'

'No, she only likes to play and eat food.'

'Don't go back into the shabono until someone else can go with you. Mother's in a mood today.'

'She is every day,' he grumped. His hair was in need of cutting, and he looked more like a girl than a boy, not even fifty-fifty any more. In a few months he'd be two-thirds girl to one-third boy. I didn't say this to him, of course.

I headed for the plantain trees. Three women were picking fruit and they paid me no attention as I went by, and that started me thinking about how we'd all four been accepted as part of the landscape by the Yayomi. Zeppi was still a big attraction, with his tits, but the rest of us were far more likely to be ignored. I paid as little attention to the women picking plantains as they did to me, because Awomay wasn't there with them. I couldn't see Klaus either, and kept on walking, wishing Zeppi could have been a little more detailed in his directions.

I found Klaus a few minutes later, talking with the professor. Both of them were squatting on their haunches like a pair of hairless apes. They were close together, and I almost asked them if they'd been grooming fleas from each other's scalp. Klaus had begun to grow a beard since he didn't have a razor, and it was long enough now to rasp. I wondered if Mother objected to it scratching her face when they kissed, and it occurred to me that I hadn't seen them kiss since we got on the plane. The stubble made Klaus look like a pirate. They stopped talking as I came up.

'Mother's looking for you,' I said.

'Did she send you out to get me?'

'Yes.'

'And what have you been up to all day?'

'I can answer that,' said Wentzler. 'Hunting.'

Klaus's eyebrows lifted. 'Really? Did you catch anything?'

'No, but Kwaytcha did. You'll get some monkey tonight, Herr Wentzler, young and juicy, just as you ordered.'

'Excellent.'

'And fish – one big, three small.' Talk of fishing reminded me. 'Herr Wentzler, is it against the law to piss in the river? I did, and Kwaytcha tried to make me stop.'

His expression became thoughtful. 'You urinated into the river?'

'Yes, why not? Everyone craps in it. We weren't anywhere near the shabono, if that's what you mean.'

'No, no, it's something else. Have you by any chance heard of the candiru?'

'No, what is it?'

'A tiny member of the catfish family. Also known as the toothpick fish. It lives in the gills and especially the cloaca of larger fish.'

'What's a cloaca?'

'The hole in a fish where the excretory functions flush out

their wastes. The candiru is attracted to the smell of uric acid. Should you happen to urinate while swimming, any nearby candiru will enter your stream and follow it clear inside the urethra. There it'll expand its spines to establish a firm hold, and completely block your bladder. The pain is said to be legendary, and of course the longer-term torture is uremic poisoning from the blockage. The only remedy, they say, is penile amputation.'

'Ouch,' Klaus said, pulling a face. 'Erich, any tickling sensation inside the old fellow?'

'No . . .' I gulped. 'It really does that?'

Wentzler shrugged. 'I've never seen it, merely heard about the results. I must say, I find it hard to believe that a candiru could possibly swim up a stream of urine falling through the air. It would be like a salmon attempting to climb Niagara Falls. Urinating while underwater – now, that's a different thing altogether. You were standing at the time, I take it.' I nodded. 'Then count yourself fortunate, my boy, and consider young Kwaytcha your friend and benefactor for looking after you.'

Klaus said, 'Really, Gerhard, you might have told us about this earlier. Every time I swim I take a piss. Are you telling me I'm lucky not to have attracted the attention of this disgusting creature?'

'I'm saying I have no idea at all if the candiru occurs in this region, or the piranha either, come to think of it, which is why I've also neglected to warn you against swimming while cut or bleeding. The piranha, as you have probably heard, will attack anything that smells of blood and strip it to the bone in minutes.'

'I think,' said Klaus, 'I'd prefer to go that way than the other.'

'Me too,' I said, resisting the urge to cup both hands over my cock.

'Should we tell him now?' asked Wentzler.

'I don't see why not,' said Klaus.

'Tell me what?'

'About our plans for leaving.' Klaus enjoyed the look on my face.

'Leaving? To go home?'

'For the Orinoco, at any rate, and from there we can be picked up.'

'But I thought the only way to the Orinoco is through some other tribe's territory.'

'It is. The Iriri and the Yayomi are mortal enemies, and have been for as long as anyone can remember. Those are the people across whose land we'd have to portage our canoes, and I can assure you we wouldn't get far. The Iriri are the most hostile tribe in all of Amazonas. We'd be butchered instantly. Even the Yayomi fear them, although they won't admit it. The river system inhabited by the Yayomi and the system occupied by the Iriri are quite separate, so they tend not to brush up against each other, thank God.'

'Then how do we get across from one system to the next without getting killed?'

'Aha! We allow Mother Nature to perform that task for us.' He was smiling broadly, showing his teeth.

'I don't understand.'

'The rainy season,' Wentzler said.

'Rainy season?'

'Due to begin in about a month. Torrential rain, like nothing you've ever seen, every day for months on end. The Indians much prefer the dry season. In the rainy season the

ground is always muddy, the heat intensifies, the insects mul-
tiply, and snakes migrate from the ground into the trees,
where they become angry and bite as you pass by. The rainy
season is nature's way of saying she cares nothing for the comfort of man or beast.'

'I still don't follow.'

Wentzler began scratching in the dirt with a stick. 'This is
the Yayomi's river system, and this is the Iriri's. These are
approximate renderings, you understand. I doubt that either
one has been mapped properly.' He stabbed at the place where
one set of scratchings came closest to the other set. 'Here is
where the portage must be made, the only place possible.'

'The place where we'll be killed,' I reminded him.

'Perhaps, perhaps not. The rainy season is a peculiar thing,
I've noticed. Every five to seven years, there comes a rainy season unlike any other, a terrible deluge that goes on and on,
night and day, almost without stopping. The ground becomes
so saturated it rejects any further moisture, which in turn
feeds the river systems to overflowing. The country resem-
bles a lake dotted with treetops. The shabono will be
inundated, possibly for weeks. Everyone will be thoroughly
miserable until the waters recede, at which time a new
shabono will be built, probably on a new site offering even
higher ground, and life will go on as before.'

'Get to the point, Gerhard,' urged Klaus.

'The point, yes. When this occurs, the two river systems,
each running exclusive of the other during the dry season,
and also during normal rainy seasons, will merge. No portage
will be necessary. Our canoes will simply float from one system to the next without being bothered by the Iriri, who
doubtless will be squatting miserably in their homes, waiting

for the rain to stop. Once across the divide we simply continue west until the Orinoco is reached.'

'But . . . how many years do we have to wait until the next really rainy season?'

He erased his sketch with the stick. 'I said the phenomenon occurs every five to seven years. It's been seven years since the last deluge. I believe we can expect the necessary downpour this year. It'll begin, as I said, in a month or so.'

I looked at Klaus. He was smiling. 'It puts things in a better light, doesn't it, Erich?'

'Yes!'

'I intend letting Helga in on our little plan this evening. Chances are it'll cheer her up. No aspect of Yayomiland is to her liking, I'm sure you've noticed.'

'I know. I can't recognise her sometimes. She's not herself.'

'Precisely, and that's why this has to work. I only hope she can continue for as long as it takes to bring her back to the world she knew.'

'I hope so too. Mother has to be her old self again.' I felt tears prickling at my eyes. Wentzler and Klaus pretended not to notice the way my mouth kept twitching and my voice went funny.

Klaus continued. 'Now then, Erich, you have a special role to play in this plan; in fact, I'd go so far as to say it can't happen without your cooperation.'

'How?' I asked, getting control of myself.

'The canoes,' said Wentzler. 'We'll need two, one won't be enough for all five of us. Ask yourself, Erich, how we should come by two canoes.'

I thought for a moment. 'Steal them?'

'Stealing is a crime, even here. The Yayomi make excellent

canoes, and it costs them a great deal in sweat. Canoes are valuable objects. A Yayomi has little sense of personal property, as you've no doubt noticed, but there are three things he considers distinctly his own. His weapons, his wife and his canoe. Touch any one of them without his permission and there'll be trouble.'

'Then how do we get two of them?'

'Surely an obvious answer presents itself, Erich.'

'Make them ourselves?'

Klaus and Wentzler both laughed. I felt my face flush.

'Try again,' said Klaus.

'We . . . buy them?'

'Exactly! Now, ask yourself, "With what will I buy two canoes?"'

'I don't know. None of us has got anything any more.'

'You have,' corrected Wentzler.

'I do?'

'It's hanging around your neck.'

My hand went automatically to Father's Iron Cross.

'Oh.'

'There's a man in the shabono who doesn't like you, Erich, but he likes your military decoration. This man has a canoe. For the Iron Cross, he'll sell it to you.'

'What man?'

'His name is Tagerri. He happens to be Awomay's intended. I don't think he likes the way you and she have been making eyes at each other. I did explain to you the system for arranging marriages here. You threaten that system, and he won't allow it, but he's not a bloodthirsty fellow, even though you've already had what amounts to a shoving match.'

'We have? What does he look like?'

'He has a small birthmark on his temple, a blue patch of skin.'

The man who wanted to take my shorts from me! I was shocked. 'But he's old, at least thirty! How could he marry her?'

'Because he paid Noroni for her years ago. Can you guess how he paid for her?'

'With a canoe?'

'Tagerri happens to be the best canoe maker among the Yayomi. He wants you to go away in one of his canoes, but, of course, he can't say so outright. Because there's no such thing in Yayomi society as a gift without strings, he has to sell you the canoe. He approached me today and asked if I'd act as go-between. Incidentally, it was this that made me start thinking of the rainy season and the seven-year floods, so we must be grateful to the man. He wants your Iron Cross as payment.'

'And you think I should give it to him.'

'For two canoes, not one. The canoe he currently owns, plus another that he'll make for you. How important is your decoration, my boy? Klaus tells me it was pinned on your father's chest by Hitler himself. Could you bear to part with it?'

'I . . . to get away, yes. For Mother.'

'Good lad. You see, Klaus, how even one so young as Erich here understands the basic need for compromise. Thank you, Erich, for being so level-headed about this. The price is high, from your point of view, but so too are the stakes, don't you agree?'

'Yes.'

'Your mother, all of us, will thank you.'

'You'll thank yourself,' added Klaus.

'I'll tell Tagerri this afternoon,' said Wentzler. 'It takes time to make a good canoe, and we'll want both of them ready when the rains come. Whatever you do, don't lose that Iron Cross. It's our ticket for departure.'

Wentzler and Klaus went over the plan again, calculating the odds, convincing themselves it would work. I thought about Awomay. Suddenly she'd been made unobtainable. That man with the birthmark, Tagerri, would hold her, and put himself inside her. She wouldn't want that. No young girl would. It wasn't fair, not to her and not to me. And to add insult to injury, Tagerri would end up with not only the girl I wanted, but my Iron Cross too. Against all of that I had to weigh the importance of us getting away, especially Mother, who would die if we didn't, I was fairly sure; either die or go mad. She had to be looked after, taken back to a world of electricity and medicine, and if the price was high, that was just too bad.

That evening, Wentzler came to me and told me Tagerri had agreed to the terms and tomorrow would begin searching for a suitable tree from which to carve a second canoe.

'I believe our plan is going to work,' he said, looking excited.

I asked him, 'Why do you want to go home now, Herr Professor? You've been here so long.'

'I've asked myself that question, and the answer is plain. If you and your family hadn't dropped in on the Yayomi I wouldn't have considered it. But here you all are, and seeing white faces again, and hearing German, has made me homesick. I have enough knowledge in my head now to proceed with my book. One can't write a book in the jungle. No, the time for leave-taking has arrived. A man can resist fate if he so chooses, but it's wiser not to.'

I left the professor and went across to Mother's hammock. Klaus was telling her about the plan, and Zeppi was there too, listening closely. When Klaus was finished, Zeppi said, 'Can I take Mitzi? I don't want to leave her behind.' His monkey was curled around Zeppi's neck. The little thing seemed genuinely to love him.

'Certainly you may. Now then, Helga, what do you think of Gerhard's plan?'

Mother said nothing for a while. It was hard to see her face in the failing light. We waited, and finally she said, 'Will there be room for Heinrich?'

We all stared at her. Mother's skin was the colour of dirty chalk. I hadn't seen her bathe today, so that might have accounted for it.

Klaus said softly, 'Heinrich is not with us, Helga. Heinrich died in Russia three years ago, remember?'

She shook her head, quick little shakes from side to side, like she was shaking a fly off the end of her nose. 'No, he was here a moment ago. We spoke with each other. He said I should have waited for him.'

'Waited? Waited for what? My brother's dead, Helga. He wasn't here just now. You didn't speak with him, nor he with you, unless you mean in your imagination. Is that what you meant, Helga?'

'Go away,' she said. She didn't sound angry, not even irritated. She just didn't want us crowding around her. 'Go away, all of you.'

'Of course. We'll go and get some food in a minute, won't

we, boys? But the plan, Helga, what do you think of the plan?'

She looked up at the dark hole above us and smiled. 'Heinrich will come for me. He said so. The rest of you can go with that man.'

She meant Wentzler. Klaus looked stricken. He spoke slowly, the way you would to a child who simply doesn't understand. 'Helga, don't you think that's a foolish way to talk? We must all leave together or it won't work. When the rains come, we'll get in our canoes and ... float away downriver. Won't that be marvellous?'

She looked at him. 'Heinrich said I should have waited for him to come home and not married you. It isn't a real marriage because he isn't dead, so the ceremony meant nothing. It meant nothing, Klaus, do you hear me?'

'The Church would disagree, Helga. It was a perfectly legitimate ceremony ...'

'He isn't dead. The Russians captured him. He still lives. They took him to Siberia. He works hard and they don't give him enough food. He's building a dam. There are other prisoners too, Germans, some of them ...'

'Helga, listen to me. The Russians took many prisoners, yes, but every German was marched east until he dropped from hunger and exhaustion and was shot. They killed tens of thousands that way. This thing you have in your head, this voice that calls itself Heinrich, it isn't real. Heinrich is gone forever.'

'You tell me this,' she said, 'but you don't know. You don't know anything. We are not married. We never were. My husband is Heinrich, the father of my children. God has brought us here to make me see that.'

Klaus chewed his lips, but stayed calm. 'God had nothing to do with our being here. That was an accident. Why would God do that, Helga?'

'To make us stay apart.'

'Stay apart?'

'In front of these filthy people. I see them sneaking away in the morning, going out there, not even bothering to hide properly before they do what they do. Filthy.'

'Most of them are man and wife, Helga. It's not so different to what we're used to. They have no bedrooms, no privacy . . .'

'God brought us here. You and I, we haven't done anything wrong, haven't gone out there like the rest of them . . . We aren't married. The Church will agree. There'll be an annulment . . . There'll be an annulment granted on grounds of nonconsummation . . .'

'Helga, your boys . . . our boys are here with us. Do you think they want to hear this . . . this silliness coming from you? I'm your husband, Helga. We were married in Ciudad Bolivar. Nothing can change that, and nothing should.'

'Married with a false name!' said Mother. She almost spat the words out. 'Brandt! Who is Brandt? Not me, not you. No one is Brandt! Klaus Brandt married me, but you aren't Klaus Brandt, so what does it mean? Nothing! We are *not* married, not legally, and not in the eyes of God.'

There was a little smile playing around her lips, almost a smirk. Mother knew she had Klaus rattled and was enjoying it. 'Poor Klaus, with no wife now and no family, just relations. How dare you tell me what you think is real. None of it was ever real. The marriage was a fake and *you* are a fake.'

'Helga . . .'

'And don't think I don't know what you did. I know, but I didn't want to know, so I pretended.'

'I have no idea what you're referring to, Helga. If you'd just stop for a minute and look at things realistically . . .'

'What you did there, where you worked, that *place*.'

'Now, Helga, you know very well that my work was nothing you or anyone else has any knowledge of.'

'I went there to visit you after Heinrich was reported missing. I wanted to talk to you, but you were never able to leave, so I went to that place, that . . . factory of death.'

Klaus's voice hardened. 'Helga, you're imagining things. At no time did you visit me. Don't you think I would have remembered?'

'You never saw me. I never saw you. I came by bus, then walked out from the town to the gates. I never went inside. There was a terrible smell in the air. Smoke kept falling from the sky, heavy smoke, too heavy to rise . . . I knew that smell. My uncle had a farm . . .'

'Helga, what does this have to do with anything?'

'He had a man who worked for him. The man lost an arm in a threshing machine and died. He had no family, no one to claim him. Uncle had to bear the cost of burying him, but a dog had run off with the arm so he went into his coffin without it. Later, Uncle found the arm and burned it. I was there, only a little girl, but I remember the smell, that same smell . . . of burning flesh.'

Klaus laughed. 'What nonsense you do talk. Come on now, why don't we all go and eat something? That'll make us feel much better. You know, you've been losing weight, Helga, because you haven't been eating enough, and that isn't healthy. I'm a doctor, and doctors know what's best for good health.'

He laughed again, and both times it sounded strange, a laugh that wasn't a laugh, more like air escaping from a split football.

'You're no more a doctor than I am,' said Mother. 'Doctors make people better. You're a . . . a . . .'

'Helga!'

'. . . a boiler attendant! A coal shoveller!'

'Stop it! You're making a fool of yourself.'

'Doctor of *furnaces*!' she shrieked.

The Yayomi became aware of the argument then and began watching to find out why Klaus and Mother were fighting. They were like the people back home who peeked out from behind their lace curtains at what was going on across the street, but the Yayomi had no curtains to hide behind and so they simply stared, and waited. Most of what Mother had said was so peculiar I didn't know what she meant. I'd never heard the story about the farmer's helper and the dog with the arm. It was a good story, so why hadn't she told me? Maybe Klaus was right and Mother was spouting nonsense that made sense only to her, like some kind of dream that was happening while her eyes were still open. Her mouth was a thin line now, and I knew she wouldn't say another word, not to Klaus, not to anyone.

Wentzler was coming over, so he must have heard Mother screeching. 'Is everything all right?'

'Certainly everything is all right, Gerhard. What wouldn't be all right?'

If Wentzler had just come from Germany he would have realised that a family argument was going on, and left us alone, but he'd been among the Yayomi for too long. They knew everything that everyone else did, and they made no bones about knowing and wanting to know more. They stared, they asked questions, they waited around until they found out everything. Wentzler was like that now, not at all embarrassed to be standing there, waiting for an explanation. I could see Klaus was getting more and more upset because he wouldn't go away. It was almost funny.

After a minute I said, 'Klaus told Mother the plan.'

'Ah, and she doesn't like it?'

'She wants to leave sooner.'

'Impossible.' He spoke directly to Mother then. 'Absolutely impossible, Frau Brandt. The success of the plan depends entirely on the water level. We must wait for the rains and hope they're exceptionally hard this year.'

Mother said nothing, of course, and wouldn't even look at him. Wentzler was no fool. He saw that something was wrong, and saw also that no one wanted to tell him what it was. He still didn't go away, though.

'Klaus, may I have a word with you?'

'Very well.'

I think Klaus was happy enough to walk away from Mother and everything she'd said, all those peculiar comments about him not being a real doctor. I knew that wasn't so, because I remembered Father saying he'd seen Klaus's certificate from the University of Frankfurt. And that business about talking with Father, that he wasn't dead and she wasn't married to Klaus. Mother was having a nervous breakdown, I think.

I'd heard about such things. Frau Schellenberg down the street from us had one after she found out her husband had been seeing another woman for a long time in another town and even had another family there with her. I thought it was a bit selfish of Mother to have a nervous breakdown now, just when there was a plan to leave. It should have cheered her up to hear about the coming flood that would carry us all across Iriri territory to the Orinoco.

Zeppi, who hadn't said a word all through the argument, now opened his mouth to whisper in my ear, 'Why doesn't Mother like Klaus any more?'

'She does,' I whispered back, 'but she's not well in her head at the moment, so she says things she doesn't mean.' Mother was close by and I felt guilty about our whispering.

'Will she say them to us?' Zeppi looked worried. He hated to be in Mother's bad books. When that happened his whole world fell apart.

'She might. If she does, just ignore her.'

I could see Awomay watching me from a short distance away. We locked eyes and didn't move, either of us, for a long time. That's what the poets call the look of love. I hated that I'd sold her love for two canoes. That's how I saw the deal Wentzler had made with Tagerri. It had nothing to do with my Iron Cross. Then the canoe maker himself, Tagerri, came over and started talking to her. He must have seen us looking at each other because he stood between us, his back to me. I turned away.

Klaus and Wentzler had drifted off into the shadows. Zeppi was lost in thought, no doubt worrying about the possibility of Mother shouting at him. He stood there, a pretty little girlie-boy with his pet monkey chattering in his ear and pulling at his hair, and it struck me that there never was a more helpless person in the world than Zeppi. If Mother got worse I'd have to protect him from her. Klaus would be too busy protecting himself. It didn't occur to me that I might need a little of the same. If I needed protecting, though, it wouldn't be from Mother, it'd be from Tagerri. I didn't trust him, even if a deal had been struck.

There was a gathering over to one side of the shabono, and like everyone else, I wanted to know what it was all about, so I went over there and found Klaus and Wentzler in the thick of it. The chief, Manokwo, was talking to them, and dozens more were listening. As I came closer I heard Wentzler, who was translating, say to Klaus, 'No matter what explanation you give, he'll want to see results. You'll simply have to force the issue with her. Too much depends on it.'

Manokwo was talking again, pointing across at Mother still sitting in her hammock. I stood beside Klaus. I had the impression he was being accused of something.

Wentzler said, 'If he doesn't have proof that she's your wife, he'll take her for himself. He says all dolphins fuck, he's actually seen them, and even if they've grown arms and legs and walk on land, they should fuck. Excuse me, but I'm translating literally.' Manokwo said more, and Wentzler changed it into German. 'He knows the two boys aren't from your loins because I said so.'

'You did?'

'I . . . believe I chatted about it with someone or other. I was trying to impress them with your generosity of spirit, taking on the responsibility of your brother's children.'

'You shouldn't have done that, Gerhard.'

'In retrospect, I agree, but it seemed harmless at the time.'

'All those lectures you've given us about walking a fine line so as not to upset our hosts, keeping them happy in their belief that we're dolphins . . . and now you say you opened your mouth and jeopardised everything.'

'What can I do but agree with you? It was a mistake.'

Wentzler looked very uncomfortable, but he wasn't trying to weasel his way out of the situation, so I felt sorry for him instead of being angry like Klaus.

Klaus looked over at Monokwo, who was still talking. 'What's he saying now?'

'That a woman with such a . . . beautiful hairy . . . snatch . . . excuse me again, should have a hard cock put inside it twice a day. Anything less is an insult to her . . . furry cunt. Excuse me again, but they do put these things crudely.'

'I don't care about that. What should I do?'

'Shall I tell him your wife really is your wife, but she's been sick lately, a special dolphin sickness that results in her being unwilling or unable to make love?'

'Better make it unable. He already has a wife, doesn't he? What does he want another one for?'

'Why does a rajah have a harem, a king a mistress? Variety, my dear Klaus, the male prerogative, if he can afford it, and Manokwo can afford it. He wants Frau Brandt for his new wife, and you'd better be prepared to stand up to him.'

'How?'

'First, with words. We must bluff him into thinking that there's a legitimate reason why you and she don't engage in the conjugal act. Shall I go ahead with the sick dolphin story?'

'You may as well. Make it convincing.'

Wentzler spoke for some time in the Yayomi tongue. Everyone was listening very closely. Manokwo spoke again, and Wentzler said, 'If she's sick, he'll ask Noroni, who's the tribal healer, to make some medicine for her. He wants to know if it's a head sickness, a belly sickness or a . . . cunt sickness. Noroni has all kinds of cures for all kinds of sicknesses.'

'What kind should it be?'

'I'd recommend against the last two. I've seen Noroni at work, and he tends to place his hands on the area in question, to rub away the demons of sickness.'

'All right, make it a head sickness. Tell him.'

Manokwo called for Noroni, who came forward. Awomay was close behind her father, but she didn't look at me. I guessed Tagerri was somewhere close by too, keeping an eye on her. Manokwo and Noroni discussed the matter of the dolphin woman who wouldn't or couldn't fuck, and what to do about it. The nearest fire had more wood dumped on it so everyone could follow what was happening. The entire shabono was taking part now, despite the fact that the evening meal was supposed to be prepared around this time. The fact that all the other fires were being neglected showed me how important the talking was.

Noroni went over to his family's area and came back with a small woven bag. 'His bag of tricks,' I heard Wentzler say. 'Now he wants us to bring Frau Brandt over. This is going to be the hard part. Will she cooperate, do you think?'

'I couldn't say,' Klaus admitted. 'She really does have a mental condition at the moment, you know. Having a savage prance around and rub her skull might not be the best thing.'

'You can't back out now, and neither can she. You'd better go over there and explain the situation. Persuade her to submit to a ritual performance, for the sake of us all. It won't hurt her, not physically.'

Klaus did as he was told. I went with him to Mother, and he quickly gave her the facts. She'd lost some of her anger, and instead seemed amused to see Klaus so uncomfortable. 'Are they making mock of you as a man, Klaus? How sad. Tell them that my real husband wants me to wait for him.'

'They won't understand. Let their healer fellow practise his mumbo-jumbo for a few minutes, and then you should, I don't know . . . fall over in a faint or something, as if whatever he did had some kind of effect on you.'

'And what will you do if I don't?'

'Do? Nothing. What can I do, Helga? You're the one who's put us in this position with your . . . refusals. They don't understand any of that, your prudishness . . . excuse me, your modesty. They require a performance, something magical.'

'You're not a doctor and I'm not an actress. Tell them I don't love you.'

'Don't you understand what's happening here? That big savage Manokwo wants you for his second wife! If you declare yourself no longer in love with me, he'll take that as consent for him to take my place.'

'He could no more take the place of Heinrich than you could.'

'But don't you see . . . Christ, Helga, this isn't our world, these aren't our people, and whatever happens here happens on their terms! For God's sake, try to get hold of yourself and do as I say. You're in danger, isn't that obvious?'

'So you say. God says otherwise. I have nothing to fear at all from anyone. Heinrich is alive and will find me. Nothing bad will happen to me until then.'

Klaus turned to me. I'd never seen him look so uncertain, so lost. His eyes asked me to try to make her see reason, so I went to her and said, 'Mother, Klaus is right. All you have to do is pretend to have your sickness cured, and then you should . . . you should be like a wife to Klaus, then everything will be all right.'

She gave me the same pitying look she'd given Klaus. 'Pretend to be sick,' she said. 'Pretend to be cured, then pretend to be someone's wife. I'm your father's wife, Erich, and always will be.'

'Yes, but . . . can't you just do a little bit of playacting?'

She turned away from me, saying, 'You have both insulted me by insulting Heinrich. A brother and a son, and you both want to betray him. I won't allow it.'

I looked at Klaus, who was looking at Mother. Both of us were thinking the same thing – Mother was mad. It wasn't simply peculiar temper tantrums and unhappiness because we were in a place we shouldn't be. It was another kind of thing altogether. How could she not see what had to be done to save the situation? Why was she being so obstinate?

Like a stupid dog in the middle of the road, she insisted on staying right where she was, no matter how many people whistled and called from the kerb to get her out of danger. It was so stupid, this behaviour, that I hated her for a moment, the way you hate a wasp in the house that won't go out the window you opened for it and instead keeps buzzing back and forth, threatening to sting you even though you tried to help it get away. And the fact that this was my own mother I found myself hating made it worse than any ordinary hatred, because underneath it was love for the woman she'd been, and guilt for not being able to keep her from being stupid this way.

All the time I'd been learning how to go about naked and swim in the river and shoot darts through a blowpipe, Mother had been sinking into a pit of poison, letting it seep into her brain until she couldn't see what was real any more.

'Mother, please . . . please do this. It's so silly not to . . .'

'You're silly,' she said. 'You and Klaus, you're both silly, and that man, he's silly too. Go away and stop this silliness. I don't want to look at you.'

Klaus pleaded with her. 'Helga, for the last time, will you please do as we ask, for your own sake and the sake of the boys, if for no other reason . . .'

'Not for you? Hypocrite. Go away.'

She shut her eyes and lay back in her hammock.

I felt my heart shrinking inside my chest, becoming smaller and smaller until it was a tiny thing, the size of a walnut, with no more room inside it for Mother, who wouldn't want to be there anyway. She wanted to be in the heart of her dead husband, my dead father. And that somehow made her a dead woman. She lay in her hammock and lived and breathed and thought of her dead man and didn't even know she had just died herself, in a way. Mad people don't know they're mad, or so it seemed. I wanted to hit her to wake her up, make her come back to the place where the unmad people lived, but I couldn't do it, couldn't touch her, lying there naked and white and mad, with the bushy blond hair that Manokwo wanted to put his big brown cock into standing up like a hedgehog.

And next to me stood Klaus, who couldn't do anything either. A fully grown man, a doctor, and he didn't know what to do, couldn't reach out and take hold of Mother and pull her back away from the madness. He could only watch her fall asleep in the middle of the road. And I wanted to hit him too, because he was no more able to change things than me, half his age and far less wise. We were both helpless, and both of us ashamed of it. At that moment he was more like my brother than my stepfather, and I almost felt sorry for him, but that feeling wasn't as big as the feeling that I wanted to hit him for what he couldn't do.

'All right,' said Klaus very softly, then more firmly, 'All right then.'

He went back to Wentzler and Manokwo and the crowd, and I followed.

'She won't do anything,' said Klaus. His voice was neutral.

Wentzler said, 'Nothing?'

'Nothing. To her, none of this is real.'

'But you must make her realise that nothing could be *more* real. You're aware of what will happen if she doesn't openly declare herself your wife?'

'I'm aware, she isn't. She's mad, Gerhard, I swear.'

'But she's your wife ... You can't allow this to happen.'

'I tried, she refused, and she doesn't consider herself my wife, in any case.'

'But ... what do I tell Manokwo?'

'Please yourself, my friend.'

Wentzler was getting quite upset, more so than Klaus had been, or me, for that matter. Maybe it was a question of how much showed on the surface, I don't know, but Wentzler allowed a lot to show – in fact, he got very agitated. 'That man standing there is going to have your wife, Brandt. He's going to take her into the bushes and spread her legs, do you understand what I'm saying? He wants her and, by God, he'll have her, and he won't even think twice about it, won't be aware that he's doing anything wrong, because you won't take steps to stop him. You don't have to face him in mortal combat, you just need to trick him, for God's sake, and yet you won't make the least effort to spare your wife this humiliation.'

'I've told you, I tried ...'

'Of course you did, all of two minutes' worth of trying, and then you gave up.'

'She won't listen to reason! Try for yourself if you think I've done such a bad job. Erich, tell him we both tried ...'

'It's true, Herr Wentzler. She won't listen. She thinks my father's still alive, but he isn't, he died in Russia, and now she just wants to lie down in the middle of the road ...'

'What are you talking about? Do you want your own mother to be used by a Yayomi? What kind of son would allow that?'

'What can I do?' I said. I felt like crying. It wasn't my fault and it wasn't Klaus's fault. It was Mother's fault, but Wentzler wanted to blame us for it. Zeppi was at my side. He'd left Mother, finally, and come over to where everyone else was gathered. Tears were running down his face. He didn't understand anything, but he knew that Mother was going to be hurt somehow, and he understood that Manokwo was the one responsible. I put a hand on his shoulder and felt the trembling that ran through him like ripples.

Wentzler said to Klaus, 'Are you telling me that you've given up?'

'Not given up, no, more like been given no reason to continue.'

'Brandt, you can't do this.'

'I've done nothing. She's made her choice.'

'But you say she's mad. The mad can't choose anything.'

'Then you fix it, Herr Wentzler, and stop making me out to be a coward! I simply have no way of influencing events from this point forward, and I acknowledge that. A coward would never face the truth that way.'

Wentzler seemed at a loss for words; then he turned to Manokwo and spoke with him for a short time. When they were finished, Wentzler said to Klaus, 'I've told him your wife thanks him for the offer of Noroni's medicine, but she respectfully declines. This kind of sickness has come over her before and will eventually pass away because she's familiar with the ways of the demon causing it. Nothing upsets this demon more than to be ignored, and when he gets upset enough at the lack of treatment, he'll go away. I had to give a specific time for these events to take place. The Yayomi have no numbers beyond two, so I told him that in two days Frau Brandt will be well again. You have that much time in which to resolve this ridiculous state of affairs. After that, I can't be responsible.'

'Thank you. No one can blame me for any of this. The blame lies elsewhere. Her mind has been ... distracted from the moment we came here. It may be that she was already ... disturbed. I've had no contact with her, you understand, for several years, not since after my brother died. I thought I should do the correct thing, the way Heinrich would have wanted, and now this. Who but a madwoman would actually believe her dead husband is still living?'

The crowd was breaking up, the Yayomi going back to the business of preparing a meal for the evening, and soon Klaus and Wentzler stood alone, with Klaus still talking. I'd never heard him talk so much, so quickly, with such a need to be understood.

'What can a man do when he plans for the best and receives the worst? Good intentions, what are they worth? A man makes his plans, taking care not to allow past mistakes to muddy the waters, does what he knows is the right thing, at considerable risk to himself, mind, given his past and the current world situation, and spends good money to bring about a result he can live with. He does all that, but then fate steps in. A man has a new family and a new life all mapped out. He wings his way toward a brighter tomorrow, and what happens? Fate claws him from the sky and slams him to earth. What happens next? Fate again. His wife goes mad, or else was already mad and only needed a nudge to go over the edge. And his new son, a fine young boy, what happens there?

Not a boy at all, not even a girl, no, a hybrid, a freakish thing only savages could admire . . .'

Wentzler and I stood with mouths agape as he continued. 'They think he's wonderful, a little godling of their very own – boy, girl, dolphin, all rolled into one, and this was not something that happened overnight, oh no, it was kept from me by my wife. She knew what I'd think of something like that, a doctor who knows the difference between the proper configuration of the human body and unfortunate accidents, genetic mistakes. She hid it all away and accepted my offer, took my hand in marriage – which I didn't have to offer, by any means, no, I could have had any number of younger women, but I wanted to do the right thing by Heinrich, you see – took my hand with a smile on her lips, but failed to tell me of the thing she knew would have made me refuse.'

Klaus was very much in earnest now. 'You know, Wentzler, a fellow in my position, the position I occupied in the Reich, must be above suspicion, his background pure, no taint of Jewish or mongrel blood allowed, those are the rules, damn necessary rules given the state of the world with its mixing of races, the bastardisation of the Aryan strain with inferior breeds. What would my position have been worth if something like this had occurred while I was still at the top? Instant disgrace, removal from my official duties, important duties, Gerhard, the very essence of the Führer's program for racial purification, a sweeping of the continent to remove every last trace of inferior blood. What could have given me greater satisfaction than that, I ask you?'

'I don't know,' said Wentzler. He was looking at Klaus in a peculiar way as he rambled on and on, becoming like a crazy person himself.

'A great work of extermination was expected of me, Gerhard, great work but exhausting physically, you understand, emotionally uplifting by its nature, but terribly demanding in practice because of the numbers, the endless numbers. Later on, when the war was lost and I had to flee, I asked myself what greater need I could serve, with Germany in ruins and all hope of starting a new era of Aryan mastery gone ... and it came to me again, that feeling of enlightenment – of sacred duty, if you will ... I would reach back into the smoking past and bring forth from the ashes the family of my brother, pluck them from darkness and bring them into the light, to share that light with me and go on, in Heinrich's name ... and that's what I did, but now the results are set before me, such disappointing results from so unselfish an act. How to explain it, Gerhard? How to reconcile intention with outcome?'

Zeppi had run away after hearing himself referred to as a freak, but Wentzler and I were turned to stone by Klaus's ranting.

Wentzler said, 'A terrible shock for you, all of it.'

Klaus nodded, appreciating the sentiment. Then Wentzler walked away from him toward the cooking fires. Klaus watched him go, a little surprised, then turned to me. I couldn't take my eyes off him, the way it's said that a rabbit can't avoid the gaze of a snake, yet I didn't feel threatened by him. He said to me, 'Erich, whatever the failings of the others, you must know that I see you as a perfect example. None of my ... my dissatisfaction is directed at you. You're a splendid specimen of Aryan boyhood. I have high hopes for you.' He really meant it, every word.

'This dreadful business with your mother, if you can think of a way out ... Naturally, I don't want to see her condition worsen, which it most certainly will if Manokwo so much as touches her. We need a plan, Erich, but nothing from an adventure book, nothing impossible. These people are primitives and must be dealt with on their level, since we don't have a division of panzers to wipe them out.' He laughed at that, then settled down again. 'So, Erich, any suggestions?'

'Steal two canoes tonight and go downriver.'

'But downriver leads to Iriri country. You heard what Wentzler said about them.'

'He said if we carried the canoes across from one river system to the next they'd catch us. I'm saying just go downriver and keep on going past that place where the systems come close together.'

'And then?'

'Then we'll be far away from here.'

'And from anywhere else, I'm sure; without weapons or food or any idea where we might be. That won't work. It's not a plan, it's merely a reaction to the absence of a plan. We must do better than that.'

'I'll ask Mother,' I said, leaving him.

Behind me, he said, 'That's a complete waste of time. She won't understand!'

I went to Mother and sat by her hammock. Her eyes were open. Zeppi was in the next hammock and I knew he'd been sobbing. What was strange was that Mother hadn't comforted him. That more than anything she'd said or done so far, or anything Klaus had to say about her state of mind, brought her condition home to me. Before, whenever Zeppi stubbed his toe she was there to kiss it better. Now, it was as if she'd retreated from everything and everyone, gone back deep inside herself like a tortoise into its shell.

'Mother? May I speak with you?'

She didn't say anything for a moment, then shrugged, 'If you wish.'

'We need to steal some canoes and go away from here, Mother.'

'Why?'

'Why? Because if we don't, something bad will happen. To you.'

'What will happen that hasn't already happened?'

'Well, that man, Manokwo, he'll . . . hurt you.'

'No one can hurt me now. When I was blind I could be hurt, but only because I wouldn't let myself admit I was blind. Now I'm not blind any more, so nothing can hurt me. My eyes are open.'

'Mother, we have to go away, just you and me and Zeppi. One canoe.'

'I don't like canoes. I went in a canoe once when I was little, or it might have been a rowboat. It tipped over. Someone stood up and over it went.'

'We'll be very careful.'

'No.'

'But you have to, Mother, or Manokwo, he'll . . . he wants you to be his wife.'

'God would never allow such a thing. Heinrich has told me so.'

'If Father's alive, in Russia the way you said, how could he be telling you anything at all? You can't hear him, you just think you can.'

She turned her head a little to look at me, then reached out and put a hand on my shoulder. She was smiling. 'Erich, I know you're worried for me, but really, there's no need.

Nothing bad will happen. All of this is a test. If we have courage, everything will be all right, for you, for me, for Zeppi. Please don't worry about it.'

I put my hand over hers. Only a madwoman would speak this way. I felt a kind of humming in my head. It told me that I mustn't believe her. I had to ignore her smile and her hand on my shoulder and her calm way of talking. It was all a part of her madness, and I couldn't be caught up in it.

'Zeppi's very upset,' I told her. 'He's been crying. Klaus called him a freak.'

It was a test for Mother, not a test from God, a test from me. I wanted to see how she'd react. If she called Zeppi to her side and stroked his hair and told him to take no notice of anything Klaus said, then she was still Mother somewhere inside, and maybe she could be Mother again. But all she did was sigh and say, 'He must grow up. You help him, Erich, I'm too tired.'

And with that, she turned away and closed her eyes and fell asleep, really asleep, not pretending. Zeppi was watching from his hammock. He'd heard everything. I put a finger to my lips so he wouldn't wake her, then went to the fires and brought back some food for him, just a few cooked plantains on a big leaf. He wolfed them down and I tousled his hair. 'Go to sleep now,' I said.

'Are we going to take a canoe?'

'No, that won't work. I'll think of something else. Nothing will happen tonight.'

He actually trusted me so much he closed his eyes, folded his arms across his breasts and fell asleep. I went back to the fires and took some food for myself, then went looking for Wentzler. I couldn't see Klaus anywhere.

Wentzler was lying in his hammock, wide awake. 'Herr Wentzler? I think my mother is mad. I don't know what to do. She won't leave here.'

'She doesn't appreciate the seriousness of the situation,' he agreed. 'As for what can be done, I haven't a clue, I regret to tell you.'

Had I expected help? I didn't know. I think I went to him because he was an adult. Now I was learning that adults don't always have answers, and are sometimes the cause of the problem. It was upsetting to learn this. Who could Zeppi depend on now? Only me. And who could I depend on? Only myself. I felt sick. For a moment I felt as though I was wrapped in a sleeping bag, a tightly laced cocoon that was suffocating me, holding me rigid inside it, unable to move. Then, simply by thinking about it and deciding, I cut my way out of the bag and could breathe again. I felt different, taller, but at the same time more helpless, without the answers I needed to make me feel safe, to make me feel that tomorrow everything would be better.

'I do have some advice for you, however,' said Wentzler. 'Become a Yayomi. Camouflage yourself, as I've done. You can never be truly Indian, but you may become sufficiently alike so as not to cause offence. Do you follow?'

'Don't be a dolphin any more?'

'Don't count on being perceived as such. The Yayomi have a practical side that allows them to be amazed when they wish to be amazed, and bored with whatever amazed them when they lose interest. And what ceases to amaze them had damn well better not offend them. Now do you follow?'

'Yes. Thank you, Herr Professor.'

'You and your brother, if you can convince him to follow in

your steps, may survive. I intend giving your uncle the same advice. As for your mother, I can tell you nothing that might comfort you.'

'I know.'

'Good. It's far better to know than not to know, whatever the knowing brings.'

SEVEN

THE TWO DAYS WENTZLER had managed to buy for Mother's recovery were wasted, at least for that purpose. She spent quite a bit of time on her knees praying, with Zeppi watching from his hammock until he couldn't stand it any more and ran off to play with his monkey or swim in the river. The sight of Mother with her face lowered over her joined palms made me ill. I tried a few times to talk with her, but all she did was tell me not to worry, Heinrich and God had things in hand.

Wentzler told me that Tagerri had suggested that I go with him into the jungle to help pick a tree for the second canoe, but I said no, and Wentzler agreed that was wise. If Tagerri should happen to come back alone, wearing my Iron Cross and telling a sad tale about a jaguar or anaconda that had carried me off, who among the Yayomi would disbelieve him? When Tagerri was told I wouldn't go with him, he looked sour and walked away into the trees with one of the old machetes Wentzler had given the tribe eleven years ago.

I had another reason not to go, of course, and that was to spend some time with Awomay while her husband-to-be was away. Wentzler was no fool. He told me he was young once and knew which direction my thoughts were taking, and he warned me against doing anything so foolish, even for a girl as pretty as Awomay. 'Tagerri has half-a-dozen family members watching you both at all times, depend on it. The least infraction of the rules of betrothal and he'll challenge you to a fight. You simply wouldn't have a chance. Stay away from her.'

I said I would, and actually meant it at the time, but it was hard not to feel it was my right to be with her if she wanted that too. But in the end I went hunting again with her brother. Just before Kwaytcha came over to me with his zabatana and darts and made the suggestion that I go with him – a simple twitch of the head that I understood instantly – I'd seen him talking with his father, Noroni, and I had the feeling that Noroni had told him to get me away from the shabono while Tagerri was gone so that I wouldn't be tempted to get up to mischief with Awomay. He was only an anxious man wanting his daughter to make a good marriage. Good from Noroni's and Tagerri's point of view, that is. Women among the Yayomi had little or no say in how things were done, according to Wentzler, but I suppose it's that way for women everywhere.

So I went with Kwaytcha and we came back late in the afternoon with two big waterbirds and a monkey. Kwaytcha had downed them all, but he'd spent some time helping me sharpen my aim with the blowpipe, and I was definitely getting better. He chatted freely with me, even if I couldn't understand a word, and I think he told me I'd bring down something edible before long. We bathed before returning to the shabono, and I took care not to piss in the water.

Every hour spent with Kwaytcha in the world beneath the tree canopy was an hour I didn't have to think about Mother or Zeppi. Maybe it was selfish of me, but Wentzler had told me to become a Yayomi, and he was the one person who knew anything worth knowing. I avoided thinking about Klaus as well, because I didn't know what to think about him. Was he my new father or wasn't he? Did I want him to be? It seemed somehow to be less important than before. Klaus was the one who'd wanted to be a husband and father. He was already unhappy with his choices because they had turned out to be a madwoman and a hermaphrodite, and it could be that he'd end up not wanting me for a son either, since I only wanted to be an Indian. I was Zeppi's brother, not Klaus's stepson, and not even Mother's son any more. All of that was falling away, being left behind with my sandal tracks on the jungle floor.

When we came back to the shabono I found Mother on her knees again. I didn't talk to her, there wouldn't have been any point. Manokwo was watching her from his hammock on the other side of the central space, and he gave me a nod as I came through with Kwaytcha. I had the feeling he approved of me as a future stepson, probably because I was trying to learn the Yayomi ways. I didn't want to be Manokwo's boy any more than I wanted to be Klaus's, but Wentzler's words came back to me and I nodded in return. If he liked me, I was safe, that's what it amounted to.

I pulled two long feathers from one of the birds, took one to Zeppi and tied it in his hair, then tied the other in my own, at the back where it wouldn't be a nuisance. It was my first step in making us both Yayomi. I'd be more convincing once I had weapons of my own, and perhaps some of the body paint the others wore. I wanted my white skin to disappear

under a layer of red and black. I'd already seen where they got
the colours from. The red came from the seeds of a certain
bush which they crushed and moistened, and the black was
dampened charcoal from the cooking fires. But it wasn't up to
me to put the paint on myself. The Yayomi painted each other.

I went looking for Klaus and found him where Zeppi and
I had found him before, along one of the more distant path-
ways, sitting under the trees with his black bag beside him
and a dreamy look on his face. He seemed pleased to see me,
and I had to remind myself that he knew nothing of what
went on inside my head. It was unsettling, though, to be
greeted with a smile and a wave as I approached. He looked
like a man who has gone to the beach and had every stitch of
clothing washed away by the tide, but who stands guard over
the family picnic basket as if nothing had happened.

'Erich! I was looking for you earlier. Where've you been?'

'I went hunting with Kwaytcha.'

'Sit down, sit down with me.'

I sat next to him.

'Hunting, eh? Excellent. I should do something like that
myself, get away from the river and those damn Yayomi for a
while. Wentzler's no company either. The fellow's been avoiding me all day. You'd think a couple of university graduates –
fellow Germans, on top of it – would want to stick together,
wouldn't you? Not old Wentzler. I think he's finally realised I
don't approve of the way he's gone native. Studying primitives
is a perfectly legitimate activity, but running around naked
for eleven years? All right, we look like naked savages ourselves, but that's simply a matter of accommodating the
climate. Inside we're still German, still civilised. Can't say the
same for Wentzler, dear me, no.'

A fly was buzzing around a spot of blood on the inside of his arm where he must have been bitten by an insect. He brushed it away. There were other insect bites in the same place. 'Still, only another month or so to go before the rainy season. I have a sneaking feeling that Wentzler won't come after all, even if it was his idea. I think he prefers it here. He doesn't want to write a book, he just wants to hide out in the wilderness. What was that theory of yours, a murderer on the run? I'm beginning to think you may be right.'

'Who do you think he might have killed?' I asked, just to keep him talking.

'Who? God knows. No, actually, God doesn't know. God doesn't know anything, for the simple and obvious reason that he doesn't exist. Don't tell your mother I said so. She'd be upset. No, wrong again. She'd just smile that condescending smile and give me that pitying look, you know, the one that says I'm living in total ignorance of what's real. Silly woman. Sorry, Erich. I shouldn't have said that. We must feel sympathy for Helga and her . . . condition.'

He stroked his new beard thoughtfully. 'It's all been too much for her. The mind snaps when it has to handle more strain than it can bear. Some cope better than others, of course, but it's clear she was already pretty far gone, wouldn't you say? That's what comes of hiding the facts about little Miss Zeppi from the world. A facade can't be maintained indefinitely. Sooner or later it has to crack, and then the real person oozes out from behind it for all the world to see. It's simply a matter of time, a very short time in Helga's case. I can talk to you like this, man to man, can't I, Erich? You're a sensible lad, and clever, and above all a survivor like myself. Some people aren't. Zeppi, for example, and Helga. But you and I, we're going to be all right, because we have what it takes to survive no matter what. Why are you looking at me that way?'

'What way?'

He brushed the fly from his arm again. '*That* way, the way you're looking at me now. Here, have a look yourself.'

He opened the clasp on his bag, reached inside and brought out a small mirror. 'Know what this is for? Checking the breath on dead men. No mist on the mirror, no breath. No breath, no life. Dead man. Here.'

He pushed it at me. I took it and saw myself for the first time in I don't know how long. My hair hung in my face like dirty yellow straw, and my skin had been darkened by sun and smoke. My face was thinner, the expression more serious. It wasn't me, it was some twin brother who'd been lurking inside me all the time. It was his face I saw.

I handed the mirror back and Klaus returned it to his bag. I asked him, 'Why do you carry that thing everywhere? The Yayomi have been scared of it ever since Waneeri said it bit him. You could leave it at the shabono and I'm sure nobody would touch it.'

'Perhaps, but one can't trust the Indians to remain scared of a demon in a bag. Sooner or later someone would get up the courage to look inside, and my equipment would be scattered far and wide as they dug through it looking for the demon. It's better off with me, and I'm better off with it.' He laughed, then went on, 'A doctor's bag is what defines him, like a soldier's gun and a musician's instrument. Without my bag, what am I? Just some fellow lost in the jungle. You have a feather in your hair, Erich, why is that? You're not going native like Wentzler, are you?'

'I might be, just for a little while, until we leave.'

'Not a good idea. The more like a Yayomi you look, the less like a dolphin, and if you aren't a dolphin, you're vulnerable, just a guest eating their food and taking up space. Better to maintain a certain mystique. Keep the bastards guessing, that's the safest thing.'

'Herr Wentzler doesn't think so. He says all that dolphin business is probably already wearing off, and we'd better be useful to them when it finally dawns on them that we're only people. I'm going to be a hunter.'

'Oh yes? And Zeppi, what will he be? And what the hell use does Wentzler think he is around here?'

'That's different. He was never a dolphin. Anyway, they like the stories he tells.'

'Listen to this conversation! We're discussing absurdities! As for me, I'm going to remain myself, and the Yayomi can go hang. I won't lower myself to their level, not for anything.'

If I hadn't known better, I'd have said he was drunk. His words weren't slurred, but his personality had changed somehow, become less sympathetic, and he was a lot more careless with his tongue.

'Klaus, how many men did you kill in the war?'

'Kill? None at all, nor women and children.'

'But how many Jews? You said you did a great work of extermination.'

'Aaah, Jews! I thought you were talking about people. Who knows how many. It isn't important what one man accomplishes in work as vast as that. The solution to the Jewish problem required a machine with many arms and a single mind, a national commitment, if you will, to taking care of things once and for all. I was one of those arms, not even a very important one, but I played my part, I'm proud to say.

Too bad the Allies couldn't allow us a little more time to accomplish our ends. Another year, possibly less, and history would have been made. Not a single Jew would have survived, from the North Sea to the Caspian, and perhaps beyond.'

I pictured Klaus's machine of many arms. It looked like an octopus, with all the arms busily feeding Jews into its beak. I wondered what it would be like to be bitten in half, to see that awful bloodstained beak coming closer and closer, biting other people in half and swallowing them, and now it's your turn . . .

'Erich, you're shivering. You can't possibly be cold. Do you have a fever?'

'No . . .' I remembered something Father used to say. 'Someone walked over my grave . . . that's all.'

'Interesting expression. No man knows where his grave will be, or even if he'll have one. Jews, for instance, did they deserve a piece of land that otherwise would serve a genuine purpose, farming, for example? No, a sheer waste of good soil.'

'What about their relocation settlements? Couldn't they have graveyards there?'

'Settlements? My dear Erich, you must learn to distinguish between the euphemisms of propaganda, and reality. The Jews were resettled all right, but not in the east, not on the plains of Poland as we described to them, good God no, that would have meant moving thousands of Poles, and we already had our hands full moving tens of thousands of Jews. What am I saying . . . *hundreds* of thousands.'

'Then where did you put them?'

'They were resettled as promised – in the atmosphere.'

I waited for him to explain, but he took one look at me and burst out laughing. 'Oh, Erich, surely you can't have thought there was any real alternative. We did what we had to do, for a better Europe and ultimately a better world.'

'Mother said there was a burning smell at that place she went to visit you . . .'

'And it brought back a painful memory from her childhood. I do regret that.'

'What's going to happen to her?'

'To Helga? I hold out little hope for a recovery. If we could get her to a hospital there might be a chance, but that's out of the question, I'm afraid.'

'No, I mean about Manokwo.'

'Oh, that. I doubt he'll make good on his threat. I've consulted with Wentzler on this, and he says the Yayomi men have no patience at all with a woman who doesn't work, and Helga is certainly not capable of that. It's all bluff. These Indians are all posture and no action most of the time, a bunch of blowhards, and the biggest blowhard of all is usually the chief. That's how he got to be chief, by bluffing his way to the top, if "top" is the correct word in this case. A rooster struts on top of a rubbish heap and imagines himself a king. Everything is relative.'

'But what if he isn't bluffing?'

'Erich, Erich, you worry too much. Think ahead to our escape plan, keep it in the forefront of your thoughts. That's what I'm doing. There's a way out of this, and we're going to take it when the time comes, make no mistake. This,' he swept his arm across the scenery, 'is not for us. Our destiny lies elsewhere.'

I saw that he wouldn't answer my question, or couldn't. It was obvious he didn't think of himself as Mother's husband any more, and I was glad about that, because he didn't deserve her, even if she'd gone mad. He thought he was so wonderful for having killed a lot of Jews, but he didn't want to get into an argument with Manokwo over what should happen to his own wife, so how much of a man was he after all? And when we were in Ciudad Bolivar I'd thought us lucky to be with him. He was smiling at me, but I couldn't look at him.

'Yes,' he said, 'it's depressing to have to wait so long, but we must be patient, you and I.'

'What about the others? We're getting a second canoe so everyone can go.'

'Of course we are, yes, certainly, all together and indivisible.'

He laughed his leaky football laugh. I'd had enough. I stood up and walked back down the path, too angry to speak. There was probably nothing Klaus could do for Mother's madness, even if he was a doctor, but he might at least have been thinking of ways to keep Manokwo from taking her as a second wife. Mother was a very irritating person to be around now that she was mad, but that was no excuse for Klaus, who was her husband after all, even if they had been married under a false name. And the other thing that made me angry was the fact that I didn't have any idea how to save Mother from Manokwo either.

He was a big man, for an Indian, very solid, and I doubted that he'd been made chief of the Yayomi just because he was a bigger blowhard than the other men. No, he was a better fighter, he had to be, and I didn't have the least talent in that direction. I don't mean that I was bullied at school, but I never went out of my way to make enemies or jump into a fight on anyone else's behalf either. Hitting people had always seemed like a stupid thing to do. There were times I was able to talk my way out of a confrontation with some idiot or other, and at least two occasions when I had to fight, but these were both draws, because my opponents were as untrained in fist fighting as me. So I couldn't fight Manokwo like the hero in an adventure book, and that made me angry.

Not tough enough to fight, not smart enough to argue my way around Manokwo, because I didn't speak the language. But did that matter? Wentzler spoke Yayomi. If I could think of a way to outsmart Manokwo, Wentzler would be my ally, as long as it didn't put him at risk. But what plan? I stopped walking, wanting to concentrate, and a big buzzing beetle flew straight into my forehead. It bounced off and kept on flying. I barely noticed it, my mind was racing so. It would have to be a plan that used as its main weapon the fact that the Yayomi were superstitious and could probably be persuaded to believe just about anything, for a while, anyway. Something that would make Manokwo scared to touch Mother for at least a month, until the rainy season started and we could sneak away.

What might Manokwo be afraid of? What would make him set Mother aside as the object of his lust? I thought and thought, but nothing came to me. Even if a squadron of beetles had aimed themselves at my head and dive-bombed it, they wouldn't have shaken free a single plan that made sense. I stood there on the path, sweating and anxious and useless, a perfect fool and weakling. I slapped myself across the face to bring out an idea, anything to keep Mother from being used like a whore, but all I got was a stinging cheek.

That night we saw the dark side of the Yayomi. It was what a policeman would have called a domestic argument: a Yayomi man who'd found out that his wife was going off into the jungle to have sex with another man was bent on seeking punishment for her crime.

Things got going even before the evening meal was ready. A man called Isiway (Wentzler started explaining it all to me from the moment it began) jumped up and began screaming in front of everyone that his wife, Taroomi, was going off behind his back to do it with some other man called Mapeway, and Isiway wanted to get his own back on both of them for having wronged him.

The accused man, Mapeway, jumped up and started screaming that if Isiway was any good as a husband (Wentzler interpreted this as 'cocksman') then Taroomi wouldn't have been interested in going with ('fucking') another man, so it was all Isiway's fault for having a cock that couldn't take care of his wife's needs.

That made Isiway even angrier, and he accused Mapeway of casting a spell on his wife to make Taroomi no longer interested in her husband. Mapeway said this was not true, that no magic had been used at all, because magic wasn't needed when a lazy cock was to blame. That made everyone laugh. All the cooking fires had been neglected as the entire population of the shabono gathered around the shouting men to enjoy their argument. Wentzler called it 'the court of public opinion.'

They kept shouting back and forth, then Mapeway said Taroomi had to stand up and say in front of everyone why it was that she'd done it with Mapeway, because being accused of casting bad spells was a serious charge. She stood up then, and I saw it was the woman who'd suckled a little monkey on one tit and her baby on the other. She didn't look at all happy to be the centre of attention, and screamed even louder than the men, which got the baby on her hip started, so there was a lot of noise inside the shabono's walls. Taroomi said between howls that she'd gone with Mapeway because her husband Isiway beat her too much when she didn't please him, and Mapeway was much nicer to her, calling her his 'tasty little dog in heat' and his 'lovely juicy puppy fuck', which were compliments that Isiway never paid her. Instead he called her 'lazy ugly monkey turd' and so forth, which upset her and drove her into the arms of Mapeway.

She was very insistent that she hadn't felt any spell cast over her, and in any case, Mapeway was better looking and a better lover than Isiway. Some of the audience cheered when she said this, and Wentzler said they were related to Mapeway. Isiway's relations, he pointed out to me, were stony-faced.

It was clear that Isiway wasn't happy with his wife's explanation, and he said that it was magic of such a superior type that had snared her that she hadn't been aware of it, and still wasn't, which was why she was saying such bad and untruthful things about her husband and such nice things about Mapeway. There would have to be a fight to settle the issue, and this time Mapeway wouldn't have the chance to cast any spells to weaken Isiway, because the fight would take place there and then, in front of everyone.

This got the audience very excited. Wentzler said the Yayomi enjoyed a good fight between two evenly matched men every bit as much as white people liked a professional boxing match. Isiway and Mapeway ran to the pole frame supporting the shabono's roof and both pulled out poles about three metres in length and as thick as their arms. Then they faced each other, screaming insults and being supported by all their male relatives on both sides. Mapeway, as the accused party, was by law entitled to the first blow, and after he'd run out of insults he struck at Isiway, who didn't even try to dodge the blow, which came straight down onto the top of his head.

I heard a horrible *bonk* sound as it hit. Isiway staggered to one side but didn't fall, then he straightened up and got ready to hit Mapeway, who also didn't make any kind of move to get out of the way as Isiway's pole began coming down. It hit him in the same place, making the same sound, and Mapeway also staggered back and forth a bit before recovering. Both men had blood running down from their hair onto their faces and necks, and both smeared it across their chests before getting ready for the second round of blows. It was the stupidest kind of contest I could ever have imagined, but Wentzler said it was the traditional way of settling disputes among the Yayomi.

The two men squared off and Mapeway struck again. This time Isiway went down onto one knee, but he quickly got back up again while his supporters screamed themselves hoarse. He took a moment to recover himself, then lifted his pole to hit Mapeway, who stood with his bloodied chest pushed out and a confident look on his face. The pole came down faster than before, and the sound as it hit Mapeway on the top of his head was awful, like the sound of an axe splitting wood. He stood for a moment, still with his lips curled into a sneer, then he simply dropped like a sack of turnips right where he stood, and the fight was over.

Isiway began prancing around, chanting some kind of victory song, and his relations cheered him and joined in the singing. Mapeway lay where he fell, untended by his family, in disgrace because he'd lost, which meant, Wentzler explained, that everything he'd said was a lie. An honest man would have won the pole fight, and Mapeway's relations were embarrassed by his loss, so they wouldn't go near him until later, when the excitement had died down.

But the show wasn't over. Streaming blood, acting as if he was mad with joy at having won, Isiway announced that his wife must also be punished for having made her husband feel so very bad. Taroomi started wailing when she heard that, and I expected to see her given a good beating, only not with the pole. I was right about that – he used a machete instead and cut off her ears, while his wife squatted on the ground screaming in front of him.

First he sawed off her left ear, holding it out away from her head so he wouldn't cut her scalp, then he started on the right ear, but she fainted and collapsed in a heap like Mapeway, so Isiway had to turn her over to get to the ear. He sawed it off the same way, then held them both up in his hand and gave a speech which Wentzler said was all about being right when the faithless wife and bad neighbour were absolutely and totally wrong – the poles said so, and the butchered ears were the final proof. Taroomi lay in a pool of blood, still unconscious, but Mapeway was stirring. He sat up and saw Taroomi without her ears, and I waited to see what he'd do about it, but he did nothing. Justice had been done, Wentzler said, and there was nothing more to do or say about the matter.

I felt a bit sick. Would Manokwo do that to Mother if she upset him? The thought of it made me want to run directly at him and shoot him through the heart, but of course I had no gun, nothing at all to make things happen the way I wanted them to, the way Isiway had done. I knew I couldn't just stand there and let someone hit me over the head. I found myself thinking of the Yayomi with less respect because of that fight, especially when, five minutes later, Isiway and Mapeway could be seen running in circles together, arms around each other's shoulders, laughing and shouting like the best of friends, and the woman they both loved or wanted or whatever it was that Indians felt, lay on the ground with her ears cut off. It didn't make sense.

'They aren't more foolish than us, Erich, don't think that,' Wentzler said. 'Have you never heard of a pistol duel where both sides are allowed to take a shot in turn? That practice is no more absurd than this. Both men will have huge lumps on their heads tomorrow, and they'll be very proud of them, even to the point of cutting their hair away on top so everyone can see the wounds.'

'But the woman ... she's got no *ears* now.'

'Unfortunately, no, but then, she's only a woman. That's the way of things here.'

'I want to go away. I want to leave here and never come back.'

'And so you shall, Erich, once the waters have risen high enough for our plan.'

'But by then ... it'll be too late for Mother.'

'I know. I'm sorry, but I can't help you.'

'It should be Klaus. He should be the one to stop it!'

'Probably, but what should he do? He blames your mother for the situation she finds herself in. If she'd only consent to act like his wife in a manner that the Yayomi could understand ...'

'But she *hates* him! Why should she do that with him if she hates him?'

'Please lower your voice. I understand her point of view, and yours, and Klaus's, and Manokwo's. They're irreconcilable. That's the conundrum we face here.'

'She hates him because he killed all those Jews.'

'Really? Are you quite sure? I haven't formed the opinion that your mother is a friend of the Jews.'

'She isn't. Nobody is, but killing them all like that . . . Today he told me there were hundreds of thousands! Resettled in the atmosphere, he said . . .'

'Did he now.'

'And he won't do anything, I know it. He thinks it doesn't matter what happens to her because of . . . the way she is.'

'And what would you do, if you could?'

'I don't know. Outsmart Manokwo somehow. Trick him into waiting until it's too late, until the rains come and we're gone.'

'Trick him how?'

I had nothing to say. The shabono had quietened down a lot now that the fight was over. I watched some women carry Taroomi away and put her in her hammock. They didn't bother cleaning up the blood that had spilled all over her shoulders and down her belly. What sort of people were these who could show so little sympathy for their own kind? They seemed to have the emotions of children and hearts of solid wood.

Wentzler must have read my face. 'Erich,' he said, 'they differ from us only in the limitations imposed upon them by stone, as opposed to iron and steel. If Isiway hadn't had the use of a machete to cut off his wife's ears, he'd have used a freshwater mussel shell, which would probably have caused her even more pain.'

'But why did he have to do that? It didn't fix anything.'

'Fix? Nothing broken can ever truly be fixed again. Taroomi will always fear and hate Isiway, and Mapeway, even though he's pretending for now to be Isiway's friend again, will want revenge for his humiliation. None of this can ever be fixed, and it will all lead to more breakage, more pain. Nothing can change that.'

I said goodnight to the professor and went to my hammock. He was right – broken things couldn't be put back together the way they used to be. Mother was broken. Her marriage to Klaus was broken. The family was broken. It had all started when Father was killed. If he hadn't died, Mother wouldn't have been tempted to remarry, and none of us would be here now.

I looked up at the sky through the shabono's giant hole, half expecting to see it shatter into a million pieces like a black mirror hit from behind by the fist of God. Soon the food would be ready and everyone would eat as if nothing had happened, as if no blood had been spilled and no lives changed. At least the sky would never break and fall in pieces, I could depend on that. Everything else was either broken or waiting to be. It was calming, in a way, to think like that. More breakage would follow, but it wasn't my fault. Things just happened that way.

Mother's final day of freedom dawned like those before it, and she got up and prayed. She hadn't eaten in two days. Klaus couldn't persuade her, and neither could I. She hardly spoke at all, except silently to God. Everything that happened that day happened slowly, as if each passing moment was being measured out.

Most of the men went hunting, but I stayed behind. Tagerri and some of his friends had dragged a log from the jungle the day before and he was working on it, shaping another canoe.

The other women in the plantain garden were watching over Awomay to make sure she didn't come near me. The truth was, I didn't care. Mother's situation filled all my thoughts that day. Zeppi played with Mitzi, but even the monkey's antics couldn't make him smile.

Manokwo came to watch while Mother prayed. He seemed puzzled by her behaviour and asked the professor what she was doing. Wentzler explained, and Manokwo said something about laziness always having an excuse, and that tomorrow she would have no time for talking to gods. Tomorrow she would be his wife, unless she made it clear that Klaus was indeed her husband as he claimed, which Manokwo doubted. He was looking forward very much, he told Wentzler, to having a dolphin woman for a wife, but he wanted Mother to understand that their children, when they came, would have to look like humans, not dolphins.

He was very nice about it all, not gloating or rubbing his hands together. I hated him anyway. But I hated Klaus more for doing nothing. He was nowhere to be seen, probably somewhere in the jungle, regretting that he ever wrote to Mother with an offer of marriage.

As the afternoon wore on, everything became less real. Even the air stopped moving, and all the leaves and fronds of the jungle were still. I could hear thunder a long way off, but the sky was clear. The river, when I went down to bathe in it, was flowing like warm chocolate with hardly a ripple on its surface. The parrots in the trees were silent, and very few were flying. Then, as I watched, the sky began turning a yellowish-green shade, and clouds began building up behind the treetops, lumpy clouds of steel grey shot with a blue so deep it was almost black. The sound of thunder was louder now, and as the clouds rolled closer I saw lightning flickering inside them like veins of gold in boiling rock.

The colour of the river changed from brown to muddy green as the clouds thudded and thumped overhead. I had to find cover, but I didn't want to go back inside the shabono, so I went into the jungle as the first drops of rain began to fall, big fat drops that made a sound as they hit the earth, so big they bounced off the bigger leaves in little explosions of water. It started as a pattering sound, then became a drumming, steady and strong, and the light overhead was so dim it was like walking through a room full of trees in the dark. I followed a familiar path that was already running like a small creek with water.

Then the wind came, and suddenly every tree and plant was waving and creaking back and forth and rubbing their branches together. The leaves all began to flutter and rustle so fast they made a hissing sound behind the falling rain, and behind the rain was the wind, moaning and whistling like something alive and in pain. Lightning flickered and flashed every few seconds, and more thunder came crashing and rolling along behind, a continuous sound that made me think of grinding wheels and slapping sails.

I slowed to a walk along the path, placing my feet carefully, feeling water run over them, filling the spaces between my toes with warm dirt. Sudden flashes of brightness made the thrashing trees on either side seem like creatures flailing around in agony. Rain fell onto my head and shoulders like stinging needles. Somehow I found all this exciting. It wasn't like any rainstorm I'd ever known before. Here the falling water seemed to fill the air itself, make it heavy and hard to breathe. It was like walking through an underwater jungle where my ears were filled with the rumbling of nearby surf and the smashing of waves against coral reefs. I was a dolphin, with legs instead of fins, plodding through a seaweed jungle.

I saw Klaus beneath his usual tree, sitting with his back against the trunk, face upturned to receive rain into his open mouth. His eyes were shut against the stinging drops. I was close enough to see rain bouncing from his white teeth and handsome nose. I didn't want him to see me, I don't know why, so I hid behind a nearby tree while his eyes were still closed, and watched him, hating him silently and at the same time feeling sorry for him because he was alone (he thought) in the jungle in the middle of a storm.

He dropped his head to take the force of rain on top of his skull. Droplets ran from his nose and chin onto his belly, and for a while it looked as if he was asleep, his head hung so far forward. Then he lifted it and opened his eyes. He turned his streaming head left and right, looking at nothing in particular, his forehead plastered with hair. While I watched, he opened his medical bag and reached inside, hunching his body over it to keep the rain from getting in. He found what he wanted and brought it out. A lightning flash seemed to make the thing in his hand twinkle like a test tube filled with sparks. Another flash, and I saw what it was – a hypodermic syringe.

He held it up to the flashing overhead as if to check that it was what it appeared to be, then with his other hand he brought up to the needle's point a tiny upside-down bottle, and capped it. He drew the plunger back, draining fluid from the little bottle, then set both things, still joined together, carefully to one side.

The bag was opened again and a length of thin rubber hose brought out. He tied this around his upper arm and pulled it tight with his teeth, then picked up the syringe. The empty bottle was plucked from the needle's tip, then he squirted a little liquid into the air to be sure there were no bubbles inside the syringe's chamber. Satisfied, he brought the needle to his arm and carefully slid it under the skin inside his elbow joint. His face was awful, grinning teeth holding the rubber hose tight while he injected himself, then his lips slackened and the hose fell away. Klaus's face seemed to relax all at once as it tipped upward again to take the full force of the rain.

His eyelids fluttered like butterflies, then stayed open. He eased the needle from his arm and smiled. Who was he smiling at? What was his sickness that needed self-doctoring? Maybe he was dying of something. Thinking this, I was glad, and I wanted him to know I was glad, so I stepped out from behind my tree and stood there, waiting for him to notice me.

It took a long time, at least a minute, before he saw me there. The expression on his face didn't change, as if he'd known all along I was watching, or else he couldn't be bothered being surprised. We stared at each other for another minute or so, then he beckoned to me and I went closer. He put the syringe and bottle and rubber hose back into his bag and snapped it shut, then looked at me. His mouth opened and shut several times, and I realised he was talking but I couldn't hear a word. He looked like a fish in a bowl, yawping and yawping with its mouth, over and over again without making a sound. The storm was too noisy, his voice too weak, and he ended up gesturing for me to come even closer, but I didn't want to.

I stayed where I was, watching him. He sagged against the tree, as if giving up, and turned his face away from mine. His hand came up again, but this time, instead of beckoning me forward, he shooed me away. The movement of his hand was slow and lazy, a hand waving underwater like seaweed surging with the tide.

Now that he wanted me gone, I stepped closer, just out of reach, and we continued our staring game. His face, slick with rain, had no expression at all, and his body seemed as limp as a fallen puppet's. Klaus was a puppet man, his strings snipped or broken, left to rot in the jungle with splayed-out limbs and a face washed free of paint and varnish. He couldn't move without his strings, and I liked the look of helplessness he wore, lying at my feet that way, breath moving in and out of his chest, lips parted, eyes half closed again. Whatever sickness he had inside him, I didn't want it, so I stepped away before he could cough all over me. I imagined a cloud of darkness spewing from his mouth, a poisonous mass swarming with microbes, the churning smoke of death itself.

He was smiling at me now, and I knew it was because I'd stepped away as if afraid of him. Klaus was amused by my fear, mocking me with his eyes and the smile playing around his silent lips. I wanted to kick his teeth in, wipe the smile from his face with a rock. I was shivering again, but not with cold. It was hatred that made me shake so, and I knew the only way to make it go away was to strike Klaus, transfer the shivering along my arm and fist into his slack and defenceless body.

But I couldn't. He was like a child, without the strength to resist, and I couldn't hit him. A part of me wanted to pick him up and carry him home. I didn't like that, didn't want to feel sorry for him in any way. He was a weak man, a coward, and sickness was the right thing for him to have been struck by. I didn't have to bother. If I walked away and left him there, he might even die. Could I do that, walk away and forget about him?

His eyes weren't focused on me any more. He was looking behind me, a slight frown creasing his forehead. I turned and saw Awomay. She looked like an otter I'd seen once at the zoo, sleek and brown and curious, running with water, alert but friendly. The moment I saw her I stopped thinking about Klaus. She was standing by a tree, lightning flashes flickering across her breasts and belly. I went toward her and she turned away, then began to jog along the path. I followed, but in a moment of darkness I lost sight of her. Any footprints that might have been left on the path were lost under the shallow stream it had become.

I stopped. 'Awomay!'

I heard nothing but thunder and rain, the lashing of trees in the wind. A twig hit me in the neck. She'd disappeared, but I sensed it was deliberate. She wanted me to find her. Her running away had been to tease me. Another twig, on the shoulder this time. She was throwing them at me from cover somewhere. I spun in a circle, looking for her among the trees and vines.

'I can't see you! Come out!'

But she wouldn't. Another twig hit my back. I turned but still couldn't see her. I liked this game, but at the same time I wanted it to end. I wanted her within reaching distance, not scampering around, hidden from me by leaves and noise and darkness. 'I love you!' I called out, but that didn't make any difference to Awomay. I might as well have been telling her it was Tuesday. 'Please come out!' She wouldn't and I got angry. It was a silly game, a childish game, this hide and seek in the middle of a storm, and I had no more interest in it, or in her. 'Piss off, then!' I yelled at the trees. 'I don't care! Stay away from me! Cow!' Still no sign of her, so I turned back to the path, and found her right behind me.

She said something, took my hand and led me away. I followed like a dog on a leash. She went where the trees grew thickest and we had to go forward in single file. I had no idea which direction we were travelling in. All I could see was her lovely arse going up and down in front of me, and her back and shoulders wet with rain, and her hair, black and thick as a horse's mane, and the green ribbon I gave her clinging wetly to her narrow waist. We came to a small clearing and stopped. She turned around to face me, smiling, and it was clear that the next move was mine. Her face told me she'd done a brave and foolish thing in bringing me here, but she didn't care.

I looked at those three little sticks stuck into the flesh around her mouth. I wanted to kiss her, but those sticks were in the way, and, in any case, the professor had told me the Yayomi never kissed. They patted and stroked and sometimes hugged, but never kissed. I stepped forward for a hug. She stood absolutely still when my arms went around her. Her breasts were like two little pillows pushed against me, but her back felt stiff and tense. I must have done it wrong. I let her go. She still didn't move, but the smile continued. I didn't know what to do next.

She pointed at my cock, which was rising, and asked me something I couldn't understand, then she grabbed it and started working the skin back and forth, which completed the hardening in about five seconds. Then she bent down to look closely at it. There was nothing sexy about what she was doing. She wanted to see if it worked the same way as an uncircumcised cock. She kept tugging to see if the skin would cover the tip, but of course it wouldn't, not when it was that hard, and finally she seemed to accept that it was a different kind of cock, but one that functioned normally despite its strange appearance.

Awomay lay down on the ground on her back, pulling me down with her by my cock, and opened her legs. Her vagina was pink inside, the edges like formless lips, and it was surprisingly long from top to bottom, not like a hole at all, which is what they call it in jokes, more like a crevice. I couldn't see where exactly my cock was supposed to go – into the top part, the middle, the bottom? It was all one long wet crease, opened out for me like a book. Her legs were stuck sideways, she was so far open, and she was still smiling, but tugging more urgently on my cock. I stopped holding back to look down at her and sank onto her body like a weary man sinks onto a bed, and found that I needn't have worried about where exactly to put myself, because Awomay guided me inside her.

My cock entered what felt like a very firm and warm jelly mould pressed between walls of muscle that gripped me as tightly as the legs that swung across my back and locked themselves at the ankles, grinding a little at the base of my spine. Her arms were on my shoulders, slapping me, and her eyes were screwed shut. Her lips were parted but she wasn't smiling now, more like clenching her teeth in pain, but none of it was hurting her, I could tell, because she kept pulling at me, making me go in and out of her body faster, and the little sticks in her face trembled every time our bellies slammed into each other.

I couldn't feel the rain or the wind. I couldn't feel the wet ground under my knees, only Awomay's insides, and after a few thrusts more I emptied myself there. I think I yelled. Awomay made no sound, just released me and let her arms and legs flop sideways. I sank onto her for a moment, panting, then she pushed me off. The rain washed sweat off us both.

She got up and said something, then started walking away.

I got up in a hurry and followed. Without her I would have been completely lost. Branches slapped at my face as we passed through the undergrowth, but I didn't mind. I watched Awomay's shoulders and back as before, loving them, wanting to pick off the wet pieces of dirt and leaves stuck there, but she moved so quickly I didn't get the chance. Then we were at the river. Awomay waded in and squatted until the water covered her up to her neck. She was washing away the evidence. I went in and squatted next to her, feeling the current loosen dirt from my skin and carry it away.

We left the water together. I took hold of her hand but she shook me off and started walking again, following the bank, and soon we were in sight of the curving shore where the Yayomi kept their canoes. Pulled up in ranks, they were filled to overflowing with rainwater, like long cattle troughs. There was nobody nearby. The rain still came pelting down, the thunder rolled and lightning flashed.

Awomay turned and pushed at my chest, telling me not to follow her any more now that we were so close to home. She didn't want anyone seeing us together, which was very sensible, so I stopped there and watched her walking away. When she was halfway up the slope, someone called her name. Awomay turned. I saw Tagerri come from the nearest trees, carrying a machete, and my stomach lurched. Of all the people to have seen us, it had to be him. He must have been working on the new canoe – I saw the roughly trimmed trunk of a tree just beyond the other canoes – when the storm came and had gone to stand under cover until it passed.

His face was twisted with fury. I was afraid of him. He wanted to hack me to death with the machete and then cut off Awomay's ears, even if she wasn't his wife yet. She was rooted to the spot, too scared to move as he came closer, swinging the blade back and forth like an angry cat swings its tail. It wasn't clear which one of us he'd go to first, then he turned in my direction, and my bowels wanted to spill themselves I was so frightened.

Tagerri's lips were peeled back from his teeth in a horrible grin, and his eyes never left mine. His body seemed to bulge with muscle, especially his arms and neck, and the machete's handle was gripped so tightly in his hand I could see the knuckles showing white under his brown skin. My legs wouldn't move, whether from paralysing fear or because I didn't want to turn and run from him in front of Awomay, I didn't know. I stood where I was, not moving an inch, waiting for a solution to the problem. My brain fizzed and whirred, looking for a way out, and when Tagerri was three metres or so away, the answer came.

I took hold of my Iron Cross and quickly pulled it up and over my head, then held it out like a man with a crucifix defending himself from a vampire. Tagerri stopped, his eyes fastened on the medal, then he shook his head and kept on marching toward me. I backed away, still holding up the Iron Cross, hoping he'd change his mind when he got closer, but it wasn't working that way at all, because Tagerri lifted his own arm, the one with the machete, and grinned even wider as he took the last few steps that would put him within cutting distance of me.

The machete was raised to take that first swipe, and I couldn't move. I was going to die less than half an hour after losing my virginity, and it wasn't fair. It was my own fault for being too proud to run, too concerned with how things looked to Awomay. I tried to blame her as well, but couldn't.

All the fault was mine, and my only comfort was knowing that I would die without the least illusion as to why. I did it to myself, and so I deserved what was coming. The machete was lifted as high as Tagerri could take it above his head, and he paused for a second or two, enjoying the look of fear and hopelessness on my face.

Then, as the blade began to move forward and down, a white light filled my eyes and a white heat blasted me backwards. It lifted me up and away from the mud and threw me on my back, stunned and blind.

The machete blow must have struck me so fast I didn't see it coming. It had split my skull in two, opened my brain to the sky and rain, and now I was dead, or dying, and it was all over. I could feel heat along the front of my body and cool mud along the back, but my head didn't hurt at all, which is why I knew I must be dead after all, because a split skull would have hurt a lot if I was alive. I stared up at the air above me, surprised that I could see again after being blinded by the white light of death. I felt raindrops pattering on my face, hitting my eyes and washing them, my dead man's eyes.

It was at an end, everything I'd worried about and fretted over – Zeppi and Mother and everything else that had gone wrong in Venezuela. Someone else would have to step in and fix things. It was a great relief, frankly, to know that I needn't care any more.

Awomay was bending over me, searching my face for signs of life. She wouldn't find any. I hoped she'd cry, right there above me, so I could see how much she was going to miss me now that I was dead. Her tears would be the last thing I saw before my split brain shut down completely and let me drift away to wherever dead people went, if they went anywhere.

But I wanted to see those tears first, and they weren't coming. Her hand took me by the cheeks and shook me. I thought that was no way to treat a dead man, and was annoyed with her thoughtlessness, the lack of tenderness in her fingers, then I decided to forgive her, because Yayomi ways were not my ways, and everything she did might be perfectly acceptable to a Yayomi, under the circumstances.

Then she prodded me in the guts, and I went, 'Ooooph . . . !'

This surprised me again. How could a corpse produce such a sound? I reasoned that it was only a physical reaction to her prodding, a release of wind from my dead lungs.

She smacked me across the face – once, twice, three times! I thought that was outrageous by any standards, and brought up my hand to grab her wrist before she could do it again. I had to use my left hand because my right hand felt peculiar, as if a sharp object was digging into it. Then I remembered the Iron Cross. It was still clenched between my fingers. I could feel it. I could feel everything, and see everything . . . so how could I be dead?

I opened my mouth. Air rushed into my lungs like a river of cold fire that filled my head as well as my chest, and when it came out again carried with it the loudest scream I'd ever heard. 'Aaaaaaaaaaaaaaaaaaggghhhhh!' I did it again, screamed as loud as I could without knowing why, only that I was able to scream and that meant I was alive after all.

I sat up, pulled myself from the mud like Adam, and marvelled at my body. There it all was below my eyes – the belly and legs and arms, the feet and hands, one clutching an Iron Cross. I was alive . . . I was alive! And Tagerri was dead.

He lay a short distance from me like a toppled statue. I knew just by looking at him that he was dead. His machete hadn't even come close to me, hadn't even swung down. The blade had taken a lightning bolt through its tip, and thousands of volts had run down through Tagerri's arm, through his body, down his legs and into the mud. Tagerri had ended his life as a human filament. I stood up, my whole body tingling with blood that moved and flowed and announced my aliveness, and looked down at the man who had wanted to kill me.

His eyes were open and slightly bulging. A piece of tongue, half bitten off, lay across his lips. His skin had a greyish tone to it, and beneath it there wasn't the faintest stirring of blood. I looked at the Iron Cross in my hand, amazed that the electricity coursing through Tagerri hadn't leapt across the short space separating us, drawn to its metal. By rights I should have been lying dead beside him, two fools in the rain with metal in their hands. His had been raised much higher than mine, and the mass of metal in it had been greater. Still, I'd been lucky.

I turned to Awomay. Her face was filled with worry, I couldn't understand why. She hadn't wanted to marry Tagerri or she wouldn't have done what she did with me. 'It's all right,' I told her. 'He's dead. A lightning strike. Electricity.' She ran toward the shabono without looking back. I stayed where I was, staring at Tagerri, wondering who, now that the Yayomi's best canoe maker was gone, would make my second canoe. Maybe, since Tagerri had been prepared to sell me two canoes for the Iron Cross, someone else might want to do the same. I slipped the ribbon over my head and let the medal dangle over my breastbone as before.

Did I really want to sell it now? After all, it had saved my life. If I hadn't taken it off and held it out toward Tagerri, he might not have hesitated that extra split second, the time it took for a lightning bolt to snake down from the clouds and kill him stone dead. Father would have been pleased that his Iron Cross had saved me. Mother would say that Father's spirit in heaven had sent down the lightning to do just that, and the fact that I hadn't been struck, despite having metal in my hand, was proof of it.

People were pouring from the shabono like ants from a kicked-in nest, and they all streamed down to the river and surrounded Tagerri and me. They looked at his body and they looked at me. Awomay was telling them what had happened, more excited than I'd ever seen her before. Mother wasn't there, but Zeppi and his monkey were.

Wentzler was among the crowd, and after listening to Awomay he came to my side, a look of confusion on his face. 'Erich, enlighten me if you would. The young lady says you killed Tagerri.'

'Killed him? Me? No, *he* was trying to kill *me*, and when he lifted his machete it was struck by lightning! I got knocked over backwards when it happened.'

'Trying to kill you? Why?'

'Well . . . it's about Awomay . . .'

'Aaah.'

'Tagerri saw us together and got angry. He was really going to kill me, Herr Wentzler.'

'I believe you, but Awomay has embroidered the story somewhat. According to her, Tagerri approached you with the machete and said your time to die had come because you had lain with his intended. Is . . . is that part correct? None of my business, of course.'

'Umm . . . yes.'

'You weren't about to be intimidated, is what she's saying, and you told him to beware your mighty dolphin powers of death. You gave him fair warning, Awomay says, but Tagerri sneered at you and said he thought you were bluffing, that you had no such powers, and with that, you took the charm you always wear around your neck and pointed it at him, where-upon Tagerri was hit by a blinding light from the sky and died. Awomay's doing a wonderful job defending you morally and inflating your reputation for magic at the same time. She's say-ing you must have powerful friends among the sky gods as well as the water gods. Did you point the Iron Cross at him?'

'I was offering it to him, not pointing it. I wanted him to take it and let me live, that's all, then he was struck by the lightning.'

'Fantastic! This is how legends are born. A little misinter-pretation, a little exaggeration, a lot of admiration and a dash of self-interest. You've become some kind of superhuman entity, Erich. I hope you're prepared for instant canonisation.'

The Yayomi were all looking at me with what could only be called awe. It was very funny, but I didn't laugh. Instead, I stared back at them with my sternest expression, one at a time. And they couldn't look me in the eye! Wentzler was right! I'd become someone else, someone other than the dolphin boy they'd grown used to. Now I was something far more danger-ous. I felt myself getting taller by the minute . . . It was wonderful! There was a dead man at my feet and I didn't care! And best of all, it meant that now I could do something for Mother, extend the two-day breathing space Wentzler had arranged before the chief could take over as her new husband. Manokwo wouldn't want to offend the mother of a son able to strike dead anyone who angered him. It was perfect!

'Herr Wentzler, would you say a few words to Manokwo for me?'

'Certainly.'

Manokwo was staring like all the rest at the body of Tagerri. Wentzler spoke to him and he came closer. I could already see a new respect for me in his eyes.

'Tell him that my mother will not become his wife as planned. My mother will not become his wife at any time. Tell him.'

Wentzler did so, and Manokwo was not pleased.

'He says, Erich, that a woman, even a dolphin woman, must have a husband to lie with or the earth would have no children and would be an empty place except for the animals and birds, who would miss the opportunity to be hunted and eaten by humans, which is an honour for them.'

'Tell him I don't care about any of that nonsense. Ask him how he knows that animals like being eaten by us. Tell him it's all a crock of shit.'

'Erich, watch how you talk, please. I'll tell him no such thing. He, and the rest of the tribe, would be tremendously insulted. Think of something else for me to tell him, some explanation for your mother being unavailable for marriage. The Yayomi will accept anything associated with an interesting story. You can't simply say no to them without also saying why.'

'All right . . . Tell him my mother is pregnant with a new dolphin baby and doesn't want to lie with him or any other man. And tell him that the reason Klaus doesn't lie with her is because he's sick. Dolphin men get sick for a while after they lie with their wives to make a dolphin baby, because . . . because it's very hard work mounting a dolphin woman and it makes the husband exhausted and sick, at least until the baby comes, which won't be until after the rains. Then Klaus and Mother will act like husband and wife again. Tell

Manokwo his interest in my mother is very flattering, but he didn't have all the facts of the matter, so now that he knows, I'd appreciate it if he wouldn't look at her all the time. If he does, I'll be angry.'

Manokwo and the professor spoke for some time. Manokwo still seemed upset, despite the explanation. Everyone else was listening closely to the conversation. Finally, Wentzler said to me, 'He understands, now that you've explained things to him, but he wishes you'd told him earlier. He still wants a new wife with yellow hair, and he asks that you summon from the river a sister or cousin of Frau Brandt's to be with him in the shabono and lie with him as his wife. Let me make clear to you that he's intensely disappointed and quite angry that he wasn't told about the dolphin baby in the beginning.'

'What should I say? I can't bring him another blond lady to be his wife.'

'Then think of a good reason why you can't, or better yet, tell him you can do as he wishes but the sister of your mother has to swim upstream from a faraway place and won't be here until after the rains. That's my suggestion.'

'I've got a better one. Tell him that Zeppi will turn into a girl completely after the rains and she'll be his new wife.'

'Zeppi? Are you sure he should be involved?'

'He won't mind. He won't even understand.'

'But perhaps you should ask him first.'

'He's twelve years old and not very bright, frankly. I'm almost seventeen and...I can kill people with lightning! What Zeppi doesn't know won't hurt him.'

My brother was poking a little fearfully at Tagerri with his big toe and couldn't hear us. Wentzler looked dubious. 'I think you should say your mother's sister is swimming upstream to be with Manokwo.'

'That woman won't ever be here, but Zeppi's right under Manokwo's nose. He's very pretty and he has blond hair. Manokwo won't have to use his imagination at all. It'll be a more convincing story this way, with Zeppi right here and already halfway to becoming a girl.'

'I don't approve, I have to say.'

He was starting to irritate me. 'Herr Professor, I'm the one with the friendly gods behind him, so I think my plan should be the one we use, if you don't mind my saying so. Tell Manokwo that all baby dolphins of our kind are born male, but when they get to be around Zeppi's age half of them transform themselves into females, which is what's happening to Zeppi. Say that it's a slow process, which is why Manokwo will have to wait until after the rains for Zeppi to be his wife. That's an interesting story to give him, don't you think? I'll bet you he believes it. Tell him.'

Wentzler sniffed and huffed to let me know he wasn't happy, then spoke at length with Manokwo, whose face brightened a bit by the end of the telling.

'He believes you,' said Wentzler. 'I just hope this doesn't jeopardise your brother in any way.'

'It won't. We've got them where we want them now, thanks to Tagerri. Silly bastard, to run around in the middle of a thunderstorm with a machete in his hand.'

'You also had a metallic object in yours.'

'But a lot smaller,' I said. I didn't like the way he was calling me a silly bastard too. I didn't say anything, though. I had to keep Wentzler as a friend, since he was the only way of communicating with the Yayomi.

'Oh, and one more thing, Herr Professor. Would you mind telling Noroni that I'm going to be his daughter's husband now that Tagerri's dead? Don't ask him, tell him.'

'I'll suggest politely that you wish to ask for Awomay's hand in marriage. You don't know these people yet, Erich. Kindly be led by me in these matters.'

'All right, do it your way then.'

I didn't like his attitude. Here was I, a supernatural dolphin boy with lightning in my fingertips, and the Yayomi were obviously scared and respectful of me, and Wentzler wanted to treat them with kid gloves instead of laying down the law. The storm was passing, patches of blue appearing overhead, and the last of the rain pattered to a stop as Wentzler and I glared at each other. He didn't like taking orders from me because I was much younger than him. Too bad. He'd been here eleven years and hadn't even made the Yayomi respect him enough to let him take a wife. I'd been here only a few weeks, killed one of them and was ready to dictate terms. He didn't like that either. But, as I said, I needed him, maybe even more than he needed me. I wasn't so impressed with myself that I intended turning my interpreter against me. I would be the sultan, and Wentzler would be my grand vizier, just like in *The Arabian Nights*.

EIGHT

THE NEXT DAY NORONI, after a very longwinded speech delivered to Wentzler and myself, agreed that since Tagerri was dead, I should step into his footprints and be Awomay's husband. He wanted to give me a dowry to go along with his daughter, namely a set of weapons made by Kwaytcha and the promise of more lessons in their use from my soon-to-be brother-in-law. Usually a man had to pay the father for a girl, but in my case the rules were reversed. I said that the arrangement was very satisfactory, and we were married straightaway.

There was no ceremony, and nobody said anything to the two of us that might have been called an official pronouncement. Awomay came over to my hammock and sat on it. Kwaytcha came with her, then went away after leaving his bow and arrows and zabatana and darts propped against the nearest pole. I asked Wentzler if that was all there was to getting married, and he said it was, then he said, 'Congratulations.'

I took Awomay to meet Mother. This should have been an

important moment for Mother, the firstborn son bringing his bride to her for approval, but Mother just looked right through Awomay and me and started another silent prayer, her lips moving quickly, hands pressed together. She was still mad, maybe worse than before. If Manokwo had come for her as planned, she would have gone completely insane, crazy enough to foam at the mouth and be considered for a strait-jacket, I'm sure of it. This way she was left alone to continue being mad in her own quiet way. If I thought about it, the situation made me angry, then sad, so I made a choice not to think about it any more.

I was a married man now, so the thing that was on my mind the most was getting Awomay off into the jungle again for more of what we'd done yesterday. But first there was a funeral I had to attend, along with everyone else in the shabono. As much as a marriage was casual, a funeral among the Yayomi was filled with ritual acts and a strict following of age-old rules. Professor Wentzler explained it all as the day went on, and because it would have been an insult to the family of the man I killed to walk away from his funeral, I had to postpone my plans for Awomay and stay inside the shabono. I have to admit, though, that what I saw there was very interesting, in a disgusting kind of way.

First a big fire was built, right in the middle of the shabono, and Tagerri's body, already smelling very bad, was placed inside it, then the fire was lit. It burned for a long time, and more wood was added to keep it good and hot. I smelled what Mother had talked about in her fight with Klaus, the smell of burning human flesh. It wasn't as bad as she made out, not so different to the smell of cooking animal meat. Maybe she meant that burning Jews smelled different to any other type of burning human, but I couldn't see why that should be so. I'd talk to Klaus about that later.

He was back with us again, had come in at sundown the day before and been dumbfounded to learn that I was a lightning warrior and soon to be married. He didn't talk to me about any of it, only chatted for a few minutes with Wentzler, then went to his hammock and fell asleep. Sick or not, I think he should have spoken to me. He hadn't gone anywhere near Mother either, I noticed.

Tagerri's body hissed and crackled like bacon, and made me hungry just thinking about it. Even when the war was over you couldn't get things like bacon unless you were rich or had connections to a black marketeer or you were a whore. I stood there watching a man burn, and all I could think of was lovely crisp bacon. His whole chest and stomach exploded out suddenly, I don't know why, trapped air and gases getting heated inside, perhaps, but it created a lot of muttering among the Yayomi. Wentzler explained, 'It isn't a good sign when the corpse ruptures like that. It suggests that his soul was still inside when the fire was set. Now everyone feels worried that Tagerri's spirit will haunt the shabono.'

'Tell them that if it does, I'll kill him all over again.'

'The best thing you can do is keep quiet. Maintain your presence here with silence, not threats and boasting. The Yayomi men are all braggarts, it's required of them, but they do have respect for the odd man who prefers to remain quiet.'

'Have you noticed that Waneeri's been looking at me a lot?'

'Waneeri is Tagerri's cousin. They were rather good friends too, as it happens. Don't worry, he won't challenge you over Tagerri's death. You're too powerful now, and he won't bother your family either, he's still scared of the demon inside Klaus's bag. But don't provoke him by staring back. Just ignore him.'

'What happens to Tagerri after he's just bones?'

'It's quite fascinating, actually. There'll be an extended chapter in my book about funeral practices.'

'But what happens?'

'You'll see.'

What I saw was this: Tagerri's bones were pulled out of the ashes when they were cool enough and put in a shallow wooden trough, then pounded with poles until they were nothing but grey powder. The powder was then tipped into a bowl of plantain soup, and all of Tagerri's family drank from it! I was relieved when the professor said I wouldn't have to drink any, that it was for close friends and kin only. Waneeri took an especially long swallow, and his eyes were on mine while he did it. I let the look pass, the way Wentzler had said to. It was late afternoon by then, and nobody had done anything that might be called work all day, no hunting or fishing or plantain gathering. Everything had stopped for Tagerri, so to speak. The fire kept smouldering, and the smell of his flesh was still heavy in the air.

When the last of the plantain soup was drunk, there wasn't much anyone could do, so I took Awomay's hand and we went for a stroll together. She was acting very strangely, not looking into my face for more than a few seconds at a time, and I wondered why. Wentzler had explained to me that Yayomi women were expected to be very submissive to their husbands and fathers, even their brothers, and to give them whatever they needed, when they needed it. That sounded like slavery to me. Mother had always given Father what he wanted for dinner, but if he got home late she'd yell at him

about his dinner going cold or getting overcooked and dry.
He took it all without a word, sometimes even apologised,
but that wasn't how a Yayomi man was supposed to act.

I decided then that I wouldn't behave like a Yayomi. Being
married to one of them didn't mean I was an Indian; I had no
intention of bossing Awomay around, or hitting her with a
stick if she didn't do something quickly enough, the way I'd
seen a lot of the men doing to their wives. I loved her, so I'd be
good to her, and she'd probably appreciate it and love me all
the more for being such a nice husband.

Wentzler hadn't given me any advice about being married
when I'd asked him. He'd just given me a wink and said he
thought I'd learned the most important part yesterday. He
didn't often make a joke, so I laughed when he said it. I was
liking him quite a bit more than I used to, probably because
Klaus had become something of a hermit, hiding away in the
jungle and dosing himself with medicine, and above all avoiding the problem with Mother and Manokwo. I didn't hate him
for that any more, but I'd lost most of my respect for him. I
suppose Wentzler was a kind of substitute father, now that
Klaus's marriage to Mother had turned into a shambles.

Awomay and I hid ourselves for the rest of the afternoon
and had our honeymoon. Like any other married couple
(except for Klaus and Mother) we made love a lot, although I
have to say that 'making love' is a silly way to put it. We fucked
all over the place in a little clearing in the jungle, just like
yesterday, only this time we took a lot longer doing it, then
doing it again, and before returning to the shabono near sundown, doing it again. We got up to so many tricks she lost one
of the little sticks that stuck out of the holes in her face.
When she realised it was gone, Awomay got very upset, and

kept a hand over the little hole in her face while she went around in circles looking for the stick. She found it again before it got too dark and stuck it in the little hole under her lip, then she smiled at me. It was like a white woman not wanting her husband to look at her until she had her makeup on. Her happiness at finding the stick again made me love her even more.

There were plenty of looks given us when we came through the hole in the wall, and some of the Yayomi shouted things at us that I think were pretty suggestive. Waneeri and his brothers and cousins, those who'd drunk Tagerri's powdered bones, didn't say anything, or even look at us. I ignored them. Awomay and I both ate like horses that evening, which caused more comments. Wentzler told me they didn't need translating.

The next day, Noroni, the man who'd had the vision of dolphins coming ashore, and who'd gone to find us that first day, the man who was now my father-in-law, did me the honour of painting me in red and black. It was some kind of official acceptance of me as a member of the tribe. Wentzler let me know that he'd been painted too, once, but it had taken almost a year of living with the Yayomi before they'd permitted it. He was letting me know how different, how speeded up, things were for me, but at the same time he was trying to tell me not to get too big a head about it all. He was the senior figure among the white men here, was his message to me, because Wentzler knew everything there was to know about living with the Yayomi, and I didn't, even if they were treating me like a favourite son. It was all perfectly clear and acceptable to me. Quite a bond was growing between us.

Noroni took his time painting me, and all the children watched as my white skin, even my face, was decorated with patches and lines and squiggles of black and red. Awomay stayed away while it was being done. I saw her bringing firewood in, and later some plantains, then she sat with the other women while they wove something or other. I would have preferred to spend my second day of marriage like the first, but apparently the Yayomi had very short honeymoons.

When the job was done I went to show Mother, and she actually spoke to me. She said, 'Erich, you shame me. Please, wash it off, all of it.'

'I can't, Mother, not without offending them. Noroni took a long time doing it. I'm going to skip bathing today, so it won't wash off.'

'Your father would be ashamed.'

'I don't think so,' I said. I meant it, too. I wasn't trying to start an argument.

'You shame me,' she said again, her voice sounding old and weary. I noticed some grey hairs among the blond on her head and was shocked. Mother was getting older by the day, it seemed. I put it down to everything she'd suffered since coming here. Her new marriage hadn't worked out at all, in fact, she despised her new husband, and on top of that, her younger son had been revealed as a hermaphrodite, and her older son was a painted savage with a wife of his own who wore little sticks in her face. It was more than she could stand. I appreciated the moment we shared that day, though, even if she used it to criticise me. It was better than having her ignore me by concentrating on her prayers.

I wondered what it was exactly that she was praying for, her lips moving, eyes shut tight. Whatever it was, it hadn't happened. We were still there, and everything – from Mother's point of view, anyway – was an impossible, horrible mess. She waited for God to fix it, and aged a little every day while she waited.

'Where is Klaus?' she asked.

'I don't know. He's been a bit sick lately, I think.'

Mother didn't seem concerned about that. 'Tell him his crimes have been noted.'

'What crimes are those, Mother? Crimes against the Jews? I don't think he sees that as a crime.'

'Crimes against his family. Taking his brother's wife in a mock marriage. Bringing us here to die among these awful people. I suppose they're people. Why have you become like them?'

'When in Rome, do as the Romans do,' I said, smiling.

'You fool. Little fool. Your soul is dying and you aren't even aware. That girl, that brown thing with the scarred face, she's destroying you, Erich.'

'They aren't scars, they're just little holes, and she isn't destroying me. She's very nice, really. Herr Wentzler told me that Awomay and all the other women wish you'd join them when they do their chores.'

It was a lie. He told me that the women regarded Mother as some kind of beached dolphin whose mind was being taken away a little at a time by the new dolphin growing inside her. They wanted nothing to do with her, and the only reason she hadn't been driven out of the shabono to do her mumbling elsewhere was because of me. Mother may have been a dolphin, but she was a lazy dolphin who wasted all the hours of daylight doing nothing when there was so very much for females, dolphin or human, to be doing. But I didn't want to tell her any of that.

'Keep them away from me,' she said. 'All of them, including Klaus. I won't let him touch me.'

'He hasn't tried to, Mother. Klaus keeps to himself nowadays.'

'The moment he touches me, he'll be punished.'

'Yes, Mother.'

'For everything he's done.'

'Of course.'

'Everything!'

'I have to go now, Mother.'

She turned away as if I'd already disappeared from sight. I waited a minute longer to see if she'd look up at me again, but she didn't. She just stared at nothing across the width of the shabono. By the end of that minute I'd lost a little of the sadness I usually felt for Mother. It was a bit of a shock to realise I was caring less and less for her as a human, let alone as my own mother.

I wondered what would happen if she was taken away to an asylum like Otto Fruenmeyer. Would she refuse to eat, and die of self-starvation the way they say he did? I could see her doing that. I doubted that I'd cry about it if she did, the way Frau Fruenmeyer had when she was told the bad news about Otto. Or would it be good news instead, to be told that Mother was dead? How could I even think like that? Since coming among the Yayomi I'd found that I could think about all kinds of things that would have made me ashamed before. Like the boy in Klaus's mirror, I wasn't me any more, and not only on the outside where all the red and black dye was.

On the inside I was someone else too, an older person. I wasn't ashamed to be that person, even if he looked at his mother and wondered about how he'd feel if she was taken away to die in an asylum, and knew that he wouldn't care all that much. Pieces of me were falling away, being lost. I didn't know if they were good pieces or bad pieces, or if their falling away was something that happened to everyone. What I did know was, when the last piece that used to be me had fallen away, the thing that was left, the Erich that remained, would still be me, only different. Better or worse, I couldn't say. In fact, I didn't care.

Now time began passing more quickly. Every morning I took Awomay into the jungle and we did it. To be honest, I think we did it more than she cared to, but she had to do it anyway because I was her husband. I didn't know much about how it was supposed to be done, or if I was doing it right, or what Awomay thought about it all. She seemed affectionate enough.

The Yayomi never kissed, as I said, but she did like to pat my head and pull on my blond hair. This was a bit irritating at first, but I got used to it. Usually we did it once each morning, then strolled back to the shabono. We saw other married couples doing this too, but all the couples ignored each other. Wentzler said this was their way of coping with private acts that couldn't be screened by walls. What they chose not to see wasn't there.

Every day I went out with Kwaytcha to learn more about handling the weapons he'd given me, and every day I got better. He didn't have much to say to me, but I could tell that his few words were to let me know I wasn't embarrassing him the way I used to. I actually began killing things, monkeys and some dark-feathered birds that lived on the ground, like skinny turkeys. They were good eating. I began catching fish with my pronged arrows, three or four a day sometimes. Everything that was caught, by me or by Kwaytcha or anyone else, was given over to the women for sharing out equally. A hunter gave his catch to his own wife or family, but they made sure that those families whose hunter hadn't managed to kill anything got just as much as them. I thought it was a very fair system, one that meant nobody went hungry.

Manokwo always got first choice of the food once it was cooked, because he was the chief, but that was due to simple respect, not fear. Manokwo himself was a pretty fair hunter, and usually brought home a monkey or something else good to eat. Before coming to Venezuela I had thought that a tribal chief was someone who sat around on a throne of bones and animal hides, giving orders, but Manokwo was nothing like that. As well as being a hunter like all the other men, he was actually a very good teller of jokes. Wentzler translated some of them for me, but they didn't make much sense, usually being about having sex with animals that were betraying their animal husbands.

I didn't think that was a very funny subject, especially considering the way the Yayomi treated women who betrayed their husbands, but Wentzler said it was normal to make fun of serious topics by making the characters animals instead of humans. I thought it was silly, and he said, 'You're not Yayomi, that's why.'

He was right, of course. I was never going to be one of them. I made no effort at all to learn the language. You didn't need words to hunt and fuck, and in any case, we were all going to sneak away when the rains came. Our second canoe sat where Tagerri had left it on the day he died, and nobody took over the job of shaping and hollowing out the log, probably for fear of catching a lightning bolt like he did. And I found out we didn't have a first canoe either, because

Waneeri took over Tagerri's own canoe, the one he was going to trade for my Iron Cross along with making me a second one. We'd have to buy two canoes when the time came, or else steal them.

The problem with Mother and Manokwo had been solved, thanks to Tagerri and the lightning bolt, but the problem of Mother herself hadn't. She hardly ate at all and was growing very thin, and her hair was turning a little greyer every day. It was Klaus who'd first persuaded her to go into the river and take off her clothes and bathe, but now that he was always off somewhere, she didn't bother, and her skin was soon as grey as her hair with smoke and grease and dirt. It was very depressing to see her that way, but when I tried to make her go to the river and wash herself, she hissed at me, hissed like a snake, the way the Yayomi did when they were angry. She hadn't used words for almost a week by then, except when talking with God.

Klaus. What to make of him? He was friendly enough, but he wouldn't learn to hunt or fish. I thought he went into hiding every morning because he was ashamed at the way he hadn't defended Mother when Manokwo wanted to take her from him. If he didn't want to be with the rest of us, I didn't care. It made me stronger than him, somehow. When I wanted company, I had Wentzler, who was ready to talk with me at any time about anything. Zeppi was available too, but his conversation was not worth listening to.

Manokwo paid attention to Zeppi now. Zeppi was going to be his wife after the rains, and he was waiting for the rest of his transformation from boy to girl to happen. Every other day or so Manokwo would beckon Zeppi over to him and squat down to look directly at his little cock and balls to see if they showed any sign yet of falling off or shrinking away to nothing, or folding themselves up into a vagina. His wife paid a lot of attention to Zeppi too, feeding him and letting him trail around after her like a little boy following his mother. She didn't seem at all jealous of him, and whenever Manokwo examined Zeppi's privates, she did too, and they both talked about it afterwards. It was funny to watch them with their faces close together right in front of Zeppi's cock, then later on looking puzzled and disappointed. Zeppi didn't seem to mind – in fact, he liked the attention, I think.

All in all, time was passing pleasantly enough. We had several more very loud thunderstorms like the one that killed Tagerri, and whenever they came along, everyone stayed inside the shabono. They always kept their faces turned away from me when there was thunder and lightning around, just to make sure I didn't take offence at their looking and strike them dead. That was funny too. What wasn't so funny was the way the floor of the shabono turned into a muddy mess. I asked Wentzler if this was the beginning of the rainy season and he said no, this was just normal rain. When the real rains came, he said, I'd see the difference and look back on today with a sentimental eye. I only half believed him.

Klaus came into the shabono late one afternoon, clutching his black bag, rain running off him in little waterfalls. He sat on his hammock and looked at me with something like panic in his eyes. I waited to see what he'd do next, but all he did was lie back and stare at the leaves above him. The shabono roof wasn't completely waterproof, and whenever it rained lots of people had to shift their hammocks to stay dry. Klaus's hammock was under a leak, but he didn't bother moving, just arranged his legs in a crooked and uncomfortable-looking position to allow the drops to pass between his knees.

I couldn't be sure if he was too lazy to shift the hammock or too concerned with whatever was on his mind to take the time. He lay there shuddering, and I started to wonder if he had a cold. That could be very bad for us. It was colds and other simple little sicknesses that wiped out the Indians after Columbus landed in the New World, as everyone knows. The Yayomi, even after all this time, might not be immune to cold germs, and if Klaus infected them they might start dying.

I went and stood beside him. His hammock ends were vibrating like violin strings with his shivering, and now he was covered in sweat, not rain. He looked up at me, then shut his eyes, then opened them again, and his eyeballs started dancing around in his face like one of those little games where the ball bearing bounces around from one side of a little flat box to the other while you try to steer it into a tiny hole to win. If the Yayomi caught something and started dying, we'd be blamed.

'Klaus? Klaus, what's the matter with you?'

He didn't say anything, only lay there shivering and swivelling his eyeballs.

I hurried over to Wentzler. 'Something's wrong with Klaus.'

'Yes?'

'He's shivering. I think he's caught a fever or a cold or something.'

'Klaus has caught nothing. He gave it to himself.'

'Gave what? What do you mean, to himself?'

'These are symptoms of withdrawal. He'll be like this for some time, I'm afraid.'

'But what is it?'

'Klaus is addicted to morphine, I regret to tell you.'

'Morphine?'

'You've surely heard of it. Doctors have ready access to such things. Klaus has been addicted for some time. He told me so himself.'

'But why?'

'Why are some men drunkards and others whore chasers? I have no answer for you, Erich. His supply has run out, that's all, and now he must cope with the results of withdrawal from his drug. It won't be pretty to watch.'

'So it isn't a sickness, with germs?'

'You won't catch it, and nobody else will either.'

'Morphine, that's what they give wounded soldiers, isn't it?'

'That is its intended use, yes, to conquer pain. Klaus has used it unwisely, to make his thoughts and memories more bearable, I suspect. You've noticed the marks on his inner arm?'

'Sort of.'

'Injections, self-administered.'

'I saw him once, injecting himself. I thought he was sick . . .'

'And so he is, very sick indeed, but not contagious.'

I saw Klaus suddenly begin thrashing about in his hammock, so violently that he spun himself right out of it and onto the muddy ground. He lay still for a moment, then his arms and legs began punching and kicking at the air and his heels drummed on the ground uncontrollably.

'Typical symptoms, from what I've heard,' said Wentzler. 'He warned me it would be coming soon. Shall we go and pick him up?'

Klaus was still thrashing around in the mud, making such a windmill of his limbs that we couldn't get close enough to lift him until he exhausted himself ten minutes or so later.

Then we placed him in his hammock, and he started shivering all over again, with his hands clutching and unclutching at nothing. His head thrashed from side to side like a painted clown head in a carnival inviting you to throw a ball into its mouth.

Zeppi came over and asked, 'What's wrong?'

'Uncle Klaus isn't very well. Herr Wentzler and I are looking after him.'

'But why is he doing that?'

'Because he can't help it. Go away and keep Mother company.'

'She won't talk to me.'

'Well, I'm sorry, but you can't help here.'

He waited a little longer, watching Klaus jerk around like a puppet with tangled strings, then went away. Wentzler and I stood on either side of Klaus to stop him from falling out again. Other people were coming over, fascinated by his twitchings and moanings. Noroni came closer than the rest, and spoke with Wentzler.

'He asked if there's a demon inside our friend. I told him no. If I said yes, Noroni would do a dance of healing, and Klaus doesn't need smoke blown over him and a lot of chanting and carrying-on. I told Noroni that when a dolphin mother is growing a baby inside her, the husband is the one who feels the pain as it gets bigger. He believes me. We already told him Klaus wasn't able to make love because the original insemination was so painful, and now we have him suffering some more through the pregnancy. Noroni says he knows now why there are so few dolphins in the river.'

It was a clever story, building on the nonsense we'd already told the Yayomi, and I had to admire Wentzler for his quick mind. We really were very much alike when it came to spinning yarns that explained things the Yayomi couldn't possibly understand. Klaus was quiet for the moment, and more Yayomi came closer.

While we waited for the next convulsion, Wentzler explained, 'For these people there's no such thing as a natural illness. If anyone becomes sick, they are considered the victim of a spell cast by an enemy, and the business of casting out the spell's demon is a very noisy affair, believe me. It can go on for days, and if the victim dies, as they usually do, then the task becomes one of vengeance. It has to be determined which among the neighbouring shabonos is responsible, and who specifically in that shabono. There's always someone who might have had bad feelings toward the victim for one reason or another, no matter how trivial, and once the identity of that person is decided upon by the shaman – in the case of this shabono, it's Noroni – he or she must be killed, or at the very least, someone else from that shabono must be killed to atone for the death here. Then that shabono is obligated, at some time or another, to raid this shabono in retaliation for that killing.'

'How stupid it all is.'

'From our perspective, yes. From their perspective, no.'

'But it just goes back and forth, the killing, for no good reason.'

'And what was the reason for the recent war you and Klaus have told me about?'

'The Jews,' I said. 'They were responsible.'

'Yes? And what was it that they did to warrant killing so many? I have it right, don't I? Hasn't Klaus admitted to herding Jews together like cattle and slaughtering them by the tens of thousands, or was it the hundreds of thousands?'

'They were poisoning our society,' I told him. 'That's what everyone said.'

'That's what the Noronis of Germany said, perhaps, and quite possibly they even believed it, but you and I know that the Noronis here assign blame for all kinds of things in absolute ignorance, isn't that so?'

'But that's here. In Europe it's different.'

'You think so?'

'Herr Professor, you don't talk like a German at all.'

'Oh, I'm a German, all right. Maybe not such a German as our shivering friend here, but most definitely a German. The family tree has been carefully cultivated, its many branches documented over four hundred years. My father and grand-father always insisted on teaching me how far back the Wentzlers have extended. Oh, yes, they were very proud to be German, and so am I. You mustn't think, Erich, that a dissent-ing squawk among the cawing of a million crows is the voice of the enemy. There are differing opinions in any society, whether that society puts its faith in blowpipes or artillery. And I still don't have my answer. What did they do, all those Jews, that was so bad they had to be exterminated in such numbers?'

I thought about it, but couldn't come up with an answer that would have satisfied someone as clever as Wentzler, so I said, 'When Klaus gets better, he'll tell you.'

'Very good. If anyone should know the answer, it'll be people like him, the ones who did the killing, am I right?'

'Yes,' I said, not sure if he was or not.

He just smiled at me in a peculiar way. I think Wentzler liked me, but he wasn't about to let me think I was anywhere near as smart as him. He was annoying that way.

Klaus came to life again and we had to hold him inside the netting of his hammock while he thrashed about the same as before. His knuckles hit me on the nose accidentally, and I wanted to punch him right back, but didn't, because he wasn't even aware of it. He wasn't aware of anything except whatever was inside him, gnawing at him like a hungry rat. He did this several times more as the sun lowered itself and the rain finally stopped.

I looked at him shivering and trembling next to me. Klaus was a drug addict, something I'd heard about but never expected to see for myself, especially in the family. Now I was glad he wasn't really married to Mother. Drug addicts were filthy creatures, so I'd been told, moral degenerates who thought about nothing but their dirty drugs. I'd always pictured them as small and pale-skinned, living in cellars and darkened rooms, never seeing the sun, not really human at all, but Klaus didn't look like that, at least not until he'd run out of morphine. It just went to show that the things you're told aren't always true. Klaus was tall and handsome and suntanned, not some slobbering drug-addicted dwarf. But how could anything about him be believed after this? In fact, how could I believe anything about anything?

For five days Klaus lived through his own private hell. The Yayomi soon got bored with his moaning and yelling and flailing around, and ignored him. Wentzler and I fed him a tiny portion of food and a lot of water every day. He shat himself twice and pissed all over himself more times than I can remember. We cleaned him up each time and waited for it to happen again. Sometimes he was able to get up from his hammock and walk about the shabono, but he looked like a living skeleton, he'd lost so much weight, and his eyes had sunk so far back into his face they looked like little blue marbles hiding there. He hardly ever spoke, only staggered around in circles for a while then went back to his hammock. By the sixth day he was sleeping for longer periods and we could relax a bit. Wentzler said the worst appeared to be over, but Klaus's health would be fragile for some time yet, and we'd have to keep watch over him until he was better.

'You seem to know a lot about it,' I said. 'Do you have medical experience?'

'An acquaintance of mine was going to be a doctor. While he was in training he stupidly picked up the habit of morphine. He got away with it for a year, then was caught. The hospital didn't want to make a fuss with the authorities, so they handed him over to the family and told them to keep their mouths shut. My friend went through exactly what your uncle has experienced, but at least he had clean sheets under him every day. I'm told it always happens like this, the breaking of the chemical bond. It's quite pathetic, really. I was glad about one thing, though.'

'What was that?'

'I was in love with my friend's fiancee, and I wanted her to see him for the weakling and fool that he was, so I invited her to visit and see for herself what a drug addict looks like during the withdrawal phase. It was a mistake, as it turned out.'

'Why?'

'The silly girl felt sorry for him instead of being disgusted and turning to me for comfort. She went ahead and married him once he was well again. Never try to manipulate the feelings of others, Erich, especially in the name of love.'

'Were they happy?'

'I have no idea. I buried myself in my studies and did my best to forget my friend and his wife. I wonder how they fared in the war.'

'Where did they live?'

'Berlin.'

'Then they might be dead. All the bombing.'

'I suppose I'll find out all about them, and my own family, when I get back.'

On the seventh day, Klaus opened his eyes and for once didn't have the look of a hunted animal. He saw me and said, 'Erich, good morning.'

'It's afternoon.'

'Is it? God, I feel weak as a kitten . . . and thirsty! Be a good lad and get me some water, would you?'

I fetched some for him and he drank it down like a man dying of thirst, then belched loudly. 'Excuse me. Have I been sick?'

'Yes, very.'

'For how long?'

'A week. Are you hungry?'

'Not yet, my stomach's in knots. Has anything happened while I was sick?'

'A search plane came. I waved at them and they dropped a message. A rescue party's going to come by boat and pick us up.'

He sat up so fast he almost fell out of his hammock. 'My God, really . . .? How marvellous! How soon will they be here? Was it a Zamex plane?'

'I thought so at first, then I saw it was just a big bird, a heron, I think.'

'A heron . . .? So . . . there won't be a rescue party?'

'No.'

He slumped back into his hammock. 'Why are you teasing me, Erich? That was unkind, a vicious little trick to play on me. Why?'

'I felt like it.'

He looked at me. 'You're painted like a savage.'

'This is the second time. The first lot washed off in the river after a while. Noroni painted me again yesterday. He says he'll tattoo my face if I want.'

'Don't be ridiculous. When we get out of here you'll have a hard time explaining away a tattooed face. You'd be laughed at everywhere you went.'

'I think I'll have it done, though.'

I wanted to make him angry, so I could get angry back at him.

'How long have you been a drug addict, Uncle?'

'I'm not your uncle now, I'm your stepfather. Well, perhaps I'm also your uncle still, but . . .'

'You're not my stepfather. You married Mother under the name of Brandt. You aren't a Brandt, you're a Linden. You're Uncle Klaus Linden.'

'Why are you making such a fuss over minor legalities? Stop it. Stop calling me Uncle. Where is everyone else? Where's Helga?'

'Mother left a few minutes ago. I think she's gone to the river to wash. I hope so. She hasn't been for a long time. She was getting very smelly. Then again, maybe she went to take a shit.'

'Don't talk that way about your mother!'

'She doesn't hear me. She only hears God. How long were you taking it, the morphine?'

'None of your business. It's over and done with now, anyway.'

'You ran out, that's why.'

'Has something happened while I was sick? You're not yourself. This isn't the Erich I knew. Explain yourself.'

'I don't have to tell you anything.'

I walked away. Let someone else listen to him, I couldn't be bothered.

Wentzler saw me passing by. 'How is he, awake?'

'Yes. I don't want to talk to him.'

I left the shabono and went to the river. Mother wasn't there, and it occurred to me that I hadn't seen Zeppi in quite a while either. I started wandering along the river bank, not especially worried about either of them. I just wanted to be away from Klaus, now that he was himself again. I still wanted to blame him for what had happened to Mother, even though I had to admit to myself that the madness might have happened in any case.

Maybe Sigmund Freud would know the answer to that. Of course, he was a Jew and couldn't be trusted. He was dead, anyway. Father had read the news of his death out loud from the newspaper and said good riddance to a Jew who thought every daughter lusted for her father and every son lusted for his mother. Only a filthy Jew would think that way, he'd said. I couldn't recall ever having lusted for Mother, even after seeing her naked. It made me feel a bit sick even to think about it, frankly, which only goes to show what a lot of rubbish Freud must have written.

I was walking past the canoes and out along the bank. A short distance on, I saw a few drops of blood on the ground. I didn't think anything about it until, after another twenty or thirty metres, I saw some more.

I kept walking, wondering if someone was carrying some game they'd killed and was leaving a trail. The next splash I saw was so fresh it still glistened in a shaft of sunlight, so whatever was bleeding was being taken away from the shabono, not toward it. So it wasn't food. All kills were taken straight to the rest of the tribe for sharing out. Was someone hurt? Was it human blood, not animal? But why would some-one who was injured be going away from the shabono instead of toward it, where they could get attention?

More blood. Whoever it was, they were following the river bank, just like me. Could it be that some intruder from another shabono further inland had kidnapped one of the Yayomi women and was dragging her home with him? I'd been told about raiding parties that made sneak attacks to take women. I hadn't seen any sign of a struggle, but that didn't mean anything, because time and again Kwaytcha had shown that he could see things on the jungle floor, tracks and so forth, that were completely invisible to me.

Now I was a little frightened. How many of them might there be? I'd heard of raiding parties a dozen or more strong, and although they tried not to hurt the women, since that's who they came for, they liked to kill or injure men as part of the fun. Should I go any further and risk catching up with them, or should I run back to the shabono and alert the tribe? I stopped dead, undecided, knowing only that what I'd dis-covered was important, too important to keep to myself. The local Yayomi were my people now, in a way, and I had a responsibility to help protect them from other Yayomi – or even worse, the Iriri! – marauding into their territory. They might have kidnapped Awomay! This might be her blood! I felt a wave of rage sweep over me, but it wasn't strong enough to make me go charging ahead to catch them. I didn't have my weapons with me for one thing, and for another, what could one man do against many? And I still wasn't positive that I was reading the signs correctly.

I decided to go on a little further, to see if there was any indication, footprints or something else, that would let me know I wasn't imagining things. I had respect in the shabono, and it would easily be lost if I came running in, yelling about invaders and kidnappers that weren't even there. I went on, heart hammering inside my chest. And saw Mother.

She was standing with her feet in the river, her back toward me. I stopped and watched as she dragged her toes back and forth in the shallows. It made her look very young, like a little girl again. But she was no girl, because flowing down the insides of her legs was blood. It didn't alarm me to see the blood there. This was the blood I'd been following, and it wasn't from a wound. Mother was having her monthlies, and even though she'd never taken to daily bathing like everyone else, she obviously couldn't put up with fresh blood trickling down her legs, and so she'd come to a private place, away from the usual bathing spots, to clean herself. It was a sensible thing to do, and it made me wonder exactly how mad she really was.

I didn't want to move for fear of letting her know I was there, so I stayed perfectly still and watched as she began wading out into deeper water. Two huge dragonflies, one blue and one silver-green, were buzzing in circles around her as she waded out until her hips were beneath the surface. Her hands went down out of sight to clean herself, and the dragonflies continued to circle like tiny coloured planes around and around, as if she was so wonderful a sight they couldn't leave.

Watching her, I realised I still loved Mother in spite of

everything. I hated the way she behaved, and the way she talked, when she *did* talk, but those irritating things meant nothing next to the fact that she was my mother, crazy or not, and I owed her my love, or at least a part of it. How do you know how much to love someone when they change from one day to the next, from a loving mother to a complaining hag? But she looked like my mother again out there in the river, her shoulders moving slightly as she scrubbed gently at herself underwater. I expected to see blood rising up around her on the surface, but couldn't see any. Her hair hung in limp curls, and below the hair her back moved a little, this way and that. A kind of peace came over me, as if the hands that touched her were also comforting me in a kindly way. Everything would be all right for Mother once we stole the canoes and paddled off through sheets of falling rain that would wash away the past and leave all of us new and clean again.

The dragonflies suddenly streaked for shore.

Mother's back went rigid, then she screamed. It was an awful sound, like the sound made by horses in the slaughter- house back home as the hammer came smashing down between their eyes. Mother's scream rose from the pit of her stomach and came rushing from her upturned mouth like a jet of foam, boiling and jagged and ear-splitting, loud enough to reach the stratosphere. The water around her waist was seething with movement that couldn't have come from her own hands, a frothing and churning that quickly turned pink, then red. I watched with open mouth and eyes that under- stood nothing as Mother rose out of the water, rose straight up into the air until I could see the crease of her bottom and the flashing silver-grey skirt that seemed to start there, a ballerina skirt of leaping fish, then she sank down again as the fish, a shining mass of them now, thrashed and darted and flung themselves at her buttocks and thighs, biting and tearing in a frenzy of hunger, flesh eaters maddened by blood, the ones Wentzler had warned me about, the boiling cloud of razors called piranha.

Her scream ended suddenly, and Mother sank deeper into the water, up to her shoulders, up to her neck. The fish milled around her in a pinkish haze of movement, until her blond hair, stained with pink froth, sank from sight, and the waters were still again.

NINE

I WAS FALLING INTO a bowl of leaves. The bowl of leaves was the shabono roof, and I was staring up into it, not falling. I was in my hammock. Klaus's face came into view above me like the prow of a ship about to run me down. His nostrils looked like the holes in the bows that lead to the chain locker. He opened his lips and words fell down one after the other like an anchor and chain, rattling and clanking from one word to the next, smashing into my face, driving me back underwater.

'Where is she, Erich? Where's Helga?'

I tried to talk, but couldn't. Words were rising from my belly, crawling up through my gut pipes, crowding together in my throat. My lips were forced apart by them, and the words escaped. 'Gone ... fish ...'

'What do you mean, gone fishing? That's absurd. Think, Erich. They found you by the river. Helga has disappeared. The Indians are saying there was blood along the bank. What happened?'

'The fish . . .'

'What fish? What about them?'

'Piranha . . .'

'Don't be foolish. The blood was on the bank. Piranha don't leave the water.'

'She was . . . bleeding.'

'From what, a wound? What wound? How could she be wounded?'

I swallowed a few times. The words were coming up easier now. 'From . . . bleeding from . . . herself.'

'You're not making sense. Were you hurt? They found you lying on the ground, unconscious. What do you remember, Erich? This is important.'

'She's dead . . . They ate her.'

'Pardon me?'

'Piranha. She was having her . . . you know, *bleeding* . . . and they attacked her.'

He stared at me, then his face withdrew and was replaced by Wentzler's.

'Erich, this is true? You saw it?'

'I saw it . . .'

'You've been in some kind of comatose state, Klaus tells me. No bruises, just . . . unconscious. Do you want some water?'

'Please.'

He fetched me some and helped me to sit up and drink it. Klaus was nearby, looking at me as if I was to blame.

'Erich, some of the Yayomi are saying you followed your mother and killed her. Dozens of them heard her scream.'

'It was the piranha. I *saw* it.'

'And I believe you. It's just that piranha aren't usually found in these waters.'

'There were hundreds . . . It only took a minute . . .'

'I'll tell them something they'll want to believe.'

'Tell them the truth! They might be attacked too.'

'Yayomi truth, Erich, is whatever they choose to accept. Trust me, please.'

He went away, and Klaus came over. 'All right, I can believe you now. My God . . . to die that way . . . Did she suffer long?'

'Less than a minute, a lot less, I think. It's hard to say . . .'

'My God, my God . . . and they want to blame you.'

'But that's so stupid. Why would they think that?'

'It's Waneeri. He's the one who found you. He says there were signs of a struggle on the bank.'

'He's lying. He hates me.'

'Wentzler has been trying to cast doubt on his story, but there was nothing he could say until you woke up. What happened – to you, I mean?'

'I don't know. I saw Mother . . . and then I was here.'

'That's all you can recall?'

I wanted Klaus to go away and stop looking at me. I wanted to see him go away and cry for Mother. That way I might be able to forgive him a little for not loving her enough. He shook his head. 'This place, what a pit. Nothing but bad luck. Do you want me to tell Zeppi?'

'I'll tell him. Where is he?'

'With his friends. He has quite an entourage following him around these days.'

Klaus wasn't shocked enough or sad enough over Mother. Had he ever really loved her? Why bring us across the ocean if he hadn't? Did he fall out of love with her when she wouldn't go into the jungle with him and be his wife? I couldn't ask him. You can only ask personal questions of someone you like. And then there was my own behaviour, my own failure to do what was right. Instead of watching Mother bathe, I should have remembered what Wentzler told me about going into the river with a wound. I should have screamed at her, 'Get out! Get out before they come for you!' But I didn't. I'd forgotten. And she died a horrible death because of it.

Wentzler returned and said, 'I've told them that your mother felt her baby coming and went to the river to give birth. That accounts for the blood. You were with her when she went into the water, and you saw the baby come out, then both of them, mother and baby, swam away. Before she left, your mother told you they'd be back after the rains, then she made you fall fast asleep, because you wanted to go with them, but she insisted that you stay here with your father and Zeppi to make sure everything goes as planned, by which I mean your story about Zeppi turning into a girl after the rains and marrying Manokwo.'

'That should keep them happy,' said Klaus. 'The more ridiculous the story, the more they're willing to accept it. These people are so gullible it's pathetic.'

Wentzler ignored him. 'Try not to act heartbroken, Erich. Everyone will be watching. A son whose mother has gone away should be sad, but not too sad, because she'll be coming back. If they catch you moping they'll suspect something is wrong. If they get wind of the fact that Frau Brandt is dead, they'll suspect that all of you are merely human.'

'Don't forget the way I killed Tagerri.'

'That story improves with the telling. A few days ago I heard one of the women tell another that you and Awomay are going to make a baby with fins and a long nose, a dolphin baby, but it won't be able to strike anyone down with lightning because

Awomay is only a girl, not a dolphin, so the son – they automatically assume it'll be a son – won't have the same powers as the father. He'll be a remarkable swimmer, though.'

Klaus snorted. Wentzler looked at him and said, 'Herr Brandt, I assume you'll be able to mask your sorrow over the death of your wife?'

'Are you being funny, Wentzler?'

'Not at all. She'll be coming back with your new baby in time for Zeppi's wedding, so you mustn't miss her too much. And now that her baby's been born, it coincides perfectly with the end to your own ... illness, the illness you had while your wife was pregnant, remember? The Yayomi have been told that's how it is with dolphin marriages and birthing.'

'I know what they think. We don't need to go over and over these idiotic lies. I'm surprised you're so willing to heap all these untruths onto your native friends, Wentzler. I rather thought you admired them, yet here you are telling them one outrageous lie after another.'

'It's necessary. I thought you understood that.'

'A lie is still a lie, in my opinion. Still, if you can live with it, so can I.'

'So glad to have your cooperation.'

I thought they were going to have a real argument, something that would end in a brawl, but they chose to ignore each other instead, and soon Klaus went away.

'Where's Awomay?' I asked. 'She should be here.' I was a bit upset that she hadn't come anywhere near me.

'Don't forget, everyone has heard Waneeri's story about how you killed your mother. She's staying away until it's been accepted by Manokwo that you didn't. They're all discussing my story – my lies, as Klaus would have it – as we speak.'

'I forgot about the blood. I should have shouted something, made her get out of the water, but I forgot ...'

'Blaming yourself won't help anyone, least of all her.'

He was right, I suppose, but I blamed myself anyway. Then something occurred to me. 'It was Waneeri who found me?'

'Yes.'

'Why was he there, in that spot?'

'Perhaps he was the closest when her screaming was heard.'

'I'll bet he was following me. He wants to kill me for killing Tagerri.'

'He could have killed you when he found you unconscious, if he'd wanted to. Of course, that generally isn't the way a Yayomi would kill a man. Too cowardly. I don't doubt that Waneeri may have been following you, though. You'll need to watch out for him from now on.'

'Who carried me back here?'

'Kwaytcha and Noroni carried you between them. They're your family too now.'

He searched my face for a moment. 'Erich, you've seen your mother die. Are you ... are you all right? What I mean to say is, will you be able to carry on as if she has simply gone away for a while? You realise how important this is.'

'I can do it.'

'My grandmother used to say, "Cope now, cry later."'

'I don't need to cry.'

'If you say so.'

'And I don't need to be lying here like a sick person.'

I got out of my hammock and went looking for Awomay. I found her with the other women, all talking nonstop, presumably about Mother and me. They shut up when I came closer, which was not very bright of them, since I couldn't

understand the language anyhow. Awomay saw the look on
my face and came to me, but when she was standing right in
front of me I didn't want to be near her, so I turned away,
walked across the shabono and went out through the hole.

I wanted to be alone, to think about everything that had
happened today, and to store it all away somewhere deep
inside myself, where it wouldn't get in the way of whatever
might happen next. Everything was happening so quickly. I
was having to shed memories and emotions, lighten the load
I had to carry in my head, just to keep up with events. Cope
now, cry later.

I was walking in no particular direction, and a few minutes
later found Zeppi and his friends. They'd obviously spent all
day in each other's company and didn't know anything about
what had happened. All four were lying in the sun on the
river bank. Zeppi's monkey let out a screech as I came closer.
They weren't doing anything, just lying there, the head of one
on the stomach of the nearest, the way Yayomi children often
lazed around together, but their eyes were wary as I
approached. Maybe there was something in my face that let
them know I wasn't happy.

Zeppi got up on one elbow. 'Hello,' he said, smiling.

I stopped beside him. 'Have you been enjoying yourself,
Zeppi?'

'We went for a swim. Mitzi ran up and down on shore,
making such a fuss. She wanted to come with us, but monkeys don't like water. It was so funny.'

'I have some awful news.'

'What news?'

'Mother's dead.'

I couldn't help myself. I hadn't wanted it to come out that

way, but seeing him with his friends, without a care in the world, made me angry. Zeppi's face creased a little as he tried to understand.

'No she isn't . . . Stop it . . .'

'She's dead,' I repeated, but then common sense made me pause. There was no point in telling him how she died. Knowing Zeppi, he'd have nightmares about it, and in any case, we had to keep the Yayomi thinking she'd only gone away, not died. If Zeppi got hysterical, they might be suspicious. 'Dead to us, that is.'

'What do you mean? Stop saying that . . .'

'What I mean is that Mother has decided to go away. You know how strange she's been acting lately, well, she decided to get on a floating log and go away downriver to see if she could find some white people to rescue us. So she's gone.'

'Gone away? Did Klaus go too?'

'No, Klaus stayed here.'

'But why did she go?'

'Didn't I just tell you? Mother was a little crazy, and she thought she could find white people downriver, so she left. On a floating log.'

'Will she find some?'

It was typical of him to ask such a nonsensical question, but I was beginning to feel sorry for him, and already regretted most of what I'd said. 'Who knows? She may be lucky, she may not.' I was spinning lies to my brother, telling him stories calculated to jibe with what he might believe in his babyish mind. He couldn't have coped with the thought of Mother being devoured by fish with razor teeth, so I told him a lie he could live with, in the same way that Wentzler was obliged to spin fairy tales about us to the Yayomi – to keep them happy.

That was what I told myself, but maybe my explanation was simply another lie, one I tried to fool myself with. I didn't want to think about it any more. I started walking away.

'When will she get back?' Zeppi called after me.

'How would I know?' I flung over my shoulder.

'Did she say goodbye?'

I turned and yelled, 'What do you think?' then turned again and kept going. The sun was low in the sky by then, sinking toward the treetops. Today had been the worst day of my life, by anyone's standards, and yet I was on my feet, not lying in my hammock weeping about it. The old Erich couldn't have done that. The old Erich was as dead as Mother. The new Erich walked into the future one step at a time, knowing nothing, fearing plenty, wondering and planning, aware that at any moment the ground might swallow him up and turn all wondering and every plan into ashes and dust. The new Erich didn't even care about that the way he should have, wasn't surprised that he didn't care.

Still some distance from the shabono, I saw Awomay coming to meet me. She waited on the path as I came closer. I couldn't read her face. Maybe she wanted to let me know she was sorry for not having tended to me while I was unconscious, instead of leaving that job to Klaus and Wentzler. It didn't matter, because I didn't care. When I got close enough I took her arm and steered her off the path, into the jungle, deeper and deeper, then stopped and pushed her shoulders forward until she bent over, and I had her. When we were done she still wore the same expression on her face, and I felt that nothing had changed in the last five minutes. I don't know why I thought fucking would change anything, but then again, I didn't care.

*

After the evening meal I joined Wentzler and Klaus. They didn't like each other, but they were both white men among brown people, so it was only natural that they should drift together anyway. Klaus talked about how he missed cigarettes; he wouldn't touch the native tobacco no matter how much he wanted nicotine. The stuff the Yayomi had wasn't smoked, it was wedged under the lower lip and left there to get filled with saliva and spat out as tobacco juice. Most of the men and older boys sucked on a tobacco wad when they felt like it, even some of the women. I was glad Awomay didn't have a craving for it like her father. Noroni was always dribbling and spitting. It was disgusting.

Klaus droned on and on about cigarettes, and how he could never get his favourites, Balkan Sobranies, after 1943. Wentzler and I got bored listening to him talk about such trivial stuff on the evening of the day his wife had died. There was something wrong with such a topic after Mother's awful death, and I decided to shut him up by asking him the same question Wentzler had asked me.

'Klaus!' I said. He was taken aback by my tone. 'What exactly was it that the Jews did again?'

'What do you mean? They did so many things.'

'What, exactly? Don't tell me about them killing Christ. Jesus was a Jew.'

'The ancient arguments against them are irrelevant, I agree. The modern Jew is no less an abomination, however.'

'And why is that?' asked Wentzler.

'You don't know?' Klaus seemed amazed, then he said, 'Of course, you've been tremendously isolated here.'

'The Jews I knew,' said Wentzler, 'they didn't seem so bad.

What's the difference, a peeled penis? Zeppi and Erich have that. There must be something more.'

Klaus shook his head at our ignorance. 'A couple of children,' he said. 'Very well, class, pay attention. A line must be drawn under the Jews, their existence snuffed out, every one. Then the rest of us can breathe clean air again.' He paused, already losing the thread of his argument. 'God's chosen people,' he sneered, 'what a laugh! For the last few years of the war there was a river of Jews flowing from everywhere to nowhere, an avalanche of Jews. No one can say it was easy work ridding ourselves of them that way, and the work was never completed, sad to say, but my God, we shifted a lot of them, an incredible number, entire families, entire neighbourhoods and villages and districts, a world of Jews on the march with their pathetic belongings, a suitcase army.'

He paused, remembering, and enjoying the memory. 'They were like bewildered cattle when they came spilling from the railway cars. Blinking stupidly, following orders. This way, that way, the living and the dead and the soon-to-be-dead. Scarecrows in the end, nothing but walking cadavers, really. Useless, utterly useless, more like shadows than men. And still they made work for us, making us pick them up on the end of a shovel to be flung into the great beyond, swallowed by fire for a clean removal of their every filthy atom. Did I tell you we had three furnaces operating day and night? Shadrach, Meshach and Abednego, we called them, and God didn't protect any Israelites inside those burning walls, let me assure you.'

I looked at Wentzler, but he was looking into the flames of our fire. I thought he hadn't even been listening, but then he said to Klaus, 'So many? You aren't exaggerating even a little?'

'My dear Wentzler, one couldn't exaggerate what happened. It would take a Dante to describe the hellishness of it, the never-ending grind of getting rid of them. It was like taking a swatter to rid yourself of a roomful of flies, swatting this way, swatting that way, until in desperation you hit upon a plan, the perfect plan that will kill them all, methodically and cheaply, with a minimum of fuss. You set fire to the room. But then you need to sweep up the ashes. Really, there's no easy way to accomplish a task so great.'

'And you yourself, Klaus, you took part in this slaughter?'

'Certainly. It was my duty as a German and as a National Socialist.'

'But as a doctor, surely your oath never to do harm would have prevented you from taking part?'

'Where's the harm in killing Jews? The real harm lies in *not* killing them. They've been a crawling plague on the planet for too long. The Führer had the courage to call a halt to their plans, the stock manipulations and all manner of swindling practices they'd developed expertise in. They've been stopped in their tracks, even if unacceptable numbers of them still remain. Mark my words, they'll be regrouping for a generation or two, planning a return to their former position of influence, but, gentlemen, so will we.'

His voice was different now, taut with excitement. 'In Argentina there are men, good men, making preparations of their own for a Fourth Reich, I have it on the highest authority. Though we may be scattered and hunted for the time being, each of us knows another, who knows another, and so on, a vast web of contacts scattered far and wide, waiting for the right moment to proclaim ourselves. We'll be liberated from the outer darkness on that day and will never stand in the shadows again. Erich, yours may be the generation to bring back greatness to the Aryan world. It's been a glorious beginning, but the work is far from over. Are you up to the challenge, Erich? I married your mother so I could bring you under my wing. We haven't spoken of this, but I've always admired your spirit, your intelligence, the very qualities of Aryanness you possess so casually, so naturally.'

His face was shining now. 'Think about it, Erich, and you'll come to the same conclusion I have – it's your destiny to carry on the great struggle against the Jews. Too grand a word? I don't think so. A place is being prepared for you, my boy. Your credentials are impeccable. Hero father decorated by the Führer himself, mother lost in tragic circumstances, uncle on record as having assisted mightily in the great work of exter-mination. That Iron Cross hangs about your neck like an amulet, a holy relic of the war against the Semites. The rest of the uniform is yours if you care to wear it, Erich. The fit will be perfect!'

Wentzler interrupted. 'In your capacity as a man of healing, Klaus, did you at any time administer medical treatment to a Jew? I don't ask this to embarrass you, just out of curiosity.'

'I take the question as it was intended. Yes, I gave medical treatment to many Jews under my care at the camp. There was one, a skinny fellow even among a society of skinny fel-lows, and he had cancer of the bone in his arm, horribly disfiguring. I gave him a new arm. Yes, you heard correctly, a new arm. Not a word of thanks for my efforts, naturally.'

'A new arm? I think this isn't possible, not unless there have been incredible developments in surgery since I've been away.'

'The incredible developments, Gerhard, were mine to cre-ate, and I took the opportunity to do so. I removed the bad arm and immediately took a healthy arm to graft onto the stump. It was work of fantastic complexity, all the nerve endings and blood vessels, you know, but after more than seven hours it was done. To my knowledge, no one before or since has attempted such a thing.'

'Did it work?' I asked.

'Certainly, for a time, then it began to rot. The work was simply too fine, too detailed to be achieved successfully with current instruments and procedures, but I do hold out hope for the future development of similar surgeries. The field is brand-new, and early accomplishments will be elusive.'

'The healthy arm you replaced the diseased arm with,' said Wentzler, 'was that also a Jewish arm?'

'How could it be otherwise? Jews and only Jews were my subjects.'

'It came from the body of a deceased Jew?'

'What use would a dead arm be to me? It came from a living Jew, a comparatively healthy specimen. I wanted to give the patient every chance, and a fresh arm, if I may put it so crudely, was essential for the success of the operation.'

Even by firelight I could see the enthusiasm in his face, the light burning in his eyes. He wanted me to congratulate him, thank him for starting the great extermination, wanted me to pledge myself to carrying on the good work he'd begun. I could think of no words to say. I could only stare at him. Klaus was like a statue that depicts everything noble and great, a beautiful man of bronze with eyes fixed on the distant horizon, seeking challenges there to overcome. But inside, the statue is hollow, and stirring there in the darkness is a terrible creature, a worm that must have blood, and more blood, or it ceases to thrive. Klaus's worm had grown fat and repulsive inside him.

He went on, 'We began with a general cleansing of the European genetic pattern, which involved ridding ourselves of mental defectives and those with gross physical deformations. What kind of children would they have had? Far better to do away with such aberrations, to avoid the possibility of breeding, or simply to improve the view for the rest of us, don't you think? Would you take pleasure in walking down the street and seeing something grotesque? No, it would make you uncomfortable, a perfectly normal reaction to physical deformity.'

'What about people with big ears that stick out,' said Wentzler, 'or people who are just plain ugly or funny-looking?'

'Corrective surgery is the answer for those unfortunates. Anything that's correctable by the scalpel is permitted; in fact, I see it as the duty of the state to assist such people with free medical treatments. I told you about my own efforts to help the fellow with the bad arm. If it can be fixed, it can live. There you have my answer in a nutshell. Provided, of course, that the patient has no mental deficiencies.'

'People with webbed fingers?'

'Correctable, even today. There have been great strides taken in such procedures, correcting nature's simple mistakes with the scalpel. Human flesh can be manipulated, but not human nature, hence the need to be rid of the Jews.'

'People with clubbed feet?'

'A perfect example of what I'm talking about. There are corrective procedures for such things. Reichsminister Goebbels himself had such an affliction.'

'What about people with too many fingers or toes?'

'A simple process of removal, best performed soon after birth.'

'People born with two heads?'

'You're joking. Such abominations must be disposed of immediately.'

'What about . . . Zeppi?'

There was a long silence, then Klaus gave his leaky football laugh.

'Ah, yes, little Zeppi of the golden curls. You'd like to hear me say, wouldn't you, that he should be disposed of. I'll say no such thing. The answer is, of course, to assist Zeppi in becoming one thing or the other, male or female. It isn't impossible, you know. Such procedures have already been attempted, but these are few in number to date, naturally. Ernst Muller in Berlin was pursuing such avenues of surgical enquiry. A man of genius, Muller, a credit to the Reich. I believe his efforts were interrupted by the war.'

'So nothing could be done for Zeppi, is this what you're saying?'

'At the moment, probably not.'

'But at some future time, when more sophisticated operations are possible?'

'Perhaps, yes, at some future time. Until then it's kinder to remove them, to end their suffering. Life unworthy of life should perish. I have no doubt at all in my mind.'

'I see.'

'You see nothing. It may be, Gerhard, that having avoided the war entirely you lack the necessary perspective for such musings. To change the world, you must be in it up to the neck, my friend, not lazing away your time doing nothing but eating bananas like a chimpanzee and contemplating the remote possibility of one day writing a book about banana eaters.'

'You're referring to plantains, I take it. They're not bananas, not quite. A scientific mind such as yours should be aware of that.'

'My mind is aware of many things that yours, apparently, is not.' Klaus stood up. 'Goodnight to you.'

'An interesting man,' said Wentzler, watching Klaus walk across the shabono to his hammock. 'And you're his nephew,' he added, turning to me.

'I didn't ask to be.'

'No one asks to be what they are. They simply are . . . whatever they are.'

I didn't understand his point, but it seemed wiser to say nothing. Wentzler stared at the fire for a while, then said goodnight and left me. I went over to Zeppi's hammock. He was asleep already, with Mitzi in his arms, also sleeping, her little furry head resting on Zeppi's breasts. It wasn't a picture of abnormality. It looked perfectly all right to me.

I made a decision the next day that was calculated to offend Klaus. He wanted me to be some kind of politician one day, but I didn't want to be, and getting tattooed was the strongest way of saying so. Would someone run for political office with a tattooed face? Never. So I went to Noroni and pointed to my chin, then at the tattoos on his cheekbones, and he understood.

Soon I was lying down in the shade while Noroni prepared his equipment, which was nothing but a bowl of water, two little sticks, one with a sharp thorn jammed at a right angle into the end of it, and a little pile of charcoal from last night's fires. He took the stick with the thorn in it and held it over my chin, then smacked it with the other stick. That drove the thorn into my flesh and I jumped. Noroni grinned and said something that I think meant we hadn't even started yet, so don't be such a weakling about the pain.

He hit the stick again, and again, and quickly built up a rhythm that was almost as fast as someone playing castanets – *prickprickprickprickprickprick* – until the thorn seemed to dance all over my chin like a maddened biting insect. I felt blood flowing down onto my throat, and the area around my chin felt as if it was burning. Noroni stopped every now and then to wash away the blood. After a while, the pain was so bad it didn't hurt as much, which sounds strange, but it's true. I pictured a creature of some kind that had bitten me on the chin and continued to hang there. It was important not to move or the creature would bite deeper.

Noroni washed me again, then started applying a mixture of charcoal and water to my chin, painting it on slowly and carefully with a springy little stick that he'd cut off square at the end, like a calligraphy pen. I didn't know much about tattooing, but I supposed the charcoal dye was entering my skin through all the tiny thorn holes. I didn't know what kind of pattern he was creating, but I trusted him to do a good job, the way he had when he painted me.

All the Yayomi who were tattooed had designs that I liked, interesting lines and zigzags and squiggles, so they seemed to have perfected tattooing as an art form. I knew that Mother would have hated to see such a thing on me even more than would Klaus, and the very fact that I was doing it brought home to me the reality of her death. I didn't want to think about that any more, so I let the animal attached to my chin bite as hard as he pleased, daring him to make me feel pain.

It took all morning, but at last Noroni was finished. I wanted to ask Klaus for his mirror so I could see, but he was nowhere around, so I went to ask Wentzler if he would describe what he saw on my chin.

'A large red and black scab, very fresh,' he said.

'But what's under it?'

'I can't see. You'll have to wait until the scab heals and falls off.'

'But that'll take days!'

'Quite so. Are you sure this was a good idea, Erich?'

'Yes. Why don't you get one too?'

'I must admit, I've sometimes been tempted. The Yayomi aren't masters of the art, like the Japanese, but they do excellent work with simple tattoos.'

'Go on then. When we leave you can take away a little bit of the Yayomi with you.'

'I don't think so. I'm far too conservative.'

'Have one on your chest, or your back. It doesn't have to be anywhere that shows.'

'I'll think about it. Does it hurt?'

'You get used to it.'

'What made you take the plunge?'

'I don't know, I just felt like it. It makes me feel different.'

He looked at the scab on my chin, then into my eyes. 'These things Klaus has been telling us, have they given you nightmares?'

'Of course not. Nothing he says could scare me.'

'How do you feel about the man, quite apart from his conversation?'

'I don't feel anything about him.'

Wentzler didn't look convinced. He said, 'You know to keep out of the river with that bleeding chin?'

'I'm not stupid.'

'Good. Do you have plans for the rest of the day?'

'No.'

'Would you care to accompany Isiway and myself on a special gathering trip?'

'Gathering what?'

'A kind of tree bark that has unique properties.'

'What are they?'

'I'll explain as we go.'

He obviously wanted me to go with him, so I agreed, even though what I really wanted to do was take Awomay off into the jungle and have her as many times as it took to make the pain in my chin go away.

We started out soon after, with Isiway in the lead. He carried the machete he'd used to cut off his wife's ears, but he didn't look threatening today. He and Wentzler kept up a line of chatter as we walked, and some of it was about me.

'Isiway says you look like someone who ate a big fat leech and had it burst in his mouth. He says your wife won't let you near her, you look so awful.'

'Tell him thank you very much. Tell him his wife looks awful with no ears.'

Wentzler spoke to Isiway, who laughed out loud.

'He thought it was funny?' I asked.

'What I said was, you had a dolphin joke to tell – why did the chicken cross the road? I changed it to – why did the anteater swim across the river? When I told him – to get to the other side – he liked it. He'll tell everyone now, wait and see.'

Isiway kept repeating the joke out loud to himself and cackling over it every time. He finally stopped as we moved away from the river. It was sad that Wentzler had to tell bad jokes on my behalf like that. Kwaytcha and Noroni and Awomay should have been my closest friends, but I couldn't talk to them, and it hardly seemed worthwhile learning how to if we were planning to leave soon. I heard Klaus's voice in my head telling me that the reason I didn't really consider any Yayomi my friend had nothing to do with language and everything to do with race. I thought he was wrong, but there was one person I was beginning to feel guilty about, and that was Awomay.

She was my wife, so what did I intend doing with her when we left? I hadn't even considered that when I married her, I only wanted to have her, and now that I'd had her, I was thinking of leaving without her. It wasn't right. Wentzler, who seemed to have strong notions of right and wrong, hadn't criticised me, but he was probably not happy about what I'd done. Maybe he thought it was all right to leave an Indian wife behind. I knew Klaus would think that way.

We tramped for quite a while, then Isiway stopped and pointed to a tree. It wasn't a tall tree, and I couldn't see the difference between it and a dozen others, but it was obviously the kind he was looking for. He started hacking at the slender trunk with his machete. Wentzler and I didn't seem to be expected to do anything, so we sat down and watched Isiway working. He only stopped once, to tell the anteater joke to himself again, and laugh. It was so silly it made Wentzler and me laugh too.

'Herr Wentzler, I have a question.'

'Isn't it time you called me Gerhard?'

'All right, I will. The question is – what will I do with Awomay?'

'Erich, if I was your age and had a wife as shapely as Awomay, I certainly wouldn't need to ask that question.'

'No, I mean when we leave here. Should I ask her to come along?'

'First of all, Yayomi women are never asked to do anything by their husbands, they're told, and Awomay would think it most peculiar that you were giving her a choice. Secondly, if you let slip our plans, she won't be able to keep from telling everyone. There are few secrets among Yayomi, and none at all between the women. Thirdly, since you don't speak the language, I'd have to translate for you, and frankly, I refuse to do so. You'll simply have to walk away from your marriage as if it had never been. Right up until the last moment, the plan must be kept to ourselves or it won't work. I'm sorry. Does that answer your question?'

'I suppose so.'

'Don't sound so miserable. After you've gone, Awomay will be a prime catch for one of the men, even if she's pregnant by then. Usually a man wouldn't be interested in raising another's child, but, let's not forget, this baby will be half dolphin. Awomay's status within the shabono will be high, you can be sure of that.'

'What if they chase us when we leave?'

'Provided we can sneak away without being seen, I doubt that there'll be any pursuit. The Yayomi will probably build a story around our disappearance, something to do with the dolphins returning to their world once the waters rose, because there wasn't enough dry land around for their human shapes to feel comfortable on. Awomay will be sad, yes, but not for long. It simply has to be that way, Erich.'

What he said made sense, so I decided not to think about

it any more. Isiway gave the tree a few last blows with his machete and it toppled. Without pausing for breath, he cut a long slit along the length of the trunk and began peeling back the bark.

'Here's where we can lend a hand,' said Gerhard, and we got up to help. Peeling the bark was easy because under the outer layer was a second layer that wasn't like bark at all. It was yellowish and slippery to the touch, and peeled away from the bark itself without any trouble. Soon the tree trunk was as naked as the leg of a stork, and the two layers of bark had been separated. The slippery stuff, about two kilograms of it, was gathered up and put into a woven bag Isiway carried, and then we started back.

It was midday when we arrived at the shabono, and Isiway began preparing the mushy bark by pounding it with the end of a pole until it was like thick glue. He added something else to the mixture, something green that Gerhard told me was crushed seeds from another tree, and pounded it some more, spitting into it once in a while, then he laid it all out on a flat stone near the biggest cooking fire, where it began to give off quite a bit of steam as it warmed. When no more steam came from the gummy-looking mixture that was left, Isiway picked it up like a mass of bread dough and rolled it this way and that on the hot stone, stopping to pound it with the heel of his palm every now and then. By midafternoon he was satisfied with the result and set it to one side, a small green brick that was now dry in appearance, not at all like the stuff he'd begun with.

Gerhard still hadn't told me what all the preparation was about. 'Just wait and see,' was all he'd say.

I got impatient and went away to find Awomay, but she

was busy with the women. When they saw me coming some of them started giggling and nudging each other, and pointing me out to Awomay, who turned to look at me. I didn't need Gerhard to tell me they were saying something like, 'Look, here he comes again. He can't keep his hands off you, can he.' I felt like a fool, and walked straight past them, ignoring Awomay completely. If she was to be left behind, I had to start controlling my need for her, or I'd miss her too much. It was hard not to think about her body, though, and how good it felt to slide inside her. Leaving wasn't going to be so easy.

I left the shabono and went down to the river where Mother had died. There were lots of brightly coloured dragonflies, and I noticed something that I'd missed while watching Mother bathing here. The water was very still, almost without a ripple, a kind of backwater set off from the main body of the river, which ran strong and deep. If Mother had bathed in the same place everyone else did, where the current was fairly swift, chances were that the blood seeping from her would have been carried quickly away and dispersed, and the piranha would never have been able to smell it, or trace it back to the place it came from. Mother's need for privacy was most likely what had led to her death. I sat on the bank and stared at the water and the dragonflies that darted about just above the surface.

The scab on my chin was hard and itchy and still very sore, and I had to make myself resist the urge to keep touching it. All in all, the rest of the day was one frustrating hour after another, and I kept myself to myself until sundown, then went back to the shabono.

Entering through the hole in the wall, I saw Gerhard, who saw me at the same time and beckoned me over. He was with

Klaus, and they were both watching Isiway and another man crumble the green brick into powder. It went from a solid substance to a rough green powder simply by being rolled between their fingers, and they took that powder and ground it between stones until it was finer than sand. I made myself ask no questions, just watched like the others, because if I'd asked, Gerhard would only have told me again to wait and see.

The sky was dark above our heads by the time Isiway carefully scooped up every tiny particle of the green powder and put it into a little pouch, something like the ones the Yayomi carried their poison darts in. I thought I'd discovered what the powder was, and said to Gerhard, 'It's their poison, isn't it?' He shook his head, smiled and said, 'Wait and see. Tomorrow you'll learn what it's for.'

That really annoyed me, so I went to my hammock and pushed back and forth crossly with my foot. Zeppi came over with his monkey and asked me how far down the river I thought Mother had got by now, and I told him I didn't know. He went away and Awomay joined me, getting into the hammock right alongside me. Feeling her skin all down one side of my body, I got hard, even though I didn't want to, not right there with dozens of people all around, even if there were lots of shadows cast by the fires. Awomay couldn't help but notice my cock banging against her thigh, and she reached down and squeezed it, which just about made me faint from pleasure.

Then she started pulling on it, sometimes gently, sometimes not so gently; in fact, she squeezed so tightly every now and then it made me gasp, and that made her laugh, the little tease. She wasn't doing it with enough rhythm to make me come, and I didn't think it would be dignified for me to take care of myself while lying right next to her, so in the end I swung my legs out of the hammock, turned my back on her and waited for the log standing up in front of my belly to go down. Awomay started stroking my back then, but all that did was irritate me, so I jerked away from her hand. She gave a little hiss of anger, slapped me between the shoulderblades and swung herself out of the hammock.

I didn't turn to watch her leave. I had to remind myself that one day soon I'd turn away from Awomay and never see her again. I felt like crying. I hadn't cried when Mother was killed, and yet here I was, feeling sorry for myself just because my chin hurt and Gerhard wouldn't give me a straight answer and my little cocktease of a wife would soon be lost to me forever. It was enough to make me feel ashamed, and the shame was enough to make me angry, so when Zeppi came strolling back to ask another stupid question I told him to buzz off quick or I'd take his monkey and rip its head off. He put his hand around precious little Mitzi's head and said that if I did, he'd pull my head off too.

That made me laugh, and after that I felt better, but for the rest of the evening, until everyone was asleep, I talked to no one. It was almost enough to make a fellow start praying, just to have a silent conversation with someone who'd understand. But since I didn't believe in God, I couldn't, so until I finally fell asleep I was alone, the sound of breathing all around me.

TEN

IN THE MORNING ALL the men began painting themselves in black and red. Kwaytcha insisted that I paint him, after he'd painted me, and I started work on him, using my fingers for the broad patches of colour and a little squared-off stick for the fine details. I made my design on Kwaytcha's back and chest as close to the usual Yayomi patterns as possible, for fear of doing something that might not please him, but I did give the edges of the black areas a series of pothook projections like the ones I'd admired in school when we were studying the Ancient Greeks.

Kwaytcha was very pleased with what he saw, and ran around showing himself to everyone. At about this time I began to wonder if this was the start of a war party, which made me nervous. I was grateful to the Yayomi for allowing me to be their guest, but I didn't want to do any killing on their behalf. I didn't even know if I could.

I went to Gerhard and said, 'All right, tell me what's going on. Why are we all painted like this?'

'I'm not,' he said smugly, 'and neither is Klaus.'

'Well, why are the rest of us painted? We aren't going to have a raiding party against another shabono, are we?'

'If that was the case they'd be stroking their weapons and talking to them and jumping up and down with excitement. This is another type of occasion entirely.'

'Something to do with the green powder?'

'Correct. You waited, and now you'll see.'

Some of the men weren't content simply to be painted, and added parrot and toucan feathers to their armbands, so many they almost looked like little brightly coloured wings growing there, and others put on beautiful feathered headdresses that made them a metre taller. I was getting annoyed all over again at the delay, then Manokwo came out to the centre of the shabono and held up the little pouch Isiway had put the green powder in last night.

There was a lot of yelling when he did that, and the men all squatted down in a circle. Mapeway, the man who'd had the pole fight with Isiway, came forward with a long tube, like a zabatana but only a third the length. One end of the tube was open, and the other had a tapered seed pod with the end cut off stuck onto it, like a nozzle. Gerhard winked at me.

Manokwo put his fingertip into the green powder and picked up a little of it, then placed it into the open end of the tube. Mapeway was sitting opposite him with a look of expectation on his face. Manokwo lifted the tube and offered Mapeway the seed-pod end. Mapeway put the end into his left nostril. Manokwo took a deep breath, then blew as hard as he could into the tube. Instantly Mapeway's head jerked back. The green powder had been blown straight up his nose, which struck me as a ridiculous thing to have done to you, especially since it looked so painful. But Mapeway then stuck the nozzle into his other nostril, and Manokwo, who'd already loaded more powder into the other end, blew that lot up Mapeway's nose too.

Mapeway dropped his end of the tube and rolled away, green slime dribbling from his nose onto his upper lip, and as he rolled, getting his new paintwork all covered in dirt, he moaned and groaned like a man in terrible pain.

Another man took his place, and the same thing happened, ending in the same dropping of the tube, the green nostril slime, the moaning and so forth. I asked Gerhard what the green powder was, and why they had it blown up their noses if it hurt them so badly.

'The pain is temporary,' he said, 'and easily outweighed by the pleasure that follows.'

'Pleasure?' The first two men to have taken the green powder were outside the circle now, the latest one still rolling on his back, the first one crawling on hands and knees, apparently going nowhere in particular. 'What pleasure?'

'It's a drug, Erich, a narcotic. Although it doesn't look like it, those fellows are having a wonderful time, seeing things that you and I can't see, talking to them as well, in all likelihood.'

'Is it like morphine?'

'Only insofar as it's made from the product of a plant. They call it yoppo. I'm not sure it's addictive, but they take it as often as anyone cares to make a batch.'

'Look at Mapeway!'

Mapeway was climbing an invisible tree. The other one was torn between staring into space or consulting the dirt between his toes. 'What do they think they're doing?'

'Who can say? They may not even remember themselves, once the drug wears off.'

'But you must have asked them, for your book.'

'Well, yes . . . but they weren't very forthcoming. A few of them spoke of talking with spirit people, but it was all very vague, rather like asking an alcoholic to recall exactly what he was thinking about during his last bout of drinking. It's a wholly subjective experience.'

'Have you had it?'

'Once. I found it not to my liking.'

'Why, what happened?'

'It's rather difficult to describe.'

More men had yoppo blown up their nose, then went reeling away as if they'd had a nail driven into their forehead. It was a hilarious sight, and Gerhard had to lay a hand on my arm to stop me from laughing. I didn't feel like laughing after Noroni took over the tube from Manokwo and blew powder up the chief's nose, because after Manokwo went away with green slime running into his mouth, Noroni gave me a signal that meant only one thing – it was my turn.

'What should I do?'

Gerhard shrugged. 'You can refuse, but refusing a Yayomi anything he offers you is generally considered a dreadful insult. The yoppo won't actually hurt you, it'll just feel like it at first. Pain without a source of pain, is how I would describe it.'

I didn't want to take it, but insulting the Yayomi was out of the question, so I squatted in front of Noroni and lifted the end of the tube, which was covered in green snot. The men who had taken yoppo before me now had a green mess running clear down their chests to their navels. It didn't seem possible for so much snot to come out of a nose, but the proof was all around me.

I put the tube into my nostril and saw Noroni take a breath ... then someone hit me between the eyes with a hammer, so hard I was knocked backwards and found myself looking up at the sky. Someone put his hands under my shoulders and sat me up straight again, then put the tube into my other nostril. A voice inside me was begging Noroni *no no no no* but he blew more yoppo into my skull anyway. I couldn't breathe. My lungs had collapsed. Long fingers of fire were creeping from the bridge of my nose up into my brain, flowing across the outer membrane, looking for a way inside, and somewhere in the region of my ears they found it, and poured into the deepest part of me like an invading army, to ransack my grey matter and rummage through every chest of memories stored there since the day I was born.

Little Erich, that was me, with my short pants and a baby brother squalling on my knee while a photograph was taken of us both by Father, who warned us not to move. No chance of my moving, since all my breath was gone. It seemed like a good idea to stay where I was, wherever that might be, because I didn't want to spoil the picture. Then Father put down the camera and offered me the Iron Cross that was already around my neck, but that didn't seem to matter at all. He said to me as he pressed it into my hand, 'The Führer himself has held this in his hand. Never let it leave you.' I told him I wouldn't; in fact, it was already around my neck and had been for weeks.

'Good,' he said, and then he hung his head. 'It wasn't me who blew up those Russian tanks, it was Haeckel. His tank was in the lead, so he had the best kills laid out for him. I hit plenty, but for every one of mine Haeckel hit two, maybe even three. He couldn't miss that day. We were out in front of the rest, protected by God, I think, because not one Russian came anywhere near to hitting us, yet we got almost twenty of them, like knocking over toys on the parlour carpet, but it was Haeckel that got most of them, before he was finally hit. The entire crew, wiped out. Then I was hit, and everyone but me died. I claimed the lion's share of our combined score. It wasn't cheating. I'd killed plenty, just not as many as Haeckel. It was a contest between us, a friendly rivalry. Really, he wouldn't have minded. What use is an Iron Cross to a dead man? I lied for it, but the Führer touched it with his hands, and now it's yours. Earn it.' I said I would, but he wasn't there any more.

Someone picked me up in his arms. It wasn't Father. Father was gone. It was Gerhard, and he laid me in my hammock. My head hung sideways. It wasn't attached to the rest of me. I could see Klaus with the yoppo tube stuck in his nose. He fell over backwards. I wanted to laugh, it was so funny, but I couldn't. There was a peculiar wetness all down my chin. Had the tattooing scab broken open and bled again? The blood had run down over my chest as well, but it wasn't coming from my chin. It was coming from my nose. I had the world's worst nosebleed, only the blood was green. It flowed and flowed.

Father should have wiped my nose for me the way he did when I was little, but he was too busy shooting at Russian tanks with his panzer, then too busy lying about it. Why had he told me? I didn't want to know that about him. I forgave him. I'd have to earn my Iron Cross, though, to make up for his lies. Now I remembered when he'd told me about his shame. I'd been asleep, fast asleep, the night of the day when he'd given the medal to me for safekeeping, and he'd sat beside my bed and murmured the story to me, but I was asleep, and in the morning I remembered nothing of it, until now. How strange, I thought.

Klaus was crawling away from the yoppo tube on all fours. He crawled in circles, looking like a hairless monkey searching for a tail that wasn't there. Yayomi men were standing up and falling down like dancers in a ballet being machine-gunned by a dissatisfied audience. They were trying very hard to dance, but couldn't, could only jerk around in circles and lean against poles and drip green slime down their chests before taking a bullet and falling down again. I wanted Father to come back, but he wouldn't, so I called for Mother to come, and she loomed above me big as a pink cloud, and raised my head to her big pink breast for me to suck, but my mouth was filled with snot so I couldn't drink.

Mother shook her head at me, but she was smiling, so it was all right. I wanted to ask her if it hurt very much to be eaten by the razor fish, but the words wouldn't come, blocked by green snot in the back of my throat. She said to me, 'Who's my precious little one,' and I wanted to shout out loud that it was *me me me* but couldn't, so I closed my eyes instead and milk rushed into my mouth, warm milk, warm as blood, filling me steadily like a rubber balloon fitted over a tap, filled me and filled me until I couldn't possibly be filled any more, so full I couldn't draw breath, so full I knew I was going to burst, and then the milk all rushed out of me in a warm jet that felt so good as it left me and I could breathe again, green milk with chunks of other food mixed in. It all went down onto my shoulder. Why was my head tilted at such an odd angle? I wanted to change it, but couldn't.

Nothing could shift my head, because it was filled with too many memories, thousands of them, all leaping from the past at the same time, so many they got in each other's way and were jammed together like two fat men trying to get through a door at the same time, then three fat men, then four, and the doorway collapsed and they all fell into the room together as one truly enormous fat man with four heads and eight arms that set about pulling himself apart again until there were four fat men, then eight thin men, and all of them were Reichsminister Goebbels, the one with the club foot.

He limped closer to me and shouted into my face with his wide open slit of a mouth that my father was a hero of the Reich and I'd better be a hero too or he'd know the reason why. I told him that my father was a liar and a disgrace to the Reich who'd been given a medal he didn't deserve, and Reichsminister Goebbels got very angry. He said he was going to take it back, take it from around my neck, shouting, shouting all the time with his screeching radio voice that I was no better than a Jew for wearing a medal I hadn't earned, a medal only given to real Germans, and it had come to his attention that I wasn't a real German at all, I was a dirty little Jew, a Yid, a filthy little liar like my lying father who should have been put on a train with all the other Yids and their filthy little children and taken away to be resettled on another planet, the green planet Yayomi in the constellation of Amazonas where we belonged, where the world didn't have to look at us any more, all the filthy, lying Jews in one place, the place they all belonged forever and ever.

I shut my eyes. I shut my ears and he went away, limping a

little, looking pleased with himself because he'd made me feel ashamed at being called a filthy Jew, even if I wasn't. It didn't make any difference to Goebbels, as long as he could make me afraid. But I didn't want to be afraid, not of him, not of anyone, so I looked for a friend, a true friend who would help me if the little man with the big voice and the limp came back to shout at me again.

Where was Gerhard? He was nowhere near, but it didn't matter, because here came someone across the shabono I recognised as a friend, even if I couldn't recall his name, a friend from the past I played with so long ago his name was almost buried by the days and months and years since then . . . Noah! Noah Epstein! My friend Noah Epstein with whom I discussed the importance of Atlantis and the possibility of life on Mars until we agreed with each other about everything, everything under the sun that shone down all summer long while we talked and talked and declared ourselves the wisest of the wise, certainly smarter than anyone else in our town, those ignorant boobs with their dull interests and narrow view of the world.

Noah Epstein, so thin and clever and funny he made me laugh when he imitated the Führer's way of speech-making, as if he had an angry lion stuck in his throat. It was a shame all the Jews had been removed from school or we would have sat next to each other like chums do. I first saw him in the park, where he was watching two pigeons mating. He saw me watching and said, 'All that wasted energy, strutting and preening. You'd think the male would just hop on and be done with it.' That's how the friendship started. It wasn't acceptable to know Jews, so we never visited each other's house, just met in the park. We always managed to avoid people who might have given disapproving looks, and if we walked past someone we automatically separated a little bit and stopped talking, to avoid trouble. Then a friend of Mother's saw us and reported me, and that was the end of that. I was told if I ever saw him in public I should cross the street and pass him by with my face turned the other way, because Noah Epstein was a dirty Jew.

And then the day finally came when I saw you, Noah Epstein, walking in public like a deer that has strayed from the forest onto the road and doesn't know if its next step will be its last. When I saw you, Noah Epstein, I crossed the street and walked by on the other side without turning my head to see if you knew it was me, and only later, only when your family sold everything it owned and moved to Poland, only then did I feel ashamed and know how much of me had gone away with you, the best part of me, the part that knew the difference between right and wrong, yet had turned away from what was right and walked along the wrong side of the street.

Noah came and stood by my hammock. 'You look awful,' he said.

He looked the same as he always had, not a day older, which was impossible, but it really was him, I swear it, with his gold-rimmed glasses, thick wavy hair and dark eyes, and the mouth that was always ready to turn down at the corners whenever he said something cutting or hilarious about someone.

'Hello, Noah. How are you?'

'Dead,' he said, and we both burst out laughing the way we used to.

'You can't be dead,' I reminded him, 'because here you are!'

'Am I?' he said, looking around as if he was surprised to find himself somewhere other than our town. 'I see you've

moved up in the world. I particularly like your open court-
yard, Erich. Very Mediterranean, if I may say so.'

I laughed again. His whole face shone with the light of
intelligence. Noah was smarter than me, but I didn't mind,
because he liked me and talked to me.

'How did Poland work out for you?' I asked.

'A net loss, as my father would put it.'

'Where was it that you went? I've forgotten.'

'Lodz, but then we were relocated. I think you've cut yourself shaving.'

'No, it's a tattoo!'

'I've got one of those too,' said Noah, always one for upstaging
a friend, and it was true, he had a long number tattooed on his
arm, which I thought was pointless and ugly, but didn't say so.

'How did you get here?' I asked. It felt wonderful just being
able to see him again, although he was beginning to lean sideways somehow.

'On the wings of a dove,' he said, smiling. His body was
leaning at such an angle now, it was surprising his glasses
didn't fall off.

'Why are you doing that?' I asked.

'Because I can,' he said. 'Bet you wish you could too.'

'Teach me!'

'All right. First, become a Jew ...' He laughed loudly at that,
and I joined in.

'No, really, tell me how.'

'It's a trade secret,' he said, and winked at me. Noah was
starting to fade away.

'Come back!' I cried out, or at least I think I did.

'I never left,' he said, pulling a comic face. He was almost
invisible now, his body like smoke.

'Noah, don't go away! Stay here . . .'

'Can't do that, old chum. Wrong side of the street. Might get caught.'

'Noah . . .'

He was gone.

I'd driven him away with my stupid questions. I should have just let him talk, the way he liked to, with as little interruption as possible; 'Setting the agenda,' he called it. I'd tried to set the agenda and had failed, but it wasn't all my fault, it was the green powder. My nasal cavities were awash with slime, my lips so gummed with the stuff, it was amazing I'd been able to hold a conversation, if I had. Of course I had! That was Noah, my one and only true friend . . . until I turned my back on him.

I couldn't cry, even though I wanted to. Tears could never be enough. He hadn't asked for an explanation of my treachery, had simply taken up with me where we left off. Maybe he hadn't seen it was me who crossed the street to avoid him . . . but I knew that he had. My entire body was filled with shame. Too late now, I told myself. It was something Noah used to say, 'Too late now, as the man said while staring at his severed leg.' That always made me laugh. I said it once in front of Mother, and she just stared at me as if I'd said something completely mad.

I opened my eyes, surprised to find that they'd been shut. The ground beneath my hammock reeked of vomit. I had to get away from it, but couldn't move, so I closed my eyes again to shut out everything. The last thing I saw was Klaus, who was standing some distance away, staring at nothing with a look on his face that said his eyes were filled with things he couldn't turn away from. Then I slid down a long tube into a deep lake, where lovely fish swam by, wishing me a good day. They spoke Yayomi, and I understood them.

It was evening again. The day was already gone, and I had separated from it before noon. It was very confusing to close my eyes on sunlight and open them to firelight. Gerhard was over by Klaus's hammock, talking with him, then he saw that I was awake and came over. I swung my legs down before he reached me, not wanting to look as weak and helpless as I felt. His face had a worried look.

'Are you all right?' he asked.

'Of course I am. Why wouldn't I be?'

'Sometimes it isn't a pleasant experience, even for a Yayomi.'

'Well, I'm fine. How's Klaus?'

'His body has recovered and been cleaned, but his mind is still wandering a bit.'

'What did I do?'

'Very little. After you were put in your hammock you just lay there. You appeared to fall asleep, so I didn't bother you after that. Was it interesting? What did you see?'

'Nothing, I just felt . . . a bit sick.' I didn't want to talk about it.

'Nothing at all? That's unusual.'

'Maybe it didn't work on me the way it's supposed to.'

'It should have. Noroni blasted a good solid pinch of powder up both your nostrils, I was watching.'

'At least I didn't insult them by not taking it.'

He nodded, looking at my face, not believing me. 'Are you hungry?'

'No, I have a headache.'

'Drink some water. Drink a lot.'

I did as he suggested and soon felt a little better. Klaus was drinking like a horse when I went over to see him. He seemed very quiet. I wondered what he had seen while under the influence of yoppo, but didn't ask.

We had quite a bit of rain, and Gerhard said the weather was building toward the start of the rainy season faster than usual this year, which was good news for our plan to get away. To be frank, what we did each day was wait for time to pass, that's all. I went into the trees with Awomay as often as I felt like it, which wasn't as often as in the beginning. I think that was because we couldn't talk to each other. Even if they were sometimes nasty to their wives, Yayomi men did talk to them, especially when their children were around. They might just as well have been sitting together in a dining room or kitchen, with the man lighting his pipe and the woman fixing dinner and the children playing with a train set.

But Awomay and I couldn't do that. She tried to teach me some words, but I always stopped her, which made her sulk. She wanted to talk to me, but I wouldn't learn a single word, because once I learned how to talk with her I wouldn't be able to leave, or else I'd have to take her with me, which was impossible. Without language in common, we stayed strangers in a way, even though we did things with each other that I'd only heard about from boys at school whose older brothers had dirty books.

The scab finally came off my chin, fell off in almost one piece while I was scratching lightly at it. The skin underneath felt peculiar because I hadn't touched it for a week, soft and new and very sensitive. I went looking for Klaus, who still carried his medical bag with him everywhere he went, a naked doctor making a house call but never able to find the house. I wanted his mirror, and when I asked for it, he opened the bag and gave it to me.

'You've done something foolish, Erich,' he said, 'and you'll have to pay a price for your foolishness. It won't be possible now for me to introduce you to those important people I told you about, the gentlemen in Argentina. You've ruined a future that could have elevated you among them ... now it can never happen.'

I didn't know what he meant until I looked into the little mirror. Noroni had tattooed three zigzag lines down my chin, and they were exactly like the SS's twin lightning flash insignia: there were three, not two, but my tattoo had the same slashing angles, the same proportions between the lines as the SS symbol.

I handed back his mirror and said, 'I don't care.' And I didn't. Klaus gave me a look that expressed his deep disappointment in me, and walked away.

I went and showed Gerhard the tattoo. 'Oh my,' he said, 'won't they just love that beauty back home.'

'It isn't what I wanted.'

'You should have given Noroni a drawing of what you did want. You're stuck with it now, unless you can muster enough whiskers to grow a beard. I see you already have a furry caterpillar resting along your lip, so a beard can't be far behind.'

'Don't joke about it! What am I going to do? Could you ask Noroni to add some more to it and make it different?'

'I wouldn't recommend that. He's very proud of his work

and he'll be insulted. You can have it worked on when we get to Caracas. They have plenty of tattoo parlours there, all along the waterfront. You might be able to change it into a hula dancer.'

Awomay found me a little later and stroked my chin, which almost made me cry. She sensed something was wrong and took me by the hand out into the jungle, where we did it very slowly, with her doing all the hard work. It was the best yet, but the fact that it was her who made it that way upset me all over again.

Once in a while I went back to the spot on the river bank where I'd watched Mother die, and stared at the water and the dragonflies that always seemed to be there. It was on my second or third trip that it suddenly occurred to me I was an orphan. First Father, then Mother. The word orphan hadn't entered my thoughts until then. Was that because Klaus was supposed to be my father? I hadn't thought of him in those terms since I'd found out he was a murderer. Was it because of Gerhard Wentzler I didn't feel like an orphan?

He was something like a father, but probably too casual about it to be mistaken for a real parent. Still, he was an adult, and he seemed to care for Zeppi and me in an offhand kind of way. I didn't want him to be my father, him or anyone else. Being an orphan simplified things a lot, if I could just accept it. For example, who was there to tell me what to do any more? If Klaus told me to do something that I didn't agree with, I'd tell him to go and jump in the lake. I was free! Zeppi too, although I didn't think he saw it like that. Zeppi wanted someone, anyone at all, to tell him what to do, so Zeppi wasn't free.

Watching the dragonflies, thinking about freedom, I asked myself why it was that the dragonflies liked this part of the river. Could it be because the water was calm there, not running along swiftly the way it did everywhere else? Maybe that made it easier for them to hunt whatever they hunted. I hadn't a clue what dragonflies ate. I'd been taught about Goethe and Schiller, but nobody had ever told me what dragonflies ate. I'd never willingly read a poem, but I really wanted to know about a dragonfly's diet. Still water must have some attraction for them. Still water, where Mother was attacked by the piranha and eaten to the bone.

Still water. Which meant that Mother, or what was left of her, might yet be there, the bones at least, lying on the bottom, not washed away by the current, because the current didn't come into the little backwater where the dragonflies hovered and hummed. She was still there, I knew it.

Did I have the courage to wade into the water and feel around with my feet for her bones? Was there any point? I knew it was cowardice that made me question the need to find out. I didn't have to do it, but now that it had popped into my head, the question needed to be answered. After all, if her skeleton was there, she'd want it taken out and buried properly, with a cross placed over the grave. To leave her where she was would have been disrespectful. I felt awful, and wished I hadn't even thought of it, but it was too late now.

I'd have to go in and find out if she was there. I knew who for – Mother, even though she was dead. It's strange how a dead person can make a living person do something he doesn't want to do. But I stayed where I was. I didn't want to feel her bones with my toes. Mother was out there, only a few metres from me, and I was too afraid to find her. What a pathetic coward. I lashed myself with words – scaredy-cat, sissy, weakling – but nothing made me set foot into the water.

Then I asked myself what Awomay would think if she knew, or Gerhard. All I had to do was keep my mouth shut and they'd never know what a coward I was. But I would know, and that's what made it so awful.

I forced one foot into the river, then the other, then the first, a little further out. Moving very slowly, I aimed for the place where I remembered seeing Mother slide under the surface. My toes were like tiny creeping moles, searching out the way ahead, sinking a little into the soft river mud with every step, then wiggling their way forward, expecting at any moment to touch something awful down there in the cloudy darkness. I moved further from the bank, the water reaching my knees, then my thighs, then my waist. It was at Mother's waist when she was attacked, but I was a little taller than her, so I was already further out than she'd been.

I must have gone too far to one side and walked right past her. I began moving sideways and immediately my right foot brushed against something. I almost fell over, but made myself stay upright, then reached out again with my foot. Something hard, narrow, slightly curved . . . a rib? I felt around some more, aware for the first time that a faint moaning sound was coming from my throat. There were more hard things lying there – definitely bones. I moved a little further sideways and my foot touched something much larger. It could only have been her skull, unless it was her pelvis.

I made myself touch it again. Round, like a vase or bowl. Her head. I could even feel hair tickling my toes, so she hadn't been eaten clear to the bone the way I'd thought.

Having found her, I couldn't tell myself I'd been mistaken. I'd have to go ahead and bring her to shore for burial, reach down into the murk and take hold of her bones with my fingers. Bones with flesh and gristle still clinging to them. I'd see her face all eaten away and her teeth showing through, and her empty eye sockets, and all of it would smell of decay and river mud and be disgustingly slippery and slimy. And who knows how hungry those piranha had been. Maybe they'd left more than just the scalp. They might have left pieces of flesh from just about anywhere. I might reach down there and touch a chunk of something, and bring it up to find that it was a breast.

I couldn't do that. I knew I couldn't.

I waded ashore, ashamed. It was too much to ask of me, that handling of dead parts, fleshy bits and pieces. A skeleton in the desert, that would have been different, nice and dry and in clear sight. You'd know what you were picking up beforehand. But a skeleton in a river, that was more than I could face, more than I could touch with my fingers. It was bad enough touching Mother with my toes, but having to take a deep breath and slip under the water and reach for her with my hands, groping like a blind man . . . that wasn't for me. I was a coward, after all. I could admit it now, and accept it. I'd try to be less of a coward in other areas to make up for being so gutless about Mother.

When I came ashore I was shivering, and it wasn't from cold. I couldn't even turn and look at the place I'd been, only walked away from the river as fast as I could.

Near the shabono I saw Gerhard, and suddenly felt guilty. I had to tell him.

'We're going to get more rain this afternoon,' he said as I

came closer. 'I can feel it. Notice how the air gets so heavy and still, even before we can see any sign of clouds?'

'I found Mother.'

'Pardon me?'

'Her bones, they're right there where it happened.'

'Her bones?'

'I went in and found her with my feet. I don't want to touch her with my hands.'

'I see . . .'

He looked at me, then out across the river. 'What do you want to do, Erich?'

'I don't know. I made myself go into the water and find her, but I can't make myself bring her out. I don't want to touch her. Could you?'

I hadn't meant to ask him that.

'Let's look at what would happen if we did bring her out,' he said, and his tone of voice, like that of a very intelligent schoolmaster, was reassuring. I hoped he'd think of a way to leave Mother where she was, some way only a clever man could think of. If he did that, I'd be grateful to him forever.

'The Yayomi have been told that Frau Brandt swam away downriver with her new dolphin baby. If we bring your mother's bones onto land for burial, there's a chance someone will either see them before we can get them into the ground, or else be so intrigued by the sight of freshly turned earth, the bones would be dug up anyway, just to see what was there. And if that happened, either of those things, we'd be in trouble for having lied to the Yayomi. We could always say it's the skeleton of someone else, some unknown person.'

'I think there's still hair on the head. They'll recognise that.'

'In that case, hard as it is to leave her there, I'd have to suggest doing exactly that. We can't risk being found out, not even for your mother. Was she a religious woman?'

'Not especially, at least not until we came here.'

'I was going to suggest putting up a marker of some kind, a cross, I suppose, on the bank where it happened, but even that might make the Yayomi suspicious, Anything they don't understand, they tend to distrust.' He paused. 'And I wouldn't mention this to Zeppi or Klaus. Both of them are unreliable, for different reasons.'

He looked at the sky, which was beginning to turn green.

I asked him, 'Why does it do that?'

'I don't know. It may be a reflection of the jungle, an atmospheric inversion of some kind. Meteorology isn't my department.'

We watched the sky turning green above us. It wasn't the same green as the jungle, so I didn't accept his theory. It was more like the pale green of the tiles on the wall of Herr Bleichroder's butcher shop. Most of the tiles were white, but there was a line of green ones about a metre from the floor. I first knew I was growing up by the way the line of green tiles was level with my face on one visit to the butcher's with Mother, and later on it was level with my chest. Now the air was thick and warm and filled with moisture, more than usual, and I could swear the hairs on the back of my neck were standing up.

'Why did you become an anthropologist?' I asked.

He thought for a moment, then said, 'It's an unusual field for a Jew to enter, I think that's why. I was always a bit contrary by nature, even as a boy. My parents said I wasn't a good Jew, and I'd have to admit they were probably right. My father was a businessman. That's what Jews are good at, everyone says so, even Jews. I didn't want that, though. Too limiting. Anthropology sounded like something worthwhile. 'The scientific study of the origins of the physical, social and cultural development and behaviour of man.' The definition was custom-made to entice me. My parents didn't approve, but they paid for my tuition anyway. I suppose they're dead now, along with all my relations.'

The air seemed to get thicker as he talked, and his words slowly bored through my brain. When he finished, I finally understood what he'd said.

'You're . . . a Jew?'

'Not a very good one. I don't observe any of the rituals. Secular is the word for my type, and others in my family were the same. But I'm a Jew, now and always. Are you shocked?'

'Yes . . .'

'I've been waiting for the right moment to tell you. Even as recently as this morning I told myself it was too risky, that a good German boy like you wouldn't hesitate to tell Klaus. You can tell him if you like. I think I can handle Klaus. One Jew has always been able to handle one Nazi, but apparently there were too many of them in the end. Are you a Nazi, Erich?'

'I . . . don't think so.'

'Never in the Hitler Youth?'

'Yes, but it was just marching and pitching tents and listening to speeches and singing songs. It was boring most of the time. Even at the end of the war when we were mobilised, our lot didn't see any action.'

'And the Führer, you never thought he was a wonderful man?'

I didn't want to admit that I had, and still did, sort of. But I didn't want to lie either, so I said nothing.

'When we leave here, Erich, it isn't going to be easy. Getting past the Iriri and keeping ourselves afloat in the floodwaters will be dangerous. We'll have to rely on each other, you and I, and that requires trust. Zeppi and Klaus aren't the ones who'll make our little plan succeed – you and I are, I think we both know that. So there should be no secrets between us. I felt like a coward not having told you sooner, but I didn't want to touch the issue, just as you don't want to touch your mother's bones. It's all so stupid, don't you think? You can't stop being a German, I can't stop being a Jew. We help each other or we kill each other, there can't be anything in between, not after what's been happening back home, all that slaughter I missed out on. Do you think Klaus would like the chance to kill one last Jew?'

'I don't know.'

'I'd have to kill him if he tried, you know. Jews don't like to die, just like anyone else. It's ironic that I left Europe before the real carnage began, and now here I am, with what sounds like one of the absolute worst of the lot. Every time I look at Klaus I wonder why it is that I don't pick up someone's bow and put an arrow through his heart. I think it's because he fascinates me. The man is pure evil, and yet he doesn't give that impression. If he hadn't told me about his exploits as a Jew killer I'd never have suspected any of it.'

'Are you going to . . . kill him?'

'Klaus deserves to die. Remember what he's told us. He should be killed ten thousand times over, but once will have to do, if I decide to do it. It all depends on Klaus. I'd have to reveal myself to him as a Jew first, that's only fair.'

'But how can you be a Jew? You aren't even circumcised.'

He laughed. 'I was born in Lapland, incredible as that may

sound. My father had business dealings there, and my mother insisted on coming along to see the Lapps herding their deer. I came out prematurely, in the middle of nowhere, delivered by Lapp women during a howling blizzard, I'm told, but that part's probably exaggeration. Maybe that's why I'm an anthropologist, because I was born in a strange land, among strange people. Anyway, when we finally came back to Germany the circumcision was put off while my father had a nervous collapse brought on by overwork. I don't think my mother ever really wanted it done, in any case. As I said, we were never orthodox. Mother insisted I be given a German name, nothing Jewish-sounding. I think she wanted me to have a protective coat, camouflage, you might say. Clever Mother. The end result – it was never taken care of. Jews aren't all alike, you know, just as all Germans aren't alike. Look at you, with your Jewish cock. Life's full of surprises, isn't it.'

I looked across the river. I couldn't look at him. He was a Jew. I hadn't liked him when we first met, then slowly I had begun to appreciate his intelligence and the advice he gave and the way he never seemed to get upset or go funny in the head like the other adults – the white ones, anyway. I had come to think of him as my friend, almost to the point of slipping him into Klaus's shoes as my new father . . . and all that time he'd been a Jew.

Everybody knows that a Jew is a snake in the grass, lying in wait, not revealing himself until he does you harm, and Gerhard had definitely lain in the tall grass, hiding himself from me even as we chatted and became friends . . . but had he harmed me? He had not. And he'd confessed at last to being a Jew. No, not confessed – he'd confided. He'd told me what he was, man to man, and I couldn't blame him for not telling me sooner, not when he learned from Klaus there'd been a war, and inside that war was another war, where one side had weapons and the other side didn't, a one-sided war, it seemed to me now. I pictured Gerhard in a relocation camp with Noah Epstein alongside him. Those two would have liked each other, with their clever comments about everything. Then Klaus entered the picture, cut off their arms and legs and swapped Noah's for Gerhard's, and Noah said to Gerhard, 'Maybe if we traded clothes they'd fit,' and they both laughed, and Klaus was so annoyed he had to shoot them all over again, but they wouldn't die, and kept making sarcastic comments about his marksmanship until Klaus went red in the face and then went insane and exploded like a firecracker, and the blood and guts went all over Noah and Gerhard, and they looked at each other and said, 'Look at this mess. These Nazis, they simply have no consideration.'

'Erich, why are you laughing?'

I stopped. I hadn't known I was. I turned and looked at him.

'I won't tell about you and Noah,' I said.

'Who's Noah?'

'No one. I won't tell Klaus or Zeppi anything.'

'I was hoping you'd say that. You know, that makes us partners.'

'Yes.'

'A Jew and a German. A Yid and a sausage eater. What a pair!'

Gerhard pointed to the sky. Dark clouds were boiling up from nowhere, stitched together with threads of lightning. 'Here it comes.'

'It looks different, somehow . . . darker. '

'That means the rainy season isn't far off now.'

'Good.'

Together we watched the gathering storm. There was a new feeling to the air, a scent of something just beginning. The clouds rose higher, assembling themselves into fantastic shapes that seemed alive. They blotted out the sun and kept rising, boiling towers of darkness built and razed in minutes, then built anew, an aerial city, formless and somehow terrifying to behold. And then, as I watched, the colossal forms rumbling and straining above me took, for a moment, the shape of a massive lopsided temple with twisted columns and a roof already collapsing under its own weight, with a final ray of sunlight stabbing through it like a message from God. Then it was swept away, destroyed in seconds, scribbled over by lightning and erased forever.

'Did you see it, Gerhard?'

'See what?'

'The clouds, they looked like a huge temple.'

'I saw a conch shell', he said, 'and then a whale.'

'You must have been looking at a different part.'

The darkness loomed above us like a sheet pulled over a dead man's face, and I felt cold, yet at the same time I was strangely happy. Gerhard's head was tipped back, watching the cloud mass tumbling and spreading like a stain across the sky. I saw the first raindrop hit his cheek like a fat exploding tear, then another hit his forehead, then pellets of surprising coldness peppered my own face and shoulders.

Together we turned and began running toward the shabono, driven along by rainfall hard as hailstones.

ELEVEN

It was raining every day now, sometimes for hours, and whenever the skies opened and poured water over the land, the Yayomi barely stirred from their hammocks. Nobody hunted, and the only thing to eat was plantain soup or plantains roasted on the fire. Every morning I went down to the river to see if the water had risen, but it hadn't.

The mornings were still fair, with blue skies. That was when the plantain gathering was done, and sometimes a little fishing, but the fish seemed to have moved out to deeper water, so canoes had to be used to find them. Even Kwaytcha, who was probably the best arrow fisherman in the shabono, brought back nothing. Noroni said it was a bad omen that the fish had moved this early in the season, and Manokwo agreed.

Manokwo was getting even more impatient for Zeppi to turn into a girl, even though he'd been told the change wouldn't happen until the end of the rainy season, a long way off yet. He let it be known that he didn't see how something as important as a change from male to female could be accomplished instantly, when the rains stopped. There should already be indications of the early stages at least, because nothing in the living world of animals and men happened instantly except death by accident or warfare. Everything else that changed from one state to another state did so at a rate slow enough to be observed, and after observing Zeppi's cock many times, Manokwo still hadn't seen anything different.

He asked Gerhard why that was, and Gerhard had to tell him that the ways of dolphins were not the same as the ways of men, and it must be that special dolphins, the kind that could change into humans, were able to change themselves at will when the time came to do so. Manokwo was unhappy anyway, because the end of the rains was a long way off and he wanted Zeppi to be his yellow-haired wife tomorrow.

Klaus had definitely changed. He avoided Gerhard and myself, as if he somehow had scented collusion in the wind and knew where it was blowing from. He remained silent for long periods, sometimes days at a time, and I made no attempt to talk with him. Whenever yoppo was used, which was often, now that the men had less time to hunt during the daylight hours, Klaus had some. I didn't want any after my first experience, and Gerhard said it was probably a good idea. But Klaus had as much as the Yayomi were willing to shoot up his nose, and it soon became a common sight to see him crawling around in the mud, his backbone lashed by rain, eyes wide, staring at things only he could see.

I thought it was very likely that Klaus would die someday at Gerhard's hands, and I wasn't really surprised to realise that I didn't care. He deserved to die, I had to admit, although he was my own uncle. I couldn't have killed him myself, because of the family connection, but if Gerhard decided Klaus's time had come, I wasn't going to stand in his way.

I decided that if Gerhard could be so very much in control of himself, so could I, and the first person I showed this to was Awomay. I simply stopped thinking about what would or wouldn't happen when we left, and instead made a deliberate effort to treat Awomay with kindness, and not just when I wanted to take her off into the jungle.

I did things such as bringing her flowers, which she didn't know what to do with until I started weaving them into her hair. The other women always giggled and covered their mouths when I did this, but Awomay was very dignified about it. I could see in her eyes that she was wondering why I'd stopped being the way I was around her. She even asked Gerhard to ask me why I'd changed, and how long it would last, and she also asked him to ask me on behalf of the other women what it would take to have their husbands start behaving the same way. It was funny when it happened, but Gerhard warned me in all seriousness not to treat Awomay like that any more, because placing her on a pedestal, as he put it, was so unlike normal behaviour from a Yayomi male that the other husbands would begin to resent me if their wives started nagging them to be treated the way Awomay was treated by me.

I took his advice to heart and once again turned a cold shoulder to my wife. She was disappointed, I could tell, but she accepted this return to the way things used to be and always would be. Gerhard said that this was the very essence of Yayomi life, its basic changelessness. They liked it that way, because that was the way it had always been. When things changed, there was a chance that the newness would turn out to be bad for them. The newness of having dolphins living among them was acceptable only because it involved the supernatural. Real change was frowned upon.

It was raining more and more, and the river was rising at last. Soon there would be so much water covering the land we could put our plan into action. No frowns should get in the way of that.

One morning, Waneeri came striding into the shabono and went directly to Manokwo. Others overheard the loud conversation between them and joined in, and soon everyone except the smallest children were milling around, listening to Waneeri yell and watching him leap up and down as he got more and more excited. Then everyone went out through the hole in the wall and headed for the river, with Gerhard and myself trailing along behind.

'What are they so excited about?' I asked.

'I think Waneeri found something interesting.'

All the canoes, including Tagerri's unfinished log, had been dragged up the shore, away from the rising water. Waneeri led everyone along the river bank to the right, still shouting and punching the air with his fists. They began gathering around the spot where Mother's bones were. Gerhard and I pushed our way through the crowd. Waneeri was telling everyone again of what he'd found, and this time Gerhard was able to translate.

'He says he went to sleep last night and the yoppo still inside him from yesterday talked to him, making his dreams green and filled with a sense of betrayal ... and the dreams told him to beware of lies from the tall dolphin boy ... that's

you, Erich ... who is filled with treachery despite having been
a guest of the Yayomi ... and who had lied to them ever since
the disappearance of his mother, the dolphin woman
... and then the dreams told Waneeri to go again to the place
he'd been before, the place he found the dolphin boy lying on
the ground with his eyes closed ... and to look into the water
in front of that place ... before the rising river has a chance to
take away the bad secret hidden there ... and so today
Waneeri did as his dreams told him to do, and came to the
place ... and went into the water and found with his toes ...
the body of the dolphin woman ... and he brought her to dry
land while he still could, with the water rising and pushing
against him he did this ... and now all the Yayomi may see for
themselves the body of the dolphin woman ... which proves
the thing that Waneeri always believed ... that the dolphin
boy murdered his own mother ... and sank her body in the
water so nobody would know of his terrible crime ...'

Waneeri took a few long strides to a pile of branches and
big jungle leaves, and pulled them aside. Something like ice
water ran down my spine. There was Mother, a few muddy
bones attached to a spine and rib cage, with her head of yellow hair still clinging to the scalp. She had no face, and one
leg and one arm had become detached. There was a long gasp
from every throat, and I felt like vomiting with fear. This was
the very thing Gerhard had said we mustn't risk happening.
Now Waneeri, who hated me for having killed his cousin, had
been drawn back to the place by his own suspicions. I didn't
for one moment believe it was the voice of the yoppo that had
brought him here. He must have been spying on me.

'Whatever you do,' warned Gerhard, 'don't panic, or even
look as if you're panicking.'

'What can we do?'

'I'm thinking.'

Manokwo went to the bones and prodded them with his foot, then squatted down and lifted a few strands of hair. He rolled them between his fingertips, then dropped them and stood up. He pointed at me and spoke a few words. Everyone turned to stare at me, and it was all I could do to stop myself from running away. Only Gerhard's whispered advice, 'Say nothing, do nothing,' kept me where I was.

Gerhard began to speak, first to Manokwo, then to Waneeri, then to everyone else. He spoke for what seemed like a long time, then he stopped. Manokwo and Waneeri and anyone else who had an opinion started arguing with each other.

'What did you say to them?'

'I said that you didn't kill your mother, that you saw her and your new baby dolphin brother swim away downriver. You saw nothing more after that because of the spell she cast over you to make you sleep, so you'd stay here and not follow them. Someone killed your mother the moment you fell asleep, because she didn't get far away before dying. You have a strong suspicion who that killer is, and you'll say so outright if the accusation of murder isn't withdrawn. You've also offered to take a test that will prove you didn't kill your mother, and you'll take that test this afternoon in front of the entire shabono. If that proof doesn't silence your accusers, you'll reveal the identity of the one who murdered her . . . I'm hoping, Erich, that the test will be so conclusive that Waneeri and the rest will simply shut up rather than have you accuse one of them of having done the deed. They haven't forgotten what happened to Tagerri when he raised his hand against you, so we have a little leeway here. It's all a game of bluff.'

'What test?'

'Um . . . I'm afraid you'll have to eat your mother's remains.'

'What . . . ?'

'No murderer would dare consume the remains of his victim. To do so would mean risking possession by the victim's ghost, and there can be no more horrible fate than that. Matricide is the worst of crimes, even here, so if you do as I've suggested, it should prove to them beyond any doubt that you're telling the truth. A mother-killer with his mother's ghost inside him, that's something no Yayomi would want to see. The whole shabono would have to be evacuated, and that's an awfully difficult thing to do right at the start of the rainy season. Take the test. They want to believe you're innocent, except for Waneeri, of course, and I've made it plain by some pointed stares in his direction that he's the one you're going to accuse. He's already a bit frightened, but I don't expect him to back away from this unless Manokwo and the rest tell him to.'

'But I can't . . .'

'Yes you can, and must, if you want to live. Klaus would have to be the one to execute you for murdering his wife, and if he doesn't want to, they'll suspect he had something to do with it as well. Take the test and all that will fade away. You have to, Erich.'

I knew he was right. Gerhard was always right.

Each step in preparation for the test was closely followed by the whole tribe. First, Mother's bones, which were carried back to the shabono by Gerhard, were burned to remove the last of her skin and hair and flesh. Then the blackened bones were set aside to cool for a little while before Gerhard and I started pulverising them by grinding them with long poles.

Zeppi, watching with his friends, asked what was happening. I told him it was just another burial ceremony, and to go away, which he did, to my relief. Klaus, who had missed all the excitement, was told by Gerhard what had happened. He was shocked when it was explained what I had to do in order to prove my innocence. 'My God, Erich, can you do it?'

'I have to.'

In my heart, I wondered if I could do such a disgusting thing. It wasn't so much the fact that the bones being reduced to powder by our efforts were Mother's, it was the fact that they were bones at all. Awomay was already making plantain soup to mix with the bone powder, just like a hausfrau preparing her husband's lunch of bread and bratwurst. Klaus stepped away from me, and I didn't blame him. Really, there was nothing he could do but wait and hope I had a hearty appetite.

Finally, the bone powder was ready to be put into the soup. There wasn't as much as I'd been dreading, only a double handful of fine grey ash. I scooped up every speck onto a broad leaf and carried it to the plantain pot. Gerhard had warned me to make a speech of some kind before adding the ashes to the soup, just to create an effect, a bit of dramatics, as he put it. So I lifted the leaf up to my face and made my speech to Mother.

'Once upon a time there was a man with two sons. The man went away to war and was killed, leaving his wife behind with the two sons to raise all by herself. Then the man's brother offered to marry the widow and help her raise the sons to be men like himself and their father. The mother and her sons went to a far-off country to be with the brother, who pretended to marry the mother, then all four of them were lost in a gigantic forest that stretched out forever, with no hope of finding their way home again. But in the forest there were people who found them and took them to their shabono, where the mother went mad and was eaten by fish, and the younger brother turned into a sister, and the older brother had to eat the bones of his own mother, so the moral of the story is, never leave home and nothing bad will happen to you. Amen.'

I lowered the leaf and poured Mother into the soup. Awomay stirred it, a worried expression on her face. I looked to see if Noroni and Kwaytcha were also worried, but couldn't find their faces among the crowd. I saw Waneeri, and he looked angry that I was going to cheat him of the satisfaction he wanted. I winked at him, not to make him angrier, but to give myself some nerve. Then I squatted down by the fire and dipped out a bowlful of the soup. I let it cool for a moment, then raised it to my lips. I closed my eyes and heard a sigh from the Yayomi as the liquid entered my mouth.

I don't know how many bowls of plantain soup I'd eaten since living at the shabono, but the truth is, this one didn't taste any different, except for a fine grittiness that wasn't usually there. The larger bits of bone ash did not combine properly with the soup and I could feel them between my teeth and on my tongue as I swallowed. I dipped my bowl again, and drank, this time with less hesitation, but not so quickly that the drama of the moment was lost. This was a performance, a courtroom drama, and I was the accused, proving his innocence with a bold move calculated to win the day.

I drank and drank, and drank some more. I drank enough for five hungry men, then couldn't force another drop past my lips. My belly felt horribly full. Seeing the trouble, Gerhard hissed at Klaus, 'Help him out, grieving husband.'

To his credit, Klaus dipped and drank two bowls also, and that more or less finished off the soup. I got to my feet, feeling a lot sicker than before I'd started.

Gerhard said, 'Don't throw up, or they'll think your mother is trying to escape from inside you. Hold that soup in, whatever you do.'

I turned in a circle, holding my bowl upside down in front of me. Gerhard then made a speech, which he repeated for my benefit. 'This proves you didn't kill your mother, which was a shameful thing for the Yayomi ever to have accused you of. However, you forgive everyone, including a certain person who started everyone thinking the wrong thing. Sometimes honest mistakes are made, and when the truth is finally known, forgiveness is in order if the matter is to be put to rest without bloodshed, which is the way it should be within the walls of the shabono. Spilled blood is for those who live outside the shabono, the enemies who raid because they are evil and cruel and envious of your happiness.

'Since the coming of the dolphin people among the Yayomi there have been no raiding parties to make your lives miserable and your women weep, and this is because the dolphin people have brought good fortune to the Yayomi, and made their enemies afraid. Now the rains are here and there will be no more raiding parties until the dry season returns, all thanks to the dolphin people, who are happy to be with their friends the Yayomi and have forgiven them the terrible story they believed for half a day. If they had believed it for longer, the dolphin boy Eri might have brought down lightning from the sky to strike the shabono and set it afire and burn it to the ground, and then the Yayomi would have no shelter from the rain, which would be a just punishment for their mistaken belief. But that did not happen, because all has been forgiven and all present here are friends, just as before.'

This speech seemed to satisfy everyone, and Manokwo then made a speech for Gerhard to relay to me, a long and rambling speech that emphasised the special place the Yayomi had in the grand scheme of things, as everyone in the world knows, and which had been proved true by the arrival of the dolphin people, who were friends of the Yayomi and very welcome to stay forever. The Yayomi were very sad that the dolphin mother was dead, and even more sad that a terrible mistake was made, but that was in the past, already forgotten, and now everyone would be as one family, which was the way of happiness.

I was now officially an innocent man. The skies chose that moment to open for the afternoon rain, and within a minute the population of the shabono had scattered to their hammocks to chew tobacco and play with their parrots and doze until it was done. Zeppi and his pals came flying back into the shabono and raced for shelter, Mitzi clinging to Zeppi's hair as he ran, his little breasts bouncing and pearled with raindrops. He came to me, panting happily, and gasped, 'We ran all the way back!'

'Very good, Zeppi.'

'Is the burying thing over?'

'It was a cremation, not a burial.'

'Who was it?'

'Just a woman.'

'Why do they burn them?'

'Because they think that allowing a body to rot away in the soil is a bad thing to do to a dead person.'

'Oh.'

'Run along, will you. I've got a stomach ache.'

He left me swinging slowly in my hammock as rain poured from the eaves of the shabono's roof and my belly complained of its burden. The thing about plantain soup is, it makes you fart for a long time afterwards. Over the next few hours, wind from the huge meal I'd had left me in wisps and blasts, gradually easing the bloatedness. Once, Mother had carried me in her belly, then let me out through her vagina. Now I carried Mother in my belly, and in time would let her out through my arse.

Knowing it wouldn't be long now before we could leave, my life entered a strange new phase, one in which I saw everything and everyone around me as being not quite real. The only real thing was the escape plan. We weren't in a prison, and we weren't captives of the Yayomi, but Gerhard had made it clear that all our unfulfillable promises of Zeppi's sexual transformation made it absolutely necessary that we get away before the time came for that to happen.

True to Gerhard's prediction, the rains were more severe than usual this year. The regular afternoon rainstorm was a thunderous affair, with the earth floor of the shabono reduced to mud that didn't have a chance to dry out before the following afternoon's downpour. Everybody's feet and legs were constantly covered in mud. The only refuge was in your hammock, and that's where everyone stayed for hours at a time, looking miserable but resigned, not even talking, the thunder was so loud. The air was hotter than ever, since the rain had no cooling effect at all when it came and only made the humidity worse.

Gerhard began re-experiencing symptoms of malarial fever, and asked Klaus for some more quinine, but Klaus, without even looking into the bag at his side, told him there was none left. I didn't believe it, and neither did Gerhard, to judge by his expression, but he refused to look crestfallen or worried or angry, instead made a joke about it by saying, 'As soon as the rain stops I'll dash down to the pharmacist's and get some more.' Klaus didn't even smile.

Gerhard took himself away to his hammock and proceeded to add to the dampness beneath him with floods of sweating. I toyed with the notion of stealing drugs from Klaus's bag, but his medications were labelled in Portuguese, and I couldn't be sure that whatever pills I found would be the right kind. In any case, Klaus kept the bag within arm's length, day and night, so thieving from it was probably impossible. I felt bad for Gerhard, though, as I watched him dripping into the mud below his hammock and muttering. If I despised Klaus before, I detested him doubly after this.

Late one morning, about an hour before we could expect the day's rainfall to begin, Zeppi came to me with his face flushed and his hands held over his privates.

'Erich, my willie hurts and it won't go away . . .'

'Let me see.'

He opened his hands. His cock was swollen to twice its normal size.

'It really really hurts,' he said, tears squeezing past his eyes.

'Did something bite it, a spider or an insect?'

'I don't think so. Make it stop, Erich.'

'Come with me.'

We went to Klaus, who was staring into space.

'Klaus, Zeppi has something wrong.'

He turned his head to look at us. 'Wrong?'

'With his cock. It's all swollen.'

Klaus came alive in a very professional way and inspected Zeppi.

'I've no idea what this is. Does it only hurt where it's swollen?'

'In my belly too . . .' said Zeppi, his face beginning to twist in agony.

'Get Wentzler', Klaus told me.

Gerhard was in his hammock, sweating heavily from fever, his face pale. I told him about Zeppi and he made a huge effort to get to his feet. I held him up and we staggered over to the others.

Gerhard looked at Zeppi's swollen penis. 'Oh, no . . .' he said, and something in the tone of his voice made my heart drop. 'Zeppi, listen to me. Have you been peeing in the river when you swim?'

'Sometimes . . .'

'Zeppi, you were warned not to do that. This is what can happen . . .'

'It's that little fish thing?' I asked.

'The candiru, yes, I'm sure this is it. Get Noroni.'

I ran to fetch my father-in-law. When Noroni saw Zeppi's cock he looked worried and began shaking his head. Gerhard had a hurried conversation with him, then said, 'All he can recommend is yoppo, to ease the pain.'

'That isn't enough,' said Klaus. 'We must do something.'

Gerhard took Klaus and me aside and whispered, 'There's no cure, no way of getting the fish out of his penis. It's snagged in there until he . . . dies. Noroni's never seen anyone survive the candiru. It's always little boys who ignore the advice they're given . . .'

'Are you saying he has no chance at all?' Klaus asked.

'None. Noroni's going to prepare a pinch of yoppo. It's all we can do, unless you happen to have a little morphine to spare, Klaus.'

He made it clear what his opinion of Klaus was with those words, but Klaus brushed them off. He was looking more alert than I'd seen him look in weeks. 'I have nothing for pain, but I have my instruments. The yoppo will be his anaesthetic.'

'That's ridiculous,' said Gerhard.

'This doesn't concern you,' Klaus told him, then turned briskly to me. 'Erich, he's your brother. There's no one closer to him than you – therefore, I ask for your permission to operate. Please make up your mind now. The child is clearly in agony.'

'But without something to put him to sleep . . .'

'The yoppo will work if he has it in sufficient quantity. It doesn't mask the physical sensation of pain so much as it . . . moves it sideways. You've experienced it, Erich.'

'But I wasn't hurt at the time . . .'

Klaus was insistent. 'Make up your mind. I operate or he dies in agony.'

'Then . . . yes.'

What else could I say? Noroni was hurrying back with his pouch of yoppo and the nose tube. Zeppi by now was hunched over in pain. I went to him and put my arms around him. He was slick with sweat, shaking uncontrollably. I heard Klaus telling Gerhard to get the women to boil some water as quickly as possible.

'Listen, Zeppi,' I said, 'Uncle Klaus is going to get the fish out, but it might hurt a little bit, so we're going to give you some Yayomi medicine. They have to blow it up your nose. You've seen the men using it, and I've had it myself, and Gerhard and Klaus too. It feels a bit strange when they blow it up your nose, but after that everything will be fine, all right?'

'Yes . . .' he managed to squeeze out.

'Here comes Noroni now. Lift up your head, and try not to jump when he blows it in. Soon you'll be in a lot less pain.'

I didn't believe it even as I said it, but Zeppi was raising his face toward Noroni, ready to receive the tube in his nose. Half the shabono had gathered around by now. I placed the tube in Zeppi's left nostril and Noroni blew hard. Zeppi kicked once against the ground, then relaxed a little. I put the tube in his right nostril and the second blast made his legs stand out straight. His eyes were wide open, but I took that as a good sign because a few seconds ago they'd been clenched shut with pain.

Klaus looked at Zeppi's pupils. 'Wait a minute or so,' he said, 'then repeat the dosage.'

'That's too much,' protested Gerhard.

'I'm about to cut open his penis,' said Klaus. 'Put yourself in his place.'

Gerhard said nothing. His own fever had made him unfit for confrontation. I helped Noroni blast more of the green powder into Zeppi's nose, and his body became completely limp. His eyes stayed open, even though I tried to close them. He was ready. Within minutes, the water was boiling. Klaus selected several instruments from his black bag and placed them into the water with tongs, then took a small bottle of disinfectant and doused his hands and forearms. 'These conditions are deplorable,' he said. 'Pick him up now and bring him to his hammock.'

I did that, and Klaus instructed me to lay Zeppi's legs out to either side. His cock stood up like a fat little radish. 'What I really need is a table,' Klaus complained. 'The hammock will swing back and forth when I need absolute stillness.'

I got under Zeppi on all fours and lifted my back until it met evenly with his.

'How's that?'

'Most ingenious. Hold very still now while I disinfect his groin.'

I heard splashing sounds and smelled the sharp reek of disinfectant.

'Tell these savages to stand back and give me room.'

A few words were spoken and I saw many pairs of legs retreat a few steps.

'Wentzler, you'll be my assistant. Get me the small scalpel. Use the tongs.'

I heard Gerhard hurry off to the boiling pot, then heard him return.

'We begin,' said Klaus, and a second later I felt Zeppi shudder as the scalpel cut into him, then he seemed to relax again. I wondered what could possibly be going through his mind, and hoped none of it had anything to do with what was happening to his body. I hoped Zeppi was dreaming of home, visiting Frau Ulrich's sweetshop or the bakery further down the street, cramming his mouth with cream horns and candy, floating away on a sugary pink cloud of bliss.

Klaus worked quickly and offered a running commentary as he proceeded.

'Impossible to determine where along the urethra the fish

is stuck, so we'll begin halfway and work back . . . Nothing . . .
Further back, then . . . I'm afraid the fish is deeper inside than
I thought . . . Wentzler, the silver clamps, if you please . . .
Now then, we move further inside . . . It can't possibly have
gone back as far as the prostate . . . I trust you're not going to
faint . . . Wentzler?'

Gerhard collapsed next to me, his face above the beard
pale and glossy with sweat, his eyes closed.

'Uncle, do you want me to come up and help?'

'You're helping right where you are. I have everything I
need for the moment, thanks to our fainting friend. Stay very
still, Erich.'

After that he worked in silence. Every now and then Zeppi
twitched, and soon the twitchings threatened to slide him off
my back. 'This is impossible', Klaus said. 'Yoppo! Yoppo!' I saw
Noroni's legs and heard him administer more powder, and
Zeppi relaxed again. 'Better', was all Klaus said, and started work
again. Gerhard was as still as Zeppi, breath whistling in and out
of his nose. He looked as sick and feverish as I'd ever seen him.

My back was slippery with sweat, mine and Zeppi's. Also
blood, a lot of it. The redness trickled down my sides, following the curve of my ribs, and plopped off into the mud
beneath me. My arms and legs ached with the strain of supporting Zeppi's weight without moving, and my head hung
from my neck like a cannonball. Sweat ran into my eyes,
blinding me. Klaus was humming as he worked. The Yayomi
watched in absolute silence. Soon I heard thunder, then rain
began to fall. Klaus hummed louder to make himself heard
above the din, then started to sing. He sang a few verses from
one song, then a few from another – light opera, I think it was,
nothing I knew. His voice was quite good.

'Uncle, did you find the fish?'

'The fish? Oh, yes, some time ago. Forgive me, I become distracted in surgery. I forgot you were there, ha, ha! Yes, the fish has come out, an ugly little creature it was.'

'Will you finish soon?'

'Fairly soon. I must remove the excess tissue and clean up the edges first. Can you hold out a little longer, my boy?'

'Yes.'

'I need the needle and thread now, but I can get them for myself, don't worry.'

He walked away to the fire, then came back, whistling a merry tune.

'This is the last stage now, Erich, the suturing. Be patient a little longer if you would.'

'I'm all right.'

He hummed and sang and whistled. Gerhard lay where he'd fallen. No one came to take him away. He seemed to be deeply asleep. His face wasn't so pale any more, so I didn't try to waken him. I couldn't have moved an arm to touch him, in any case. I was starting to feel like a wooden table, I'd been in the position for so long.

'Almost done, Erich.'

The change in Klaus was remarkable. From mud-covered zombie he'd become a breezy, confident professional man again. I supposed it was the chance to do what he'd been trained to do, ease human suffering and use his scalpel to cut away something bad. He was a doctor again, not a butcher.

I realised I was preparing an argument for Gerhard. Klaus had saved Zeppi from a horrible death, from awful pain and suffering, just as a doctor was supposed to do. If only we could get him back to civilisation he could be a proper doctor again and help people, not sit around blasting yoppo up his nose. This could be a new beginning for Klaus, if I helped him stay on the straight and narrow. He was my uncle, after all, and I owed him that much.

'Done!' cried Klaus, stepping away from the hammock. 'Erich, come out from under and see!'

I eased myself away from the hammock, feeling it peel from my back like a second skin. The mud all around me was red. I stood up slowly, the muscles in my limbs screaming. From his chest to his knees, Zeppi was covered in blood. I hadn't expected as much as this. My own body was red from neck to buttocks. The air smelled of blood. The Yayomi stared at Zeppi, at Klaus and at me. I could tell they under-stood nothing of what had happened, the concept of surgery being unknown to them. They'd be amazed by the results of Klaus's science when Zeppi woke up and was well again. Klaus nudged Gerhard with his foot and he stirred.

'It's all over, Wentzler. Take a look, if you think you can do so without fainting again.'

I was delaying my first close look at Zeppi. My stomach felt queasy, my head a little light. I wanted Gerhard and myself to look at the same time, for mutual support. Gerhard got slowly to his feet, looking sheepish.

'Sorry . . . Was I out for long?'

He turned to Zeppi and his jaw dropped.

'Don't panic,' Klaus told him. 'It's not as bad as it looks. I didn't have a nurse to mop up the blood as it came, that's all. Look,' he invited us, like a baker who'd just completed a three-tiered wedding cake. 'Look, see what has been done here. The accomplishment, the challenge . . . Look, gentlemen.'

We moved closer and looked. Zeppi's midsection was like

something from the back room of a butcher's shop. All I could make out was a massive gash between his legs, sutured with black horsehair. It looked like a ruptured sea anemone with little dead insects all over it. I felt my stomach lurch. I couldn't understand what it was I was looking at.

'Where's . . . where's his cock and balls?'

'The external genitalia have been removed,' Klaus explained, sounding very much like a proud professor of surgery lecturing his students. 'Even as far back as the prostate, every male organ is gone. What you see, gentlemen, is medical history.'

'The fish . . .' said Gerhard, barely breathing beside me.

'The fish, yes, that was most opportune. Without the fish I would never have had the opportunity, you see. History is often created by happy accidents, and such was the case here.'

'But . . . what did you *do*?'

'Do? I've made young Zeppi into what nature obviously intended he be all along. I have made him female!'

He was beaming happily, this naked man covered in red, so proud of what lay in the blood-soaked hammock before him. Rain hammered at the roof, at the earth, at my brain.

'But you . . . you only had to cut the fish out, a tiny fish . . .'

'A lesser surgeon than myself would have contented himself with that small task. However, I saw what needed to be done, the larger picture, if you will, and I knew the moment must be seized, the work done, here and now, under the most deplorable conditions possible . . . and it was done! Even Muller in Berlin has never attempted the complete procedure! Zeppi now has a vagina. This is the way he should always have been, a young *female* of the species Homo sapiens. I have done this . . . Nature gave Zeppi too much, and now I

have taken a little back and remade him as a her. She'll thank
me, I know it, when she wakes up. That may take a while,
since I have no idea what that amount of narcotic will do . . .
but it served its purpose well, don't you think? There she lies,
a sleeping beauty, male when last awake, and female when she
awakens again.'

Gerhard moved closer. I didn't dare. He said, 'Zeppi is dead.'

'No, no,' Klaus assured him, 'not dead – sleeping!'

I made myself go closer. Zeppi wasn't breathing. There was
absolutely no motion in his blood-spattered chest. His eyes
were half open, and the pupils had rolled up into his head. He
was dead. He might have been dead for a long time, dead even
as Klaus sutured his awful wound, humming and whistling. I
couldn't move. The thing in front of me wasn't Zeppi, it was a
piece of tortured flesh, cut and hacked and stitched up again
in a make-believe operation performed by a madman.

I stepped away, out from under the roof, into the shabono's
open centre, and there I emptied everything from my stomach. Then I stood and let the rain wash Zeppi's blood from
me. My head swam. Nothing of the scene behind me could
possibly be real. Zeppi was alive, somewhere near, playing
with his friends, monkey perched on his shoulder, laughing
in the sun. Klaus couldn't have done *that* to his own nephew
and sometime son. No man could be so insane as to butcher
a corpse and display it so proudly. There could never be any
understanding of what he'd done, never be any forgiveness.

In my heart I grieved for Zeppi, and in my mind I planned
how best to kill my uncle. Klaus Linden would have to die for
this, if not for those other countless butcheries he talked of.
They were someone else's loss, but Zeppi was *my* loss, *my*
tragedy. I had never loved him enough, and now he was gone,

taken from me by Klaus the mad butcher. Rain lashed my upturned face. There were no tears to wash away. The thing that had happened to Zeppi was too terrible for tears.

Behind me I heard Gerhard and Klaus arguing.

'Look a little closer, Herr *Doctor*. I think you'll see the patient has expired.'

'The patient is sedated. Don't tell me my business.'

'Oh, excuse me, I thought death *was* your business.'

'Kindly step away from him . . . her. There's still the risk of infection.'

'Certainly, Herr Doctor. Whatever you say. Is the prognosis good, in your opinion? Will Zeppi wake up and call for his monkey? What about pregnancy when he's old enough? You did include a womb in his new body, didn't you?'

'Regrettably, that was not possible.'

'Perhaps next time.'

'Perhaps.'

Gerhard approached me. 'Erich, what can I say . . .'

'Nothing. I'm going to kill him.'

'Listen, we can leave Klaus till later – he's in his own little operating theatre of the mind, taking bows, scheduling lectures, accepting the Nobel Prize for medicine – what concerns me now is that there were four dolphins, now there are two. And one of the survivors killed one of the dead, right in front of the Yayomi. They won't know what to make of this until I tell them what to make of it, but there's a good chance they won't believe me. More likely they'll think they've just witnessed an elaborate murder. Manokwo is going to be furious that once again a yellow-haired bride has slipped through his fingers. Someone's going to have to pay for that, and it won't necessarily be Klaus alone. I have a feeling the magic has worn off. We're all at risk.'

'I don't care. I'm going to kill Klaus right now, and I don't care who sees me do it.'

'Think again, Erich, if you want to survive.'

'Don't tell me what to do.'

'Understand this – if you jeopardise us any further, I'll abandon you to save myself. I don't have too much respect for unreasonable people. By using our heads we may get out of this alive. Put your feelings away for later, when we're away from here. Think hard about this. Now, I'm going to tell Manokwo some lies, and then I'm going to build a fire for Zeppi. We have to do what's expected. Dinner will be served this evening with one thing on the menu – plantain soup, you know the kind.'

He left me, and I heard him telling more lies to explain the actions of the dolphins. The crowd that had surrounded Zeppi's hammock was breaking up, the people drifting away. Two of Zeppi's friends were crying, and Mitzi was scampering about, swinging from pole to pole under the shabono roof, aware that something terrible had happened to her human. Klaus stood guard over the body, looking less assured than he had a few minutes ago. Reality was creeping in at the edges of his vision, slyly blotting out his great achievement, like clouds sliding over the sun.

As I watched him, Klaus slowly came to the realisation that he was only a naked man beside a dead boy, a boy he'd killed. His eyes betrayed him. For the moment, he was sane again.

'Do you know what you have done?' I said. I couldn't look at Zeppi, couldn't even point to him.

'It was the fish ... the toothpick fish.'

'It was you, Uncle.'

'The fish would have killed him anyway. Gerhard said so and the Indians said so ...'

'You cut the fish out. Zeppi would have lived, maybe with a scar on his cock, but he would have lived. It was the other things you did that killed him.'

'You aren't qualified to pass judgment on medical matters, Erich. I must ask you not to criticise what you don't understand.'

'Certainly, Uncle. We're going to burn Zeppi now. Please don't help us.'

I left him and joined Gerhard, who was watching Manokwo's retreating back. 'What did you tell him?' I asked.

'The truth, for once; dressed up a little, perhaps. I said Klaus had tried to cut out the candiru, but he cut too much, and Zeppi died from loss of blood. Klaus regrets robbing Manokwo of his second bride, but it couldn't be helped.'

'What did he say?'

'Nothing, that's what worries me. I think we should get away tonight. Performing the ritual cremation and soup-drinking for Zeppi will keep everyone off our backs for the rest of the day, but tomorrow morning is another matter. Tonight we have to go, flood or no flood. We've all outstayed our welcome. Are you with me?'

'Yes.'

'Who should tell Klaus, you or me?'

'You. I can't stand to look at him.'

'Done. Let's get on with building the fire.'

The rain stopped falling as we set about our work. Most of the firewood inside the shabono was wet, but we stacked it in the traditional way, as had been done for Tagerri and Mother, and placed Zeppi, bloody hammock and all, onto the small bed of wood arranged for him, then added more wood until he was hidden from view. I took a burning stick from one of the cooking fires and touched it to Zeppi's pyre. It wouldn't catch until Gerhard added more kindling; after a while, when the main body of wood had dried, it caught properly and flared up around my brother in a cradle of bright flames.

I stood back then and watched him burn, smelling the odour of roasting flesh which somehow was cleaner than the smell of blood still lingering in the air. It was dusk by now, and the fire roared in a friendly way, pushing back the darkness, lighting the inside of the shabono with a golden glow.

Unlike the previous burnings I'd seen, the Yayomi took no interest in Zeppi's pyre; in fact, they kept as far away from it as possible. Gerhard didn't need to point out this was not a good sign. While I tended to the fire, Awomay prepared plantains for soup, but when she was halfway through her work, Manokwo suddenly went to her and ordered her to stop. She obeyed him, looking sideways at me to let me know she couldn't disobey, and I nodded back to let her know I didn't blame her. He ordered Awomay to her hammock and her plantains were added to the pile for general preparation. No soup for Zeppi, was the intended message, or for the living dolphins either.

Klaus came over to stand with Gerhard and myself. I didn't want him anywhere near me, but arguing with him in front of the Yayomi would have been foolish.

'Something's wrong,' Klaus said. 'Why do they look so sullen?'

'The small matter of a dead child,' Gerhard reminded him.

'Such things happen,' Klaus said stiffly.

'Around you, all the time, I'm sure.'

'I resent your tone, Wentzler.'

'Listen, Herr Doctor, we're getting out of here tonight. The welcome mat has been withdrawn. We can discuss the reasons for it later. Erich and I are going to steal a canoe and make a run for it when everyone's asleep, right, Erich?'

'Yes.'

'You can come along with us, or stay here and entertain the Yayomi with your surgical skills. I'd suggest that your first brilliant act should be to cut your own throat before they do it for you. Coming along?'

'How could I resist such a friendly invitation?'

I waited for Gerhard to continue. 'The plan is simple. First, when the fire dies down we'll grind Zeppi's bones. The Yayomi will leave us alone while we do it, out of respect for the dead. It looks as if there won't be any need to drink the usual bone soup, but I'll give everyone a little speech about taking the ashes down to the river for dispersal, the correct thing to do for a dolphin, no? All three of us will do that, and when we get to the canoes we'll grab the nearest and run it down to the water. All the canoes have been turned upside down because of the rain, and each one has its paddles underneath, so don't forget to grab those.'

'What if they come with us?' I asked.

'I don't think they will. Rejection of us means avoiding us as much as possible. We've become the men in the room with the smelliest armpits, so the chances are good they'll let us walk out of the shabono with just Zeppi's ashes in our hands. This is important – take nothing else. That means you leave your bag behind,' he said to Klaus.

'Impossible. Those instruments are worth a lot of money. What kind of a doctor would I be without my instruments?'

'What kind of a doctor are you *with* them?'

'Stop it, both of you,' I said. 'This is not the time.'

'If they see you pick up your bag just to walk down to the

river they'll know we're not intending to come back. Use your head. The bag stays behind.'

Klaus said nothing, and Gerhard continued. 'If by some stroke of bad luck they do follow us, we'll make a dash for the canoes anyway. The Yayomi don't like being outside the shabono in the dark because they think the night air is the natural home of spirits. If we make a break for it they may be too scared to follow. Does everyone accept this plan?'

I nodded. Klaus sniffed. Gerhard added, 'Make no mistake, tonight is our last opportunity. It has to be done the right way.'

After that we watched the flames. The smell of burning flesh lessened over the next hour or so as Zeppi's body was consumed. The Yayomi ate their meal, offering none to us, and Gerhard cautioned us not to ask for any in case it provoked some kind of confrontation. He said an empty stomach was best in any case for doing risky things, because there was less chance of us shitting ourselves if things turned sour. I think he meant it as a joke.

When they finished eating, the Yayomi went back to their hammocks, but the usual chatter and horseplay were missing. They stared at us as we tended Zeppi's fire, stoking the coals as they burned lower and lower until finally the last of them was snuffed out. Gerhard whispered that if we stretched out the grinding process into the small hours of the morning we might be able to stay awake long after the last Yayomi was asleep, and simply walk out without even having to use the excuse of disposing of the bone ash in the river. It was getting on toward midnight, I estimated, and most of the people around us were already snoring.

Gerhard fetched the grinding poles and we raked out the fire to collect Zeppi's bones. His pile was smaller than

Mother's. Working by moonlight, now that all of the other fires had also burned low, we started grinding the chunks of bone to powder.

Gerhard and I did all the work. Klaus seemed to understand that I meant it when I told him not to help. He sat by his medical bag and watched us. By the time the bones had been reduced to a fine powder there was little light under the shabono's roof, so it was impossible to tell if anyone was still awake and watching us

'This is how we'll play it,' Gerhard whispered, setting down his pole. 'In case there's still someone awake, we'll take the ashes and you, Erich, will carry them over your head in a way that will make anyone watching think it's part of some dolphin ritual. Then, very slowly, walking in step with each other, we'll move toward the hole in the wall. I'll be in the lead, so I'll pull the thornbushes back, making it all look like part of the ritual, then out we'll go. At no time can we hurry. The least indication of haste and anyone watching will know we're escaping. Are we in agreement? Good. Now then, we need something to put the ashes in.'

I found a pot nearby and we scooped up what remained of Zeppi, then I held the pot above my head and we formed a single file with Klaus in the rear. Gerhard began a strange shuffling motion and we copied him. Under different circumstances it would have been funny to see three naked men take two steps forward, then dip their bodies, take another two steps forward and dip again. In this way we moved toward the exit, blocked as usual with thornbushes. We were almost there when someone stepped from the shadows and stood directly in front of us, arms folded across his chest.

It was Waneeri, and I could sense rather than see the sneer

on his face. He said a few words in a tone that couldn't be mistaken for anything but suspicion and contempt. Gerhard answered back. Neither man was talking loudly, and no one else seemed to be taking any notice.

'He says to go back and wait till morning to get rid of the ashes.'

'Tell him it's the dolphin custom to do it at night,' I suggested.

'I already did, and he says the dolphins have no customs, because you ate your mother's bones the Yayomi way, not some other way. He's not fooled by any of this.'

'We can't stop now,' Klaus hissed. 'In the morning they'll kill us if we try to go through with the plan.'

'Yes,' admitted Gerhard. 'Does anyone have a bright idea?'

'Uncle,' I said, 'Waneeri's afraid of your bag. He reached inside it once and got pricked by a scalpel, so he thinks there's a demon living in it. Let's show him the demon.'

'What demon? There's nothing in my bag but instruments.'

'Erich is right,' said Gerhard. 'Open your bag and talk to the demon. Give a little laugh as you do it, as if you can't wait to get the bag close enough to Waneeri to let the demon reach out and grab him. Act the part. There's a demon in your bag and you want Waneeri to make his acquaintance. Go on, do it, and make it convincing.'

To his credit, Klaus got directly into the spirit of the thing by opening his bag and chuckling like a demented person. How ironic – an actual madman was acting like one to save us all.

Klaus advanced on Waneeri, whispering his name like a pervert offering sweets to a little girl in a darkened alleyway, his voice cooing and purring, the words oozing from an invisible smile. Waneeri backed away from the offered bag and the oblong of darkness it contained.

Klaus ducked his head into the opening and spoke words of encouragement to the demon, then thrust the bag at Waneeri, who had heard his own name mentioned often enough in the last thirty seconds to think that a spell was being cast, a spell that would set the demon on his trail. His back was against the thornbushes and Klaus was advancing slowly toward him with the bag. Gerhard and I were on either side, unarmed but friends of the demon's master and so equally to be avoided. There was only one thing for a scared Yayomi to do. Waneeri must have scratched his hands and arms badly, he tore the thornbushes aside so quickly, then he stepped aside himself, never once taking his eyes from Klaus's bag.

'Move!' said Gerhard, and Klaus went through the hole. I went next and Gerhard followed. Passing through, I accidentally dropped the bowl of ashes and stopped for a second, then kept going. In the moonlight I saw the canoes lying in a row like black bananas. We hurried toward them, Klaus's bag bumping against his thigh as he jogged. Behind us we heard shouting as Waneeri roused his people.

'Hurry!' said Gerhard.

I heard a babble of voices from the shabono, growing louder as they came outside. The more excited among them screamed when they saw us dashing away in the moonlight, and we all abandoned stealth for speed, our bare feet splashing across muddy earth, breath whistling in our lungs. The skin between my shoulderblades was waiting for an arrow. My Iron Cross bounced painfully against my breastbone. I was scared, too scared to slow down as we streaked for the canoes.

I passed Klaus, struggling with his heavy bag. If he was too slow and was caught, I wouldn't care. In fact, it would serve him right to be left behind. I ran faster, hoping to discourage him so he'd fall behind, but Klaus seemed to get a second wind and actually passed me, hugging the bag to his chest, lips peeled back from hissing teeth, knees churning like pistons.

Gerhard reached the canoes and turned one over. He grabbed the paddles and threw them inside, then went to the bow and lifted it. Klaus arrived second, threw his bag inside and lifted the middle section, and a second later I joined them to raise the stern, only to have it jerked from my hands as Gerhard and Klaus started running for the water, maybe ten metres away. I grabbed for the stern again, held onto it and matched my speed to theirs. Klaus's bag was bouncing around in the midsection among the clattering wooden paddles, and all three of us were puffing and blowing like marathon runners. Something whiffled past my ear – an arrow!

My legs moved so much faster then that I could feel myself pushing the canoe through the air, shoving it forward faster than the other two could carry it. The voices behind us were louder, uttering screams and howls like angry monkeys. It sounded like the entire shabono was hard on our heels. Another arrow! I heard it splash into the river ahead of us. I also heard another sound, a whimpering, and it was coming from me.

'Nearly there . . .' Gerhard's voice was unrecognisable, a high-pitched gasp charged with fear. I heard his feet splash into the shallows, then Klaus's, and our progress slowed suddenly as they stopped to lower and launch the canoe. Its hull slapped hard into the water and bobbed back up again. Gerhard was already scrambling inside in a tangle of arms and legs, and Klaus followed him, grunting with effort and fear. The water was only up to my knees, and I didn't want the canoe to lose any forward momentum while Gerhard and Klaus struggled to find and dip their paddles, so I stayed outside, pushing hard with my legs, grasping the narrow wooden sides, pushing and pushing it into deeper water where the Yayomi couldn't follow without losing speed themselves, pushing and pushing until I could see paddles cutting into the water.

I took a breath and lifted myself up and out of the river. At that moment, while I was not yet out of the water, not yet inside the canoe, an arrow struck me where the cheek of my left buttock met the top of my thigh.

It felt like a hornet's sting, times one hundred. I froze for a second with the shock of it more than the pain, and let loose my grip on the canoe so that I might pull out the arrow. I should have waited until I was inside. I should have left the arrow sticking out of me, its point buried deep in my flesh, hurting more than anything I could recall in my life. By reaching back to pull it out I allowed the rough sides of the canoe to slide past me. Even as my fingers closed around the shaft and yanked, the canoe's stern was passing my face, water hissing along the hull.

The arrow came out and I gave a silent scream at the pain. I wanted to vomit but my stomach was empty. The canoe was beyond my reach now, picking up speed. The paddlers, unaware that I was not aboard, were jerking their arms in uncoordinated circles, digging and digging at the water like automatons run wild. It was then that I knew I would be taken, because the smaller the canoe became, the louder the sound of splashing behind me as Yayomi by the dozens thundered into the shallows, howling, baying like a pack of four-legged hunters from the dawn of time.

I felt the sickening fear of a creature about to be brought down, engulfed by thudding flesh and hair, ripped by eager claws, nipped and torn by flashing teeth. Just before the blow that felled me came crashing into the side of my head, I looked up and saw the circle of the moon above me, impossibly close, so close I could see every detail of its untrodden plains and airless, unscalable mountains. Then hands closed about my throat and I was driven underwater, air rushing from me like a punctured boiler, and throughout it all, with the distorted human shadows above rippling like flags as the life was strangled from me, I continued to see the moon, yellowish-white, serene and pure, an eye without a pupil blindly overseeing my death.

The eye winked out.

TWELVE

THEY DRAGGED ME BACK to the shabono and tied my wrists to one of the roof's support poles, then the fires were built up and the story of the escape gone over and over. From the way Waneeri kept re-enacting my capture, clenching his fingers in a murderous circle, he must have been the one who held me under the water until I blacked out. His face was bright with triumph, his movements exaggerated and heroic.

Waneeri and others danced around me, sometimes slapping me across the shoulders and the back of my head, but the blows were intended to humiliate me, not do me any harm. Yoppo was brought out and consumed to keep the excitement going, and the shabono was a place of pandemonium for several hours. I watched all the celebration and storytelling and wondered when and how they intended to kill me. That they would do so was never in doubt. The Yayomi had been deceived, and they never forgave such an insult. I would have to pay for that, and for the escape of Gerhard and Klaus.

I tried to imagine those two together in the canoe, and couldn't. They'd start to fight and would end up killing one another. It had all been for nothing. My head ached, my bound wrists chafed. The wound in my buttock burned and throbbed. I was hungry and at the same time filled with despair.

Awomay was allowed to feed me, but when she stayed with me to give me silent comfort she was yanked away by Manokwo. It was clear that the decision to kill me would be made by him. I had promised him my brother as a wife, and instead of Zeppi turning into a girl, he'd become pulverised bone. I had to pay for that too. Every man in the shabono did some kind of victory dance in front of me, and Waneeri pissed all over my back. Even the children mocked me, Zeppi's friends among them. Noroni and Kwaytcha were less jubilant, while Awomay sat as near to me as was allowable and stared, her face filled with sadness.

The more yoppo was blown up noses, the more extreme the dances and showing-off. I stopped watching and looked at the pole in front of my face. Soon I'd be joining Mother and Zeppi, then the Yayomi could forget there had ever been white people at the shabono and go on with their lives as if none of it had ever happened. The next time whites came, if any did, they'd probably be killed immediately to save the Yayomi the time and effort of learning how treacherous they could be.

I couldn't sit for fear of getting the wound in my buttock dirty. Even if I was going to die, I behaved as if I wasn't. Why was that? Did some inner strength make me believe I'd be saved despite all the evidence to the contrary? Why not sit and risk infection for the sake of comparative comfort? But I wouldn't do it, and recognising that I wouldn't made me realise something else – I wasn't prepared for death. I had thought I was, but my refusal to sit in the mud and dirt said otherwise. It was strange to be taught that lesson, and to know that it made absolutely no difference to my chances of survival.

My instinct was to live and breathe, and would remain that way until my head was bashed in or my throat cut. Twice already, Waneeri had taken hold of my hair and yanked my head back to draw the blade of a machete across the skin below my Adam's apple without touching it. Each time he did this he was loudly applauded. The third time he was so full of yoppo he accidentally nicked my cheek, but the cut wasn't deep.

As the hours passed I became tired, and slid my wrists down the pole so I could squat on my haunches, the leg below my injured buttock stuck straight out in front of me so the flesh around the wound wasn't stretched apart. I needed to empty my bowels but had no means of letting anyone know. They might not have set me free for that purpose anyway, choosing to let me shame myself.

My bowels clenched and wind escaped me. Some of the children found my predicament hilarious, and made farting and grunting noises. Then I saw Awomay go to the lowest part of the shabono roof and pull out a large leaf. She brought it to me and placed it between my feet. I shat onto it, not caring whether this public display of helplessness gave the Yayomi cause to laugh. Awomay slid the leaf out from under me and took it away. Manokwo hadn't stopped her because he was lying stupefied in his hammock, along with most of the other men who had overindulged in yoppo.

Things were quite a bit less rowdy by now. They needed to sleep, to make up for the hours of celebration, and one by one everyone went to their hammocks to find rest. The fires burned low again, and by the time I could make out the edges of the sky hole against the pre-dawn lightness, everyone but myself appeared to be fast asleep. I rubbed the fibre bindings around my wrists up and down the pole, but they were too thick and the pole too smooth to wear them away. The hole in the shabono wall hadn't even been plugged with thorn-bushes, I noticed. If their enemies had wanted to take the shabono now, they could have walked right in without the least effort. I waited, hoping to see naked forms slipping past the hole, unfamiliar faces painted for war looking in, but of course no such thing happened. There would be no rescue by outsiders, and when Manokwo and the rest awoke, my time would be up.

The jungle was quiet for a short while, the night creatures finding shelter, the day creatures slowly coming to life. All around me, smoke from the fires clung to the ground along with a little mist that had drifted up from the river. I could actually see it pouring over the lower section of the hole in the wall, silent and white, barely there at all.

A shadow passed in front of me, and then Awomay was sawing at the fibres on the far side of the pole with a machete. A few seconds later they parted and my arms fell to my sides.

I stood up. She looked once into my eyes, then turned away. I watched her return the machete to its resting place beside someone's hammock, then she went to her own, lay down in it and stared at me. For what she had done, Awomay might have her ears cut off, or worse. I beckoned to her, imploring her to join me. She closed her eyes and they remained closed.

I took the Iron Cross from around my neck and set it on the ground, I don't know why, maybe to appease them when they found me gone. Tagerri had died from wanting it, and I had no need of it any more. It was only a piece of metal on a dirty ribbon, and removing it from my neck felt good somehow.

I walked to the hole in the wall and stepped through, then limped to the river and dragged the nearest canoe down to the waterline, went back for the paddles and launched myself out into deeper water. There was a fierce humming in my throat, the song of freedom.

One last look back at the shabono revealed no pursuit, no movement at all. The top of the dwelling seemed to sit lightly on a bed of shifting mist, as if at any moment it might float away like a dream. I dug deep with my paddle, again and again, until the bank of canoes was left behind and I rounded a bend in the river.

Then I was alone. Awomay should have been with me but she was not, the ties of family and tribe too strong to overcome. They would suspect her, hit her until she admitted her crime, and then she would be punished. It made me angry with myself, leaving her to face all that on her own, but maybe Noroni and Kwaytcha would intervene on her behalf. There might be a stalemate, a willingness on both sides simply to forget everything associated with the white people who had pretended to be dolphins. It would be better for everyone to forget such dishonourable and devious people. It might happen that way. I would never know.

I paddled for hours without stopping. The Yayomi would waken late in the morning after their disturbed night, but that might not prevent them from setting out after me. Two valuable canoes had been stolen and, more importantly, their prisoner had escaped, a fact that brought shame upon the shabono. I acted as if pursuit was inevitable and made my arms ache with paddling. There was also a chance of catching up with Gerhard and Klaus if I made good time. They were only four or five hours ahead of me.

Two hours after setting out, by my reckoning, it began to rain, and although this made things difficult for me, I knew it would probably keep the Yayomi at home.

Rain pelted my head and shoulders, every fat raindrop a stinging pellet. After a while I was sitting in rainwater that had accumulated in the canoe, the downpour was so intense. I hoped it was cleaning my wound, not making it dirtier. Either way, it hurt all the time, but since I couldn't do anything about it, I tried to ignore it. Getting downriver was the important thing. The river itself seemed to disappear for minutes at a time behind lashing veils of rain, and the banks, when I could see them as I went flashing past on a faster than usual current, were being torn apart by the rising waters.

The nearest trunks each had a wave lapping at the lower branches as the river swirled past, attempting to uproot them. The river had begun invading the jungle and was twice as wide here as it had been where I launched the canoe. Thunder rumbled continuously overhead in a sky made invisible by rain. It was like paddling through gauze.

The passage of time had no meaning any more, not when my own weariness made me lose track for long stretches as I ploughed on. My mind was completely emptied. Every hour was the same as the one before it, and the hours yet to come. I stopped only to catch my breath and ease the weight on my wound, and to try to gauge my closeness to the banks. The last thing I wanted was to run aground among the trees. The river was flowing so hard now that such an accident might make the thin-sided canoe break up.

Sometime in the afternoon the rain began to slacken a little, and the waterscape around me could be seen more clearly. I was not alone on the river. Huge trunks went gliding by, torn away from the river's banks, sent plunging into the brown foam, roots still heavy with earth, branches heavy with leaves and vines, turning over and over as they were swept along, sometimes with monkeys clinging to their perches, wet and miserable. I saw other animals swimming, two or three tapirs churning along with their flexible snouts above the waves, even a jaguar that had managed to reach one of the drifting trees. If there had been monkeys aboard that tree they would have been in trouble. Once a green snake attached itself to my paddle and attempted to wriggle up my arm, but I shook it off before it had a chance to bite me.

My entire upper body ached, but I compared that pain to the pain Zeppi must have endured even through the yoppo, and the pain Mother must have felt as the living flesh was eaten from her bones, and told myself I was a weakling, a coward who didn't deserve the freedom given to him by a woman – a girl, really – who had done the bravest thing possible, defied the laws of her world and set free her ungrateful husband. What Awomay's pain might be as a result, I couldn't imagine. For all of them, and for myself, I paddled on.

Someone was calling my name . . .

I looked around through veils of falling rain, but saw nothing. For a few seconds I wondered if God was calling me, since no one else was near, then told myself I was being idiotic. It came again . . . 'Erich! Over here!' Then I saw the tree, over to my left and already falling behind me, the branches slowing its speed. And clinging to the tree with one arm, waving with the other, was Gerhard!

I turned my canoe, backpaddling at the same time so I wouldn't overshoot the tree, which was swinging sideways with the current. Gerhard stopped waving once he saw that I'd noticed him, needing both hands to cling onto the trunk. I paddled frantically in reverse, allowing the tree to catch up with me, and at the same time I manoeuvred clumsily to the left. When the main body of branches finally drew level with me I put all my remaining energy into reaching the trunk where Gerhard clung. He groped for the canoe as I edged closer, and only let go of the tree when one hand was firmly locked onto the side.

The canoe tipped a little with his weight, and tipped much more as he attempted to climb aboard. I leaned sideways to counteract the dangerous tipping, but we almost capsized anyway as Gerhard flung one leg, then the other, over the side and into the canoe. He lay there motionless, and I quickly steered us away from the tree before the root mass could overtake and sink us.

'Erich ... What a fantastic surprise! We thought they had you ...'

'They did. I got away. Where's Klaus?'

'Up ahead somewhere ... He has the canoe ...'

'What happened?'

'We couldn't see that tree back there in all this rain, not until we hit it ... and I was knocked overboard. He ... he was swept away ...'

'How long ago?'

'I don't know ... hours! Are you all right? Did they hurt you?'

'An arrow in the arse! It stings a little!'

He looked at me, then burst out laughing, and I joined him. We were a pair of laughing hyenas lost in a world of river and rain, and neither of us cared. When he could, Gerhard picked up a paddle and started slicing the water, and we moved along even more swiftly than before. The water in the canoe, I now saw for the first time, had a pinkish tinge. It would have been redder if the rain didn't keep diluting it. My wound wasn't hurting so much now, but it was still bleeding, and that made me worry about passing out. I kept paddling, because every minute still counted, whether to put the Yayomi further behind us or to catch up with Klaus, it didn't matter.

At last it stopped raining, and we saw that the river had widened tremendously. We could still see both banks or, rather, where trees were still visible at the water's edge. It must have been more than two kilometres wide, and back at the shabono it was only a hundred metres or so. If such volumes of water continued coming downriver, the regions upstream would also widen, which meant the Yayomi were probably in danger of losing their shabono to the flood. I liked that possibility, because it meant that punishment for Awomay would be delayed and the whole episode of my capture and escape would quickly be considered unimportant by comparison.

I felt happy again, despite my pain and the fact that we were without supplies of any kind, happy not just because my wife might escape punishment but because my best friend was in the same canoe with me, his skinny back rippling with motion as he paddled.

If I did one thing in all my life, assuming I lived, I would tell anyone who asked, and plenty who didn't, that Jews are no more separate and different from other people than a blue parrot is to a green one. A parrot is a parrot, and calling a parrot a bat is the sign of a fool. Now I was no longer a fool, and never would be again.

'Gerhard!' I called out.

He turned his head. 'What?'

'A parrot isn't a bat!'

He absorbed the lesson, frowning a little, then said, 'I know,' and kept paddling.

And I passed out.

The first thing I became aware of was land beneath my back. It was wet and yielding, probably mud, but it was land. I opened my eyes and saw only darkness. Had night come so soon? Then I saw the inside of the canoe in front of my face, and heard the tapping of rain against its hull. Gerhard had overturned it to protect me.

Where was he? I placed a hand under one side and lifted. The canoe toppled sideways and there he was, only a few metres away, staring out across the river with his back to me. I sat up and noticed a broad leaf under my wound, keeping it clear of the mud. There was blood on the leaf, but not too much.

Gerhard turned around. 'Good afternoon.'

'Good afternoon . . .'

My stomach hurt. It had been twenty-four hours since we'd eaten, but there was no possibility of catching anything in all that rain, and no chance of lighting a fire to cook it even if we could. My guts hurt more than my arse, which is saying something.

'I couldn't go on,' Gerhard said. 'Didn't have the strength.'

I nodded. 'Are you as hungry as me?' I asked. 'Because I'm so hungry I feel sick.'

'I felt that way hours ago. I'm worse now.'

'Ha, ha.'

'If you feel up to it, we can go on for a while before dark. There won't be any food downriver, but since we're going in that direction . . .'

I got to my feet. 'I'm ready.'

'You're sure? I was having trouble keeping the canoe going in a straight line without you in the stern. If you get lazy again we might be in trouble.'

'I won't. I've had a rest now.'

'Then let's go.'

We launched the canoe. I kept the leaf under me, since it was smoother than wood. Nothing had changed while I slept, not the thunder and falling rain, the swollen river or the lack of any way to tell east from west. We assumed we were heading west because that was the general direction the river took back where the Yayomi lived. It could have taken any number of twists and turns since then, of course, but we had no choice but to follow it, wherever it was leading.

'How far to where the Iriri live?' I asked.

'The story has always been that their territory began three days' paddling below the Yayomi, but that would be paddling under ordinary circumstances. For all I know, we've already covered that distance.'

We paddled on. There was no sign of the Iriri or of any other living thing apart from the few creatures we saw swimming in the flood or riding uprooted trees. The sun broke through eventually, surprisingly low in the sky, bleeding red and yellow light across the undersides of the clouds. We had perhaps an hour of daylight left, and both of us were bone tired. It was agreed that we should steer a course closer to one of the banks, so we could get ashore easily when the last of the light faded. We chose the right bank, for no particular reason, and no sooner were we within a hundred metres of it than we saw Klaus's canoe, and then Klaus.

He'd already landed and was looking at the jungle. He was quite unaware of us until I called out to him. He turned, but his expression registered neither surprise nor gladness. It was as if he'd last seen us both five minutes ago. We steered our canoe some distance in among the trees that now stood in water up to their lower branches. Smaller trees were already completely submerged, their tops leaning sideways in the current like seaweed. The land began at Klaus's feet.

He looked at me, then at Gerhard. 'How is it that you're together?'

'I got away and bumped into him along the river. Are you going further today?'

'That wouldn't be wise. It's difficult enough in daylight.'

'Then we'll join you,' said Gerhard.

'I think not,' said Klaus. 'Erich, you may stay, but not this other . . . thing.'

I turned to Gerhard. 'You told him, didn't you.'

'He didn't take it well, but then I didn't expect him to.'

'Why did you tell?'

'It just slipped out, the way it did with you. Having told one of you, it seemed silly not to tell the other. You were much nicer about it, Erich. Our Nazi friend got very excited to find himself paddling downriver with a Jew, and invited me to leave. I didn't want to, naturally, being a poor swimmer, and so I said no.'

'Why didn't you tell me this before?'

'I didn't think we'd meet up again with the good doctor, to tell you the truth.'

'But you have', said Klaus, 'and you must leave. Take your canoe. Go!'

'Too tired', said Gerhard. 'Why don't *you* go?'

'I was here first!'

They sounded like schoolboys arguing over who gets to ride the swings.

'Did he make you get out of the canoe?' I asked Gerhard.

'No, but it was while we were arguing that we hit the tree.'

'And did he try to reach you and pull you back aboard?'

'I'll let Klaus answer that.'

I looked again at my uncle. He pointed at Gerhard. 'I let the course of events continue as fate decreed', he said grandly. 'He fell out. It wasn't my job to bring him back in. All rats can swim!'

'And all Nazis can float', replied Gerhard, 'like the shit they're made from.'

'Uncle', I said, 'do you have something for a wound? I was hit by an arrow. It isn't deep, but it hurts.'

He went to his bag in the canoe and opened it. 'Come here.'

He poured some kind of antiseptic powder from a paper packet over the wound, then wrapped a length of bandage around my upper thigh and hip. 'Don't sit on the ground', he said. 'And try to keep it dry.'

'That's a tall order, Uncle.'

Klaus's face was like stone, his lips clenched in a line. He reached into the bag again, and this time brought out a scalpel.

'Wentzler, I'll have mercy on your black Jew soul and let

you leave here if you do so immediately. Any delay whatsoever and I'll cut your throat.'

'Uncle, no ...'

'Shut up, Erich. This man has profaned our friendship by
not admitting at the very beginning that he's a Jew.'

Gerhard laughed. 'The way you admitted at the very beginning that you're a Jew-killer? Somewhere deep inside you,
Brandt, there's a tiny part of your conscience left, and it
knows you're a monster. That's why you hid your real self –
shame.'

'You couldn't be more wrong, Jew. No part of me is
ashamed of any part of my life. You have ten seconds to leave.'

'I believe you,' said Gerhard. 'I was wrong about the small
piece of conscience. It isn't there.'

'Seven seconds.'

'Which makes you even more of a monster.'

'Five.'

'Uncle, stop!'

'Three ...'

I went and stood between the two, facing Klaus. 'You
mustn't do this!'

He sidestepped past me. 'Two ...'

'I dare you,' Gerhard taunted.

Again I placed myself in front of him, but again Klaus
stepped back the other way, aiming a ferocious look at
Gerhard. 'Certainly, Jew. Most happy to oblige you.' But he
made no move in Gerhard's direction.

'I'm waiting, Brandt.'

'My name is Linden, Klaus Linden! Leave now, this instant!'

Gerhard looked at me and shrugged, then walked up to
Klaus and took the scalpel from him. He tossed it over his

shoulder into the water, then slapped Klaus across the face with both hands, not just once but many times, ten or fifteen slaps that took Klaus so much by surprise that even as the last slap was delivered he still couldn't believe a Jew was doing this to him. Gerhard's advance was so fierce Klaus had to back away, and by the last slap he was on his knees, his mouth open in surprise, or maybe outrage.

He simply couldn't speak, even as Gerhard walked away. Then he made a sound, the strangest sound. It came out of him like an air-raid siren, a wailing cry that went spiralling upward into the air, getting louder and louder, until he suddenly ran out of air and stopped. Then he fell over and curled himself into a ball. I'd never seen any adult act that way. It was as shocking to me as the slapping had been to Klaus.

Gerhard wouldn't look at him, he was so filled with hate, and I couldn't blame him. Klaus was a pathetic wreck, and it was all his own fault. It was like looking at a dead man and knowing there was nothing you could do, so there was no point in feeling anything about him. Klaus was someone else now, not my uncle, just a dead man who looked something like him.

Then, as quickly as he'd fallen down, Klaus stood up again and marched toward his black bag. He reached inside and came out with another scalpel, then held the blade against his left wrist. Gerhard and I watched, waiting for him to make the one clean slice that would end his miserable life. I felt no compulsion whatever to stop him. But Klaus couldn't, or wouldn't, do it. He started to cry instead. He sobbed and sobbed, still holding the blade against his wrist, then he stopped and threw the scalpel away. Not content with that, he picked up his bag and threw that into the water too. It landed on its side and, with the top wide open, soon took in enough water to sink.

Then Klaus seemed to draw himself up, as if trying to be a man again, and went to his canoe, shoving it away from the island of mud we stood upon. He fell into it and picked up his paddle. Without looking back, he passed between the flooded trees and rejoined the main body of the river, was caught by the current there and whisked out of sight. I let my breath out. I'd been holding it for a long time.

The sky was darkening, the day ending with yet another shower of rain. Gerhard stood shivering as the first drops fell against his gaunt face and tangled beard, his bony chest and skinny legs covered in mud.

The rain fell harder. We dragged our canoe further up onto the mud in case the river should rise some more during the night, then climbed into the nearest tree that wasn't already occupied by wildlife. There we settled ourselves to spend the most uncomfortable night of our lives. I thought a lot about Klaus, but then got tired of it – Klaus was a non-man, not worth thinking about. Instead I thought of something much more important. I thought of food, and made myself even more miserable.

For another day we followed the river, and on the afternoon of that day saw Klaus again. It was raining as usual, and through the squall we saw his canoe, but the canoe was not alone. There were two more, with several Indians in each, and they were overtaking Klaus far to our left. Then the rain hid them from us, and us from them.

'Yayomi?' I asked Gerhard.

He shook his head. 'Iriri, this far down. Did I tell you they're headhunters?'

'No.'

'I probably didn't want to scare you. They'll take his head, smash the skull and pull the pieces of bone out through his mouth, the brain too, then they'll fill his head with hot sand and stitch his lips shut. His head will be about the size of his fist when they're done.'

I paddled harder than before, wanting to be away from here, grateful for the curtains of rain separating us from the Iriri. It didn't matter any more that I was tired and hungry. All that mattered was my freedom, and Gerhard's.

Somewhere up ahead our river would join another as we glided like a shadow over the drowned jungle beneath us, and that river would join another, and that river would flow into the mighty Orinoco that flows all the way to the ocean. Somewhere along that broad ribbon of river there would be a steamer, and on the deck of that steamer would be a man who would see us, and the steamer would stop and take us aboard, Gerhard and myself, and we would be made clean and whole again, and fed everything we wanted from a long table.

Then the canoe that had brought us there, our fragile hollowed stick from the forest of Yayomiland, would be left behind. It would drift with the current, lost among water that was sunshiny silver on top and muddy brown below, until one day it would reach the sea, where the water becomes green and blue, and be drawn under by waves the colour of jungle and sky.

About the author

About the book

Insights,
Interviews
& More . . .

Read on

Torsten Krol's extended biography

TORSTEN KROL is the author of *Callisto*, which *Kirkus Reviews* called "the best portrayal of an American Innocent since *Forrest Gump*." Nothing further is known about him. ∽

A Conversation with Torsten Krol

Where did your initial impulse to write The Dolphin People *come from?*

As a boy, my favorite book was *Green Mansions* by W. H. Hudson, an Edwardian adventure/romance and minor classic. I reread it many times. When I came to write my own jungle tale, I decided to avoid any kind of imitation by extending the timeline into the mid-twentieth century and steering clear of anything that might be called romance.

In Callisto *it's the U.S. administration and the surveillance community that gets the bad rap. Here it's the Nazis. One of these is history; the other a pervasive fact of life. Yet they both seem to wind you up, today, more than they do the average citizen. Why in particular the Nazis?*

Whether it's Bush and Co. or the Nazis, I have a hatred of governments that insist on rearranging the world to suit their particular ideology. The Bush-Cheney-Rumsfeld axis of idiocy doesn't compare with the Hitler-Goebbels-Himmler bunch, but it's possible something even worse could arise in the future. As a species we tend to forget yesterday's crimes.

A native Amazon tribe, a German family with Nazi sympathies, post–World War II— these all seem like rather unusual elements for a story that touches on so many important issues relevant to modern-day, progressive, civilized societies. But you pull it off wonderfully here. Can you share any ▶

> ❝ Whether it's Bush and Co. or the Nazis, I have a hatred of governments that insist on rearranging the world to suit their particular ideology. ❞

3

thoughts on why you chose characters and a setting that are so seemingly unlikely?

From boyhood I have had an obsession with World War II, in particular the Holocaust. I regard it as the blackest page in human history, the absolute nadir of human baseness. Given that many of the top Nazis fled to South America after the war, it seemed logical to combine my two interests—the war and the book. They turned out to be a natural fit.

As with Callisto, *there's no doubt that a first-person narration—here, the voice of a sixteen-year-old boy—works for the story. But it begs the question, where does the author's controlling consciousness reside? Is there a Torsten Krol—or are you just channeling?*

I have no idea where other authors keep their controlling consciousness, but I keep mine in a jar under the bed. Isn't every author channeling when he writes about someone who is not himself or depicts incidents in which he took no part? There's autobiography and then there's channeling, which is just another word for imagination plus empathy.

What were your sources for the details in The Dolphin People, *especially those of life within an Amazonian jungle tribe? Or did you make them up?*

My research into both Nazis and Indians was considerable. Worse things took place in the death camps than I have described here. The bizarre customs of Indians like

66 I have no idea where other authors keep their controlling consciousness, but I keep mine in a jar under the bed. 99

4

the Yayomi are fully documented. I invented nothing but a tribal name for them.

Patrick White, the well-known Australian author and Nobel Laureate, once said famously that after a new manuscript was completed, he never again read the book. Do you reread your novels? Do you ever think, How on earth did I catch that voice?

After the editorial process and the galleys have been taken care of, I'm happy not to look at my work again.

I know you don't like discussing writing under a pseudonym, but surely it means you miss out on many of the good things that other writers seem to enjoy: public adulation, invitations to media events, the whole hoopla of the book-publishing world?

All of that sounds to me like a lower circle of hell. I am a very private person who communicates best on the page.

Some readers have been shocked by the more gruesome details in The Dolphin People. *Others find it hard to take them seriously—or at least so many of them in the space of a single novel. One quote is that the novel reads "like* The Swiss Family Robinson *for psychopaths." Care to comment?*

I'm aware that there is almost an excess of discomforting scenes in the book, but when you combine Nazi medical experiments with somewhat bizarre Indian practices (for example, consuming the ashes of a loved ▶

one following cremation) the result is naturally going to be fairly bloody. For those readers who think I've gone over the top, I assure them it could conceivably have happened this way.

The opening lines of The Dolphin People *are lyrical, even beautiful, as is the ending. Yet terrible things happen in between. Is life on this planet doomed to be "nasty, brutish, and short," or do you hold out hope for something better?*

Life on earth has been all about advancing from the simple to the complex, at the molecular and sociological levels. Modern technology has accelerated those changes to an alarming degree (think climate change) and we are entering panic mode as we foresee what might be waiting for us down the line. Fixing things is going to require international cooperation. We're all going to have to begin reading from the same page regardless of political, national, religious, and ethnic differences. In other words, we're toast.

Your two novels released to date could scarcely be more different. Yet, at least with their favorite authors, readers tend to enjoy a certain degree of consistency—of setting, theme, etc. It might be said on the evidence of these two that you are easily bored. What might we expect from Torsten Krol farther down the track?

The next book is about my favorite frustration: organized religion. Why do we continue to believe in invisible presences that will aid us if only we placate them with

66 We're all going to have to begin reading from the same page regardless of political, national, religious, and ethnic differences. In other words, we're toast. 99

the right offerings and rituals? As an atheist I find such behavior fascinating and ridiculous. Given that I and others of similar persuasion are in a distinct minority, our disbelief is something worth examining—constantly—in order to avoid being steamrollered beneath the massive weight of received opinion. I think it requires a clearer mind and braver heart to acknowledge that we are on our own and always have been. ∾

An Excerpt from
Callisto

An excerpt from Callisto *(Harper Perennial, March 2009), a novel compared often to a number of important, treasured works of literature:*

"The best portrayal of an American Innocent since **Forrest Gump**."
    —*Kirkus Reviews* (starred review)

"Every war needs its absurd antiwar hero; Vietnam had **Tim O'Brien's Cacciato**, and now Iraq has Odell. There are other echoes, too. Think **The Good Soldier Švejk** with a touch of **Confederacy of Dunces** and maybe even a little **Catcher in the Rye**."
    —*Booklist* (starred review)

"Imagine a collaboration by **Sinclair Lewis, John Kennedy Toole**, and **Stephen Colbert**—but funnier."
    —Adam Davies, author of *The Frog King*

"A broad, rollicking satire of contemporary America reminiscent of **Vernon God Little** by **DBC Pierre**."   —*The Economist*

"A modern **Catch-22**."
    —*The Independent* (London)

"A droll, sharp-witted farce, reminiscent of **Dario Fo**."   —*The Big Issue* (London)

From Chapter One

MY NAME IS ODELL DEEFUS. I am a white person, not black like you might think from hearing the name and not seeing me. If you did see me, you wouldn't remember me for my face, which isn't the kind to stick in anyone's mind, but you might remember me for being tall. I am six-three, which makes women attracted to me, then they find out I don't talk the kind of talk they like to hear, so there goes the romance before it even started. You have to be able to talk to get anywhere. Me, I have to think awhile before I talk, but in the meantime the conversation has moved on, as they say, so forget that. I have had this difficulty all my life, with bad consequences.

I will be twenty-two years old on November 21, 2007. I will not be here then because I am riding this bus to somewhere else away from here. So far I have not said a single word to any of the other passengers. They are all asleep right now as we go speeding through the night. They most likely think I'm a tall dumb hick but they would be wrong about that. I know this because I have read *The Yearling* sixteen times now, and that is a Pulitzer Prize book which you can't be dumb and be able to read it. I have tried three other books to read but they did not satisfy like *The Yearling*. If you have not read the story, it's about a boy that adopts a fawn after its mother gets shot in the woods, and he raises it to be his pet like a dog, only it all goes bad when the fawn gets to be a year old and is a big nuisance around the place, eating the corn crop and so forth, so in the end it has to be shot, which always wets my eyelashes it's so sad. Which is more proof I am not dumb, because a dumb person would not feel all that emotion.

I am writing this on the bus in a school ▶

exercise book with lined paper in it and the Little Mermaid on the cover. I got a bunch of these because I have got a long story to tell. There is the Lion King and the Incredibles, the whole family, and there is Nemo and Friends plus Shrek and his buddy the donkey that talks, also everyone from *Toy Story*. I would've got plain covers but the store only had the cartoon kind. There is a little light bulb over my seat to do the writing by. I have got the urge to write it all down, the things that happened to me, while everyone else is asleep, write it all down before something else happens to me. I will figure out later what to do with the story, maybe send it to the *New York Times*, which is the way true things get told no matter if someone wants the story not to get told. They will not stop me or the *NY Times* either.

Okay then.

A little while back I'm driving across Kansas in a '78 Chevy Monte Carlo with an engine that sounded like it's driving piles into a riverbed. I was on my way to sign up for the Army now that they want people so bad they don't care all that much if you don't have that high school graduation certificate, which I don't, but not because of stupidity. I was not in the best frame of mind that last year of school, resulting in a bad consequence of not graduating, which was something I didn't care about at the time. But later on I did when the best job I could get was working in a grain elevator. I almost got killed in that job, low paid and dangerous with all that wheat thundering into silos two hundred foot tall. The Army wanted enlistees bad since the war in Iraq made guys quit signing up for enlistment.

They even paid a bonus now, I heard, so that was the plan, get enlisted and collect that bonus and try my hardest to be a good soldier against the mad-dog Islamites over there exploding everything they could get their hands on including their own people. I am not a bloodthirsty person, but that kind of craziness has got to stop right now. I was not a big success in the world yet, but maybe I would be if I could get some combat medals to show.

There was an enlistment office in Callisto, over there in Callisto County, so that was the direction I went, holding to a steady seventy miles per hour which the Chevy's engine operated best at. I had less than forty miles to go when it started sounding real bad, like it's about to throw a rod or something, so I had to slow down or risk the whole thing going up in smoke. You can't drive slow on the interstate highway, so I got off and went real slow and careful along the back roads, not sure exactly where I was but heading in the right direction for enlistment. Then the engine went all ragged and quit on me, so I had to pull over and shut it down. I sat there awhile watching dust blow past, then I got out and raised the hood. Everything under there was all plugged in, nothing I could see disconnected or out of place, not that I'm a mechanical expert. So the problem was somewhere inside the block, most likely an old-age problem with the odometer reading ninety-eight thousand miles, its second go-round after clocking up that first hundred thou. The engine was ticking like a time bomb, blasting heat and oil stench up at me, so I backed away, thinking maybe if I let it cool down it'll be okay for later on. It was around ►

midafternoon by then and I'd been driving most of the day, so I was ready for a break in any case.

There was nothing around to look at, Callisto County being flat and empty like most of Kansas except over in the east where they have got itty-bitty hills to look at. I leaned against the door and looked at the horizon a long ways off, not letting myself get mad about the engine quitting that way. It never does a bit of good to get mad about stuff like that, it's just a waste of time. You see some guys yelling at their car, even kicking it if they're pissed enough, but it never makes a bit of difference to the problem, so why waste your energy. Besides, this has happened before, so I am used to it. I'm thinking when I get out of the Army the first thing I'll get with my wages is a car with less than fifty thou on it and no problems yet.

It was hot in the sun with hardly no cloud cover at all, so I got in the back seat and opened my suitcase which had pretty near everything I owned in it, which just goes to show the sad state into which my life had fallen thus far. A life should not be able to fit in a single suitcase that way. There was some clothes that needed the attention of a laundromat and a quarter-empty bottle of Captain Morgan which I'm partial to and my copy of *The Yearling*, getting split pretty bad along the binding I had it so long now. I studied the Captain in his pirate outfit for a long time, asking myself if I should take a shot or save it for later, being that I only had about twenty-five dollars in my jeans. They better take me on for the Army or I was screwed, financially speaking. In the end I put the bottle down, feeling strong and sensible about it, and picked up the book instead. I have this philosophy—if you have got the choice between picking up a bottle and picking up a book, pick up the book. It is almost always the correct and sensible thing to do. There are some that live by the bottle or else they smoke dope like they can't get enough, and this behavior is a distraction from real life. That was not my way and never would be. That's why I was confident they would pass me for the physical and not worry overmuch about the high school graduation certificate. What does shooting mad-dog Islamites have to do with anything you learned in school anyway?

I started in to read, passing the time. I was at the scene where the boy, Jody, goes to visit his crippled friend, Fodderwing, to say how-do. I have looked at titty magazines and car and gun magazines and there is no satisfaction in them for a mind that craves a story. You might say that I go through *The Yearling* the way some folk with religion go through the Bible, from front to back and start all over again. There is something new to discover every time, I have found.

One time a person I was acquainted with who was not a friend started in making fun of me for reading that book. He said it was a book for little kids because it had a picture on the front of Jody with the fawn in his arms. I told him it was a Pulitzer Prize book, it said so right there under Jody and the fawn, but he wouldn't let up, kept on making these comments about how you'd have to be retarded to be reading a kid's book like that, probably he never even heard of the Pulitzer Prize, so in the end I had to set the book down and teach him a lesson. ▶

An Excerpt from *Callisto* (*continued*)

I am not often that way, getting violent,
I mean, but he asked for it the way he was
talking. I am tall like I said, but I am no
skinny beanpole to be pushed around.
This fool that was poking fun was no small
person either, but I got the better of him
all right with only a grazed cheekbone and
knuckles to show for winning the argument.
Sometimes things just have to be settled that
way. It is not the way I prefer, but there is
sometimes no choice in the matter and you
have to stand up and do what's right or else
get laughed at.

That happened back at my school, Kit
Carson High in Yoder, Wyoming. I was held
to blame and had to spend three days in
suspension for it even though it was not
my fault what happened. This is one reason
I did not do well in school, resulting in no
certificate and a string of jobs like the one
at the grain silo, but the US Army would
change all that, I hoped.

So I started to read, but then got so
hot even with the windows rolled down
I couldn't concentrate and had to put the
book aside and napped for a short time,
maybe an hour. I woke up feeling thirsty,
but not for Captain Morgan, more like an
ice-cold Coke. Not one vehicle had gone
by in that time, so it looked like rescue was
not coming down the road anytime soon.
I tried starting the engine. It caught and
I got rolling again, only the car sounded no
better than before. I kept the speed down
and limped along that way exactly thirty-
seven minutes and then it died on me same
as before, only this time fate was kind and
I come to a stop a few yards from someone's
front gate, only there was no gate, only fence
posts either side of where a gate ought to be

and a long curving dirt driveway leading to a farmhouse set way back from the road, the only one in those parts, real isolated.

I started up that driveway on foot. It was in a neglected state with a washout halfway along where the land dipped a little and you could see the spring rains runoff had done damage there. I was expecting a dog or three to come running at me like they always do from a farmhouse yard, but there was no dogs at all. It was a ramshackle place, neglected like the driveway, a two-story clapboard house with a porch on three sides, all badly in need of paint with a flaking propane tank alongside like a midget submarine. You can see places like this all across the plains states, a few big old shade trees overhanging it and liable to cause damage to the roof next time a twister comes through, and a big old barn with a beat-up Dodge pickup parked inside.

I went up some sagging steps to the porch and knocked on the screen door. The front door was open so I could see down the long hallway. There wasn't a sound coming from inside except a steady ticking from an old grandfather clock big as a coffin stood on its end halfway along the hall. I knocked again and called out, "Hello? Anyone home?" Well, there wasn't. I knocked a little louder with no result and Helloed some more, louder than before, only it brought no result still. They were all away someplace else and were the kind that leaves their door open with no fear of thieves. There are still country folk like that, but their numbers are getting dwindled real fast what with criminality being everywhere nowadays like it is.

I was thirstier now than before. Maybe there was a tap in the yard but I couldn't ▶

see it. I wanted water, which is a free
commodity and not like stealing, even if
I had to take it from the kitchen and not
from the yard. So I opened the door, calling
out again, and stepped through into the
house. There was that old farmhouse smell
from the cracked linoleum floor and faded
wallpaper, all of it needing replacement. The
clock ticked away deep and slow, like it was
measuring out time from a hundred years
ago when everything moved slower than
today.

The kitchen was right where I expected
it to be. There was mess everywhere along
the counters and the sink was crammed
with dirty dishes. This was not a proud
household. I could smell rotten food
somewhere, the old-fashioned pantry
maybe, or the trash bin that needed
emptying. Someone needed to go through
that place with a bucket and mop and a
scrub brush too, but that was none of my
business how people choose to live. There
was a swivel tap over the sink and I already
saw glasses standing like troopers on parade
on the overhead shelf. That shelf needed
cleaning too. I would not have allowed that
kind of grime if it was my place. I took
down a glass and filled it, then drunk it all
in one long swallow, then filled it again for
a more leisurely drink.

"Put it down," says a voice behind me.
It was not a scared voice, not angry either
the way you might expect seeing as I wasn't
invited. I turned nice and slow with the glass
still in my hand. The guy across the kitchen
was a little older than me. His T-shirt said
Bad to the Bone—and Proud of It. He had a
baseball bat in his hands. He hadn't shaved
in a day or two and there was a kind of

twitchiness about him that didn't appeal.
If I was a smaller man than I am I would
maybe have been a little bit alarmed by him
holding the bat like he was. I thought, At
least it isn't a gun.

"Afternoon," I said.

"Put it down."

I put the glass on the counter without
taking my eyes off of him. His hair was
standing out all wild from his head and his
eyes were strange. I waited for him to say
something else, but he just kept on staring
and holding the bat ready to slug me if
I made a move towards him.

"I had car trouble," I said to explain
myself. "I'm down at the road. I knocked
but nobody come. Thank you for the water.
I was thirsty."

He still said nothing.

"I'm Odell Deefus, from Wyoming."

"That's a nigger name."

"I knew a black kid in school called Alan
White. You can't tell just from a name."

The clock ticked on while he watched me
watching him. Then he lowered the bat.

"You can't be too careful," he said, still
not relaxed at all, but not jittery and
alarmed like he was up till then.

"I knocked, then I figured there's nobody
home. I needed that water."

"Go ahead."

I picked up the glass and drunk it down,
keeping my eyes on him but trying to look
casual. He was wearing sneakers, so that's
why I didn't hear him coming. I set the glass
on the counter. "Thank you. I'll be getting
back to my car now."

I had to walk past him on my way out
of the kitchen. He stepped back a little to
let me by. People do that when you're ▶

six-three. If I was five-eight he'd still be
giving me grief about the water and maybe
threatening to call the police, but he was
shorter than me by a good six inches and
just wanted me out of his house, which is
understandable. He followed me down the
hall past the grandfather clock, all the way
to the screen door.

When I'm on the other side of it he
seemed to find some manners at last and
says, "Overheated radiator?"

"The car's a junker. Could be anything."

"I'll take a look. I always fixed my own
cars."

"Okay."

He leaned his baseball bat against the
wall next to the doorway and come outside.
We crossed the porch, went down the rickety
steps and across the yard to the driveway.

"Hot day to get car trouble," he says.

"I know it. The engine's been sounding
bad for three hundred miles. I'm lucky I got
this far."

"Where you headed?"

"Callisto. Signing up with Uncle Sam."

"Huh?"

"The Army. They've got a recruiting
office there."

"The Army?" He made it sound like
something bad.

"I tried other work. It all goes nowhere."

"The Army'll send you to Iraq. You want
to go up against those jihadis?"

"Someone has to."

"It's Iraq's business, not ours. They don't
need no outside interference. We should
keep our nose out of it."

I heard the exact same line many times
before. It's what most people were thinking,
and I could see why, but when you need to

be making decisions about where to go in your life, that kind of argument doesn't stack up so high against serving the nation and making life better for people outside America.

"You're crazy if you do it," he says.

"I want a regular paycheck and a career. That's what they're offering."

"Someone big as you, you should get on a football team. Are you fast?"

"No."

"I bet you could block pretty good, though."

"I never cared for football that much."

It's true, I never did join the team in school, even when the coach kept on at me to be part of something proud. It's hard to be proud of something when you're from Yoder, Wyoming, population 2774. And my old man, he wanted me to be on the team so he could have something to brag about. Maybe I didn't want to do it because of that. Me and the old man never did see eye to eye about a single thing, which is why I left home after school was all over and done with. He told me good riddance, said those very words to me. It hurt when he told me that, but I never did let it show. I paid him back by leaving without saying another word, just got on a bus down to Colorado and worked there awhile in a Denver car wash with a bunch of drop-outs going nowhere. I have never once sent a letter home to him or called on the phone. If my mother was still alive I would have, but not for him, that washed-up son of a bitch. He had no call to look down on me. All he ever was, after he got busted out of the police force down in Cheyenne for reasons he never disclosed, was come home to Yoder ▶

and work at the gas station out on the interstate ringing up change. Some big achievement.

We got to the car and he looked under the hood, then said to turn the ignition. The engine rattled to life, then quit again, then restarted. "Sounds like shit," he said. "Why don't you drive it on up to the barn. I can't work on it out in this sun."

"Okay."

I kept it firing all the way up the driveway to the yard, where it quit again. He come walking up behind me, shaking his head. Together we pushed it inside the barn next to his truck. On the Dodge's door it said *Dean's Lawnmowing* with a telephone number.

"That you?"

"That's me, Dean Lowry. Get the hood up again."

He got a set of tools and started poking around in the engine bay, every now and then telling me to start it up, which it never did. After about twenty minutes he says, "I can't see where the problem is. You might need a complete overhaul on something old as this, engine rebuild, the works. Probably cost you more than the car's worth. What'd you pay for it?"

"Seven hundred."

"Hey, take it to the scrapyard and they'll give you fifty bucks for the parts, that's my advice to you."

"Getting it there's the problem."

I looked at the rear of his truck and saw the towbar. He saw me looking and says, "I'll haul you in tomorrow, it's too late today." ❧